GRYMM

www.totallyrandombooks.co.uk

GRYMM

KEITH AUSTIN

RED FOX

GRYMM

A RED FOX BOOK 978 1 849 41556 9

Published in Great Britain by Red Fox,
an imprint of Random House Children's Publishers UK
A Random House Group Company

This edition published 2012

1 3 5 7 9 10 8 6 4 2

The Random House Group Limited supports the Forest Stewardship Council
(FSC®), the leading international forest certification organization. Our books
carrying the FSC label are printed on FSC®-certified paper. FSC is the only
forest certification scheme endorsed by the leading environmental organizations,
including Greenpeace. Our paper procurement policy can be found at
www.randomhouse.co.uk/environment.

MIX
Paper from
responsible sources
FSC® C016897

Red Fox Books are published by Random House Children's Publishers UK,
61–63 Uxbridge Road, London W5 5SA

www.**kids**at**random**house.co.uk
www.**totally**random**books**.co.uk
www.**random**house.co.uk

Addresses for companies within The Random House Group Limited
can be found at: www.randomhouse.co.uk/offices.htm

THE RANDOM HOUSE GROUP Limited Reg. No. 954009

A CIP catalogue record for this book is available from the British Library.

Printed and bound by CPI Group (UK) Ltd, Croydon, CR0 4YY

I'd like to thank my partner Helen O'Neill for believing in me and for turning the garden shed into a writing den. And also my son, Calum, who asked for more after each chapter was finished. Of course, *Grymm* wouldn't exist were it not for my mother, Sheila, who encouraged me to read in the first place. And lastly, thanks to Bethnal Green Library – that palace of dreams – just for being there when I was a kid.

In olden times when wishing still helped one . . .
The Frog King by the Brothers Grimm

1

Jacob Daniels is twelve years old and none too impressed with his sister. Make that *step*sister. Right from the start let's get that clear – as clear as the clearest and most expensive, most flawless crystal. Jacob is adamant about that. Just because his mother and *her* father have shacked up, it doesn't mean she's family.

Not by a long shot.

No, sir.

No way. Not in a million years.

That's not why he thinks she's an idiot, though.

It's because she thinks she's a witch.

Yeah, sure. And Jacob's Harry bloody Potter.

Wilhelmina Lipton is fourteen and a Goth, a teenage Morticia Addams. Her mousy hair is dyed cat-black and backcombed until she looks like the Bride of Frankenstein (according to Jacob, that is). She wears shocking white make-up, black clothes and a silver ring in her nose (that caused a few family arguments, it must be said). On a chain around her neck hangs a small, five-pointed star, a pentacle.

Jacob doesn't understand why she can't just have her name there, or a heart, or some sort of locket. Honestly! What *does* she think she looks like? She's obviously watched too much *Twilight*. Jacob calls her a witch because he knows how much it irritates her. He calls her *Wilhelmina* for the same reason.

She's not, though, OK? She's 'Mina' to her father and to all her friends. Always has been, always will be. And if her new *stepbrother* 'Jakie' doesn't shut his face, she's going to turn him into a big, ugly frog. Well, a frog any-way; he's already ugly. And what's with the hair? There must be half a tonne of gel on it – he could take some-one's eye out.

Yeah, well, *she* can talk. And why doesn't she stop calling him Jakie? She only does it because she knows he hates it . . . And another thing—

'Will you two pack it in?' Mary, Jacob's mother, has turned in her seat to glare at them. Mina's father is trying to steer their well-worn four-wheel-drive and map-read at the same time. 'You're upsetting the baby. George, will you tell them? They're upsetting the baby. Again.'

Ah, now here's something – the *only* thing – that these two sworn enemies can agree on. Everything else pales into insignificance. Their newborn half-brother, Bryan, perched in his bright new blue booster seat between them, might look like any other baby – a pudgy white dough-boy with big eyes the colour and shape of those scented blocks they put in toilets – but he's really the devil's spawn, sent to Earth to make their lives even more miserable. During the nine-hour drive from the city, the little monster has already somehow broken Mina's mobile phone and vomited over Jacob's T-shirt and shorts.

Then there's the stink. How can something so *small* smell so *bad*? That's what Jacob wants to know. Maybe he'll take him in and ask the chemistry teacher when school starts again after the summer holidays.

Mina, on the other hand, has had a year of biology at secondary school and is fascinated by what happens between Bryan's mouth and Bryan's bum. Maybe that's next term's project: Bryan and his fatal effect on biodegradable matter. Perhaps they could dissect him.

And then there's the crying. Morning, noon and night; the thing never stops caterwauling. It was like listening to a vet de-sex a cat, without anaesthetic. They went to bed at night with his sobbing in their ears, and woke up the next morning to a dawn chorus of yowling that frightened birds out of trees and attracted wildlife from miles around.

'He's just a bit colicky,' their parents had explained, gazing at their little bundle of misery with tolerant smiles. It was sickening to watch.

Bryan, according to his loving half-brother and half-sister, never seemed to stop grizzling unless he was eating something he could turn into radioactive waste. Even Mina's father, a geologist with kind eyes, a bushy grey beard and even bushier ginger eyebrows, made jokes about taking samples of his son's poo to his new job at the mine. 'I could get them to run a Geiger counter over it; tell them it's a new strain.'

And what a strain it was. Every so often Bryan would turn purple, and veins would stand out on his head with the exertion of pushing another toxic bundle into his nappy. It was a performance that never failed to make Mina's top lip curl in disgust. She would bet anything that her father hadn't been this *goo-goo*, *ga-ga* when *she* was a baby.

So they bicker on through the sun-blasted desert, throwing up a long billowing plume of red dust behind them that makes their 4X4 look like it's ablaze and they're trying to outrun the flames.

But the Liptons and the Danielses aren't fleeing from a fire.

Oh, no; unknown to them they are rushing full speed towards one.

The town of Grymm perches on the very edge of the Great Desert. It is inextricably part *of* the landscape but is not of the landscape, like the dry, pale bones of some enormous dragon that have fused with the very earth of its final resting place. It is easy to believe that these desiccated remains – perhaps exposed by a freak wind – resemble a town only by accident.

Beyond Grymm to the west, the landscape turns into a vast dustbowl of many thousands of square miles. It is more or less featureless, apart from the arrow-straight dirt road that disappears into the permanent heat haze. Get one-hundred miles into it and there is nothing to see but red dust and the horizon for 360 degrees. It is an eerie feeling to stop, as many travellers do, and realize that you can see the curve of the Earth. Eerie and more than a little frightening, as if God were whispering in your ear that, next to all *this*, there's the insignificant, pathetic little speck that is *you*. God, or the devil.

Beyond Grymm to the east, it's more of the same – just not quite as much of it. Seven or eight hours' hard driving will find you in the city, in a hot hotel bath, scrubbing sand from every crease and pore, and marvelling at how it got there. That's both the dust *and* Grymm.

Legend has it that in the late 1800s it was a horse called Pilgrymm who discovered gold on the eastern threshold of the desert. Standing outside one of the impromptu canvas inns that sprang up from time to time to take advantage of the passing parade of prospectors heading further west, Pilgrymm the nag pawed at the ground and unearthed a soft yellow metal. Simple as that.

Gold!

Gold fever!

Gold rush!

And Grymm was born.

The gold is long, long gone, but other precious minerals were found there, and *that* legacy remains in the shape of the giant mine sitting just north of town and in the random hillocks of discarded earth and rock left by generations of desperate miners. Once, the area was an ants' nest of activity as they scurried in and out of holes in the ground. Since then, more than one person has gone into the low-lying hills and never been seen again. Swallowed up, quite literally, by the Earth itself.

Until they finished the bypass a few years ago, Grymm was the final watering hole for travellers before that great, flat, arid expanse swallowed them up – in a good sense. Or spat them out – for it was also the place to buy new provisions and stock up on water and petrol *after* emerging from that same wasteland. Today, only a lopsided wooden sign decorates the side of the new highway, and fewer and fewer travellers take up the offer. Perhaps it's the declining population statistic that someone has thoughtfully painted on the bottom of the sign:

~~5000~~ ~~3502~~ ~~2006~~ ~~1545~~ ~~810~~ 200

Grymm, the dripping, blood-red paint reveals, is a place you *leave*.

Thanks to the bypass, fewer and fewer people bother to make the detour to Grymm, forcing the struggling locals to rely on the mine for survival. And it's this great jagged scar in the surface of the planet that has brought George Lipton and his fractured family to the town. Three months, he has promised them. A three-month contract and then it's back to 'civilization'. And it's not like he can turn it down. Things haven't been great recently. The money's good – better than good – and they've got another mouth to feed now, haven't they?

Which brings us back to Jacob and Mina, staring moodily out of their respective windows at the monotony of the passing landscape, and blaming the screaming infant between them for their awful predicament.

Poor Mina: stranded for a summer and more in the middle of nowhere while, back home, her once-best friend, the now-nauseating bitch Nicola Elton, flutters her eyelashes at Jimmy Flynn. Mina had been flirting innocently with him in class with the aim of turning up the heat during the holidays. If he was lucky she might have even let him *kiss* her.

Of course, gorgeous Jimmy could have his pick of girls but . . . Nicola? It wasn't *fair*. It made her feel sick. And could she stop thinking about it? There's Nicola in her push-up bra! And there's Jimmy – dark-haired, dreamy-eyed, cherub-lipped Jimmy with his muscles and his tongue hanging out like one of those cartoon wolves.

And here's Wilhelmina Lipton: imprisoned in the middle of nowhere, surrounded by idiot stepbrothers, noxious half-brothers and . . . and . . . dirt. Red earth, red sand, spiky pale patches of scrub, and red rocks.

It's a cruel and unusual punishment.

Apart from that, it's *boring*.

And then there's poor Jacob: stuck in Nowheresville with the Wicked Witch of the West while the guys surfed all summer. *His* board was stuck in a friend's shed gathering dust. At least, he hoped it was gathering dust; if Calum laid so much as a *finger* on it . . . What? *What?* What could he do, stuck out here? Maybe he could get

Wilhelmina the witch to put a spell on him. Wipe his memory of the twenty-first century or something.

And what were the chances there was an internet café in this place? Out here? No chance. Zilch in a million. Even satellites would give *this* place a miss. His mother said even TV reception would be a problem. So, no TV, no internet, no telephone coverage . . . no *fun*. Like being stranded on the dark side of the *moon*.

And why?

Because they had an extra mouth to feed.

And whose fault was that? Not theirs, that was certain.

Blast baby Bryan.

It was going to be boring, boring, *boring*.

'Hey! Look at that!' said George, touching the brakes and peering through the windscreen. 'It's a dust devil – but I've never seen one *that* big before. It looks more like a tornado.'

Instead of the miniature eddies of wind and heat that occasionally appear in the desert, this one – moving from right to left across the landscape about half a mile away – was a massive whirlpool, a great greedy funnel turned blood-red by the sand it was sucking up.

Jacob pulled the iPod buds out of his ears and leaned forward. Tinny music escaped from the tiny speakers. Mina wondered what rubbish he was listening to now.

'Wow!' he said. 'That's *sick*!'

'*You're* sick,' countered Mina as she watched the dust devil power across their path. 'Sick in the head.'

'You're so—'

'George?' interrupted Mary from the front seat. 'I think it's changed direction. Has it?'

All four of them were silent as the dust devil halted its progress across their line of sight and began to move towards them. It was as if it were alive and had seen their tiny vehicle sitting there, unprotected and alone in the middle of the road.

'It has!' Mary's voice was higher and louder this time. 'It's coming this way!'

Mina and Jacob felt the hair on the backs of their necks stand up. Even Bryan seemed to notice a change in the atmosphere and stopped his mewling. Mina leaned forward as far as her seatbelt would allow and began slapping her father on the shoulder.

'Dad! Do something! Do something!'

'George?' whispered Mary.

George brought the 4WD to a stop, turned to them and shrugged. His face was a mixture of confusion, shock and amusement. 'Do what?' he said with a lopsided grin.

Instead of wavering all over the landscape, the narrow end of the dust devil's funnel seemed to have grounded itself right in front of them. It was wide enough to cover the road – and three or four car-widths to either side.

'But we can't just sit here!' yelled Mina as small pieces of grit began to rain down on the roof.

'She's right, George. Let's go.' Mary was beginning to panic. 'Let's *go*.'

The drumming on the roof grew louder as larger bits of gravel started to fall around them. Mina jumped and yelped as something cracked against the window next to her. The 'devil' was about 400 metres away, obscuring the sky and creating a sepia-tinged semi-dusk in front of them. Behind, the sun shone in a bright blue sky.

'Yeah, let's go,' barked Jacob. 'Back up or something.'

'Too late,' said George quietly as it struck them with enough force to make the steering wheel buck in his hands. For what seemed like an eternity, the jeep was buffeted by a whirling dervish of heat and sand and noise that blanked out the rest of the world. They might just as well have been deep underground.

Mina screamed.

Mary screamed.

George fought silently to stop the car from moving, his foot jammed on the brake with all his strength.

Jacob snatched a green canvas shoulder bag from the floor between his feet, hunched over it, scrunched his eyes closed and stuffed his fingers in his ears.

The noise was like the grating of gears in some enormous, celestial truck. Their world was suddenly nothing but darkness and thunder and movement as the car shifted and the wheels skidded under them. Then came a loud report, like a gunshot from a high-powered rifle, and a crack appeared in the windscreen.

'George!' Mary put a trembling hand up against the glass, as if just that simple gesture would stop the fury outside from coming inside.

'Daaaaad!' Mina was in tears, looking around in panic, wondering whether to open the door and run for it. Jacob was curled up in the corner, thinking, *Make it go away, make it go away, makeitgoaway, makeitgoaway . . .*

And then, as if in answer to his silent prayer, it was gone, spinning off to the side and leaving them sitting in the middle of the road in deathly silence. They watched as the whirlwind staggered off into the desert, almost expecting it to turn round and finish off what it had started.

'Everyone all right?' asked George after a while. There was an embarrassed hush.

Mary laughed, wiping away tears with the back of her hand. She looked back at Mina and Jacob, who were both trying desperately to regain their composure and look 'cool'. Bryan, on the other hand, had fallen asleep. 'That was amazing!' she said.

'Pity about the windscreen, though,' said George. He touched it gently. 'And I shudder to think what the bodywork's like. Still, it could have been worse.'

'Ah, but are we still in Kansas?' said Mary, laughing nervously.

'Ask the munchkins,' replied George with a grin. He turned the ignition and the engine roared into life, bringing with it the sweet, cold relief of the air-conditioning. 'Well, kids, are we?'

'Are we what?' snapped Mina. She felt stupid for losing control in front of Jacob. Jacob might have almost wet his pants but at least he hadn't screamed like a *girl*.

'In Kansas any more?'

'What *are* you on about?' snarled Mina.

'Leave them,' said Mary with an indulgent smile at Bryan, sound asleep in a baby seat between the two older children. 'They're in a world of their own sometimes.'

Yeah, thought Mina with an inward sneer as they drove on. *In some sort of parallel universe where everything was boring until something tried to kill you!*

Yeah, thought Jacob, with a sly glance at his stepsister. *In a world where your worst nightmares come true. What have I done to deserve this?*

Then they both thought, *Stupid stupid stupid Bryan.*

2

Grymm, when it finally arrived, arrived with a surprise. Mary saw it first. 'Oh! Oh, look at that. What's *that* doing way out here?'

They had turned off the main road ten minutes previously, passed between the tan walls of a canyon, rattled across a warped wooden bridge over a dry creek, and suddenly there it was on their right-hand side – a two-storey warehouse backed up hard against the final cliff face of the valley entrance. Even Mina was surprised enough to drop her hard-cultivated bored expression.

There were two dirty trucks parked off to one side and, beyond them, the paper-thin and rust-red metal bones of another unidentifiable vehicle that had all but crumbled into the dust. But what had caught their interest was the brightly coloured sign hammered above the front door: *Puzzlewick's Candle Factory*. Every letter was hand-painted in a different colour, and the 'i' in *Puzzlewick* was a burning candle. It was also utterly free of desert sand; as clean and shiny as if the owners washed it down every morning. Perhaps they did. You never knew when a carload of potential customers was going to pass by, right? It certainly stood out.

'Why,' mused Mary, 'would you start a candle factory all the way out here?'

'I once drove through a place that had three houses, two tractor dealerships and a Christmas decoration factory,' said her husband, as if that explained everything. Then, realizing that this explained nothing: 'It was for export. I think.'

'Still . . . a *candle* factory? It must be well over thirty degrees out there.'

'Then they must have one hell of an air-conditioning system. Bet our air con at home wouldn't be able to hold a candle to it. Eh, kids? Get it? Candle? Eh?'

Mina and Jacob, composure regained, looked at the factory with boredom, and at their parents with contempt.

'Lame, George, really lame,' said Jacob.

Mina, feeling that she had to defend her father against this squeaky-voiced twit, gave a short but half-hearted laugh. Jacob glanced at her, rolled his eyes, and sighed just as the baby, still innocently asleep, farted wetly.

'Goodonya, Bryan,' said Jacob, deadpan.

As Mary snorted with laughter, George shifted the jeep into gear, and they trundled on towards the outskirts of Grymm. This time it was Mina's turn to roll her eyes. How would she survive three months with these idiots? Even her father seemed to have lost his mind. So what if there was a candle factory in Grymm? The whole place could melt for all she cared. All she could think of was what Jimmy Flynn was doing *right now*.

Jacob, with a sly sideways glance at Mina, thought, *I bet she's thinking about that idiot Jim Flynn. She always gets that goofy look when he's around. She's such a girl.*

Grymm itself began a few hundred metres away, where the single-lane gravel road turned into a sealed, but potholed, main street wide enough to take four cars abreast.

The few shops, they saw, were mainly pale and peeling clapboard, shaded from the blazing sun by a covered veranda that ran along the side of the street. There were no trees but a half a dozen power poles threw long, late-evening shadows across it. The power lines between them hung low and lazy.

This was their new home? The children's spirits plunged even further. There was a hardware shop, an undertaker's, a threadbare second-hand furniture shop, a dowdy and dusty-looking sell-anything store, a souvenir shop, a dilapidated hotel with holes in the roof, a greasy-looking one-pump petrol station and . . . not much else. All the shops were closed, giving the empty street the air of a ghost town. There was also an abandoned Chinese restaurant, the Golden Dragon, that looked as though it had not cooked a meal in many a year.

'Pity that, eh, Jacob?' said Mary, turning to look at the dusty red exterior.

'Yeah.' Jacob could feel himself blushing. Just because his real father had been Asian didn't mean that he wanted to eat chow mein all the time. If anything, it made him less inclined towards anything oriental. His father had disappeared when Jacob was five. Run off back to China, they thought, away from the white woman and her half-and-half son. Whatever the reason, they had neither seen nor heard from him again. For that he hated both his father and, perhaps even more strongly, the physical legacies that marked him out for playground taunts and torment. 'Chinky Chinaman!' It might not be clever or original, but it still hurt. Just looking in a mirror was reminder enough without his mother going on about it. She'd had the sense to change his surname back from Qiu, but now . . . How could she be so . . . so . . . indifferent? She just didn't seem to *care*.

He looked without interest at the abandoned restaurant and the crude picture of a dragon drawn in gold around the windows, its great head and mouth opening up around the door.

'Yeah,' he sneered. 'Great. Perhaps Dad's working there. We'll get some free stir fry.'

Mary, knowing better than to rise to the bait, shrugged and smiled thinly at her second husband. George reached across and gave her thigh a reassuring squeeze. She looked at her watch. 'I'd have been at art class right about now,' she sighed. The children weren't the only ones with regrets.

'Hey, look at that,' said Mina, more to break the tension than from any genuine interest.

'That' was the tattered remains of a fairground, set back on a vacant lot halfway along the main street. They looked over at a row of white-faced clowns with open mouths, the kind you drop balls in to win prizes. All of them were covered in thick dust; several had had their heads caved in, leaving just a round 'O' of surprise below the nose. For some reason, Jacob thought it was one of the saddest things he had ever seen.

And there, ahead of them on this lazy Sunday afternoon, the real-estate agent, slouched outside her premises as if she knew to expect them *at that very moment*.

She looked like a ghost herself in the sun; a dark heat shimmer against the faded, almost bone-white of the town. In her hand was a set of keys on a black ring, the sort jailers used in cartoons; the keys to the dungeons where Jacob and Mina were to be incarcerated.

'That must be Thespa Grymm,' said George needlessly. 'Be nice.'

For Thespa Grymm was like no other real-estate agent you have ever seen.

Thespa Grymm had to be seen to be believed.

Thespa Grymm lived up to her name.

As Jacob and Mina clambered from the cool of the 4WD and into the furnace-like heat of the afternoon, Mary busied herself unbuckling Bryan, and George jumped out to greet the woman he had only spoken to on the phone.

'Mrs Grymm? George Lipton.'

'It's *Ms* Grymm,' said Ms Grymm in a deep, abrasive growl before turning to the children. Mina was puzzled to see something – a look of recognition, perhaps – cross the woman's pasty face. As George introduced them and they shook her pudgy hand, she half expected *Ms* Grymm to say, *Haven't we met before?* Instead, the flare of interest in her eyes died and she just grunted, like a pig.

'These are your keys,' she said, thrusting the huge

iron key ring at George. 'The big one's for the house, the small ones are for the shed and the padlock on the gate. Now, I've stocked the freezer for you, and I've got a map here somewhere. Not that you'll need it – any idiot could find it – but just in case.'

'In case?' asked George.

'In case you go getting yourself lost. Then they can't blame me.'

'Right.' George waited uneasily, a forced grin on his face, as she burrowed through the pockets of her voluminous cardigan. Mina and Jacob, feeling the heat through the soles of their shoes, stood in the shade outside the office window, with its faded photographs and bright FOR SALE, FOR LEASE, and AUCTION signs. They were both, quite simply, aghast at the apparition before them.

Thespa Grymm was about Jacob's height and as wide as she was tall. Unwashed frizzy grey hair framed a countenance as round as a smiley; a chubby, piggy-eyed face, half-smoked cigarette dangling from humourless lips. On the right of her chin sat a pitted wart from which erupted three black hairs, as thick and lustrous as a cat's whiskers. As she searched, moving two packets of unopened cigarettes from pocket to pocket, she wheezed and squinted at them through a veil of blue smoke.

'It's here somewhere . . .'

'Look, it's really no bother. Just point us in the right direction; I'm sure we'll find it. We got this far,' said George lightly.

'No, no, no,' came the reply. '*Nothing's quite what it seems in Grymm.* You'll take a wrong turn and end up on the plains. We'll find what's left of you in two or three years and it'll all be my fault.'

And we can't have that, thought Mina, dismayed to discern a faint whiff of sweat coming from the woman as she hunted through any number of pockets under the heavy black cardigan. And was it any wonder? The cardigan was covering a crew-neck woollen jumper, black again, the whole ensemble completed by a black knee-length skirt and black tights full of runs. Her calves splayed out and ended in swollen ankles that disappeared tightly into a pair of brown-check carpet slippers with a hole in one toe.

Jacob looked his stepsister up and down, examining her black T-shirt, black jeans and black Doc Marten boots. 'Are you two related?' he whispered.

Mina gave a sharp tug on the rope strap of the tattered green canvas bag that Jacob had slung across his back. 'Glad to see you're still hanging onto your *comfort* bag, little boy,' she snarled.

'Ah, here it is,' exclaimed Grymm as Jacob scooted

out of Mina's reach. In her excitement, a cylinder of ash dropped off her cigarette and left a trail like volcanic rock down the long slope of her huge breasts. It wasn't the first such stain. 'I knew it was here somewhere. There.'

She held out a crumpled ball of paper that had been torn out of a notebook. They crowded round to look at the crude map scrawled on it. There was also a phone number and Thespa Grymm's name. 'Just in case you need to get in touch. Not that there's a phone at the house.'

As they digested this piece of information, breath held to avoid the clammy stink coming off her, she made them all jump by exclaiming, 'Now *who* is this beautiful boy?'

Mina Jacob and even George turned, expecting some stranger to have arrived, but were greeted by Mary, who had finally extricated Bryan from the baby seat. George smiled proudly while the other two turned to each other in astonishment.

'This is my wife, Mary. And our other son, Bryan.'

Bryan then astonished them *all* by giving Thespa Grymm a happy gurgle and a smile that lit up his sleepy face. This was very unlike Bryan, whose repertoire of facial expressions so far had extended from fierce to fiercer, with a few side trips to straining-so-hard-his-head'll-explode.

But here he was extending his pudgy arms towards the fat bulk of the Grymm woman as if she were a long-lost aunt.

'Oh, he's *gorgeous*!' gushed the leviathan. 'Can I hold him?'

Mary hesitated until Grymm grabbed at her cigarette with a pudgy hand and flicked it casually into the middle of the street. Jacob and Mina backed off, suddenly finding the prices of real estate around the town infinitely fascinating. The last thing they wanted was to get caught in the usual *isn't he lovely* crap.

Grymm pressed the baby to her face. Cheek-to-cheek like that, they looked eerily similar. When she pulled away, Bryan giggled again, one side of his face stained with her make-up and the other decorated with a red lipstick kiss. Holding him high in the air, she cooed at him and grinned lasciviously. She was looking at him, it occurred to Mina, the way her father looked at a fillet of beef. For some reason this sent shivers up her spine. She glanced at Jacob, who shrugged lazily at the unexpected exuberance.

'Oooh, he's so lovely I could *eat* him!' screeched Grymm, and pretended to take lumps out of his neck. At which Bryan giggled musically.

Mina got the uneasy feeling that this woman wasn't joking; that given half a chance she'd take him home, feed him up, and then roast him with an apple in his little, toothless, drooling mouth. Look at her! She was drooling too!

And then it was gone. Grymm handed the wriggling blob – who immediately began to cry – back to his mother, sent a not-so-sly look in the direction of the other two children, and said, 'What a pity they have to grow up.'

Mary and George caught her sideways glance and, for a second or two, the three adults stared at Mina and Jacob as if they were beings from another planet. The comically sour looks on the children's faces made their parents laugh at Grymm's 'joke'. Then the three of them fell easily into a conversation about the town, its inhabitants and where to shop for nappies.

'Would you like to come inside for a cup of tea?' asked Grymm eventually. 'We can sign the rental agreement at the same time.'

'Sure,' replied George with a grin. 'I could murder a cup after all that driving. Kids?'

'Nah, we're good, thanks.' Mina was sure this was one thing on which she and Jacob the moron would agree. As the others filed into Grymm's office, she tugged at his sleeve and tried to pull him up the street.

'What are you doing, *Wilhelmina*?' Jacob snatched his arm away. 'Off the cloth, moth!'

'Will you shut up and listen, *Jakie*, you idiot.' It *wasn't* a question, and Jacob had enough sense to recognize that his stepsister was serious. What *was* her problem? He followed her to slump, wrung out by the heat and by being trapped in a car with each other all day, on a bench outside the souvenir shop. Jacob was puzzled. He'd never seen Mina so freaked out and, to his considerable surprise, that worried him. She might be a bit of a pain sometimes but she always seemed so confident, so sure of herself. Suddenly that confidence was gone, and it frightened him. He even let the 'Jakie' jibe go.

'What's up?'

'Didn't you see that?' Mina asked. 'The way that . . . that . . . *thing* looked at Bryan? As if she wanted to eat him?'

'I thought you'd like that; you always reckoned he'd taste good in a bun.' Jacob knew it was the wrong thing to say but he didn't like the way the conversation was going. He wanted to bring it back down to what was familiar: insults, arguments, torments. But Mina was having none of it. She leaned in close and whispered, as if Grymm had supernatural hearing (which wouldn't have surprised Mina at that moment), 'No, it wasn't like that. She *meant* it. Didn't you feel it? There's something odd about her.'

'There's something odd about *you* too,' scoffed Jacob, 'but I don't think you'd actually *eat* Bryan.'

'Oh for Christ's sake, Jacob, stop being such a bloody know-all. Just this once will you *listen* to me?'

Jacob, until then slouched sullenly on the bench, sat upright; Mina never let herself be seen as vulnerable. Well, hardly ever. At least, not in front of him. He gave up trying to bring the situation back to normal.

'She did seem a bit weird. Nobody could go that crazy over baby Bryan and still be sane. She certainly didn't like *us*.'

'And you'd have to be mad not to like us, right?' This time it was Mina's turn to smile – mainly because she knew she'd managed to scare her stepbrother as well as herself.

'Right.' Jacob smiled back. 'But she's not going to *eat* Bryan, Mina. It's just an expression.'

'I know, I know, she's just a spooky old woman who loves babies but hates them when they grow up and start to answer back. And how could you not end up strange in this place? Look at it.'

They looked at it.

Nothing moved.

Nothing stirred.

There was no wind. Even the flies had disappeared, apart from a few buzzing desultorily on the inside of the souvenir-shop window. There was nothing but a sullen, sweltering, greasy heat that clung to their skin like warm slime.

'What are we going to *do* here?' Jacob said, then looked away, as if scrutinizing the barren street.

Mina caught the merest glimpse of his eyes beginning to moisten as he recalled what they'd left behind and the empty weeks and months that stretched out before them. His grip tightened on his ever-present green canvas bag. God, he was *such* a baby. So what if his dad had left him. Her mother had *died*, for God's sake. And *she* wasn't dribbling like Bryan.

The little fool was right about the Grymm woman, though. She'd overreacted. Thespa Grymm was just a badly dressed old woman with nothing to do except stand around on a scorching-hot Sunday afternoon waiting to hand over keys to strangers who would be gone before long. No wonder she acted a little mad. And maybe Mina herself was letting the whole Goth-witch thing go to her head. She looked down at her boots, now dusted with sand, and wondered if they weren't perhaps a little unsuitable for thirty-plus-degree heat. What's the point in making an anti-fashion statement if you melt while making it?

'You know something?'

'What?' Jacob seemed fascinated by the hand written

store signs on the other side of the street, advertising cheap baked beans and tinned tomatoes. He avoided looking at her.

'I can't wait to get out of these friggin' boots. I'm melting here.'

Jacob laughed, a little too loudly maybe, and then dropped his head to stare at his trainers. 'It'll be all right, won't it?'

'Of course it will. We've got each other, haven't we? What more could you want?' She stood up and gave his hair a ruffle. It wasn't meant as a friendly gesture; Jacob had just started spending longer in the bathroom, experimenting with all manner of water, waxes and gels to get his coiffure just right. And woe betide anyone who mussed up the resulting edifice. At least it brought their relationship back to what was comfortable and safe: bickering.

'Not the hair, OK? Stay away from the hair or . . .'

'Or what? You'll stab me to death with your quiff?'

'Just 'cause you look like a hedge.'

'Better than looking like I've been pulled through one backwards.'

Before Jacob could think of a suitable insult their parents and Thespa Grymm emerged from the office. George waved them over. 'Come on, kids. Let's get up to the house before it gets dark.'

'Coming,' shouted Mina.

Back at the car, Grymm was still chuckling away with Jacob's mother, praising Bryan the poo-machine to high heaven while simultaneously explaining that their furniture had arrived the day before and the delivery men had taken their best guess at where everything went.

'I'm sure we'll muddle through tonight,' said George from the driver's seat. He had Grymm's rag-tag map smoothed out on the dashboard. 'I'm good for nothing but a quick shower and bed.'

'It is a long drive, that's for certain, Mr Lipton,' said Grymm as Jacob and Mina came over. She nodded in their direction. 'Still, a few more years and you'll be able to get these two to drive.'

'As long as they're not sitting next to each other at the time, eh, kids? We'd end up upside down in a ditch.'

As they clambered into the back seat and pulled their seatbelts across, Grymm smiled at them. It wasn't a pleasant sight to begin with – it had been a long, tooth-rotting while since that mouth had seen a dentist – but Mina imagined that the woman had one smile for their parents and one for them. And the one she saved for them was more knowing; more of a sneer or smirk than a grin. Somehow they both got the idea that this woman *disapproved* of them. As if, just by existing, they had offended her. Or was it something else? Something deeper?

'Well, thank the Lord for small mercies – at least you've got the lovely Bryan to keep them apart,' said Grymm without taking her eyes off them. 'You are lucky, Mrs Lipton, to have such a beautiful baby boy. You look after him, d'you hear? Don't you dare let him out of your sight or I might just steal in and *gobble* him all up, he's so gorgeous.'

Mina gasped and Jacob found himself frozen – as if the woman's piercing gaze had pinned him to his seat like a bug; as if some awful memory had surfaced for a moment and shocked him into immobility. It was like seeing the back of a whale in the ocean and only being able to guess how big it really was under the waves. It was there, just out of reach. Something to do with . . . what?

Grymm held their gazes for a second longer, moving from face to face as if looking into their very souls. And then it was gone. She slammed the door, backed away from the vehicle and began patting herself, searching for a cigarette packet and a lighter.

Mary wound down her window. 'Thank you, Ms Grymm. It was nice to meet you.'

'And it was a joy to meet you. *All* of you.' She lit a cigarette, sucked on it like her life depended on it and leaned down to look across at George. 'It's not often we get a family like yours here in Grymm. It'll be good to have some young people around the place for a change. And do be careful on that off-road section, Mr Lipton. It can be dangerous out there, and we don't want you all dead before your three months are up, do we? Remember, *nothing's quite what it seems in Grymm.*'

'We'll be fine. Oh, and thanks again for getting some food in. Much appreciated. Maybe we'll see you around town.'

'Oh, I'm sure we'll be seeing lots of each other.' Was she looking only at Jacob and Mina when she said that? It seemed so to them.

As the car pulled away, Mary turned to her husband. 'She seemed nice. She certainly took a shine to Bryan.'

'Yes, I liked her. Despite the grim exterior. Ha! Ha! Ha! Geddit? Grymm? *Grim*? Eh, kids?'

'She was weird,' said Jacob. 'I didn't like her.'

'Just because she doesn't look like Britney Spears, I suppose? And what would you two know, anyway? You hardly said two words to the woman and then just wandered off. It was very embarrassing. You were only jealous that she made such a fuss of the baby.'

'Jealous? Are you kidding? She said she wanted to eat him!' Mina was aghast that the adults should take the old witch's side. 'And she meant it too.'

Mary's sideways glance at her husband was a text-book example of something that says so little and yet so much. In this case it said, *Your daughter's a fruit loop.* At least, that's what it looked like to Mina.

'She did! I know she did!'

'Shouting about it won't help, Wilhelmina.' Mina knew her father well enough to understand that when he used her full name she was heading for major trouble. Ordinarily this wouldn't have made much difference; Mina was of an age when her mouth refused to stay closed when more sensible parts of her brain were telling her to shut up. But today she had other things on her mind: for some reason the Grymm woman had frightened her badly and she needed time to figure out why. Even when Bryan began to cry again and Mary hissed, 'Now look what you've done,' she stared out of the window and kept her thoughts to herself.

'I wonder,' mused George as they pulled out of town, 'what bad thing I did in a previous life to deserve this?'

3

As the crow flies the house wasn't that far out of town, but because it was perched on the top of an escarpment, the road to it was a steep struggle, gravelly and serpentine, more rut than road. For the first time since leaving the city George had to engage the four-wheel drive to negotiate the twists and turns.

When they arrived, the porch light was shining like a lighthouse in the gathering dusk. Unlike the weatherboard of many of the shops in the main street, this house was built of brick – testimony to the deep pockets of the mine manager who had it built to show off back when the mine was a licence to print money. It had pitched, grey-tiled roofs, English-style gabled ends, two chimneys and several dormer windows. An ornate wooden veranda ran across the front and round the right-hand side. It looked, in comparison to the other buildings in Grymm, as if it had fallen out of the sky from another time and place.

'Oh, George!' Mary exclaimed with a clap of her hands. 'It's like a fairy-tale house. Look at the beautiful lead lights in the windows! And what's that on the end of the roof there? A gargoyle or something? Oh, isn't it just *stunning*?'

George, looking over from where he was loosening the straps on the jeep's roof-rack, squinted upwards. 'It's a horse, I think. Yeah, it's lovely. Now, are you lot going to give me a hand with this or do I have to unpack on my own?'

'It's a dragon,' said Mina pedantically.

'What?'

'On the roof. It's not a horse, it's a dragon, I think.'

'I don't like it,' sulked Jacob. 'It's . . . spooky.'

'You'll get used to it,' said his mother, giving him an affectionate hug. He was still shorter than her, but not by much. 'Come on, Jacob, give it a chance. All old houses seem spooky at first. You'll wonder what all the fuss was about this time next week. Come on, let's get unpacked. It's getting dark. *Brrr* – and cold.'

But as she walked back to help George unpack, Jacob noticed something on the thick, rough WELCOME mat and picked it up.

'Hey, Mum, there's an envelope here addressed to

you and George.' He held it up and gave it a gentle shake. 'I think there's something metal in it. It feels like . . .. like . . . jewellery or something.'

'Let's see,' said Mary, coming back to where her son was standing with the white envelope clutched in both hands. 'Well, it's . . . Are you OK? Jacob?'

Mina looked up from where she was helping her dad pull suitcases down from the roof-rack. Jacob had a far-away look in his eyes, as if he were seeing something else entirely; as if he were looking through the fabric of reality at something very, very bad indeed. It gave her the shivers, and her mind turned, unexpectedly and frighteningly, back to Thespa Grymm. *Nothing's quite what it seems . . .*

'Jacob, are you all right?' asked Mary, taking the envelope from him. 'Son?'

And then, just as quickly as it had started, it was gone. Jacob's eyes regained focus and he grinned his lopsided grin. 'Yeah, just tired from the drive, Mum.'

'Good. Now go help George and Mina with the luggage. My, my, someone's got *very* nice handwriting.'

The large white envelope was made of thick, expensive parchment and the name and address on the front were handwritten, not typed. Underneath this, in thick black ink, curlicued, Gothic and flowing, was written: *George and Mary – Welcome.*

'Short and to the point,' puffed George as he struggled past with a large suitcase and dumped it unceremoniously on the porch. On the way back he added: 'What's in it?'

'Oh, look, it's a note from the manager at the mine, welcoming us to the town. That's nice of him. *Dear George and Mary, I hope your journey wasn't too arduous and that you will be happy in your new home. Please accept the enclosed as tokens of my esteem. At the very least they will serve as souvenirs of your time in Grymm. Yours sincerely, Mr Anhanga, Mine Manager.* Isn't that sweet?'

'And the token of his esteemed esteem?' quipped George, stopping and peering over his wife's shoulder.

'Some sort of ring; one each.' She held one of them up to the light and squinted at it. 'I need to get my glasses from the car, but I think they've got the mine's logo on them. Is that real gold, do you think?'

George took a ring from her and scratched a grubby but professional thumbnail over the surface. 'Possibly, but I think it's probably iron pyrites, fool's gold . . .'

'And really, really, *really* ugly iron pyrites,' said Mina, pausing as she passed by dragging another over-stuffed suitcase. 'I wouldn't put *that* on *my* finger if you paid me.'

'Well, each to their own,' said George, stuffing the envelope and rings into the pocket of his jeans. 'Now, come on, let's get this stuff indoors before it gets dark.'

And it was all they could do to unpack the car before darkness fell. And for once, the idea of night 'falling' was apt. One moment it was dusk and the next it was as dark, as George put it, as a coalminer's underpants.

Inside, even though the removal men had been in the previous day, there was still a faint smell of mothballs about the place. Mary immediately found the kitchen and put the kettle on while George began hauling their bags up the stairs. If either Mina or Jacob had been in a better mood they might have appreciated the haphazard nature of the place, with its nooks and crannies, its cast-iron fireplaces, and lights fashioned after the brass bracket lights of the late nineteenth century. Or perhaps their unease was just another sort of appreciation. Both thought the place looked *too* good, as if the original owner had just stepped out for a walk and would at any moment stroll, ghostlike, in through the large French windows at the rear and demand to know just who they thought they were.

Mary and George, on the other hand, were ecstatic, constantly calling out to come look at this, come look at that. Even Bryan stopped crying as if in honour of the occasion.

'Hey! Hey, look at this!' shouted Mary when she went into the dining room, flicked on the lights and realized that the ceiling extended up through the two floors and ended in an octagonal glass roof vent to let the light in. 'Now, isn't that something?'

'Fascinating,' whispered Mina, so only Jacob could hear.

But their initial discomfort, which had been quickly replaced by a bloody-minded refusal to be impressed, disappeared when they discovered that a *huge* mistake had been made. No, not just huge – humungous. Titanic. Of epic proportions.

There, in one of the bedrooms, was Bryan's cot, a small chest of drawers and a pink bunny-rabbit nightlight. One of the removal men had even taken the liberty of rigging up Bryan's multicoloured stuffed-clown mobile – the maddening one that played *Greensleeves* over and over and over again – above the cot.

All well and good, but for some inexplicable, horrible, bizarre, *sick* reason they had put Jacob's bed in the same room as Mina's. Having scared them to death earlier in the day, God was now laughing at them.

'Oh well,' grinned Mary light-heartedly when they told her about their earth-shattering discovery. 'You'll just have to make do and bunk in with each other tonight.' At the sight of Jacob's horrified face, though, she snapped. 'You don't expect us to start rearranging furniture at this time of night, do you? Don't be so selfish, Jacob. I thought you found it all too *spooky*?

You don't mind, do you, Mina? It's only for one night.'

Mina, by now too tired to argue *yet again* with her stepmother (and still a little unnerved by the meeting with Thespa Grymm), agreed charitably. 'It's just one night, Jacob. Come on – *I* won't eat you.'

'Very funny, Wilhelmina Witchy-poo.' He frowned, but she guessed he was secretly relieved. As was she, deep down. First night in a strange new house in the middle of nowhere? Who wanted to sleep alone anyway? If it wasn't the house creaking in peculiar ways, it was the desert wind whispering round its corners and eaves. And then there was the Grymm woman. What a freak! That alone was enough to give you nightmares.

And there was the dark; neither of them had encountered a darkness quite so profound. It was as if somebody had flipped a switch and turned off not just the house lights but the stars themselves. The clouds that had gathered in the past hour didn't help.

After they'd had a quick microwave meal, Mary said, 'Come on, kids. Bed.' Somewhere behind her in the house they could hear Bryan's teeth-clenching wail. 'Jacob, your pyjamas are in that brown case in the corner. We're just down the hall if you need us, OK? Night-night. And don't forget to clean your teeth, Jacob.'

'Yes, yes – g'night, Mum.'

When she had gone the two enemies faced each

other in silence. It was the first time they had shared a room and neither knew quite how to go about it.

Mina began pulling clothes out of a bag. 'Hey, what was all that about earlier? You were being all weird.'

'Weird? When?' Jacob looked pointedly at Mina's clothes. 'If anyone around here's weird . . .'

'Oh, give it a rest, Jacob. When you picked up that envelope. What happened? Something did – don't say it didn't.'

'I don't know – I just felt that something bad was in it. It was like I could suddenly *see* all these bad thoughts and . . . they were *my* bad thoughts. All the stuff I . . . Look, I don't know, OK?'

'OK, OK, keep your quiff on, Elvis. Forget I asked. Do you want the bathroom first?'

'Nah, you go first. Just don't stink it out.'

'Stink? You can talk; you're worse than Bryan.'

'Nothing . . . *nothing* is worse than Bryan.'

'True. I'll be about ten minutes if you want to get changed for bed.'

'Sure.'

Mina gathered her towel, toothpaste and pyjamas together and clumped down the hallway to the bathroom. To her surprise, it was a cavernous room. Its floor, walls and ceiling were decorated in dusty pink, burgundy and pale green tiles. Right in the middle of it stood a gigantic enamelled cast-iron bath on four animal-shaped, bandy legs. It wasn't like any bathroom Mina had ever seen. Even the toilet, an old-fashioned, clunky-looking thing with a cracked wooden seat, looked like it belonged in a museum. It had a huge ceramic cistern high on the wall and a carved mahogany pull-handle on the end of a loose-linked chain.

The water in the taps was also antiquated. That is, cold – *freezing* cold. Dad would no doubt sort that out tomorrow, she thought. She hoped. Things were bad enough without throwing cold showers into the mix.

The cool tiles, the size of the room and the water – even her teeth felt icy after she'd brushed them – all conspired to send her back to the bedroom in double quick-time. At least she could snuggle under the blankets and warm up. What a weird place: like the surface of the sun during the day and bone-chillingly cold at night.

But as she entered the room she caught Jacob in the middle of changing. He'd put his pyjama bottoms on but seemed to be stuffing his head in the top's armhole.

'You are *such* an idiot.'

From underneath the top came the muffled sound of Jacob breathing heavily. Finally he wrenched it down over his head and emerged, red-faced. 'Don't you ever knock?'

'I don't usually have to knock to get into my own

room, you know. Jesus, you're making such a fuss over—Hey, what's all that?'

Mina was pointing at the bed, where Jacob's precious green bag had fallen open and spilled its guts. He leaped across and began furiously stuffing everything back in. But not before Mina got a good look at some of the contents.

'Isn't that your mum's ivory comb? The one she lost? What's it doing there? And Dad's Swiss Army knife? Jacob?'

'Just leave it alone, OK? It's none of your business. Go away and leave me alone.'

'Oh no, let's see what else you've got in there . . .' Mina grinned maliciously, and made a grab for the bag.

Jacob deflected her lunge and, turning his back to her, simply fell on the bed with the bag cuddled possessively beneath his body. 'Go away!'

Mina backed off, her face a mixture of disgust, pleasure, bafflement and bemusement, and sat on the edge of her bed. If Jacob had looked up he would have seen the face of a shark going in for an easy kill.

'You are getting odder by the day, Jacob. You know that? Other *babies* have comfort blankets but you have to have a comfort *bag*. And now *this*? It's called *stealing*, Jakie. You wait until I tell Dad. You are in so much trouble . . .'

'Tell him – see if I care,' came the muffled but angry reply. 'You're a freak! I hate you!'

'The feeling,' whispered Mina as she slid into bed and turned out the light, 'is mutual.'

They slept. Until some point that could have been ten o'clock or two o'clock, when something stirred in the gravelly yard beneath their window. Jacob was awake in an instant. He listened. There it was again: a sort of shuffling, or a snuffling, as if some wild animal were rooting around outside.

'Mina? Are you awake?' Silence. 'Mina? Did you hear that?'

'What? Go back to shleep.' Mina was slurred but, as yet, not shaken. 'It's late.'

'There's something outside. What is it?'

'The bogeyman. He's come to eat your brains. I told him it wasn't much of a meal.'

'Shut up and listen.'

Silence. And then they both heard it. A soft, slippery nuzzle, the sort of sound you'd expect a pig to make with its snout in a trough.

'Sounds like it's downstairs, under the window. What is it?'

'How would I know?' spat Mina. She was annoyed that Jacob had woken her and forced her – as the oldest – to confront whatever was making those disgusting noises. Why couldn't her father have taken up with someone with a muscle-bound seventeen-year-old instead of this snivelling kid?

Shivering in her oversized but thin black T-shirt and pyjama bottoms, she padded to the window and opened the curtains. Jacob appeared at her elbow.

'Bloody hell! Don't creep up on me like that!'

'What is it?'

'I don't know yet. Give me a chance. It's probably a stray dog or something.'

But it wasn't. A break in the dense cloud cover allowed a silver sliver of moonlight through to illuminate the scrubby back yard and two parched trees that somehow managed to cling to both the thin soil and to some semblance of life. The trunk and branches shone bone-white in the glow from the moon, grasping towards the house like the gnarled, arthritic hands and skeletal forearms of some giant buried witch. For a second Mina had the horrible idea that they were moving, thrusting up through the earth from the grave to clutch the house and crush them all.

'Look,' whispered Jacob. 'What's that?' He spoke through clenched teeth, not moving, not daring to point.

He didn't have to. Mina could see it too: a strangely

fluid black shape that moved about in the branches, leaping with uncanny agility from one tree to the next. It seemed to *flow* from spot to spot, defying the laws of the universe. It slid up and down, testing the limits of the outermost branches, which creaked alarmingly and bounced up and down.

'It's—' started Mina, before realizing she had no idea. Some kind of animal? She turned to Jacob and shrugged. And as she did so the thing in the branches froze, as if attuned to even the smallest of movements, the smallest breath on the window. Suddenly two large white eyes were turned on them and, in a blink of those same eyes, it leaped down from the trees and was swallowed up by the night.

'Well, it's gone now,' said Jacob sleepily, turning back to his bed. 'Whatever it was.'

Mina stayed at the window a little longer, watching the yard until the clouds gathered again and plunged the world back into pitch black. Something was niggling at her. The trees? The 'thing'? Was it her imagination or were they all trying to get into the room Bryan slept in?

She shrugged again, this time to herself. Behind her Jacob snored lightly. God, if she wasn't careful Grymm was going to drive her insane.

4

Mina woke to the early morning sounds of old plumbing shuddering into life and teacups clattering. For a few blissful moments she thought she was back in her bedroom in the city, a few blocks from the beach and within walking distance of her friends. And of Jimmy Flynn. *Mmmmm.*

And then she remembered.

She was in Grymm. Not so much 'mmmm' as 'grrrr'.

Sleepily, she sat up and looked around. The room was a jumble of furniture and boxes disgorging clothes. Jacob was still snoring. Their bicycles leaned drunkenly against each other in a corner. Mina snuggled back into the warmth of her bed and listened to the house coming to life.

It was all so different and yet . . . sure, everything was all over the place but it was all familiar stuff. The bikes, the clothes, the noises filtering up from the kitchen, the furniture; it was as if she was at home and someone had come in during the night and rearranged everything.

So why did she feel something was wrong?

Very wrong.

What was it, then, that was out of place? She leaped out of bed and rushed to the window. What had been out there last night? It certainly wasn't her imagination if she and Jacob had both heard it and saw it. She pulled the heavy drapes aside and the room was immediately flooded with a searing flare of sunlight that it hurt to look at. Mina closed her eyes until they got used to the brightness. Finally, when the purple dots stopped dancing on the inside of her eyelids, she cautiously opened her eyes and peered out into the yard below. There was nothing there but loose gravel and a few fresh animal droppings. A cat maybe? Nothing much bigger, that was for sure. And the trees just looked, well, not so much evil and grasping as tired and exhausted. She knew how they felt.

Mina felt her forehead. She was hot. Perhaps she was coming down with something. Or maybe the rising heat was affecting her brain. All that stuff about Thespa Grymm and eating Bryan! What *was* she thinking? But then there was that phrase that the real-estate woman used – something about nothing being what it seemed?

Yes! *Nothing is what what it seems in Grymm*. That was it. There was something odd about the woman. But then, wasn't Mina always saying how she *liked* 'oddness'?

One thing was certain: she wouldn't be telling Jacob about her worries any more. Too much ammunition for him there. And what was all that stuff with the bag! What *was* he thinking? He was such a mouthy little monster that it was hard to tell what he was really thinking, or feeling. *Honestly*, thought Mina. *Boys*.

After a visit to the archaic bathroom to get dressed and shower – happily, Dad *had* got the heater working – Mina slipped back into the bedroom just as Jacob woke. His carefully waxed hair stood up, stiff and spiky, like badly stacked hay. One squinting eye followed Mina as she sat at her dressing table and began to rummage through a small bag for make-up. It was the only part of him that moved for the next ten minutes.

'It's too bright and too hot; can you dial down the sun, please?'

'Get used to it. Use your factor hundred-plus.'

'You know,' said Jacob pensively, 'that we're five hundred miles from the nearest boy, don't you? And you're putting on make-up?'

'You never know who you might bump into. What if *Ms* Grymm's got a handsome nephew?'

'At least,' mumbled Jacob, sleepily eyeing her white

T-shirt, three-quarter-length jeans and trainers, 'he won't think you're a witch. You look . . . I dunno . . . normal. What's wrong?'

'For your information, *Jakie*, I'm only bringing myself *down* to your level because it's too hot to wear my other stuff. OK? I felt like an oven-ready turkey yesterday.'

As soon as the words left her mouth she regretted them. Jacob guffawed and sat up. 'Why only yesterday? You *always* look like a turkey! That's *so* good. A turkey.'

'Why don't you just go . . . go boil your head? And stick it in that bag of yours with all the other stuff you've . . . *stolen*.'

'If' – Jacob frowned – 'you lost the nose ring and the black stuff around your eyes, you'd actually look almost human.'

'Will you *please* leave it alone?'

'No, really,' said Jacob, relenting. 'Without all that muck on your face, you look quite nice.'

'Per-lease! Now I'm going to puke. Really. Pass the sick bag.'

'For a turkey, that is.'

Jacob laughed and headed for the bathroom before Mina could retort.

When he came back his face was pursed in confusion.

'It's strange,' he muttered, 'that we haven't heard a peep out of Bryan.'

That, Mina realized, was what had been niggling her. The silence. Mornings were usually ear-splitting torture as Bryan got ready for the day by making sure they were all awake as early as possible. And now – she looked at her watch – at a time when he was sure to have been awake for several hours, there was silence.

Suddenly there was a loud bang on the door and they both jumped about a foot in the air.

'Jacob? Mina? Come on, up you get! Time's a-wasting! Breakfast in ten!' roared George on his way to the bathroom. As they heard the bathroom door close and George start whistling an old Frank Sinatra song, the kids looked at each other and burst out laughing.

'Some things never change, then,' said Mina.

'Yeah, best give the toilet a miss for a while,' giggled Jacob as they headed downstairs. In the kitchen Mary was jiggling a couple of tea bags in white mugs.

'Where's Bryan?' said Mina casually as she and Jacob sat down.

'Oh, he was so restless last night that we took him into bed with us. I know the books say you shouldn't do that, but . . . *anyway*, he's tucked up on the couch, still asleep. This desert air must agree with him – he's been a little angel this morning.'

At that, as if someone had given him a cue, Bryan let out an enormous, bellowing scream. Mina gritted her teeth and thought she could feel her fillings vibrate. She sighed deeply and angrily, knowing what was coming next.

'Oh, he's awake,' cooed Mary. 'He must have some sixth sense so that he knows when you two are asking after him! Mina, darling, could you bring him in and give him some breakfast? I'll just warm up some baby food.'

'Why do I always have to look after him? What's wrong with idiot-boy doing it?'

'Because you're the oldest and because Bryan still has the bruises from the last time Jacob looked after him. No offence, Jacob, but I can't trust you not to drop Bryan.'

'Not a problem, Mum,' said Jacob, straight-faced.

Mina stood up quickly, deliberately making the legs of her chair scrape against the flagstoned kitchen floor. The noise was like nails down a blackboard but was nothing compared to the shrieking of Bryan – who, Jacob thought, was almost certainly being skinned alive in the next room. Mina gave him the evil eye and stomped off, slamming the kitchen door behind her.

Mary smiled thinly at her son, who shrugged innocently in return. Bryan was back to his blustering best. 'Want some breakfast, son?'

Mina found Bryan wrestling with his blankets, his arms waving about in front of him, his pudgy hands grasping at nothing, his face a violent crimson disc, eyes bulging wide, mouth a toothless maw from which issued a constant throbbing cry. For a moment she just stood there, calmly watching, letting him struggle and scream. *He only stops*, she marvelled, *long enough to draw in air to start again. God, I hate you*, she thought. *I wish you would just . . . disappear? Die? . . . God, I am such a bitch.*

'Mina?' It was her stepmother, shouting from the kitchen. 'Is he all right?'

'He's fine!' she shouted back, and then whispered, 'Nothing that a sharp axe to the head wouldn't cure, eh, Bryan?'

Back in the kitchen Mina held a screaming Bryan out in front of her as if he were radioactive. 'Here,' she snarled at Mary, 'you take him.'

'You look like a soldier with an unexploded bomb!' laughed George, who had appeared with yesterday's newspaper in his hand and was now sitting at the table. The stupid gold ring from the previous evening sparkled on a finger. *Suck-up.* Mina smiled to herself.

'An unexploded bum more like!' added Jacob as he tucked into a bacon and egg sandwich.

Mary plonked two cups of tea on the table and frowned at her family as she took Bryan in her arms.

'Poor little thing! Are the nasty people being rude about you, bubba? Are they? Are they? Are they also expecting me to get breakfast ready *and* tend to you? Are they, my little man?'

George gave Jacob one of his 'here-we-go-again' looks and buried his head in his breakfast.

Relieved of her burden, Mina raised her eyes to the heavens and opened some cupboards. 'Where's my muesli?' she demanded. 'There's no muesli. How come there's no muesli?'

'I forgot it,' said Mary with, Mina was sure, a certain amount of satisfaction. 'You'll have to go into town and get some. There's toast and jam – if you want it, make it yourself; you might have noticed that I'm a bit over-loaded here, what with looking after Bryan and running around after you lot.' At Mina's exaggerated sigh, Mary went on: 'I've made some sacrifices to be here as well, you know, Mina. No work, no art classes . . . just you lot, overflowing nappies and a sink full of washing up.'

'Great, just great.' Mina sulked into her seat and grabbed a piece of Jacob's bacon before he could stop her. George held a finger up at Jacob to stop the inevitable outburst as Mina went on, shouting to be heard over Bryan: 'I'll just eat crap from now on and get as fat as Bryan – maybe then you'll take some notice of how *I* feel.'

Bryan, now settled in his high chair, suddenly fell silent. One moment the kitchen was a hotbed of noise and familial irritation, and the next it was as if a guillotine had fallen. Silence. Everybody turned to look at the baby, who smiled a dazzling smile and shat himself with a noise like the last of the toothpaste squirting out of a gigantic tube. The smell was both instantaneous and revolting.

'Oh my God, that's disgusting!' shouted Mina as she bolted for the door with Jacob just behind her, gagging but still clutching the remains of his sandwich.

'It's not safe anywhere in this house,' he said with a laugh.

'Better get to work,' said George to Mary in a strangled voice that made it clear he was trying not to breathe in. 'Not a good look to be late on your first day.'

'Who's my little angel then?' said Mary as she moved to change her son's overflowing nappy. 'Who's my special boy?'

Outside the house, Mina and Jacob tried to dispel the smell by gulping down lungfuls of searing desert air. It was like trying to breathe warm water but it was better than the alternative.

'I will *never* get that smell out of my nose!' said Mina,

looking daggers back at the house. 'Never! That was the worst one yet. He's just gross. Gross. It was like . . . like . . .'

'Don't go there,' rasped Jacob, looking at the congealing remains of his sandwich and then tossing them into a nearby rubbish bin. 'Just don't go there, wherever you were going.' He sighed sadly. 'I will never eat bacon again.'

'So much for the desert air agreeing with him.'

'Hey, kids!' It was George, leaning out of the side door. 'I'm going to work in about fifteen; if I give you a lift part-way, can you pick up some stuff in town for Mary? We need milk and bread and stuff. Muesli, maybe? Certainly some more nappies! You can take your bikes. What do you say? Or you could stay here and help Mary with Bryan . . .'

He had saved his masterstroke until last. Go shopping or stay here; stay with Bryan.

'Yes, George! Not a problem.'

'Sure, Dad!'

'One thing, though, Jacob . . .'

'What?'

'You might want to get dressed first.'

Jacob looked down, surprised to find himself still wearing his pyjamas. He headed back towards the house. 'Cool. See you in a minute, Mina.'

'I won't hold my breath, weirdo.'

In the ensuing silence Mina realized that, from where she stood at the side of the house, she could see the town and the clump of buildings that included Thespa Grymm's real-estate office. The place, she saw, was bigger than it had first appeared. Spreading out from the main street were a dozen or so blocks of low-rise houses, in grids of four, each surrounded by a small piece of land. Faded green splotches here and there were evidence that, once upon a time, the good folk of Grymm had striven to keep the desert at bay. No longer. As more people left, the desert had crept in, covering up the outer roads, and creeping ever closer to the main street.

The town was dying in the worst possible way, slowly swallowed alive by the great arid beast on its doorstep. As she watched, a small black beetle of a car turned out of a driveway on the southern edge of town and chugged towards the thin black ribbon of the highway in the distance. She had no reason to think so, but she knew that whoever was in that car wasn't coming back.

At the mine, Grymm lived up to expectations and served up another slice of the unexpected. Rather than the simple barrier and flimsy wire fence they had imagined, the place looked like a circus had snaked in, shed its skin, and slithered off. Sun-bleached tepees and DIY tents of canvas, plastic sheets and pegs littered the approach road and sprawled off into the desert scrub. Smoke from small fires drifted through the encampment. Makeshift signs had been attached to the fence, which was topped with vicious razor-wire. Some signs looked professional, others just paint on creased cardboard. They shouted for PEACE and NO MORE NUKES. One of the biggest read: WHAT'S MINED IS YOURS. AND YOUR CHILDREN'S. AND YOUR CHILDREN'S CHILDREN'S. George laughed loudly at that one.

As the children gaped at the flotsam, faces emerged from the tents and peered at them before deciding they were of little interest and disappearing back inside.

'Ferals and hippies,' said George. 'They said a few of them had set up camp outside but I never expected anything this big.'

'What do they want?' asked Jacob.

'Peace on earth, goodwill to all men, no mining and no logging. That's what they *want*,' said George. 'What do they *need*? A good bath, by the looks of them.'

Mina scowled at him. 'Or perhaps they think we should stop looting the planet and think about the state we're leaving it in for future generations.'

'You could be right, you could be right. Don't take any crap from your old man.' Squinting through the windscreen, he slowed the vehicle to a crawl and examined the mine entrance. It looked like a maximum security prison: double gates, armed guards, two towers, powerful floodlights. The huge initials WDM hung over the main gate: Western Desert Mining.

'I think this is where we part company. Will you two be OK if I drop you here? It's not too far to town – and it's all downhill. I'll pop by the real-estate office around six o'clock. If you're not there I'll assume you've gone home. And don't forget the sunscreen, OK? It's boiling out there.'

Jacob hadn't said a word since they came to the camp, but his eyes were like saucers. Mina clapped him on the shoulder. 'C'mon, idiot.'

After wrestling the bikes down from the rack at the back of the 4WD, they watched as George drove through the first gate and across the cattle grid behind it. He was waved through by an armed guard who looked so bored that Mina suspected he'd shoot someone just for something to do. They stood there and waved until the jeep had vanished round a bend. And then they were alone. Or as alone as you can be under the watchful eye of half a dozen mine guards and a camp full of protesters.

Even standing still, they both began to feel dribbles of sweat build up in the small of their backs. The heat was palpable, like standing in a deep, body-temperature bath.

Looking around, Mina felt stupid, hot and pedestrian in her jeans, T-shirt and sneakers. And as for Jacob and his lime-green T-shirt and light blue shorts . . . They looked like a couple of coloured lollies dropped in the dirt. She felt herself blush as two young men and a woman in layers of threadbare army surplus gear strolled past towards the largest of the tents, a marquee-sized grey canvas erection, from which wafted the smells of curry and sweat. All three were deeply tanned and not a little stained and dusty. The men sported dreadlocks (one even wore a striped woollen beanie, despite the heat) and the woman had a shaved head. The younger guy looked over and smiled at her. He had the bluest eyes she had ever seen on a human being.

Mina blushed and immediately regretted not going Goth that morning, despite Jacob's compliments. The protesters seemed wild and exotic and wonderfully attractive, and she hoped they'd at least notice her silver nose ring. She wondered what she'd look like with a shaved head. Pretty cool, probably.

Jacob just found them frightening. 'C'mon, let's go,' he whispered, and began wheeling his mountain bike towards town. Mina followed reluctantly, fascinated by what she was seeing. At intervals along the road the protesters had erected poles that had been decorated with camp debris, turning them into fierce, demon-like masks and totems. Nearby, four children with knotted hair ran around an abandoned fridge, chasing each other and chuckling. In the distance, someone plucked away at an acoustic guitar, while from another quarter came the *pop-pop-popping* sound of bongos being savagely attacked.

'Mina!' hissed Jacob as she came to a stop next to a small camper van that had been completely covered with hand-painted peace signs. It was, she thought with a smile, a work of art – like finding a rose on a rubbish dump.

'Like it?' said a voice from nearby. Jacob put his head down and hurried off, rapping his shin against a bike pedal. Mina heard his curse as she turned to find a man studying her from the comfort of the van's bench seat. It had been pulled out and now sat off to one side in shadow. The man got up and came over to them. In one hand he carried a pen and a notebook and, unlike everyone else, he was dressed as if going to an office: ordinary checked shirt with the sleeves rolled down and buttoned at the wrist, a pair of green corduroy trousers and old-fashioned brown brogues. Sweat stood out on a high forehead, and behind bottle-bottomed spectacles his eyes appeared huge in comparison to his bulbous, balding head.

He looked, thought Jacob, like one of those bug-eyed movie aliens. Except this one was ET dressed as a schoolteacher! And in this heat!

'It's lovely,' said Mina. 'Did you do it?'

'Oh no, no, no – good grief, er, no, no, no.' The man's voice was well-modulated and creamy, and yet utterly lacking in confidence. It put Mina at ease almost instantly. 'Someone here, I would imagine.' He waved a well-manicured hand in the general direction of the rest of the camp.

'Mina!' Jacob's voice was now tinged with hurt, exasperation and anger. A dribble of blood ran down his shin. He didn't like strangers at the best of times, but out here his suspicions were multiplied tenfold.

'Ah, Mina,' said the stranger, and scribbled something in his notebook. 'And that's Jacob, yes? Father starting work at the, um, mine? Geologist or something?'

'Yes . . .' Suddenly the man didn't seem quite so ineffectual. 'How do you know?'

'My word, yes, dear me. S-so sorry,' he stammered, and held out a hand. He could have been, Mina realized, any age between twenty and fifty. It was hard to tell. 'I'm Eric. Eric Elland. I'm, er, well, I'm the priest, you know . . . At St Stephen's church? But I'm, ah, sort of retired now. Hence no, er, you know, dog collar.' He seemed both embarrassed and a little angry, and was suddenly unable to look her in the eye. 'There's, um, not much call for my, er, calling; not *here,* anyway. So, I'm indulging in my hobby: I'm writing a book. I'm just here trying to, er, talk to some of the protesters.'

Mina shook his hand, which was soft and sweaty. There was, she noticed, something like dried red ink around his fingernails. Or crusted blood. *And there you go again*, she thought, *thinking stuff like that out of the blue.* Where was it coming from? What with last night, the Grymm woman and Bryan's wailing, she was officially going mad. And this was only Day One of their 'exile' in the land that time forgot.

'Are you writing a story about them?'

'Oh, no, not really – well, yes and no. You see, well, I'm writing a book about the town and I thought that, well, you know, I should talk to them about the, ah, mine and the, like . . . And Grymm's such a small place that I knew you, er, must be the, er . . .'

'Newcomers?' Mina couldn't wait for him to finish the sentence – life was too short.

'Exactly! News gets around.' He smiled widely, seemingly pleased that everything had been explained to everyone's satisfaction. 'Are you going into town?'

'Yeah.'

Jacob shouted then, from even further away. 'I'm going without you! I'll see you down there!'

'You'd better be going,' said the man wryly, 'or he'll, um, explode or something. And if you'll excuse me . . .' Again he gestured impatiently off into the distance.

'Oh, yeah, sure. See you later, Mr Elland.'

'I'm sure you will.' He grinned and marched off into the detritus behind him, a solid, sweaty, overdressed figure contrasting oddly with the feral surroundings. It was like finding an accountant in a hut on Treasure Island.

She glanced round to find that Jacob was pedalling madly down the rugged, winding slopes into Grymm, his eternally present green bag swinging wildly from side to side across his back. *Damn*, thought Mina. *If the little moron kills himself there'll be no end of trouble.*

'Jacob! Wait up!'

The road from the mine to Grymm was downhill all the way, but they were drenched with sweat when they finally freewheeled into the wide main street, allowing their momentum to carry them to the milk bar just past the real-estate office.

There were a couple of dusty pick-up trucks parked further along the street, and a few raggedy, rainbow-coloured figures – almost certainly mine protesters – clustered around the faded grocery store, but apart from that it looked much the same as it had when they arrived the previous day: dead quiet. With the emphasis on *dead*. Two men scurried through the rippling heat haze at the far end of the street, like cockroaches running from shade to shade, hunched, insular, heads down, wide-brimmed hats on, not looking to the side. One slipped into the hardware store, the other into the souvenir shop. Intent on their business and nothing else, desperate to get out of the relentless heat. The newsagent had put out a couple of boards that shouted last week's headlines in bold type, but little else had changed.

Jacob was still moping as Mina locked up their bikes. It seemed a redundant gesture in a town devoid of life but they were city kids – and in the city, you left things unlocked at your peril. Jacob took off his wraparound sunglasses and wiped his face with the sleeve of his T-shirt.

'What now?' he asked. 'Even my eyeballs need a drink.'

'Well, you can stop sulking for a start. You look like an orang-utan with toothache when you sulk.'

'Better than looking like one all the time,' he snapped back.

'That's better. Communication established, Captain. The alien speaks Jacob. Beam him aboard.'

'Very funny. Did you invite your new weirdo *friend* for a milkshake?' But before Mina could reply Jacob's jaw dropped. Mouth open, eyes wide, he half whispered, 'Hey, look at that!'

'Yeah, right, you're not going to catch me like—'

'*Look! Look!* Before it disappears!'

Mina followed the line of Jacob's outstretched arm and astonished finger and saw a two-legged black Doberman, its haunches encased in a squeaking leather-and-brass wheelbarrow contraption, drag itself across the road and trundle between the grocery store and the hardware shop. The twittering of the wheels continued for a second or two and then faded away.

'*What* was that?' Mina asked – she knew – stupidly. It was a two-legged dog, of course. Or a two-wheeled dog, depending on how you looked at it. It made her flesh crawl. She also thought, not so stupidly, that the dog had been punished for some transgression. Maybe it had urinated against Thespa Grymm's leg.

Jacob raised his eyebrows at her. 'This place is freaking me out.'

'You can say that again.'

'That was sick, and not in a good way. Should we go after it?'

'Urgh, and do what? Buy it breakfast?'

'Funny. Look, I'm hungry. Can we get something to eat? What about the milk bar?' Jacob wiped his forehead with the back of a hand. 'And, phew, maybe it'll have air con.'

Maggot's Milk Bar was, unsurprisingly, empty except for a tall, stocky woman with blonde hair cut in a short bob. She was sitting behind the counter at the rear of the shop reading a well-thumbed book called *Your Doberman and You*. This was tossed aside so enthusiastically when they came in that it skidded across the polished surface of the counter and flew onto the floor in a flurry of bent pages. The cover photograph, of a seemingly smiling Doberman, stared accusingly at them, as if they were somehow responsible for the pathetic thing they'd seen scuttle across the street outside. Jacob picked it up and placed it neatly back on the counter.

'Why, thank you very much, kind sir. He's a real gentleman, isn't he?' The woman's voice was rough and ragged, as if she smoked too many cigarettes and had done so for many years.

'Yes, but only around eight-thirty on Monday mornings,' said Mina with a dismissive wave in Jacob's direction. 'Other than that . . .'

'I'm sure he's a little darling,' insisted the woman

with a smile that revealed the most perfect set of teeth Mina had ever seen. Movie stars didn't have smiles like that. They were so white, so evenly spaced, that she could have advertised toothpaste.

Then Jacob blurted out what had been uppermost on his mind since they came in. Perhaps because of the silver and black name badge pinned to the woman's pink nylon uniform. 'Are you really called Maggot?'

'That I am, dearie.'

'Is that your real name?'

'Good Lord, no. My real name's Margaret but my parents called me Maggot when I was a baby. It just stuck.'

Charming, thought Mina, *but not really any worse than the things Jacob and I call Bryan*. Though they might have to rethink the toothpaste commercial: *Maggot recommends Hardy's Ultra Plus toothpaste* didn't have a lot going for it.

'Of course, it could also be because I put maggots in the milkshakes.'

Huh? Mina and Jacob looked at each other and then at Maggot, but she had turned her back to them and was busily moving glasses and cups around on the counter. Had they heard her correctly? When she turned back she was smiling sweetly again. They *must* have misheard.

'Now what can I get you two kids? What about a

milkshake? My milkshakes are famous for miles around.'

I bet they are, thought Mina, sniggering.

Jacob smirked behind his hand. 'Yes, please,' he muttered. 'Banana, please.'

'I'll just have a glass of milk, thanks,' said Mina.

'Right you are. And what about some food? You, young lady, need to put some flesh on those bones.'

'Bacon and eggs,' said Jacob with relish. He had only recently discovered the joy of bacon and eggs and would now eat them for breakfast, lunch and dinner if given half a chance. Except when Bryan was polluting the air. And, given that he had previously hardly eaten enough to keep a sparrow alive, it was an obsession that was eagerly indulged.

'Do you have any muesli?' asked Mina. 'I really fancy some muesli, *and* some toast.' It had been an exhausting day already and she was, for once, famished.

'Right. Sit yourselves down then and I'll bring everything over. Grymm's best waitress service, don'tcha know.' And with that, Maggot slipped through a swinging door into the kitchen.

The left-hand side of the shop was taken up by a series of six wooden booths, each of which could easily fit six people. It had been a while, though, since the place had seated a full complement of thirty-six. Mina and Jacob chose the booth nearest the door.

'Did she say what I thought she said?' asked Mina as they sat down.

'Maggots in the milkshake? I thought so too. Let's hope not.'

'Did you notice her teeth?'

'Her teeth? What about her hair?'

'I was too busy looking at the teeth. What about her hair?'

'It kept moving. It's a wig, I bet.'

'Perhaps it's the same with her teeth. It'd explain why they're so perfect.'

'You think—' Jacob was cut off as the doors to the kitchen opened. Maggot staggered through with a long, thick sundae glass in each hand. She rounded the counter and hobbled towards their booth with a lop-sided gait that Jacob, with his back to her, didn't notice. Mina did.

'There you go, kids. One banana milkshake, one milk. Enjoy. Now, do I take it you two are Jacob and Wilhelmina? Here for the mine?'

'Yes,' said Mina, noticing the odd use of words. *For the mine?* 'How did you know?'

'Phooey! Small place like this? You can't kill your husband and eat him without everybody knowing your business. You arrived yesterday, didn't you?'

It was as if she had lapsed into a foreign language and

out again without batting an eyelid. Once again Jacob and Mina were left wondering if they had heard correctly. It was Mina who found her voice first.

'Er . . . yes. We met Mrs – *Ms* – Grymm yesterday afternoon. To get the keys to the house.'

'That's a lovely house, isn't it? Right there on the escarpment? Beautiful spot. We locals often picnic up there when it's not being rented. Though I would imagine it might all seem a little remote for you two.'

'Ms Grymm seemed very nice,' lied Mina in an attempt to turn the conversation back to their nemesis.

'Thespa? Now, now, you don't have to be polite with *me*, dear. Thespa seems like a miserable old witch, doesn't she? She might look like a harmless old sofa but you mark my words: underneath that overstuffed exterior beats a heart of pure, baby-eating evil. How's your milkshake, Jacob dear? Nice? Good.'

Mina, determined to ignore Maggot's disconcerting remarks, and not even sure she was really hearing them, ploughed on. What else could she do? 'Well, she seemed, er, like, er, one of a kind, for sure.'

'You are certainly right there. We keep telling her it's bad for the town's image, but will she listen? Oh, no. Listening's not Thespa's strong suit. Just because her family helped to found this place, she thinks she's the queen bee. Can't keep her rancid old nose out of anything. Something's happening in Grymm? Thespa's somewhere at the bottom of it.'

'Her family have been here all along then?' asked Mina.

'Oh yes – the Grymms have been here for more than a hundred years. To listen to her, you'd think that Thespa herself had been here that long too. Silly old cow. Oops, your bacon will be done to a frazzle if I keep chatting away like this. Back in two ticks.'

When she had gone back into the kitchen Mina and Jacob just stared at each other, not sure whether to laugh or cry. Then they both tried to talk at once.

'Did she—?'

'Did you—?'

'Maybe it's something like that Tourette's Syndrome. You know, when people can't help swearing,' mused Jacob.

'Tourette's?' Mina was astounded. 'How do *you* know about Tourette's? You're usually such a dill.'

Jacob, rather than reveal that he had heard about it from a movie he had watched at his friend's house when the parents were out, chose to be enigmatic. 'I have hidden depths,' he said.

'Yeah, like buried treasure.'

'I'm not the one with the sunken chest!'

'Be careful, *Jakie*, or I might have to kill you. Anyway, you missed something else.'

'What? There's more?'

'Not only does Maggot have a whole set of false teeth and a wig, but there's something wrong with her leg. I think it's false too. Didn't you see the way she walked?'

'I'm facing the door, *Wilhelmina* – how could I? She's got the hairiest hands I've ever seen, though. She'd give even George a run for his money in a hairiest hand contest.'

'Fool. So how's the milkshake?'

'Good.'

'Got to the maggots yet?'

'Very funny.'

The bacon, eggs, muesli and toast came and went without incident. When she had cleared the plates away, Maggot came and sat with them.

Jacob was determined to ask about something that had been eating at him since they walked in. 'Have you got a Doberman? You were reading that book and—'

'*Had* a Doberman,' she interrupted with venom. 'He ran away.'

'Ran away or wheeled away?' asked Mina.

At this, Maggot seemed overjoyed. 'Wheeled? You've seen him? Where? I've tried to entice him back but he's not been the same since the accident. He gets so close but runs away when I try to grab him. He used to be so trusting.'

'We saw him this morning, just across the road. He wheel— er, ran off between the store and the hardware shop. What happened to him? Was he hit by a car?'

'Car? No, no, no. I say *accident*, but it wasn't really. Someone cut his legs off.'

Silence. Jacob stopped drinking his milkshake. Mina's mouth gaped. This time, she couldn't stop herself rising to the bait.

'*Cut* his legs off?' she blurted.

'Yes. Very neat job it was too. Took them right out at the hips, like a chicken leg. Poor thing disappeared one day and reappeared two weeks later with no back legs. We found him on the road outside.'

'We?'

'Me and my, er, husband. Before he disappeared. It was him who rigged up that wheelbarrow sling so that Rex could get around. The dog's not been the same since.'

'Who would cut off a dog's legs? Why?' asked Mina, not expecting an answer. Jacob stared at Maggot in astonishment, absent-mindedly slurping the icy dregs at the bottom of his milkshake. Mina frowned at the noise.

'Who indeed,' agreed Maggot. 'Though I have my suspicions. It's a funny old place, is Grymm.'

'Yes, nothing's quite what it seems, is it?'

'Ah-ha! The town motto. Thespa's doing, I'm afraid. The poor old thing really does think she's the heart and soul of the town.'

'Poor *Thespa*? What about poor Rex?'

'Yes, poor Rex. But enough of that,' said Maggot, tapping a massive fist lightly on the table. 'Here we are getting gloomy on such a sunny day. How's your maggot milkshake, Jacob? Got to the chewy bits yet?'

Jacob smiled indulgently and sucked up a particularly tricky piece of ice. It had shot up through the straw and dropped into his mouth before he realized it was *moving*. He spat it back into the glass, where it landed with the dozen or so other fat maggots that writhed in the dregs.

'Jacob?' said Mina, watching him turn green.

With a strangled cry he leaped up from the booth and burst through the front door just in time for his breakfast to reappear in a long, slow arc and land with a wet splat on the road. He was retching up the remainder of his stomach contents when Rex appeared. As Jacob spat out the last bits of snot and bile, the dog began hungrily helping himself to the rest.

Yum: toast.

Yum yum: bacon.

Yummy runny eggs.

Carrots! Where did they come from?

'Ah-ha!' grated Maggot gleefully. 'All's well that ends well.'

And with that, she took a running jump and launched herself, prosthetic leg and all, at the unsuspecting dog.

5

Skulking in the shadows at the back of the butcher's shop, a tall, beefy man with a pointy bald head watched the kerfuffle opposite. He liked it that he could see them but they couldn't see him. That kept everything neat. And tidy.

'Insects,' said Cleaver Flay in a flat voice.

Flay stood like that every morning – except Sunday, of course – waiting for the clock high on the wall behind the immaculate glass counter to *tick-tock, tock-tick, tick-tock* its way to nine. At exactly 8:59:45 he would walk briskly across the sawdust-covered floor, open the red roller-blind and snap the sign beneath it from CLOSED to OPEN 9 A.M.–5 P.M. Then he would do the same to the bigger blind in the main window. The white words C. FLAY & SON would roll up and disappear like the pupils of someone fainting.

Today, there were still five minutes until opening time, but Flay could see the girl and the boy and the damned milk bar person because the spring on the smaller blind had broken yesterday when he was cleaning it.

Perhaps that was it?

Perhaps that was why Cleaver Flay, butcher extraordinaire, was in such a foul mood.

He hated it when things didn't go according to plan. His life was an ordered one, and the snapping of the spring in the blind wasn't ordered. Now he would have to go to the hardware shop.

'Worms.'

His almond eyes narrowed even more in the half-light and a lopsided sneer disfigured what would ordinarily have been full, sensuous lips. A woman's lips, almost. Lips that were meant to be kissed but hadn't been for a long, long time.

And still he stood there. Quiet as the dead. A dead man standing. Just those black eyes flicking back and forth on either side of his hooked nose. For Cleaver Flay was a man of distinct habits. He was a neat man, whose wardrobe upstairs boasted exactly eight pairs of white trousers, eight starched white shirts (sized XXXL), and sixteen blue-and-white striped butcher's aprons with tie strings that he had extended so they would reach around his enormous stomach. He needed sixteen aprons because he changed them twice a day. Because of all the blood.

And they were as clean as clean can be. As clean as Cleaver Flay's fingernails. As clean as Cleaver Flay's hands, scrubbed red raw every morning and night with a wire brush and disinfectant. As clean as Cleaver Flay's vast body, covered in animal fat every other morning and razored free of every last strand of hair.

Yes, Cleaver Flay was a fastidious man. And the blind had broken. It wasn't supposed to do that. And because it had done that he was witness to this unseemly fiasco between the worms in the dirty, dirty road opposite.

And because of the unseemly fiasco the dog had reappeared.

And because the dog had reappeared it had been caught.

And that reminded Cleaver Flay that it had escaped in the first place.

So perhaps it wasn't the roller-blind. Perhaps the roller-blind was just a symptom of what was really bothering him.

He didn't like it when they escaped. And you never knew when another order might come in from the mine. From *Mr Anhanga*.

And if it did, it would mean that he, Cleaver Flay,

might have to mix again with the insects and the worms and . . .

The clock ticked on: 8:58:30, 31, 32, 33 . . .

A low sound grew gradually louder until it filled the room. Cleaver Flay was growling '. . . and the maggots.'

8:59:44.

Cleaver Flay began to move. It was time to open up shop.

'What's the matter, Jacob. *What?*' yelled Mina. But Jacob was still leaning over the edge of the boardwalk, eyes closed. He hadn't been too articulate so far and her only guess was that he thought he'd found something revolting – not maggots, surely? – in his milkshake. Either that or he was ill.

Maggot herself, meanwhile, was sitting in the red dust, one leg splayed out at an odd angle, wig askew, grasping Rex the two-legged dog for all she was worth. She seemed unaware that Rex didn't appear too happy about being manhandled and then clasped suffocatingly to her bony bosom while his new rear end crashed around, upended in the road.

'There's my lovely boy, there's my coochums. Who's a lovely boy, then? Oh yes he is, *oh yes he is,*' crooned Maggot. She seemed oblivious to Rex's snapping jaws as he tried to bite her. Bits of carrot, bacon and general bile coated one side of her face where she had landed in Jacob's puke.

'C'mon,' whispered Mina to Jacob as she pulled him upright. 'Let's get you out of the heat.'

He allowed himself to be helped over to the rickety wooden bench that leaned against the wall between the milk bar and the newsagent's. And there they sat for a moment, watching Maggot pick herself up off the road and, with what was left of Rex now struggling feebly under one arm, roll back to her shop like a drunken sailor. At the door she hesitated, as if realizing, finally, that her face was half covered in vomit. With her free hand she scraped the bits off and, giving Jacob a knowing smile, ate them.

As the door closed behind her, Jacob was back at the roadside, retching. Mina could do nothing but gape at the space vacated by the mad Maggot.

'Did she do what I think she just did?'

'*Yeurgh*,' said Jacob. '*Yeurgh*.'

'This place . . .'

'There *were* maggots in the milkshake, Mina. There *were*! I sucked one up the straw. Aw, jeez. It moved. It moved in my mouth. Oh, that's *disgusting*.' He retched again.

'Are you sure?' Mina found herself in two minds. Ordinarily, a confession like that would have provided her with enough ammunition to make Jacob's life a misery for weeks. But now . . . now they were in Grymm. And she *did* see Maggot eat puke off her own face. Though surely . . . Maggots?

'Maybe we should go back and—'

'*No!*' shouted Jacob through a hanging curtain of spittle. 'No, I can't go back in there.'

Across the street, a flicker of life and the sound of something tapping against glass made them look up just as the big red blind in the butcher's shop window rolled up with a clatter. Behind the display they could just make out a large white figure moving to and fro in the dim interior – obviously the butcher doing whatever butchers do in butcher's shops in the middle of nowhere.

To take Jacob's mind off his experience with the maggots (if, indeed, that was what he saw) Mina nodded towards the shop. 'How do you reckon he makes a living out here?'

Jacob shrugged. He didn't know and he didn't care. He was wondering if he would ever drink a banana milkshake again. Which, at twelve years old, is a big deal.

'The mine, I suppose,' mused Mina. 'If they like their meat anything like my dad does.'

Leaving Jacob to get himself together, she wandered along the boardwalk to the twirling merry-go-round of postcards that stood just outside the newsagent's. She took one down and turned to Jacob. 'Hey, look at this.'

He plodded over, wiping his mouth with the back of his hand, and took the card she was holding. It showed an aerial view of the vast scar that ripped through the desert scrub. He could see the escarpment where their new house sat, and the low-lying mountain range that extended to the north and circled round, like a lizard's tail, to create the narrow gap they drove through into town yesterday. The mammoth trucks that hauled away the diggings looked like toys beside the devastation. Across the bottom of the photograph in blood-red type it read: *Grymm: not the end of the world, but you can see it from here!* Mina was pleased to see Jacob give a weak smile. She plucked another card from the carousel. It showed the main street of Grymm with the legend: *You'll wish you weren't here.*

'At least they have a sense of humour,' she said with a laugh that was more a grunt than anything else.

'Can I get a bottle of water?' asked Jacob. 'My mouth feels furry. And it tastes like sh—'

'Yes, yes, all right,' Mina interrupted. 'Stay there. I'll see if they have some in the newsagent's.'

She strolled into the shop just as a battered blue pick-up truck came round the corner by the real-estate office and skidded to a stop outside. Two massive, thickset men then jumped out and swept past her into the shop in a cloud of body odour and bad breath. They wore jeans and checked shirts rolled up at the arms to reveal thick, deeply tanned forearms. The steel toecaps of their scuffed working boots gleamed dully where the leather had worn through, and they were both wearing faded baseball caps. Mina could just make out the letters WDM. As for the men, between them they could have blocked out the sun. Mina couldn't even see past them into the shop. There was a counter on the left, a stand of newspapers and month-old magazines on the right, but past that it was a mystery.

What she could see, though, were the flies clustered on the sweaty backs of both men's shirts. Huge, plump flies waddled this way and that, climbing over each other, occasionally lifting off and quickly settling back down with an audible buzz but mostly just feasting on . . . what?

'Inky!' hollered one of the men into the empty shop. 'Bugleslab! You there?' His voice was like thunder and Mina could have sworn she felt the building tremble.

'Inky! We've come for the order. Look sharp. You know how Mr Anhanga don't like to be kept waiting.'

From the back of the shop came a reedy voice. It huffed and puffed and wavered with exertion. Or fear.

'I'm coming, I'm coming. Hold your horses. You're early.'

At this, the two miners turned sideways to allow the owner of the voice to pass. If Inky Bugleslab lost his voice it wouldn't be difficult to reacquaint the two of them; for if ever a man looked the way he sounded it was him. Tall, thin as a reed, his shoulders didn't seem to be much wider than his head. He was wearing stained blue trousers and a brown shirt with rings of sweat under the arms. He seemed to be about to explode with the effort of dragging two large bundles of magazines behind him. Shrink-wrapped and bound with plastic straps, stamped with the letters WDM. Bugleslab dropped them and straightened up slowly, wincing as something in his back cracked. Standing up, he seemed even taller and thinner. Straight on, his head was shaped like a long, narrow oval, with wide, watery eyes of the same shape. Above them, a high forehead was plastered with strands of greasy black hair that had been swept forward from the crown to hide his baldness.

'There you are, gentlemen – three hundred copies of' – he paused and smiled an oily smile, red-rimmed eyes flicking obviously to Mina – 'er, the new *Xbox* magazine. I do hope you enjoy them.'

There was that smile again, insincere and greasy, this time accompanied by the appearance in his mouth of what looked at first like some sort of fat, wriggling pink maggot but was in fact his tongue. It rolled itself around the edge of his lips and then disappeared back inside his head. Mina had to suppress a shudder, especially so soon after Jacob and his milkshake. The man leered in her direction but addressed himself to the miners.

'The, um, *Thomas the Tank Engine* videos you ordered will be in next week, gentlemen. Now, what can I do for you, young lady?'

The miners each picked up a bundle without a word, without effort, and knocked Mina back on her heels as they lumbered out of the shop. They tossed the magazines in the back of their truck, climbed in, and threw a screeching U-turn back the way they'd come.

The newsagent shook his head and tutted. 'Forget their manners, they do. Stuck up at the mine, you see. Fail to observe the niceties. Mind you, those mine protesters are *too* nice, if you ask me. Never much took to people who are *too* nice; you can't trust them. Anyway, I wouldn't take it to heart, young lady. Mina, is it?'

'Small town, right? Did Thespa Grymm tell you?'

'You know, I haven't seen Thespa for an age. Then again, I haven't seen much of Maggot since her husband disappeared. We're small, yes, but we're not what you might call a *close-knit community*. Keep ourselves to ourselves, we do. Though we all know about *you*: new arrivals always create a bit of interest. Especially when most people are *leaving*. And *especially* when they bring children with them. Not too many of *them* left in Grymm, that's for sure. Well, none, to tell the truth. Now, what can I get you?'

'A bottle of water, please.'

Inky pulled an ice-cold bottle of water out of the fridge behind him. As he put it on the counter, Mina noticed that he too was wearing a garishly gold ring like the one her father now wore. She could understand that he might have to wear it to work, given that the Coathanger person had given it to him, but who in their right mind would wear one of *those* trashy things if they didn't have to? Well, Inky Bugleslab, for one.

'As you're new in town, that one's free,' he whispered, the pulsating fat grub of his tongue emerging again to perch in the corner of his mouth.

'That's very nice of you, thanks.'

'Not a problem. Any friend of the mine is a friend of mine. Ha-ha-ha-ha!'

Mina tried to smile at the man while simultaneously not looking at the short fat tongue gyrating in Bugleslab's scalpel-slash of a mouth. 'By the way, who's this Mr Coathanger?'

'Ha-ha-ha-ha-ha! Very funny. No. It's *Anhanga*; not

Coathanger. He's the mine manager. You'll hear lots about him. But not from me.' And there was that worm-tongue again, slithering from one side of his mouth to the other.

Mina had had enough. She saluted him with the water bottle. 'Anyway, thanks again, Mr Bugleslab, for the water. See you later.'

Outside, Jacob took the water bottle and sat on the shaded wooden bench outside the souvenir shop drinking it down in great thankful gulps. He wasn't looking quite as green around the gills, but Mina knew he needed something to occupy his mind. She found it in the souvenir shop.

'Hey! Look at this.'

In the window was a collection of silvery-grey pewter figurines – wizards, dragons, knights and the like – all holding or somehow coveting small crystal balls that caught the late afternoon sun and threw rainbows back onto the glass. It was this multi-coloured light show that had caught Mina's eye.

'*From the mines of Grymm*,' read Jacob, his face now pressed against the glass.

'And what about this?' She beckoned him over to the other window, past the door with the words MAURIE'S MEMENTOES etched into the glass, where a display featured a showcase full of simple gold rings like

Bugleslab wore. This too had a sign over it: ONE RING TO RULE THEM ALL.

'Isn't there a copyright or something on that?' asked Jacob.

'Everywhere else maybe, but out *here*?' said Mina. 'Who's going to care?'

'I wonder if they're real gold?'

'At those prices? It's probably the same stuff that Mum and Dad's rings are made of. What's it called again? Oh, Dad mentioned it only last night, er—'

'Iron pyrites,' said a deep voice behind them, making them both jump guiltily. The elderly Asian man standing in the shop doorway smiled. 'It's iron pyrites. Fool's gold.'

'Oh, you scared the life out of me.' Mina could feel her heart thumping, and she felt stupid and angry for letting Grymm get to her.

'Sorry,' said the man, still smiling. 'Do you want to come in for a look around? No obligation to buy, of course.'

Jacob hesitated, waiting for Mina to take the lead. His mind was still full of maggots and milkshakes. 'Well, we don't have much money and—'

'No obligation to buy – and it's *air-conditioned*.' He paused, head to one side, scrutinizing them as they sweated in the heat. 'Come on, I won't eat you. Promise.'

He was right: inside it was wonderfully cool, almost cold. After the furnace outside it was a delight just to stand there and soak it up. The man bowed primly, introduced himself as 'Maurice Au, shop assistant, record-keeper, accountant and owner of Maurie's Mementoes', and slipped behind a small counter at the very back of the shop. As she browsed through the souvenirs, Mina studied him furtively. He was un-remarkable: brown trousers, beige shirt, neat grey hair. *So what is it*, she wondered, *that's odd about him?* She looked away quickly as he glanced up.

'On your right,' he said, 'is the usual souvenir stuff – postcards, posters, pictures framed and unframed, tea towels, T-shirts etcetera. On your left, the mine-based memorabilia. Got any questions, I'm not going any-where.' And with that, he began leafing through a magazine.

'Thanks,' said Mina. The shop was, as Au had said, cool. It was also dark, as if the lights were dimmed. In the gloom, the minerals and crystals from the mine glittered like treasure. They were piled high and sorted into small boxes and compartments according to shape, size, colour and price. A few gigantic versions of the crystals that both Mina and Jacob had examined through microscopes at school were given pride of place on white shelves.

It was then, when she picked up a couple of highly polished pebbles, that Mina realized what was odd about Au. She peeped at him again. *That's it*, she thought: *he looks like he's made of stone, golden stone, with black pebbles for eyes.* And then, again, she felt herself flush with embarrassment. The poor man had pockmarked skin, and there she was, making judgements about him. Still, it must once have been the world's worst case of acne. The next thought came unbidden: *I hope I don't get it that bad; Jimmy Flynn would* never *look at me then.*

'Do you make all this yourself?' asked Mina as she and Jacob moved through the shop. She didn't really care; she just wanted to get her mind off Au's granite face.

'Oh yes. Everything's made by hand, by me, from stuff from the mine.'

'So the One Ring's not gold, then?' said Jacob.

'Your sister was right – *at those prices*? Real gold would cost ten, twenty times that much. More. Try one on.'

Jacob was surprised. 'Me?'

'Why not?'

'Jewellery's for girls.'

'Is it?' asked Au, holding up his right hand and wiggling his fingers. On one of them flashed a gold ring. 'What does that make me?'

Mina sniggered. Jacob blushed.

'What about you, young lady?'

'Gold's not my thing.' She showed him the silver rings on her hands and the one through her nose.

'Not your thing? Not your thing?' said Au, putting down his magazine. His eyes shone with excitement. 'But gold's *the* most *marvellous* thing. Did you know that it's chemically inert? Imperishable? When everything else is dead and gone, when all the steel and iron in the world has rusted and rotted back into the earth, *gold*, only *gold*, will still look the same. For ever. Did you also know that all the gold ever mined would fit into *one* oil tanker weighing 125,000 tonnes? And that the gold mines of South Africa have shafts that reach down more than three and a half miles into the ground, where the temperatures reach fifty-five degrees Celsius? Even hotter than here!'

'Really?' Mina was taken aback, and a little scared, by Au's sudden enthusiasm.

'Yes. You can't build anything out of it. It's too soft for that. Essentially, it's useless. And yet . . .' He paused. Only a small hesitation but one pregnant with promise. And in that moment she could almost see inside his mind as it juggled with all the possibilities, all the permutations, all the glories of gold. Did his eyes glitter a little golden light? 'And yet men will fight and steal and cheat and lie and even *kill* to possess it.'

Mina revised her earlier opinion. It wasn't enthusiasm she was seeing, it was fanaticism. She had the distinct feeling that Au's talk of killing was somehow not just theory. Here was a man who would kill – perhaps had – to possess gold.

It was, she decided as the hair stood up on the back of her neck, time to go. Jacob was examining the dragons in the window display and not listening.

'It certainly didn't do Midas much good,' she said loudly, perhaps a little too loudly. Her voice was higher and shriller than necessary.

'Indeed it didn't. Still, it's a fascinating subject,' agreed Au.

'It sure is,' said Mina. 'Jacob? We should go now.'

'Do they get real gold from the mine here?' asked Jacob, ignoring her.

'Sadly, no. They dig out quite a bit of this stuff but no real gold, no. Not any more.'

'And you make them?' Jacob moved across the display and pointed at the rings. 'What's that writing on them?'

'Oh, that's just me trying to make them a little more interesting: they're runes. You know, like it says in the book.'

Jacob peered at one. 'What does it say?'

'Jacob! I think we should be going.'

'I don't know,' Au confessed with a grin. 'I just make them up.'

'They look pretty good,' said Jacob, screwing up his eyes to examine the tiny symbols. He stared at the ring, his brow furrowing as if something important had occurred to him but he couldn't quite put it into words. He suddenly felt very sad. And something else . . . a *place*; somewhere quiet and infinitely sorrowful . . . somewhere *dead*.

'We. Have. To. Go. *Now*,' said Mina, pulling at his bag. He hated anyone else touching it and, as he jerked away from her, it seemed to break the spell. 'Come on. We have to do some shopping. Thanks for the tour, Mr Au. See you!'

'I hope so,' said Au. 'Come back soon. Maybe a T-shirt as a souvenir of Grymm before you leave?'

'Maybe,' conceded Mina, shoving Jacob before her.

As they pushed through the door the heat hit them like a sledgehammer. Jacob felt his brow break out in sweat almost immediately. He puffed out his cheeks and fanned his T-shirt for a breeze.

Mina steered him along the street, away from the front of the shop. 'Are you all right? What happened in there?'

'Happened? Nothing. Why?'

'You went all . . . all . . . What's that stupid word you use? Munted? You went all munted, all *wrong*, for a second. Like last night. What's up with you?'

'No, I, er . . . No, don't be an idiot. I was just thinking.'

'Are you sure? You seemed pretty out of it.' Then she added, 'Which, when I think about it, probably *is* you thinking.'

'Hilarious, just hilarious. What's it like being as funny as you?'

'Wonderful. Better than being *you.*'

'Now who's being munted?'

'What *does* that mean? It's a stupid word. What does it *mean*?'

'Look it up in the dictionary.'

'It's not *in* the dictionary, you mong. You and your idiot friends made it up!'

'It *is* there! With a picture of you.'

'You're a freak.'

'Am not.'

'Am.'

'And don't touch the bag, OK?'

'OK, OK, I'll leave the loot bag alone.' Mina rummaged in her jeans pocket and dragged out a crumpled piece of paper. 'We need to get some milk, bread, shampoo, eggs – and muesli, if they've got it. You know, you still don't look so good. Do you want to sit here while I go to the shop?'

'Yeah, I think I will, if that's OK.'

'Sure, just don't melt while I'm in there – if you do I'll be able to find out what else you've got in your little baggy-waggy.'

'Get stuffed. And don't forget nappies. Lots of them. And air freshener. Lots of it.'

After Mina went into the shop, Jacob sat in the shade, as impassive as an Easter Island statue. As the shadows shortened and the temperature edged up, the heat washed over him, and into him – into his lungs like warm liquid, making it harder and harder to breathe. It wouldn't have surprised him if the whole street had started to melt. The roofs first, dripping like candle wax onto the sidewalk, and then finally only he would be left, sitting in a pool of gunky town goop.

A big, blue-black, exhausted fly buzzed him lazily before flopping onto his forearm. It too seemed done in by the day, too worn out even to rub its little front legs together.

There they sat, Jacob and the fly, each squinting at the other but each too wrung out to move. Jacob could feel bubbles of sweat tickling his forehead and top lip. The sun, now a hazy white blob, pounded the town until heat rose off it in visible waves. What wouldn't he have given for a cool pool or a beach right now? Or a muffin . . .

A muffin? Jacob sat up and looked around, as if he might spot where the thought had come from. Would a muffin thought leave a trail of crumbs? And how could he possibly be thinking about food again? Perhaps it was the growth spurt his mother was always talking about; he certainly always seemed to be hungry these days.

As he sat there salivating, a large black raven – or crow, he didn't know which – flapped desultorily out of the great blue dome of sky. Its wings moved slowly, almost too slowly to keep it aloft, as if it were struggling through thick jelly (ooh, yeah, cold jelly straight from the fridge, yum). Its head was lowered with the strain of moving its wings up and down, up and down. So much so that its progress was measured in a series of mid-air hops rather than a stately glide. Jacob felt tired just looking at it.

Finally it gave up and flopped, awkward and undignified, down on the roofline opposite. *I know how you feel*, thought Jacob as the raven gave a harsh caw and cocked its head to look at him with a beady eye. *Who are you looking at?*

It was then that Jacob noticed that the bird was perched on the roof of Fleur's, the baker's, and the muffin came to mind again. He reached for his bag, delved into it and found a handful of coins – certainly more than enough for one muffin.

Fleur's was bookended by the bedraggled and boarded-up remains of the Golden Horse Hotel and the barber's, a plain-looking shop with one of those traditional red-and-white twirling poles outside. Only the pole was no longer twirling. Jacob got the feeling that if it did start to twirl again it would only go backwards. He trotted across the street, making for the cover of the other side as if it were pouring with rain, feeling the sun burn into his shoulders even through his T-shirt.

There were no blinds or curtains in Fleur's window, just the name written large on the glass in flamboyant, swirling red-and-gold letters, and beneath that, in letters no less ornate, the words *Boulangerie-Pâtisserie*. Jacob knew what *that* meant: posh bread and cream cakes.

He squashed his face against the glass to see inside but his view was obscured by layer upon layer of cakes, breads, tarts, biscuits and cream-stuffed pastries.

There were no prices, but each tray of goodies was labelled in the same typeface as the window itself. He found himself imagining biting into the . . . well, all of them. He would start with his favourites, though: the *mille-feuilles* with their folds of golden pastry, each weighed down with thick cream and slices of strawberry. He loved the way the cream always oozed out of the sides when you bit into them.

And there, *there*, were what Fleur described as *pains aux raisins* but which Jacob knew as 'snails'. He *loved* snails. In fact, the window seemed to be full of everything Jacob adored, but under different, funny-sounding names.

Down there on the right was a chocolate log marked *bûche de Noël*. And just above it a *tarte au chocolat* – that was a chocolate tart, he guessed.

Even the bread – stacked up higgledy-piggledy on the left-hand side – looked delicious. There were a dozen baguettes and a basket of little things called brioches that he longed to break into with his fingers, smear with jam, and scoff there and then.

There was also a round flat red thing spotted with olives and those hairy fish slices. It was in the savoury tarts section and it was called a *pissaladière*.

PISSaladière?

That, thought Jacob with complete certainty, he would not be eating.

Gradually, as he took in the mountainous panorama of pastry, he began to forget everything else – Mina slipped from his mind, Bryan too; Mary and George were as insubstantial as the delicate *tuiles aux amandes* biscuits down there next to the butter cream *mocha*

Génoise gâteau and, underneath, the glistening fruit tartlets. How *do* they get the fruit to shine like that – like glazed eyes? Reaching out, he gingerly touched the glass, expecting it to be sticky, made of clear sugar. And if he pushed open the door, would it flake under the pressure and succulent bits break off in his hands?

He imagined the whole shop made of bread and cakes; given enough time, he could nibble, nibble and gnaw his way through it all. And then what a fat little Jacob he'd be; what a dainty mouthful.

The door wasn't made of bread or pastry or anything of the sort. It was a plain old wooden door with a plain old four-panelled glass window. It wasn't anything special but it did serve a very important purpose: it kept the seductive smells of baking bread and cakes from seeping out into the street. If that had happened, who knows what havoc it would have caused? Or had a whiff of muffin escaped to entice him in?

Jacob was enchanted by the first rich sniff as he cracked the door open and the fragrance of warm cinnamon mixed with the sweet, burned bouquet of melting butter beckoned him. In the time it took for the door to close behind him he had been enveloped in the shop's comforting cocoon of cooking smells. It was like diving into a swimming pool heated to just above body temperature; his whole body felt reassured, relaxed. Unlike swimming, though, you could take the delicious golden warmth down into your lungs, up into your nose. He breathed in the aroma and let it suffuse his whole body. *Bliss*.

Standing there with his eyes closed, sucking it all in, Jacob began to make out a new smell – something that was familiar but didn't quite fit. Something sweet and dark. He was so busy wrinkling his nose and trying to separate the new aroma from the rest that he didn't see or hear the old woman shuffle up to him until she spoke.

'*Fee fi fo fum, I smell* . . . What do *you* smell, Jacob?'

He jerked backwards, almost crashing into the window display. 'Sorry, s–sorry. I was just . . . I was . . . just . . . er . . .'

The woman cackled and leaned heavily on a simple black walking stick. If she could have straightened up she would have been taller than Jacob but her back was hunched so badly she was almost bent double, and had to look up at him. She was dressed from neck to toe in black. All she needed was a broomsti— The word was elbowed aside in his brain by a finger bun with strawberry icing. *Tsk-tsk-tsk*, it said, and did a sexy little dance to show off its succulent body. *Good enough to eat*, it said.

Good enough to eat.

'You just wanted a taste, right? A finger bun, perhaps?

Or what about a *mille-feuilles*? You'd *love* to try one of those, wouldn't you?'

Jacob couldn't deny it, and began to dig into his pocket for his money.

'Now, don't you worry your little head none,' said the crone. She shuffled over to the display and, with surprising agility, snaked an arm through the shelves and came back with a plump pastry in her gnarled fist. 'There you are. On the house for the newcomer. Go on. It'll fatten you up.'

Jacob politely took the pastry, thanked the woman, and bit into it, holding one hand underneath to catch the inevitable flakes and blobs of cream. As he did so, he studied his unexpected benefactor almost as intensely as she studied him. There was something familiar about her but, like any memories of Mina and the rest, it stayed out of reach. His mind was focusing only on the goodies on display in front of him and how many of them he could stuff into his mouth – he had fleeting glimpses of himself as a little round beach-ball of a boy, blown up to the point of bursting, pudgy arms and legs splayed out like a cartoon – but beyond that was a thick white fog that hid his previous life.

Not that he minded. Eating fit to burst seemed like a jolly good idea.

Chomp-chomp-chomp-BANG!

But it wouldn't get that far; the old woman wouldn't let it get that far, he knew that.

Far too messy.

Better instead to . . . what? The words vanished again, chased away by a regiment of cream buns oozing cream and dripping red.

'More?' crooned the crone, laying a bony hand on his smooth forearm and gently tugging him towards a pair of plastic swing doors behind the counter at the rear of the shop. Her voice changed then, subtly becoming more sing-song, as if reciting a nursery rhyme. Or a spell. 'We have such titbits for you. Fatten you up, we will, we will, for the kill, we will.'

Jacob was mesmerized, his feet plodding slowly, heavily, his jaw working overtime on the pastry in his hand. He had this idea that he must just eat, eat, *eat eat* . . . and that all the best titbits were through the swing doors where large, shiny ovens pumped out too much heat for the sad little air-conditioner, and where pastry machines rattled and swished and swirled and ground, and made a racket that wouldn't have been out of place in a workshop producing aircraft parts, and where enormous metal bowls twirled around, their gluey batters mixed together by curved brass arms that spun in the opposite direction.

There was, through doors that would seal his fate (he

knew that in some far, dark, deep recess, but was happy with the knowledge), an assembly line, a conveyor belt for cakes manned by workers – Jacob understood somewhere in his befogged brain – who weren't *human*. Who had, quite literally, been cooked up from scratch – a great mass of life-sized, raisin-eyed *gingerbread* men, swarming through the thick, hot, scented air like a shoal of fish, never bumping into each other, always turning at the last moment to avoid collisions, kneading dough, cutting pastry shapes, splashing water into the batter mix, feeding pastry blobs into the rolling machines.

But he didn't mind, didn't mind at all . . . not when he could become a real-life SpongeBlob full of goodies and buns and . . .

As the old woman pushed him towards the doors with a bony claw, he managed to turn his head a fraction and catch sight of something that stirred a long-buried memory. On a low shelf, almost hidden by a battalion of baguettes, was a juicy-looking gingerbread house. The roof and the windows were picked out in thin swirls of white icing, and the chimney was a red-bricked column of marzipan. And he fancied he caught a glimpse of a liquorice witch enticing a sponge boy and puff-pastry girl with promises of food, with a splendid array of milk and pancakes, with sugar, apples and nuts.

Liquorice!

That was the scent he had recognized earlier. The old woman smelled of liquorice. But before the thought could process its way through his head and change into fear or disgust or shock a voice boomed out across the room.

'Ah, Pruneau! What 'ave you there, *ma petite?*'

Jacob, too mesmerized to be startled, stared dumbly ahead as a hugely fat man waddled out from behind a stack of trays holding hundreds of chocolate brownies, brandy snaps and fruit tartlets.

Imagine a snowman made of dough.

Imagine that it has pieces of perfectly round black coal for eyes.

Imagine that it has a little waxed moustache, like the brusque swirl of black marker pen.

Imagine that below that there is another short, sharp, thin, cruel flick of the same pen for a mouth.

Imagine that this snowman is dressed as a baker, complete with tall white hat.

Imagine that and you have imagined Malahide Fleur, baker *par excellence*.

'A boy! Good day, boy!' Fleur stood where he was, knowing that his bulk was an imposing presence, and somehow *preened*. Here was a man proud of his size. None of this obesity lark for Fleur; Fleur *was* his bulk. Without it he was nothing. What was a baker who didn't enjoy his wares to the full? 'You are the new *boy*, yes? In the big house on the hill, yes?'

Jacob could only nod. The bush telegraph worked well in a town like Grymm.

'With the sister and the brother? Another *boy*?'

Another nod.

'Bryan, yes? *Oui, mon petit chou?* I would meet this Bryan – I would, yes, yes, yes, I would. Is he a chubby thing? Is he chubby and doughy and fat? Unlike . . . unlike *you*!'

Fleur shambled over and pinched Jacob's arm between two of the fattest fingers he had ever seen. They looked like overstuffed white sausages, and seemed to have no fingernails. Deep down in the doughy flesh was the yellow glint of a ring. A tacky gold ring.

Jacob flinched at the touch. It wasn't pleasant. It was like being stroked by a sticky cake mix that left bits of itself behind. The man was like a walking, talking, waddling lump of his own bread mix before it was cooked.

Fleur seemed offended by Jacob's lack of fat. He turned to the witchy woman. 'He needs feeding up, of course! Come along, *boy*. I 'ave just the thing. Well done, Pruneau. Monsieur Anhanga will be pleased. *Fee fi fo fum!*'

Malahide Fleur had always wanted to be the world's greatest baker and pastry cook — a boyhood dream fostered by his father, who had owned a small bakery. *His* vision, though, was a little different to his son's. For where Fleur senior wanted only to perfect his small repertoire of breads and cakes, Malahide desired something far more ambitious. He wanted to experiment, to create new tastes and new sensations, things nobody had ever tasted before.

He had always been, as his mother put it, big-boned. Though Malahide Fleur looked as if he had no bones at all — underneath his rotund white head with its short white hair was a body that, after the age of about sixteen, grew out rather than up.

For not only was Fleur an exceptional baker; he was also an exceptional eater who *loved* his own cooking. Unable to imagine in his wildest dreams just how big his son would get in later life, Fleur senior indulged his young son's cravings. It was an idyllic time for the young boy, working proudly in the kitchen alongside a father who let him eat what he liked and who actively encouraged the boy's bizarre recipes and new techniques.

Well, until the unfortunate mix-up with the hell-hot chilli-and-chive croissant that left poor Madame

Alabaster Fresnoy in hospital having her stomach pumped and her burning lower regions washed out. Not something that you want done at the age of ninety-two. And not something you want to *do* to a ninety-two-year-old, as Mary-An, the clinic's nurse, discovered when six false teeth and a plastic doll's arm came shooting out of the woman's bottom. As if that wasn't bad enough, Mrs Fresnoy recognized the arm as one she'd lost as a child of seven. 'That's been up there for eighty-five years!' she exclaimed with glee as Mary-An passed out and hit the floor with a bang.

'I've still got that doll at home, you know,' the old lady confided to the doctor. 'She'll be glad to get that arm back.'

It was one of many memories that swirled around Fleur's brain, but rack it as he might, he couldn't remember how he had ended up in Grymm. Not that it mattered. He had gone about as far as he legally could in the 'outside world', as he liked to call anything beyond the town. *Here*, however, *here* he had expanded his repertoire beyond even *his* wildest imaginings, thanks to Mr Anhanga. A man of taste, was Mr Anhanga. Of very special tastes.

Four and twenty blackbirds baked in a pie was nothing compared to what he had planned for the mineworkers that weekend. Blackbirds indeed. Flay thought he was *so* clever – but you watch, just you watch Malahide Fleur.

But then the bell in the shop had tinkled . . . Was that a *boy* out there? A fat boy, hopefully . . . OH, that would be too, too perfect. Four and twenty fat boys baked in a pie? Mr Anhanga *would* be pleased, he was sure of that. And that fool Flay would be left in his wake.

On the move, Fleur looked like a galleon in full sail on a particularly choppy sea. Though not that many galleons had bums you could park a motorbike in. Sideways.

'*Fee fi fo fum* . . .' said Fleur.

Mina, meanwhile, was scanning the shelves of the grocery store for anything that wasn't in a can or a microwavable packet. It was a thankless task, made harder by the fact that most of the shelves were empty, half empty or stocked with bathroom products past their sell-by date. Not an easy thing to do, she thought, with those scented toilet blocks that, by rights, should survive the end of the world.

The shop was long and wooden and thin, and criss-crossed by shelves. It had once had a benign but respectable beige and green colour scheme, but time and neglect and the heat had worn it threadbare. At the far end, behind an old-fashioned wood-topped counter, stood a short, fair-haired man with a face like an over-anxious spaniel. He wore a faded blue T-shirt and, Mina noticed when she got to the checkout, baggy stone-coloured shorts from which protruded the knobbliest knees she had ever seen. His legs, which were all skin and bone and throbbing purple veins the size and shape of monster tapeworms, were tap-tap-tapping out a constant, nervous rhythm. He was so much on edge that Mina reckoned if she talked too loudly he would have just bolted out the back door.

'Hi. Nappies?' she asked. The man pointed at the furthest aisle with a finger and his chin. His eyes were, she imagined, as wide and round and frightened as those of a rabbit about to get turned into a bloody red rabbit-shaped smear by a car. What *was* his problem?

Finally she had everything that she could possibly get and approached the counter again. The man gave a thin smile. A grubby badge on his T-shirt said his name was Doug.

'That – that'll be t-t-twenty-two sixty,' he said. His breath was like the aforementioned rabbit after three days rotting in the Grymm sunshine. It smelled of death and fear and gloom. Mina held her breath and paid. He took an age giving her change. It probably wasn't an age but it is when you're holding your breath.

'See you later,' she said, turning away quickly, trying

to take a few surreptitious breaths of air that didn't smell of week-old roadkill.

'Not us, you won't,' he said. It was the first time he had seemed even slightly relaxed. No, *relieved*. 'Last few days and then we're gone. Leaving. Going back to the city. Closing Friday.' He giggled, but there wasn't anything the least bit happy about it. It was a giggle born of barely repressed hysteria. 'Better get in quick or all the good stuff will be gone.'

Mina backed away from him, smiling inanely. So even the store – such as it was – was closing. How long before Grymm dried up and blew away altogether? She turned and headed for the exit.

'Tell your mother,' shouted Doug to her retreating back, 'that we can organize regular food parcels from civilization, if she wants.'

Outside, glad to be away from the slightly mad Doug and his half-empty shop, she scanned the street. There were a few people from the protest camp milling around outside Inky Bugleslab's place, and Eric Elland – notebook in hand – chatting to a couple of miners on the way to the café, but Jacob wasn't anywhere to be seen. Of course! Of course! It was always the way. She was the oldest and therefore she was 'in charge'. And she would have put any amount of money on Jacob finding a way to get her into trouble. Again.

'Jacob? *Jacob!!!!!!*'

As she shouted up and down the street, a battered four-wheel-drive turned the corner further up and headed towards her, rattling past in a whirling cloud of dust that had Mina coughing and rubbing her eyes. She cursed the driver, and herself, and Jacob and Bryan, and her father for bringing them to this godforsaken hole. She wanted to grab each and every one of them by the shoulders and give them a piece of her mind. Except Bryan perhaps; he'd just sit there and gurgle and, no doubt, burp, puke and fart. All at once.

Mina rubbed, blinked and gradually cleared her eyes of dust. The jeep, which seemed to have its own mass and weight strapped to the roof rack, stopped at the gas station and a man jumped out. Travellers heading east, she decided, stopping for petrol.

She walked slowly along the deserted street, keeping one eye on the jeep while scanning around for Jacob. There seemed little point in shouting. How far away could he be? And despite everything she didn't want to look like a lunatic, hollering up at the blistering blue sky.

As she watched through the rippling heat haze, a small dark form came beetling out of the gas-station office, greeted the driver and moved to the rear of the vehicle. The faint clank of metal against metal reached

Mina as the attendant, still only a black smear to her irritatingly desiccated eyeballs, began to 'fill her up'.

There was a tent and camping equipment attached to the jeep's roof rack and, incongruously, a long-armed pink monkey with a stupidly happy face suckered to the inside of the side window, staring out at her. The driver, a tall man with a neat haircut, short-sleeved blue shirt and beige shorts, was nattering good-naturedly to the attendant. She couldn't hear what they were saying but the man was leaning lazily against his jeep's dirty bodywork and laughing at whatever the attendant was saying. The bizarre thing, though, was that Mina could now see the jeep and its occupant – stupid pink monkey included – in almost frightening detail. The bright sunlight seemed to etch every particle on her eyes with extraordinary clarity – and yet the attendant remained a smudge, a characterless blur. He was wearing baggy overalls of some kind . . . No, no, he was wearing a shirt with a nametag on it. No, it was overalls . . .

Mina shook her head. Perhaps there was still a piece of grit in her eye. She rubbed it and looked again. It was the same. The number plate on the jeep stood out as clear as day. She could make out the name above the office door – JOHN SMITH PTY. And yet the pump man himself remained a mere blemish.

And then she heard the sound of a bell just up ahead. *Jacob?*

She trotted along past the 4WD, feeling a dribble of sweat run down her back between her shoulder blades. Where was he, the idiot? She could still see their bicycles, locked to the defunct telegraph pole at the far end of the street, so he hadn't gone home. So where . . . ?

At the baker's she stopped – it smelled *divine* – and looked in through the window. There he was, talking to an old woman and an enormously fat man in a chef's hat! She strode to the door and pulled it open— Oh, my, those aromas!

'Jacob, what are—? Her voice died on her lips, but it was enough to break the spell. The seductive sights and smells of Fleur's shop slipped off Jacob's mind like the tentacles of some enormous squid releasing its prey.

'What?' He turned, frowning, his eyes a million miles away but gradually focusing on her. 'I, er . . . Mina?'

'What *are* you doing? Are you *hungry*? Oh, hello!'

Jacob leaped back from Malahide Fleur with a start. He wasn't sure what had happened but he somehow knew that he'd had a narrow escape from . . . what?

'No, um, er, I was looking for you,' muttered Jacob, still a little stunned.

'In the baker's? Though it does smell very nice

in here. Those – what are they? – smell like heaven.'

'We needed bread, didn't we?' asked Jacob, edging towards the door and trying to drag Mina with him. Fleur and the woman, Pruneau, just watched them silently. Jacob, whose imagination often ran away with him, could almost see them willing the sights and sounds of their shop to overpower Mina. He imagined them standing there impassively as tendrils of seductive aromas crept around them and advanced on their prey. Surely this wasn't happening . . .

'Mina, we should be going. Did you get bread?'

'Wait a minute,' she slurred in reply. He noticed her eyes glazing, as if she were looking inwards at the same sexy finger buns that he'd dribbled over earlier. 'Perhaps we need some pastries—'

'No,' he said, and gave the soft flesh of her upper arm a vicious pinch. 'No, we *don't*!'

'*Yow! Jacob!* That hurt!' There were tears in Mina's eyes now, and she looked from her arm to him in shock and puzzlement. 'What did you do that for?'

'We've got to go!' he repeated, dragging her by the arm towards the door. 'Come *on*!'

Mina snatched her arm away from him, threw one embarrassed look back at Fleur and stormed out of the shop. As she brushed past Jacob, she stamped on his foot and hissed, 'I hate you so much!'

Jacob also gave one last look at Fleur. The baker's coal-like eyes stared at him impassively, but the razor-blade mouth slithered around enough for the words '*Fee fi fo fum*' to slither out.

Jacob dashed into the steaming heat of the day; Mina, who had stormed up the street, turned to face him. She still grasped one white plastic bag in each hand. Her face was flushed – and Jacob knew it wasn't from the heat. She was, to begin with, speechless, her face changing from stunned surprise to anger, to hate, to . . . who knew where next. She looked, Jacob thought, like a bulldog chewing a wasp.

'What,' demanded Mina with undisguised fury, 'was all that about? You made me look like a complete idiot in there. What must that man think of us? I tell you what he'll think – he'll think we're mad, that's what he'll think. Because we are! Because *you are*!'

'But he was . . .' Jacob couldn't continue. Because he was what? Planning to feed them fit to burst and then cook them in a pie? What was he thinking? Maybe Mina had a point. Maybe he was going mad.

'He was what? What? Going to sell us some bread? The bastard! Jesus, Jacob! I knew you were a moron but this takes the biscuit – no pun intended. What are the oldies going to think when they hear about this? In town for one day and we piss off the baker?'

'I . . . I don't know, OK? I don't know!' Now Jacob was shouting too, more in embarrassment than anger. 'I thought he was going to . . . Look, I was hungry and I went in there and . . . well . . . I got scared. Did you see him?'

'The fat baker? Ooh, scary! How could I miss him? He was like a massive marshmallow – and he was standing there looking at you like you had two heads. And then . . . Oh my God, look at my arm! It's going to go black and blue. You are *so* going to die.'

Jacob could see her point: where he had pinched her arm there was a large red mark. He tried to reach out to her – something was wrong and he wasn't sure what it was.

'Don't you *dare* touch me!' she yelled before stomping off into the sunlight, her shadow a black puddle trailing behind her. The town, thought Jacob, and everything in it looked like it had been dropped into individual puddles of jet-black oil. The sky was no longer a creamy blue. Instead, a yellowy white gauze seemed to have been pulled down over everything. As he stood in silence and watched Mina go, he felt he could have reached out from under the sidewalk canopy and touched the burning air.

Behind him a familiar doorbell tinkled and he turned round to find Malahide Fleur peeking through a crack in the bakery door. It was just enough to see an eye, a portion of pastry-face and that lipless mouth. Jacob turned and ran up the street after his stepsister.

'Mina! Wait up!'

'Jacob,' hissed Mina, stopping in the shade and turning to face him with a look that could kill. 'You are pushing your luck. Look at my arm! Look at it!'

He looked. It was a bright, almost fluorescent, shade of puce. It wasn't going to be pretty but . . . but couldn't she see what, well, what would have happened if . . . if what?

'I hate you, Jacob, I really do. You are such a . . . *baby* sometimes. Now hold these bags while I get the rest of the stuff on *your* mother's shopping list. Can you do that? Can you stay here and be good while I do that? Can you?'

The ride back up to the house proved harder than they'd imagined. It was the wrong time of the day to be cycling anywhere, let alone uphill in a dry desert heat that seared the lungs with every intake of breath. It didn't help, either, that Jacob was silently trying to work out what had happened in the baker's shop and Mina was angrily sulking.

At the protesters' camp they stopped for a while and got their breath back while studiously ignoring each other, but by the time the house appeared up on the rise they were both pink-faced and drenched in sweat. Mina, unable to throw her bicycle down in a huff because of the bags of shopping hanging from the handlebars, contented herself with stomping into the house and announcing loudly that 'Jakie' had gone insane and attacked her.

And so the afternoon and evening of their first day in Grymm passed in a flurry of arguments punctuated by long periods of sulky silence. Mary was preoccupied with Bryan, who seemed to have turned into a buzz saw with the throttle stuck open, so heartily did he cry, and George returned from his first day at work tired and pensive.

Mina shut herself in the bedroom and Jacob fidgeted on the sofa in the lounge, trying to concentrate on the schoolwork he'd promised to do but in reality merely sweating and fuming quietly under a ceiling fan that seemed to do nothing but move the warm air from one side of the room to the other.

'I don't understand what's wrong with him,' said Mary to her husband as Bryan yowled like a banshee in her arms. 'I know he's never been the quietest of babies but he just hasn't stopped all day. I tried to get the kids to take him off my hands but Mina just ran off to her bedroom, and I can't trust Jacob not to, you know . . .

not after last time.'

'Hmmm,' muttered George, who was looking into his empty beer glass as if it were a crystal ball. 'Perhaps he's teething. Bryan, not Jacob. Though they'd have to be big old teeth for him to make that sort of noise. Or maybe it's as simple as just being too hot. Why has this house not got air-con? Did it say air-con in the ad?'

'I can't remember. Ms Grymm would know.'

'Well, it's too late now. Christ, that boy's got some lungs on him. So what did the kids get up to today? Did they make it all the way into town?'

'And back again, yes. Seems they had something to eat at the café, which is run by a "very weird" woman called Maggot.'

'Charming.'

'Yes, well, the stories they come out with would curl your hair. They haven't taken too kindly to the town, that's for sure. Full of weirdos and lunatics, according to Jacob.'

'And Mina?'

'Says Jacob is the weirdo and lunatic. Still, they got the shopping I needed, which was something. Though we're going to have to do something about that as Mina says the shop's going to close soon. And, of course, they argued all the way there and all the way back, as far as I can make out. As a result of which Jacob pinched Mina's arm hard enough to bring out a huge bruise. She's pretty angry with him.'

'She's angry with everyone, that girl. Hormones, I suppose. Were you like this at that age?'

'No, I was perfect.'

'Of course you were, my sweet. Do I need to talk to them?'

'Probably. I don't know what they argued about exactly, or what made Jacob pinch her so badly, but it is a really nasty bruise. Looks a bit like a sunset I once saw in southern China with Jacob's father.'

'Very funny. Look, shall we just thaw something out again tonight? I'm a bit worn out from all the driving yesterday and I can't be bothered cooking.'

'Not a problem. And so how was work on day one?'

'Not too bad. Didn't get to meet the manager . . .' Here George held up his right hand and waggled it in the air. 'Even put his crappy Welcome ring on for nothing – and was just shown the ropes, really. Looks easy enough. Bit too easy, to tell the truth. He's got them – us – searching the area for fresh deposits of everything from iron to uranium to bloody Kryptonite, for all I know. The readings look like nonsense. I mean, the area's already been dug up to kingdom come and back.

It's intriguing, not quite what I was expecting . . . I'm sure it'll be fine. Probably just first-day nerves. It's interesting that the iron pyrites side of the operation seems mostly automated – none of the guys I'm working with has anything to do with it, anyway. To be honest I don't know that it's a viable operation.'

'Well, as long as it lasts for the next three months,' said Mary, half joking.

'Yes, and as long as they pay the wages! Anyway, enough of that. I'll have a word with the kids before dinner. You'd think they'd be used to each other by now, wouldn't you? It gives me a headache just thinking about them. Have you ever wondered what our lives would be like without them? Without all the bitching and moaning?'

'*George!*' said Mary, taken aback by the thought.

'I know, I know. I'm sorry. Long day.'

'Mind you' – Mary cocked an eye towards the dining-room ceiling and contemplated the night sky through the glass – 'I wouldn't mind if they did a bit more around the house. Now *that* would be nice. Maybe I could set up the easel again. This would be a good place to paint.'

'Yeah, dream on. Maybe when Bryan's twenty.'

'Cheery thought, that. Anyway, I'm going to put him down for a while and get dinner ready. And look on the bright side – he can't cry any *more*.'

Whereupon Bryan proved her wrong by increasing the volume again.

'Christ, Bryan, what a noise!' said George. 'Who's hanging onto your testicles, son?'

Dinner was a frustrating affair, with neither Mary nor George willing to listen to the children's tales of Thespa Grymm wanting to eat Bryan or Malahide Fleur hypnotizing Jacob with buns so he could eat *him*. And as for maggots in the milkshake . . .

'What is the matter with you two?' thundered George. 'You've never been the best of friends, but this – this is ridiculous.' He pulled off another piece of pizza and stuck it angrily into his hairy maw.

'But Dad,' pleaded Mina, 'you've got to admit this place is weird. That Inky Bugleslab at the newsagent's is . . . just. . . *urgh*.' She shivered theatrically at the memory, taking pains to make sure the sleeve of her T-shirt didn't obscure her bruise.

'For your information I had to go get something from the newsagent's this afternoon,' said George, 'and I met Mr Bugleslab.'

'You did?'

'Yes, and he seemed fine to me. Pity about the hair-cut but you can't have everything. I also stopped in at the baker's and got some buns and stuff for the boys at the mine. He's a big lad, that Fleur, but by gum he can make a cake. Either you and Jacob have let your imaginations run away with you or you're just making mischief for the sake of it. Either way it's got to stop. And you, Jacob, if you hurt your sister like that again I will beat the living daylights out of you – see how you like it.'

Jacob, stunned to hear his stepfather threaten him for the first time ever, just gaped like a goldfish and looked at his mother, who merely gave a don't-look-at-me-you-deserve-it shrug. Even Mina, who had been playing up the 'injury' to get her stepbrother in as much trouble as possible, was shocked. It was another of those moments when time telescoped, and hours if not days of contemplation, irritation, astonishment and inner turmoil all fitted into the few seconds George took to let his threat sink in. Mina even frowned at Jacob in surprised support. She wanted him in trouble, but this . . . this was something else. And Jacob's mother just sat there with that stupid half-smile on her face instead of protecting her idiot son.

'But, Mum, I—' stammered Jacob.

George ignored him and ploughed on. 'And while we're all here together, let's get a few more things straight. You will *both* help your mother out more around the house and with Bryan. Especially with Bryan.'

'Help with Bryan?' Mina's sounded like someone had asked her to dispose of uranium fuel rods with plastic washing-up gloves. There was something very, very wrong about this. 'I tried that today and he broke my phone.'

'Just as well it doesn't work out here then,' laughed Jacob. It was the laugh of someone who was trying to inject something familiar into a situation that was rapidly getting out of hand; the laugh of someone who wasn't quite sure that what he was laughing about was really that funny; a laugh on the verge of tears.

'I am *so* going to—'

'Look,' interrupted Mary, who could see that George was about to explode with anger, 'it's just that we both think you should start doing a bit more to help out around the house.'

'What Mary is trying to say, but in a nice way, is that we are fed up to the back teeth with you two. And if it carries on, I am going to take you out into the desert and shoot you both in the back of the head. Is that clear?'

Mina and Jacob just looked at him in shocked silence.

He just grinned right back at them. 'In a manner of speaking.'

'But Dad—'

'Is. That. Clear? Good. Now, for a change you can do the washing-up, and then it's bed for you both. And don't even think I'm going to help you change bedrooms at this time of night. You are stuck in the same room. Might do you some good; you might even grow up a bit. Now get out of here – I'm sick to death of the sight of you.'

Later, Jacob and Mina sat facing each other in the bedroom. Mina, on the edge of her bed with her legs drawn up, hugged her knees tightly with both arms and glared. Jacob sheepishly clutched his ever-present bag to his chest.

'Look, the pinch seemed like the right thing to do at the time. There was something about him . . . and that woman. They weren't *normal*.'

'Normal? You're not normal, *Jakie*. And who knows what's normal in this place? We're in the middle of the bloody desert and the real-estate agent says she wants to eat Bryan! With any luck she'll finish him off and then make you the dessert.'

'Very funny, *Wilhelmina*. Didn't you feel anything in the baker's? Nothing seemed odd to you?'

Mina hesitated. She didn't want to give Jacob the satisfaction of . . . well, *anything*. But she was inclined to believe that Jacob *thought* something had happened. That said, she couldn't help herself: 'I think you have a thing

125

about fat people, that's what I think. And stealing stuff. Pick up anything good for your little baggy-waggy today, thief?'

'Leave me alone!'

'And what's my punishment for, well, for doing nothing except being pinched by an idiot? It's another night in this room . . . with *you*. What was Dad thinking?'

'I don't know, but he seemed pretty pissed off at us. I've never seen him like that before. It was like he really would take us out into the desert and, you know . . .' He mimed being shot in the head.

'Well, if he doesn't shoot you, I will. I mean, what have I done to deserve this? You, this room, being stuck here for three months, and . . .'

'*WAAAAAAAGHH!*'

'. . . Bryan. God I hate my life.'

They slept. And again, at some point in the night, something stirred in the back yard. Jacob listened. Mina listened. The sound reminded Jacob of someone slurping spaghetti. In unspoken agreement they went to the window again, quietly, hoping to surprise whatever it was that snuffled outside their room at night. Or more likely hoping there was nothing there.

They pulled the curtains back. The arthritic trees still

stood there, gnarled, ghostly hands breaking through the soil to grab the house and drag it down to hell or worse, but so did something else – a group of small jet-black creatures, like upright black cats, swarming around each other like a shoal of fish in a feeding frenzy or a pack of skinny dogs fighting over a meal.

And the noises, the muffled sounds that reached them through the closed window, were a mixture of snapping and snarling but also whispered words – like English but also like some extinct language that was once used to raise the dead. It was a susurration of evil, accompanied, as the things slithered wetly around and over and under each other, by a sticky ripping noise; as if they were all covered in Velcro and every bodily contact left something of themselves – flesh, fur, drool – behind.

Jacob found himself thinking of his milkshake, and fought to keep the bile down. They were like large black maggots wriggling and writhing in the moonlight.

Then one of them, realizing they were being observed, looked up and snarled, baring pale yellow teeth like fangs. Its eyes were red slits and the lower half of its face was smeared with something black and sticky. In its mouth was something that looked like the badly chewed hand of a plastic doll. Then, as if responding to a silent signal, they all stopped and turned to face the window.

They see us, thought Mina. *They see us!*

Fee fi fo fum, thought Jacob. *Fee fi fo fum.*

And then the pack parted and they understood.

They understood that the unimaginable was happening.

They understood that the doll's hand wasn't a doll's hand at all.

For, resting on the ground in the middle of the pack, pale, naked and unusually quiet, was Bryan, his pale oversized baby's head lolling awkwardly, impossibly, to one side. His right hand was missing, his arm ending in a torn, bloody stump. One of the things, the imps, grinned lasciviously and, with a throaty chortle, went back to its meal, making Bryan flop around like a rag doll with its red cotton stuffing hanging out. Only it wasn't cotton.

Mina's scream echoed across the plain below and bounced like an escaped rubber ball around the dead streets of Grymm.

6

'This is ridiculous,' muttered Mina the next morning when she and Jacob confirmed they had had the same dream about the baby-eating imps. She launched herself out of bed and skipped over to the window, just to make sure.

'Nothing. Dust, dust and more dust. Just like yesterday.'

Jacob eyed her from the bed. The edge of the bruise peeked out from the arm of her T-shirt. For once he felt bad about inflicting pain on his stepsister; or was it that he wasn't now entirely sure *why* he'd done it. It all seemed so far away, so fuzzy. What *had* happened to him in the bakery?

'We must really not like Grymm,' he joked, though his voice came out higher and more shrill than he expected.

'Or Bryan!' laughed Mina. 'Still, I can't hear him crying – or farting – so maybe it's doing him some good. He's obviously become a morning person.'

Jacob, warmed by the fact that Mina seemed to have shaken off the bad feelings of the previous night, sat up and rubbed his eyes. 'Still, it's odd, having the same dream, isn't it? Don't you think it's a bit spooky?'

'Yes. Of course it is. There's something wrong here. But now we're even. I didn't believe you about the baker yesterday, but when I said Thespa Grymm was a witch who wanted to eat Bryan, did you back me up? No. So we're even.'

'Yes, yes, you were right. Happy now? You think Ms Grymm wants to eat Bryan and I thought Fleur wanted to eat me. So is it them, or is it us?'

Mina exhaled slowly and backed away, plonking herself down on her own bed and plunging her head in her hands. Jacob reached surreptitiously under the bed-clothes and pulled out his green bag. *Christ*, thought Mina as she watched him through her fingers, *he even sleeps with it!*

'Maybe we *are* just letting our imagination run away with us,' suggested Jacob. 'It's a new place, new people, and . . . Well, as your dad says, we're not giving it much of a chance, are we?'

'You might be right. Maybe we're making too much

of it. Look, let's get up and have some breakfast. If I'm starving, you must be ravenous. You want to use the bathroom first? Might even beat Dad to it. Just don't start whistling in there.'

Half an hour later they walked into the kitchen to a scene eerily reminiscent of the previous day. Mary stood by the kitchen sink, dunking tea bags, while George sat at the table shovelling the last of his bacon and eggs into his maw.

'Morning!' said Mina brightly.

'Morning!' echoed Jacob.

'My, my, my, we are chipper this morning!' Mary smiled. 'You two kissed and made up?'

'Kissed?' Jacob made the face of a man condemned to eat his own intestines. 'Urgh.'

'I'd rather eat Bryan,' added Mina, and smiled slyly at Jacob to see if he got the joke.

'Who, dear?' asked Mary.

'Bryan,' Mina repeated. 'Bawling Bryan.'

'Butter-ball Bryan,' said Jacob, joining in.

'Bryan?' Mary stopped dunking the tea bags. 'I'm afraid I don't get it. Bryan who?'

'Baby Bryan! Your baby – our, er, brother. He's very quiet again. Is he on the sofa?' Mina's voice rose, heading towards shrill.

'I'm afraid I'm not with you, dear,' said Mary with a

worried glance at her husband, who was perplexedly chewing a last gristly bit of bacon.

Jacob glanced at Mina, who was half smiling, half angry, looking frantically from Mary to George and back again. His pulse throbbed in his temples.

'What do you mean?' said Mina, her voice cracking. 'Bryan your son. Bryan our bloody half-brother. Cries all the time? Poos radioactive Velcro? *That* Bryan.'

'Mum?' said Jacob. Something had occurred to him. Something so impossible, so terrifying that he felt very small and *very* insignificant. Every detail of last night came back in a rush and he felt like vomiting. He felt as if some small part of his mind, at the very back, was spinning off its axis like a broken rollercoaster at a fair.

'What, Jacob?' Mary looked sick and was swallowing hard, like someone trying to fight back the urge to throw up.

In turn, her son had gone deathly pale. Dark circles appeared under his eyes and he looked a hundred years old. 'Where's Bryan?'

'Not you too,' said Mary. 'Where is this all going? I don't understand. George?'

'Don't look at me,' said George around a mouthful of egg. 'I have no idea what they're on about.'

Mina and Jacob jumped up, rushed into the next

room and came back with even more puzzled looks on their faces.

'Where is he?' asked Jacob. 'Where's Bryan?'

Mary, now white-faced and on the verge of tears, just looked at them uncomprehendingly.

'Bryan!' shouted Mina. 'Your *son*? Our stinky half-brother? Is this a joke?'

'Mina,' interrupted Jacob in a small, frightened voice. 'They're not kidding. They don't know . . .'

The tea bags Mary was holding hung from one hand, dripping onto the floor. Her legs trembled and she covered her eyes with the other shaking hand.

'Right, that's enough!' George slammed his knife and fork down and stood up so fast his chair fell backwards. He stomped across to Mary and helped her into a seat. She put her face in her hands and began to sob. 'This stops right now. Is this because we took all your stupid electronic gadgets away from you? Well, it's not funny and it's not clever. I don't know where you got this stupid idea, but enough is enough. I don't want to hear any more about it, right? Jesus! We've not even been here one day and you've managed to upset your mother.'

'She's not *my* mother,' shouted Mina. The outburst took even her by surprise. 'I wish we'd never come here. *My* mum would never have come here. I *hate* it. I *hate* it here. And I hate *you*.' She glared at everyone and then stomped out of the room. Slamming doors charted her progress through the house.

'Jacob?' said George quietly.

'Yeah?'

'Come with me. Now.'

Outside the kitchen, with the door firmly closed behind them, George took his stepson by the shoulders and looked him straight in the eye. Jacob was shocked to see that his stepfather was on the verge of tears. He blinked once and they ran down his cheeks.

'Jacob,' he whispered in a mixture of barely controlled anger and unfathomable sadness, 'what did you think you were doing? Are you two *that* stupid? That callous? You should both know better than to pull a stunt like that. You're not babies.'

'I kn-know,' stammered Jacob, tears now welling up in his eyes too. 'But—'

'No buts, Jacob, not this time. Maybe one day, in the future, we can talk about the . . . er, you know . . . miscarriages . . . more openly but, well, it's all still a bit too raw. OK? You know how much your mother and I would have liked another child, but . . . but after what happened it looks like it's just not going to happen. Making a joke of it like this isn't going to help. OK? Mary *needs* this time. *We* need this. We need this time to get over things, make a new start. And you coming up with stupid stunts like this, well . . .'

'OK, George,' Jacob agreed. Something momentous had happened but he knew it would be useless to argue. They would never believe it. He wasn't sure he believed it himself. 'I'm sorry . . . I'm sorry. We just didn't think.'

The words sounded hollow in his mouth, let alone his ears, but they seemed to mollify George.

'Yes, well. Look, tell Mina I'll be leaving for work in about half an hour if she wants to come. Maybe you two can have breakfast in town again. Do a bit of exploring. Use up some of this excess energy you seem to have. You never know, you might get through a whole day without trying to kill each other. Just get out from under your mum's feet for the day, eh?'

'Yeah,' said Jacob with a sad smile. He was planning ahead already. 'Maybe we'll bump into Ms Grymm.'

'I'm sure Mina would *love* that. Go on. Off you go.' George patted his arm affectionately and whispered, 'Try to get her to come and apologize, smooth things over, eh?'

Jacob smiled through brimming tears. 'Mina? Apologize?'

'It's a tough call, I know, but do your best. And no more of this Bryan business. OK?'

'OK. No more Bryan.'

'No more Bryan' just about summed it up. Jacob, more in hope than anything else, got dressed and searched the house from top to bottom. Fearing the worst and expecting scenes of carnage to confront him, he thundered along the hallway to Bryan's room and threw the door open. It was empty. There was no Bryan, no cot, no clothes, no mobile. Instead, a few boxes were scattered about. He tried his parents' room too, easing the unfamiliar handle down, not knowing if the door was a squeaker or not. It opened quietly and revealed a large room dominated by a double bed. Like the other rooms, everything was either in boxes or hanging out of boxes, but there was no sign of Bryan. He had vanished from the face of the earth. He had been erased. His cot was gone. The nappies and clothes were gone. The irritating clown mobile had vanished too. There wasn't a skerrick of proof that he had *ever* existed.

Jacob was rummaging through the rubbish bins outside for evidence of nappies – surely nothing could erase Bryan's toxic dumps – when Mina strolled round the corner. Her eyes were red-rimmed and she held a scrunched-up handkerchief.

'What *are* you doing?' she asked, pointedly ignoring her earlier outburst despite the physical evidence of it.

'I thought there might be a nappy or something . . .

you know.' He shrugged helplessly, embarrassed. 'Your dad's pretty pissed off with you. He wants you to apologize to Mum. *My* mum.'

'Yeah, over my dead—' Memories of Bryan's bloody body flopping around stopped her from going any further. Were they memories? Or was it really just a dream? 'Jacob, what happened last night?'

Jacob shrugged again and moved away from the ripe smell of the bins. He stared out across the nothingness to Grymm.

'He's dead, isn't he?' Mina whispered.

Jacob turned on her, his face a dark cloud, eyes shining. 'Don't say that! Don't ever say that! He's not dead, all right? He's *not*!'

'All right, all right. Jeez, anyone would think you actually liked him.'

Jacob blushed at that, knowing she was right. They'd been horrible to him and about him since before he was born. How many times had they wished him gone? And now he was. 'It doesn't make it fair. What she did.'

'Who?'

'Thespa Grymm.'

'What makes you think it was Ms Grymm? It could have been the baker, or Inky Bugleslab, or any of the other lunatics in this town. And what is this "it" that they did? And whatever "it" was, *how* did they do it? And why only make Dad and Mary forget? Why not us too?'

'Perhaps she – they – whoever – wants to torture us,' mused Jacob. 'Perhaps only one of us will wake up tomorrow; the other one'll be gone. Just like Bryan. And my mum and your dad will only remember the one that's left.'

Mina stared at him, the possibility that Grymm might not be finished with them dawning on her. She began to stalk up and down, unable to contain the adrenalin from the rush of fear. She felt cold, despite the crushing heat.

'And then, the day after that—'

'Yes, yes,' she cut him short. 'Thanks, Jacob, thanks very much. I get the picture. So what do we do?'

'You're asking *me*? You know, you seem a lot more worried now that it might affect *you*. What do we do about Bryan?'

'Bryan?' She gave a mirthless laugh. 'Bryan's gone. We need to save ourselves.'

Jacob sneered and turned away, shaking his head in disgust.

'What? What did I say?'

He pivoted and pointed an accusing finger at her. Mina got the impression that her stepbrother had become older, wiser and more grown-up overnight. He, in turn, felt as if he had glimpsed behind her mask for the first time. And what he saw there was . . . what? Not a know-it-all teenager but someone as confused and scared as he was. He hoped it was fear that was making her so selfish.

'You know, sometimes you're— *Oh!*' His tirade died as a bright light flashed in his face. He held a hand up to shade his eyes as Mina looked down at the source of the irritation. Her pendant. She held it up and it turned slowly between them, shining in the sun.

'Of course!' shouted Mina. She, uncharacteristically, hugged Jacob. 'Of course! We *were* supposed to forget but the pentacle saved us.'

'What are you talking about?'

'Most people don't know this, but pentacles,' said Mina in the irritatingly condescending tone she used to explain things to her idiot stepbrother, 'weren't used *by* witches; they were used as a protection *against* witches. It proves that Ms Grymm is a witch! And whatever magic she used to wipe out Bryan didn't work on us.'

'And if I'd slept in my own room last night—'

'You wouldn't remember him either. I'd be going off my brain alone today. Jacob,' she gushed, grabbing him again and crushing him in another tight embrace, 'you're a genius!'

Jacob huffed and puffed and tried to disentangle

himself, embarrassed by the unexpected attention.

'What's all the noise? Are you two all right?' said George as he came round the corner, car keys jangling in one hand. The two jumped apart guiltily, adding to his confusion. He looked at each of them in turn. 'What are we celebrating?'

'Nothing,' they said simultaneously.

'*The wolf also shall dwell with the lamb, and the leopard shall lie down with the kid,*' George recited.

'What?' Again simultaneously.

'It's the Bible. Isaiah, I think. Some prophecy or another about peace breaking out on earth when the wolf and the lamb start hanging out together without eating one another. This must be what they meant.'

'*Dad!*' chided Mina, throwing an arm around his chunky waist and cuddling him affectionately. 'We're not that bad, are we?'

'Yes you are,' said George with a serious grin as they walked towards the dusty 4WD. 'Ever since me and Mary got together you two have been a pain in the bum. You know that, don't you? We love you both but it *is* a bit like living in a war zone.'

'Yeah, I know,' she said, an admission that led George and Jacob to do a double-take. George because it wasn't something he heard very often, and Jacob because he'd begun to wonder if Thespa Grymm had also swapped

Mina for a robot in the night. 'Sorry, Dad.'

'And that little stunt this morning really took the biscuit. Of course, if it carries on I'm going to get out my gun and a couple of shovels and bury you both way out *there*,' said George, pointing airily out into the western wasteland. He looked at them with such a serious look that they both fell silent. Coming on top of Bryan, this was too frightening for words.

'Ha-ha-ha! Gotcha! Of course I wouldn't; I mean, I haven't got a gun, for a start! But it's probably what you deserve for doing something so cruel. Right? Right, Mina?'

Jacob was relieved to see her bristle at this and begin to protest (it *was* the same old Mina), so he surreptitiously jabbed her in the back. She glared poisonously, but got the message. 'Yeah, well, it *was* a bit off, I know. I don't know what came over us.'

'Maybe this little détente between you two can also be extended to include Mary then? She's not taken this business too well, you know. Not on top of the miscarr— Well, you know, and the move and the drive and all the other . . . *disappointments*. I know you both miss the city but Mary's given up her art classes – and you know how much she enjoyed them. An apology wouldn't go amiss. You too, Jacob.'

'OK, George.'

'We will, Dad, I promise.'

'Good. Well, get ready; we'll be going in five minutes,' said George as he made his way back to the house. 'Put your bikes on the rack, OK?'

'I suppose we should go see Thespa Grymm. As a first resort?' said Mina after George had disappeared inside.

Jacob hesitated. While confronting Grymm had seemed a good idea to start with, he was beginning to have second thoughts. How do you face up to an adult and accuse her of making your brother disappear?

Mina saw the fear on his face. 'Look, we don't have to accuse her of anything. We'll just chat to her and then mention Bryan. See what she says. Something's really wrong here, Jacob, don't forget that. And we're the only ones who can find out what. Nobody's going to believe us. We're on our own.'

'OK, but you go first.'

'We'll go together.'

But it wasn't to be. They left George at the mine entrance again and cycled into town, this time getting a few friendly shouts of hello from the people at the tent city. Freewheeling along the downhill stretch, they stopped, parked their bikes but found Grymm's office closed. They rang the bell and heard it buzz, faint and bee-like, in the back of the shop, but there was no answer.

'She's not here,' Jacob said as they tried to peer through the windows. He stepped back and looked at the upstairs windows, flicking his sweaty T-shirt to stop it sticking to his back. The 50+ sun cream he had put on earlier had already turned into a sort of milky, snot-coloured gunk and was dripping down his forehead. He took off his baseball cap and wiped the mixture of cream and sweat back up into his black hair.

'We didn't dream yesterday, did we? Maybe it was yesterday that wasn't real. Maybe there never was any Bryan,' Mina said.

'If you dreamed it, so did I.' Jacob settled his cap back on his head with a firm slap. 'And he has to be real; *nobody* could dream up Bryan, or his bum. So, what now? She's gone – and maybe taken Bryan with her. It's the perfect crime when the victim never even existed. You might be right. Perhaps she *is* a witch.'

'Well, she's not going to get away with it. We'll ask around. The newsagent! He'll know.'

'Is he as weird as the rest of them?' asked Jacob.

'Pretty much,' said Mina as they headed towards the shop. As they entered, though, the blue-eyed dread-locked boy from the day before was leaving. He gave Mina a dazzling smile and a soft 'Hi' before sauntering off into the blistering heat.

Jacob saw Mina blushing and sighed irritably.

'Puh-lease . . .' he groaned.

Inky Bugleslab was sitting behind the counter reading a three-month-old magazine and rolling a cold bottle of water back and forth across the wide expanse of his forehead. It was dark inside but still warm. Inky seemingly didn't believe in air conditioning. Jacob and Mina had to take off their sunglasses to see him properly.

'Wilhelmina,' he rasped in his reedy voice. 'So good to see you again. And this must be Jacob. Hello, young man. Magazine? Water? Newspaper? It's about a week old but no news is good news, eh? Ha-ha-ha-ha!'

'Thanks, Mr Bugleslab' – Mina smiled as the newsagent stood up and peered at them both like they were insects under a microscope – 'but we're wondering if you knew where we could find Ms Grymm.'

'Inky, please call me Inky.'

Jacob was astonished to realize that Inky Bugleslab, tall as he was, still hadn't finished getting to his feet. The man was a human skyscraper! He looked like a white balloon on a very long stick. A balloon on which someone had used an old black marker to draw really bad hair. Mina, on the other hand, was disgusted to see that he was still in the same blue trousers and sweat-stained brown shirt that he had been wearing the previous day. For a girl who showered three or four times a day, and changed her clothes just as often, this was sacrilege.

'Thespa?' he whispered, drawing the word out in a snakelike hiss. 'Thespa? Well, I can't say I've seen her today, that's for sure.'

'Oh, we were hoping to catch her but her office is closed.'

'Oh, she never works on a Monday. You know what real-estate agents are like. Four days a week but never met a poor one, eh?'

'But today's Tuesday,' protested Jacob.

'Is it? How time flies. She should be there then.'

'Does she live nearby?' persisted Mina. 'Maybe we could visit her at home.'

'She lives above the shop. So if she's not there, she's not there. But look, about Thespa—' He stopped, looked at the ceiling and furrowed his vast white brow in thought. Tendrils of greasy black hair, combed from back to front, lay plastered to his forehead like ink runs, and his maggot of a tongue popped into the corner of his mouth and wriggled. 'Look, about Thespa . . . . I'd try to keep Thespa at arm's length, if I were you. Bit of an old witch, you see. Never much cared for her. Just 'cause the town got named after *her* lot, she thinks she's the life and soul. She's not. Not any more. History, history, she's history.'

'So you don't know where she is, or where we can find her?' said Mina.

'Not right now, no.'

'Do you know who might be able to help me?'

'Aah!' Inky Bugleslab's eyes lit up and he leaned forward as if to impart some great secret that nobody else should hear. 'Cleaver,' he said. It was as if the word were a boiled sweet and he was rolling it around in his mouth to get the most flavour from it. Suck it and see!

'Cleaver. Flay.'

'The butcher?' Something stirred in Mina's memory. It was just after Jacob threw up yesterday – the quick flash of a bright red roller-blind rattling up across the road.

'Cleaver Flay's the one you need to talk to. He and Thespa go way back. They're old . . . *friends*. Talk to Cleaver.'

Mina looked across the road at the butcher's shop and gulped.

Close up, it was even worse. Cleaver Flay's window display, thought Mina, was a celebration of the many ways in which dead animals can be dissected and displayed to their best advantage. Or rather, *our* best advantage.

Mina, whose flirtations with vegetarianism had led

146

her to view meat with suspicion, could only marvel at the lustrous spread conjured up in the window of Flay's no-horse-town butcher's shop. Plump hearts, almost mauve, were packed tightly into a bright white tray, glistening as if they had been freshly sprayed with blood – or were still trying to pump it.

Large slices of brown liver were stacked one on top of another, their pitted surfaces seemingly still trying to suck up the watery juices in which they lay.

'This,' muttered Mina, 'is freaking me out.'

'Tell me about it,' growled Jacob.

Next to the liver a tray of shiny kidneys oozed together, their protruding white cores of fat all pointing in the same direction. They looked to Mina like a parade of dead soldiers propped to attention. A tray of pork and herb sausages reminded her of the fat fingers of the two miners in Inky's shop.

Behind them, a dozen or so chicken legs danced to some unheard music, looking like the limbs of a troupe of elderly synchronized swimmers, their pale, flabby legs and loose skin poking out of a pool of pale blood. And all over the display bright green splotches of plastic parsley sprigs relieved the red and white monotony.

It was not just neatly done, she realized, it was done with an almost inhuman precision; with a passion and attention to detail that made everything seem to throb with life. It wasn't, however, a sight for the squeamish.

Especially if, the previous day, you'd sucked a live maggot up through your straw. Jacob turned away. His flesh, which had only just returned to normal, paled again and the green tinge under his eyes reappeared. 'I'm not going in there.'

This was said with a decisiveness that was remarkable, thought Mina, for a boy who had trouble deciding which of his increasingly smelly socks to put on in the morning.

'Will you be all right out here? I won't be long, but one of us has got to talk to this Flay if we're going to find Thespa Grymm.'

Silence.

'Jacob?'

'Yeah, yeah,' he said. He seemed distracted but was just trying to think of anything but maggots and slick, slippery-looking cuts of meat. *Cornflakes, cold water, dry bread, black tea—*

'Jacob?'

'Yes! I heard you! I'll wait for you here.' He plopped down in the shade, back against the weatherboard, and closed his eyes. Then, knowing that he had been too brusque, he smiled feebly. 'I'll be OK in a minute. Honest. You go. I'll be right here.'

Mina, for once, wasn't offended. The meat in the

window hadn't affected her in the same way but it *had* made her uneasy. She got the feeling, as the animal parts pressed and slithered against each other, that the whole display was almost breathing. She'd watched a documentary once about eels and how their nervous systems kept the bits alive even after they'd been cut into pieces. It reminded her of that. Chillingly, Flay had succeeded in making everything appear as fresh as if it had, only that morning, still been attached to a cow or a chicken or a sheep. Or a dog.

Braced for a close, foul atmosphere inside, Mina was surprised to find it fresh and cold. The door swung open and a bell attached to it tinkled merrily as it closed behind her. There was clean sawdust on the floor and the glass counter contained a large selection of gourmet sausages, sauces, chutneys and pâtés, all labelled *Homemade* in neat, distinct handwriting.

'Can I help you?' The man who emerged through the door at the back was enormous in every way. He wore a spotless butcher's apron and a straw boater decorated with a red ribbon. His head, Mina was certain, was completely bald. There was something else about that head, and it wasn't the hooked nose or the fleshy lips. Nor was it the close-set eyes, which were just slight indents in acres of white flesh.

Or was it . . . ? That was it! His eyes!

No, no, that wasn't it. It was his eyebrows – he had none. Which led her to another conclusion – a leap of logic so bizarre that she wondered where it had come from: there wasn't a single hair on him.

Anywhere.

That, Mina knew without hesitation. And, as if confirming her realization, she had a sudden image of Cleaver Flay standing in front of a bathroom mirror with a cut-throat razor sparkling in his huge hand, his bald dome of a head slathered in animal fat. Smiling at her – for now she *was* the mirror – he began to carefully shave every last trace of hair from his head.

And then came the second revelation: Flay was missing two fingers on his left hand and the index finger from his right, and yet he wielded the razor like a surgeon delicately slicing the heart out of a transplant patient.

'Are you all right, miss?'

The voice, deep and growling, came from far, far away. Mina shook herself out of her reverie to find Flay standing over her, sizing her up like a piece of meat. She jumped back in surprise.

'You . . .' he said, retreating a little. His eyes, she noticed, kept straying to the big clock on the wall behind the counter. It was as if he *had* to look at it. 'You . . . you . . . were somewhere else, I think.'

'Sorry, I spaced out for a moment there; it's been a peculiar day.'

'Spaced out. Spaced out.' Flay tried the unfamiliar words on for size. Agreed they were perhaps appropriate. 'Yes. Spaced. Out.'

'Sorry about that.' She held her hand to him. 'I'm Mina.'

'Mina?' replied Flay, puzzled. He reluctantly took her hand in his. The index finger was, indeed, missing. Mina found herself staring at it and had to concentrate to bring her attention back to the man it was attached to. Or not attached, as it were.

'It's short for Wilhelmina. Who knows what my parents were thinking about when they picked that.'

'It's a nice name. My mother was called Wilhelmina.'

Mina gaped at him. 'You're kidding.'

'Yes. I've never met another Wilhelmina. It's a horrible name. Anyone with that name deserves to be turned into meatballs. Mina-balls, two dollars a kilo. Yum.'

'*What?*' Mina was so taken aback she didn't realize for a moment that Flay was staring at her, bewildered.

'Are you feeling all right, miss? Perhaps you should sit down.'

'What did you say?'

'That you should sit down. You look tired.'

'No, before that.'

'I said you had a nice name and asked what I could

get you today; we have some lovely chicken in ginger and soy. Are you sure you're all right?'

'Yes, yes. I thought, I just . . . I think I might just get my brother to come in. He must be melting out there.' She nodded towards the window, where Jacob was huffing and puffing in the heat. As the sun struck the dusty street it seemed to flare up, creating a wavering, hazy glare against which Jacob was an insubstantial blur, a surreal charcoal drawing of a human being.

Flay just looked at her, unblinking. Was this worm expecting him to say something?

Jacob, when Mina had dragged him in, just stared, his mouth agape, mesmerized by his first sight of Flay.

He had no eyebrows!

And he was . . . just so . . . *huge*.

And so . . . *pink*.

And so *clean*.

And his *hands*.

'Just you two and your parents, is it?' Flay said.

'Yes,' said Mina, and then remembered. 'Well, and Bryan, our baby brother.'

'You have a *baby brother*? A *baby* brother?' Flay peered at her intently, interest flaring in eyes that, until now, had reminded Mina of the dead black eyes of a fish laid out on a slab of ice. 'A baby brother,' he drooled, a changed man. 'A baby brother – how wonderful for you. How old is he?'

'Er, six months.' Six long, horrible months.

'And is he on solids yet?'

'What?'

'Is he still breastfeeding? I think it's so important that babies are breastfed as long as possible; it strengthens the bond between infant and mother.'

Mina gaped at the man but found herself replying, 'Yes, he is. Why?'

'I just like babies.' Flay shrugged as if this were an affliction he couldn't cure. It was also horribly, obviously, scarily *untrue*. 'You must bring him round some time. Soon.'

'Yes, yes, we will,' promised Mina, knowing it was a promise she would never keep, even if they found Bryan.

'Now what can I do for you? Some nice mince? A steak?'

'I was wondering if you could tell us where we might find Thespa Grymm.'

'That old crone? No.' Flay felt anger well up inside. Thespa! Thespa again! Why didn't this filthy, bothersome insect just leave? He was at his wits' end – and beginning to think that perhaps he should just fillet her. Her and her stupid, staring, mute brother. They could be broken down, segmented, jointed, boiled and disposed of up at the mine before anyone missed them.

'Pity. I was hoping to track her down, like, today. There's a problem with—'

'I feel sick,' said Jacob.

Fear flared in Flay's face, and Jacob's feet hardly touched the floor as the butcher hustled the boy through to a bright parlour behind the shop. Here, he was deposited in front of a white sink in a small but immaculate kitchenette. Jacob closed his eyes and took a few deep breaths.

Trailing behind, Mina watched as Flay pulled on a pair of yellow washing-up gloves (the empty fingers flopping around comically), took a crystal-clean glass down from a shelf and filled it up with water.

'There.' Flay was unsmiling, willing Jacob to drink up and go. He didn't want them there, that was for sure. The little worms were interrupting his day. He looked over at the clock in the parlour; his whole schedule had been disrupted.

Mina saw his gaze flicker to the clock – identical to the one in the shop and, she guessed, on exactly the same time, to the second. 'I think we've both been over-doing it a bit. Can I have a glass too?'

Flay angrily filled another glass and thrust it at her. 'It happens. To newcomers; they don't realize how hot it is and how much water they lose doing . . . nothing. Have you finished?'

Mina gulped down the rest of the water. It might have started as a ruse but she could feel it seeping into her body, into all the dehydrated, sandy corners, washing away all the irritating, sharp-edged oddities that had lodged in her head. Refreshed, she handed the empty glass back. He would wash it until it sparkled, she knew. And then probably disinfect his hands.

She was right. Flay *was* in a tizz. He would have to clean the whole place that night; you can't have worms in your shop and expect them not to shed a hair or a flake of skin. Who knew what had dropped out of the boy's nose? He put down the glass, grabbed the carbolic soap, and began to scrub.

As he did so, Mina examined the room. There was a small table and a few chairs. A couple of prints of ye olde English countryside scenes – mostly featuring cattle but one featuring a pig of huge proportions – hung on plain walls.

Flay returned, one eye on the clock and the other seemingly rolling around in his head as he examined the room for evidence of anything Mina or Jacob had touched or dropped.

'So I was saying, my dad asked me to find Ms Grymm. You see, there's a problem with my baby brother's room up at the house,' lied Mina.

'A baby brother . . .' Flay drooled again. 'Lucky you.

You know, I might be able to find Thespa for you. I'll have to make a phone call first. Can you wait here?'

'Sure.' She was a bit taken aback at the unexpected eagerness and the joyously grim grin that lit Flay's face. He seemed to glow from within, as if all his Christmases had come at once and then he'd won the lottery. With surprising grace for such a big man, he swept out through a door she hadn't noticed before, wallpapered over and hidden in the far corner of the room. Mina was astonished. Perhaps finding Thespa Grymm wouldn't be so hard after all.

'That was genius, Jacob,' she whispered when Flay was gone. 'You were perfect.'

'But I *do* feel sick,' said Jacob. 'All this meat. After yesterday I can't stop thinking about maggots. I need some fresh air, Mina, or I *will* chunder.'

'OK. But wait for me outside, OK? Don't go anywhere!'

Seconds after Jacob had gone, Flay reappeared through the secret door, alerted by the shop bell.

'Jacob's gone,' explained Mina. 'I thought if he was going to be sick it would be better if he did it outside.'

Flay grunted assent and disappeared again. A moment later Mina heard something. A faint whimper – indistinct, almost inaudible, but there. A mewling sound, as if from a hungry baby or an animal in distress. Coming

156

from the secret door that Flay, in his haste, had failed to close properly.

Mina looked around the room. Was this some sort of test? Was Flay watching her? *Don't be stupid*, she told herself. *He's done nothing wrong. He's weird, sure, but no weirder than anyone else we've met in Grymm. And if he comes back as I get to the door, I can always say I got up to close it. That's believable enough.*

She walked nonchalantly across to the opening. At floor level a finger of frosty air crept through the gap like the tendrils of some alien plant life. It was the entrance to a large industrial fridge. But where was the noise coming from? Surely there was nothing alive in there. And, stranger still, where had Flay gone? The door swung open noiselessly. It was, indeed, a fridge – the cold made her breath linger in front of her face – but it was the biggest one Mina had ever seen; she'd been to school dances in rooms smaller than this.

There were slabs of meat hanging from hooks on both sides as she entered. Covered in a thin crust of frost were the rock-hard carcasses of a cow, a pig and a sheep. Legless, headless and emptied of their innards, they looked nothing like the animals they'd been in life. They certainly weren't as frightful as the big ginger kangaroo that hung alongside the other animals. Unlike them, it hadn't been gutted. Unlike them, its limbs hadn't been sawn off. Unlike them, it was a fresh kill, not yet frozen solid. It just dangled there like an old shirt on a hook – only this hook was curved and vicious and metal, and skewered the dead beast right through the head, the glittering point emerging where the right eye should have been.

Mina covered her mouth with a hand to keep the bile down and pushed past the bizarre tableau to the far end of the fridge, where yet another doorway beckoned. It was as if the fridge were no more than a frozen tunnel with blast-proof doors at either end. She pushed down hard on the long steel handle, levered the door open, and tumbled through the gap in a gasp of cold air and warm relief.

The space on the other side was cavernous. The freezer she'd just passed through wasn't a tunnel; it was a wardrobe. There'd be a lion and a witch along any minute.

How come they hadn't noticed this place from the street? It was twice as high as the shop, a warehouse-sized space with a wide walkway all the way round the four walls, rickety metal stairs, and opaque skylights high above that muted what little sunlight got through them to a dirty grey wash. Somewhere above, metal rattled against metal.

On the right-hand side was a makeshift office – a Portakabin affair, from which the glare of a desk lamp emerged, along with Cleaver Flay's voice, murmuring quietly on the telephone.

But the most astonishing aspect of it wasn't its size.

And it wasn't that there were things moving around in what sounded like cages upstairs.

It wasn't even the dozens of chains, saws, knives, pots, pans, trays, cleavers and cauldrons that hung from the walls in clinical rows, descending in size.

It was that the whole place, and nearly everything in it, was painted a deep ruby red. Even the floor. It looked like an anteroom to hell. But a lot neater.

And the smell. It was like a cross between a kitchen, a farmyard and a hospital.

The mewling noises she had heard earlier were louder now, still muffled but audible above the bubbling sounds coming from the stout iron stove to Mina's left. There, big black pots and pans hubbled and bubbled while something in the ovens hissed and spat. She recalled her father's attempts at cooking and how everything he put on the stove overflowed at some point. There wasn't a pot or a pan or a frying pan in *their* kitchen that didn't carry the scars of their experience with George. On Flay's stove, by contrast, it was as if the utensils knew better than to boil over.

Just past that, the flayed skin of a cow was stretched tightly on some sort of frame and a heavy metal fan was blowing air at it. Behind that, just glimpsed, was what looked like another skin, this one hanging lopsidedly on a hanger and still heavy with blood, fat and muscle fibre. Before she turned away Mina could have sworn it still had a face. A vaguely *human* face.

She really didn't want to know what sort of animal *that* was.

It was time to leave – but there it was again, the pathetic cry of a wounded animal. Before she knew it, she was halfway up the stairs and standing on an L-shaped platform that swayed precariously on struts descending from the ceiling. It didn't feel safe at all but Mina felt compelled to keep going. Something up there needed help.

And then she saw them: cage after cage after cage of livestock. There were so many caged animals that there was only enough room on the edge of the platform for one person to walk.

There were chickens galore, pigs, piglets, rabbits and ducks. And all were labelled and organized according to age, gender and type. It was very Flay, thought Mina just as something else occurred to her: a menagerie such as this should have been chaos, full of clucking and quacking. Instead, apart from the odd cry, there was almost complete silence, as if they were terrified.

Then, at the very far end of the platform, she saw it.

Struggling to stand in a cage not much larger than itself was a small deer, a Bambi. It tottered towards the cage door on its thin, wobbly legs and stuck its nose against the chicken wire. Ordinarily, Mina would have gone into ooh-aah mode just about then, but what she saw in the depths of the cage forestalled that: like Maggot's dog, the fawn was missing its back legs.

'What are you doing?' Flay's voice boomed in her ear and she turned to find him right next to her.

Jacob was sitting in the shade outside the butcher's, forcing down the urge to be sick, watching droplets of sweat splash from his nose onto the boardwalk and day-dreaming about going to the beach with his surfboard, when a voice brought him back to reality.

'Makes you want to, er, head for the beach, does it not?' Jacob looked up to find the retired priest-cum-writer – Eglund? Ellmand? – standing above him, still wearing heavy corduroy trousers and a shirt buttoned up to the neck, as if he couldn't bear to not be wearing even a *version* of his priest's dog collar. There were sweat patches under his arms and his forehead shone wetly in the relentless sunlight. And yet he still had his shirt-sleeves done up at the wrist. What a weirdo.

'You read my mind.'

'On your own? What have you done with, um, Mina?' Elland – that was it.

Jacob sighed and cocked his head towards the shop door. 'In there, talking to the butcher. She won't be long. We're trying to find Thespa Grymm.'

'What for?'

The man seemed friendly enough but Jacob certainly wasn't about to trust him. Not completely. Not here. Not in Grymm. That said, he was a *priest*. Or used to be. And they were trustworthy, weren't they? But there was something about him that didn't ring true. Or rang a bit too true. Why would anyone want to write a book about *this place*? He rubbed his eyes with the heels of his hands and changed the subject. 'Oh, our parents just want to check something out with the lease, I think. I didn't take much notice. Hey, why is there a funfair here? We saw it on the way in. It's a strange place to have one.'

Elland laughed a stuttering, grim laugh. 'Hmmm, yes, indeed. As odd as things get here; *that* is, ah, up there with the oddest. Do you want to, um, take a look? It's not far, and I'll tell you what I, er, know. For what it's worth.'

Jacob was torn, but also, as the man rightly surmised, bored out of his skull. And he was a man of God, right? Jacob was slowly persuading himself, he knew.

'It's fascinating,' Elland assured him in a kind, quiet tone that positively dripped with — Jacob smiled at the ridiculousness of it, but that was what it reminded him of — it suddenly dripped with honey. It was relaxing and comforting, and Jacob felt any hesitation or reservations melt away. 'It's not far — we'll be able to see your, ah, sister when she comes out.'

Jacob glanced sideways at the man as he stood up. Was there something familiar about him around the eyes? A softening? An ageing? More laughter lines? And that voice . . . it was so . . . so— *Oh!* Jacob blushed deeply and, to cover his embarrassment, nodded, grabbed his bag and stepped out into the punishing sun.

'Sure. Let's go.'

Elland had to trot to keep up as Jacob, furious with himself, strode towards the funfair. His *mother*! He was thinking about his *mother*! The eyes! The voice! What a mummy's boy! He'd be crying and sucking his thumb next. Maybe Bryan hadn't just disappeared; maybe Jacob had absorbed him overnight like a paper towel. What a freak! He'd be pooing his pants and finger-painting with it before the day was out. He laughed as the image brought back memories of the day Bryan had done just that. Jacob hadn't seen anyone look quite so pleased with themselves. Well, no one covered in shit, anyway.

'Nice to see someone in, er, Grymm, um, laughing.'

Elland smiled. 'What's so funny?'

'I was remembering something my brother did.'

'Brother? I didn't know you had a brother.'

'Nobody does. He's just a baby. Bryan.'

'Lovely. You're very lucky.'

'Yeah,' said Jacob earnestly, and with not a little wonder. 'Yes, yes, we are.'

A tattered, greying sign drooping low between two poles announced that they had reached the entrance to THE MOST MAGNIFICENT PAN-DEMONIUM FUNFAIR. The word 'Pan-Demonium' was the biggest and the loudest, shouting its name in letters made up of snakes, clowns, harlequins, dragons and other monsters of myth, legend and fable. It would once have been a dazzling display, Jacob decided, simultaneously exciting and forbidding.

'So what happened?' he asked, positioning himself so he could always see the butcher's shop.

'Well, they arrived just before the new road was opened,' said Elland, his odd, stuttering speech pattern suddenly silenced as he told his story, 'when Grymm was going through a sort of pre-bypass boom, what with the usual travellers, the mine and the people working on the road itself. I think they were on their way to join a larger carnival for a summer season on the coast.' He gestured around him as they passed under the banner. 'It wasn't exactly the biggest fair in the world.'

Indeed it wasn't. It was jammed on vacant land between two buildings, very narrow but long. Beyond the row of clown heads Jacob had seen yesterday were a fortune-teller's tent, a wheel of fortune with the little rolled-up pieces of paper still stuck in its holes, a darts stall, a hook-a-duck stall, hoopla rings and, on the far right-hand side of the clearing, a firing range with the guns missing. Everything was covered in dust and bleached to drabness by long exposure to the sun.

'Looks like they left in a hurry,' said Jacob.

'Yes indeed. Here one minute, gone the next. They just cleared out overnight.' Elland ducked into the sagging darkness of the fortune-teller's tent – YOUR FUTURE REVEALED BY THE AMAZING MADAME MICAIAH – and came out holding the jagged remnants of a crystal ball. 'Left it *all* behind. Someone said Thespa Grymm tried to make inquiries about them but—'

'Thespa Grymm? She's probably *behind* it,' blurted Jacob, and immediately regretted it.

Elland just gave him a friendly look and another hint of a smile. 'Oh, Thespa's not so bad when you, um, get to know her,' he said. 'Thinks she knows everything about *her* town, but she doesn't, oh no, no, not by a long chalk. Still, nothing's quite what it seems here in Grymm, is it?'

Jacob strolled over to the faded clowns, their shocked

expressions for ever stilled, and traced his finger in the thick dirt that covered them. He had thought them sad yesterday, but they were even sadder today because they reminded him of the little clowns on Bryan's cot mobile. How he had hated those things and their music. And how he had hated that the giggling Bryan seemed to find them endlessly fascinating. Now, less than twenty-four hours later, all he wanted was to hear them again. He'd even wind the damn thing up just to see the look on Bryan's face.

'There must have been at least twenty people running this place,' said Elland. 'Look out the back here.'

Jacob followed him as he pushed through a rotting tarpaulin. Behind it stood four abandoned caravans and a wrecked trailer. Like the rusting hulk they had seen next to the candle factory, they seemed to be falling in on themselves, collapsing back into the earth.

'God,' breathed Jacob.

'Oh, I think *God* had very little to do with it,' whispered Elland sadly. 'I think G-God was, er, absent without leave that day.'

Back at the front, Jacob imagined what it must have been like when it was up and running. There would have been shouts ('Roll-up! Roll-up!') and the piercing crack of guns as amateur sharpshooters tried to win fluffy toys for their girlfriends; the man at the darts stall laughing ('Come on, young man, you can do better than *that*! Have another go! You never know your luck!').

And after the last ball had rolled down the gullet of the last clown, after the last plastic duck had been hooked ('Number six! Bad luck, son!'), after they had fed the goldfish and closed down for the night, they would have heard a sound like a million spiders scuttling in the same direction.

Jacob realized he could see them, as if he were a ghost observing something appalling that happened long after he'd died. The town was giving him a history lesson; these . . . *these* were the things on which Grymm is built.

And, like a ghost, he couldn't warn, only witness, as jet-black shadows like the ones they had dreamed about the previous night came sweeping into the camp and the fair like a tide, overwhelming, silencing, dragging. The funfair people didn't stand a chance. Jacob felt a chill wash over him as he realized that one of the shadows, standing further off, seemed to be directing the operation. It was darker than the rest, a presence so jet-black that it seemed not to be there at all. It was an absence, a hole in the fabric of the universe that burned with mischief and malice. It was laughing at the bedlam around it, directing its minions with a glance, a wave, a whisper.

'*Yessss, boss. Gone in a second, boss. Hushhhhh now. Yuk-yuk-yuk.*'

And then the funfair folk were gone, dragged off into the night, the cherry-red eyes of the shadow turned towards him! It pointed a long, taloned finger at *him*; a finger on which gleamed a yellow ring as bright as the sun but somehow still dirty, like molten gold mixed with crumbs of crushed coal.

'*Welcome,*' it said in a voice that rumbled up from the bowels of the planet.

'Jacob?'

'Wha – what?'

'Are you OK?' asked Elland. 'What happened?'

Jacob tried to work his jaw and throat but produced nothing. Those eyes! So venomous. So *cruel*. And they *welcomed* him.

'I think I know what happened to the funfair people,' he said at last. 'And I don't think it was Thespa Grymm. Unless she's . . .' What if Thespa Grymm *was* the black being? What if *that* was what they were up against?

'Unless she's what?' asked Elland, his ever-present notepad at the ready, as if to take down information for his book. His eyes goggled eagerly behind the thick lenses of his glasses.

'I've got to talk to Mina,' said Jacob, heading back towards Flay's shop. 'Let's go.'

* * *

Mina jumped backwards, grabbing onto the metal railings as the suspended walkway swayed alarmingly under her surprise and Flay's bulk. For some reason he didn't seem angry with her so she decided to do something drastic: tell the truth

'I, er, I heard some noises so I thought . . . And then I . . . Look, I was just being nosy, Mr Flay. I'm sorry.'

'Not to worry at all.' He paused and waved dismissively. 'So what do you think of my little place? Nice, isn't it? I see you've met Flora.'

'Flora?'

'Flora the fawn; she's one of my favourites.'

'Where are her legs?'

'They went up to the mine: *special order.*'

'They what? You chopped her legs off?'

Flay sighed. 'It might seem cruel, but look at it this way: she's still alive. Anywhere else she'd be a carcass hanging in a cold room by now.' He shrugged and the whole hanging platform shook a little. 'When they put that bypass in, this town could have died. Instead, we turned to the mine, learned to adapt, to . . . *specialize.* And Flora gets to live a little longer.' Then he frowned and looked around, searching for something else to show her. 'There's a one-legged chicken about here somewhere too.'

Mina was too astonished to speak. Instead she pushed past the butcher and hurried to the stairs. 'I've g-g-got to go,' she said when she found her voice. 'Jacob will be wondering where I am.'

'Wait a bit longer, why don't you? I'm waiting for a phone call that might tell us where Thespa is. Come on. I'll give you the tour.'

And with that, he laid his huge, three-fingered hand on her arm and pulled her firmly down the stairs and over to a row of industrial fridges along the wall on the far right. Mina tried to keep a smile on her face as he proudly showed her his collection of tongues in brine, brains soaking in salted water, stacks of pigs' trotters and calves' feet, and jars and jars of eyeballs, lungs and testicles.

Soon they were back at the ovens, where Flay took a large wooden spoon down from a rack and began stirring what looked like a large pot of bleached white bedsheets.

'Tripe!' he exclaimed. His mutilated hand tightened on Mina's shoulder. 'Food of the gods, my little Wormina. Do you know what tripe is?'

'No.' If it's possible to imbue one two-letter, single-syllable word with disgust, implying that whatever he tells her will go in one ear and straight out the other, Mina managed it.

He told her anyway. 'Tripe is the lining of the four stomachs – the rumen, the omasum, the reticulum and the obomasum – of cud-chewing animals. The tripe from the omasum, by the way, is also known as Bible tripe. It's sold parboiled and bleached, which is what I'm doing here. Want some? It's a little slippery but you get used to it.'

'No. Thank you.'

'Ah-ha! There's the phone. This could be just what we've been waiting for.'

Flay had become a positive chatterbox in his happiness, and he hummed a happy tune as he pulled Mina into the office. It too was spotless. There were tall, grey metal filing cabinets at the far end, a desk against the wall with a chair. The old-fashioned black telephone – the clunky round-dial type you only see in black-and-white movies – sat neatly on the desk next to a lined ledger, a fountain pen and an inkwell. Flay hadn't quite entered the twenty-first century. Hell, he hadn't got far into the twentieth yet.

'Flay,' he growled into the big black receiver.

Mina had the distinct feeling that this phone call wasn't about Thespa at all.

'. . . Does it matter?' he said. 'Brian, I think. Yes, I'll find out.' He shook Mina roughly. 'What's your brother's name again, Wormina?'

'B–B–Bryan. With a Y.'

'Bryan,' said Flay into the bulky handset. He paused. 'Well, like veal, I would suspect. The best veal comes from calves fed on milk until they're slaughtered so . . .'

In a flash Mina understood. Or thought she did. Was Flay trying to fill a very special order from the mine? Was that why he was so interested in whether Bryan was still being breast fed?

Veal?

Brisket of Bryan?

Her gasp of surprise made Flay look up. His rubbery face squinted at her and she knew that he knew that she knew that . . .

'Yes, sir,' he was saying. 'Of course, sir.'

Mina looked around, panicked. Would she end up swinging next to the kangaroo in the freezer? And would Jacob and Bryan – if he even still existed – be next?

Slowly she leaned towards the desk and, with desperate fingertips, tipped the inkwell over so that the deep blue liquid ran across the desk and down Flay's pristine trouser leg. With a strangled cry, he dropped the phone, let go of her, and stared at his leg as if it were on fire.

'Worm!' he roared.

But the worm had turned. And was out the door.

And running across the red floor to the stove, where she grabbed the wooden handle of one of the pots and dragged it off the edge. The pot exploded against the floor behind her, sending out a cloud of steam and a scalding shower of water that shot three metres into the air. Hot tripe slithered this way and that as if alive. At the door to the freezer she turned and saw Flay come hurtling out of the office. His face, already in agonies over the mess she had made of his trousers, contorted in rage and indecision.

'*Noooooooo!*'

She threw open the freezer door, ducked through, and slammed it shut. Would Flay pursue her or feel the need to clean up the mess?

In the kitchen on the other side she pulled out the knife drawer and threw that to the floor too. That done, she raced through to the front of the shop and burst out into the street. The heat hit her like a sledgehammer.

'Jacob! Quick, let's . . .' The words died on her lips. Jacob wasn't there. Again. Couldn't he sit still for more than a minute? 'Jacob? *Jacob!!!!!!*'

7

Elland had been correct: you could still see the butcher's shop from where they stood. And there was Mina running along the street, shouting for him. Her jet-black bird's-nest of hair was even more astray than ever and her eyes were bugging out. He should never have left her.

'C'mon,' he said to Elland. 'She looks like she needs help. Keep away from the door of the baker's though. Mina! Mina!'

They caught up with her in the middle of the street – three insignificant figures under a cobalt sky, their ankles hidden by the cloud of red dust thrown up by their running. Jacob knew he was in trouble and could feel a headache coming on. The weight of the sun on their heads didn't help.

'Where did you get to?' shouted Mina. She slapped

him several times on the arms and then grabbed him in a bear hug. 'Oh, Jacob, you won't believe what happened.'

'What? What happened?'

'It's a long story.'

'Do tell,' said Elland. He took a pen from his shirt pocket. 'I love a g-good story!'

Mina looked up, startled to find him there, so focused was she on Jacob. She glanced over her shoulder. 'I think not. I think I've upset the butcher. Well, his tripe, anyway.'

Jacob followed her gaze and gasped.

Cleaver Flay was not a happy man. His normally full, rubbery lips were pursed tighter than a duck's bottom, and above his almond-shaped eyes his brow was knitted together just as tautly. He was wearing his usual cleaner-than-clean white shirt, white (now ink-stained) trousers, blue-and-white striped butcher's apron and straw boater, but in addition he had strapped around his midriff a wide belt with long pouches for his knives.

Only the handles and the first few centimetres of the shining steel blades were visible above the worn leather, but it was enough for them to realize that he had enough razor-sharp equipment on him to dismember a small cow.

Oddly, he also wore the bright yellow washing-up

gloves that Mina had seen him use earlier. On anyone else they would have looked ridiculous with the empty fingers waving around uselessly, but on Flay they only added to his menace. Along with the fact that just above them, his hairless forearms, revealed by the rolled-up shirtsleeves, were like the muscled thighs of a horse. Putting his vast, beefy bulk into motion, he began striding towards them.

And he growled, 'Maggotsssss.'

Mina, though, had no intention of getting any closer to Cleaver Flay than was absolutely necessary. They dashed along the other side of the street, pushed past half a dozen young mine protesters, who scattered in their wake, and were a couple of metres away from their bikes when the door to the real-estate office opened and Thespa Grymm stepped out.

'In here. In here,' she hissed. Mina and Jacob hesitated, but their momentum and a shove from Elland forced them into her office. With a bang that rattled the glass in the window, Grymm pulled the door closed just as Cleaver Flay appeared.

'Wormsss,' he snarled through the glass.

Turning the key in the lock, she blew him a kiss and then addressed the children.

'Hello, my dears,' she chortled in her gravelly voice. 'Don't worry about *him* – we're old friends.

You're safe enough. I hear you've been looking for me.'

She was wearing the same shabby black ensemble as the day before, one stockinged toe still sticking out of the hole in her slippers, one hand grasping a cigarette that shed ash all over her clothes. She smiled and sucked on it with gusto. 'Why don't you two come right inside and have a cup of tea? You've had a busy couple of days, and a cup of tea and a biscuit will keep your strength up. God knows, you're going to need it.'

She studied each of them and then turned her attention to Elland, who was standing rigidly and sweatily next to them. He looked like a mannequin dressed for winter in the middle of summer.

'Mr Elland. How *nice* to see *you* again. It's been far too long,' said Grymm in a voice that meant quite the opposite.

'Thespa,' muttered Elland in much the same manner. 'Long time no, er, see.'

'Don't let me keep you.' She grimaced as she went back to the front of the office, peeked out for Cleaver Flay and, finding nothing there, opened the door. It was an invitation that the former priest couldn't turn down, even though the children could see he was aching to stay and take copious notes on whatever was happening.

At the door he turned and addressed them while waving his notepad in the air. 'It was, er, nice to see you,

177

Mina and Jacob. Do let me know how you get on.'

'He means that quite literally,' said Grymm as the door closed behind him. 'Him and his stupid *book*. *Really!* Who does he think will want to read it? If it's anything like his sermons used to be, people will expire through boredom before the end of chapter one. Humph! OK. Now. Who's for a coffee? Jacob? Mina? Tea? No? Suit yourselves.' She moved to one side and pointed the way into her rear office. 'Shall we? We have a lot to talk about.'

'Yeah,' snapped Jacob. 'Like what you've done with Bryan.' Although he sounded and looked angry, Mina knew him well enough to notice the tiny hitch in his voice that betrayed his utter terror. And she didn't blame him; her hands were shaking and a cold shiver ran up the back of them and flowed up her arms and across her scalp.

'I'm not sure what you're talking about, young man,' said Thespa Grymm. She turned to Mina. 'Is he always like this? No manners?'

'For once, *Ms* Grymm, I'm with Jacob.' Mina was confused by the woman's attitude but determined not to let her sense her fear. She pointed an accusing finger at her, hoping Jacob wouldn't notice how it shook. 'Where the f— I mean, where the hell is Bryan?'

'Your language, *Wilhelmina*, is atrocious. What would

your father think? Mary, I'm sure, would be scandalized. Let's go inside and discuss this like civilized people. And please – call me Thespa.'

'*Civilized people?*' Mina was so aghast at this that her shock completely overcame her fear. '*Civilized people?*'

'You know, you remind me of a parrot I once had,' said Thespa. 'Lovely thing but of particularly limited vocabulary. *Pieces of eight, pieces of eight* – drove me mad in the end. Had to, er, let it go. I think it reached the end of the street before the hawks got it.'

'You don't say. *If* we come with you, will you tell us where Bryan is?'

'You look exhausted. Why not just come in, have a drink, and we can talk about things in any manner you see fit – *civilized* or otherwise?'

With a glance at each other the children made a mutual, unspoken, decision that discretion was probably the better part of valour: they would look around for something, anything, that could be used against Thespa once they'd found out the truth about Bryan.

'OK,' said Mina, leading the way deeper into the building. 'We agree.'

'But no coffee,' continued Jacob as he followed her. 'Got any Coke?'

'Coke?' Now it was Thespa's turn to be aghast.

'Aren't you excited enough already? What is *wrong* with this generation?'

Her office was not what they expected. There was carpet on the floor – unusual in that climate – floral wallpaper, a desk, armchairs, sofa, a sprawl of glossy magazines on a low coffee table, and framed black-and-white prints of the town of Grymm in its heyday. A ceiling fan spun lazily above them. The room smelled of paper and cleaning fluids – and stale cigarette smoke that no amount of cleaning would ever remove. It was also only a little less steamy than the street outside. No wonder a small cloud of sweat-stink followed Thespa as she stomped around behind the desk and flopped into a chair which groaned in protest at her bulk.

'Help yourself to a drink from the fridge, Jacob, there's a lad.' She served herself from a coffee percolator that puffed and popped away, breathing soothing rich fumes into the air, and propped her elbows on the desk. She cupped her mug in her hands and sniffed at its contents.

'Ahh, that's better.' She slurped a noisy mouthful and put the mug down with a bang that slopped coffee onto the table. 'Anyone want a cigarette? Mina? No? Ha-ha-ha-ha-ha-ha-ha-ha! Look at your face! Go on – I won't tell.'

Mina was in no mood for games. 'What's happening? What are you doing to us? Where's Bryan?'

'That's a lot of questions, to which the answers are: (a) all sorts of things; (b) nothing; and (c) who? But I understand your frustration – Grymm can be a little trying at the best of times.'

'I don't believe you.'

'Nothing I can do about that, I'm afraid. You do or you don't. And if you don't now, you will eventually. Grymm gets to everyone in the end. Let's start with this Bryan: who is he?'

'Don't play games with us. He's our brother – half-brother – he's six months old and he's gone, disappeared as if he never existed – and *you* did it! When we got here the other day you said you wanted to *eat* him.'

'Me?' Thespa's confusion seemed genuine. She pulled out a cigarette, lit it with a disposable lighter and sucked on it like a vacuum cleaner. Her first breath hung in the air between them like a small grey-blue cloud until she waved it away. 'I don't have him. It – whatever "it" might be – has certainly nothing to do with *me*. What makes you think it has anything to do with me?'

'You said you wanted to eat him!' repeated Jacob, not liking that the words sounded – and tasted – odd in his mouth. What was he accusing this woman of? 'When we got here. You said he was so lovely you could eat him! And then you did! Or someone did. Because you're a witch!'

Thespa settled back into her chair and looked them over. She frowned at Jacob and then locked eyes with Mina. After a moment's silence she seemed to come to a decision. 'Listen. Both of you. I can assure you – I *promise* you – that I don't have your brother and that I have no idea where he might be. I don't remember him being there when you came into town.'

'But—'

'No buts, Mina. You must listen to me now. I *believe* you. I believe everything you've told me. And, why? Well, you've no doubt realized by now that Grymm isn't your everyday sort of town, right?'

'With knobs on.'

'Thank you, Jacob. Your contribution to this conversation is priceless.'

There was another awkward silence until Mina broke it. 'So who *are* you? You're not the real-estate agent, that's for sure.'

'Actually I am. Things are a little slow at the moment but I'm sure it will pick up.'

'Out here?'

'I'm an optimist. Grymm *was* a thriving community. A *good* community. A *caring* community. Mostly. Until the bypass. And the goings-on at the *mine*.' She spat out the word 'mine' like it was poisoned.

'That's it!' Mina sat forward and squinted at her. 'It's

the mine, isn't it? Everyone talks about the mine, the mine, the mine, as if it's the only thing keeping the town going. Flay got on the phone to the mine as soon as he heard I had – have – a little brother. He called that Coathanger person.'

'He did, did he?' said Thespa. 'And it's not Coathanger, it's Anhanga. *Mr Anhanga.*'

'That's him. What's happening up there?'

'I wish I could tell you. He's digging something out of the ground. Whatever it is, it's torn the town apart. The people you've met here were all good, decent people – more or less – until Anhanga started at the mine. Whatever we had here has been corrupted. Some have succumbed more than others, as you've seen.' At that she nodded with inexplicable tenderness and sadness in the direction of the front door. 'That's not the Cleaver Flay I knew. Cleaver was . . . Well, let's not go into that.'

'*Nothing is what it seems,*' Mina mused. 'It's what you said to us as soon as we arrived. But Flay . . . he's done, doing, stuff that . . .' Images of mutilated dogs and deer came to mind, not to mention the tripe. She couldn't go on. 'Well, it's just not right.'

'No, it's not. But I can't be around all the time to keep him . . . *straight.*'

'Straight?'

'On the straight and narrow. He just needs the right person to be whispering in his ear . . .'

'You mean you can *control* him?' Only Jacob — a veteran of many a video game, including a favourite one in which the 'hero' could possess people with his farts — could make such a concept sound so normal.

Thespa smiled, and an ectoplasmic cloud of cigarette smoke tumbled out through her ruined teeth. Jacob was sure her hairy wart gave a little shudder too.

'No, not really. Well, yes, perhaps. I appeal, I think, to his better nature. And he does have one, you know. Such a nice man, was Cleaver Flay. Now, now, Mina, harrumphing like that will get you nowhere. The Flay you met isn't the real Flay; the real Flay is somewhere deep inside, struggling to get out.'

'You could have fooled me,' said Jacob.

'Well, that's not a hard ask, is it?' Thespa grinned, and then became deadly serious again. 'Look, I like you. God knows why because you are hateful, ungrateful, selfish little monsters. But you do need to *shut up and listen*! I'll try to keep it simple so that even Jacob can understand.'

'I'm not—' began Jacob, but was silenced by a look from Thespa Grymm that would have melted rock.

'There's a war going on, age-old and never-ending, between good and evil. And one of the battles is being played out right here in Grymm. But there are rules.

At least on our side.' She studied both children hard, looking from one to the other as if weighing up whether to reveal something of great importance. Finally, and with a little nod of her head, she went on, 'Have you ever heard the word *timshel*?'

Uncomprehending silence was her only answer.

'It's from the Hebrew and it's perhaps the most important word in the world. Certainly it explains Grymm.'

'What does it mean?' asked Mina, with a sideways glance at Jacob. Could they believe anything of what they were hearing? Jacob shrugged.

'It's from a translation of the Bible and it means "thou mayest". Or, possibly, "thou must". Scholars have argued over the exact translation for years.'

'And?'

'And it's why I don't try too hard to influence Cleaver or any of the other poor souls struggling with their inner demons in Grymm. Ultimately it's their choice. *Timshel* – it's what makes gods of us all. For if thou "mayest" do evil then, conversely, thou "mayest not" do evil. It's – for want of a better word – *God's* ultimate gift to us: *choice*. Do you see? If nothing is pre-ordained, then we have no one to blame – no gods or similar, um, entities – other than ourselves. And that's important. For us as individuals. For us as a society.

As a world. When we choose *not* to do evil then we have won.'

'Wow,' whispered Jacob. 'Deep.'

Thespa laughed. 'Deep indeed, Jacob.'

'So Fleur and Flay and . . . whoever,' said Mina, 'they're all choosing . . .' She hunted around for the right metaphor before Jacob found it for her.

'The dark side?' suggested Jacob.

'In a manner of speaking, yes.'

'And Bryan's disappearance?'

'I'm not sure about that. I can't say anything like that has happened before now.'

'That's rubbish. *This* is rubbish,' said Mina.

'It's not, I'm afraid.' Thespa shrugged. 'It's how it's always been. And probably always will be. I sometimes think that God created Grymm as a test of our resolve to do good when doing evil is so much easier and so much more . . . rewarding. It's a battle I think we might be losing.'

'Why do you say that?'

'Look, we Grymms have been here for many, many years, and although our influence has always been somewhat . . . greater than our numbers, shall we say, we can only try to point people in the right direction. The original Grymm family came from Pendle Hill, in the north of England. The story goes that great old

Mother Grymm was lucky to escape being burned at the stake.'

'See?' said Mina to Jacob. 'I told you she was a *witch*.'

'Oh, that's so old-fashioned a word. Conjures up all sorts of bats and cats and broomsticks and things. Nonsense, really. Let's just say my connection to Grymm is more than skin deep. There's certainly always been a Grymm in, um, Grymm. At least, after the white man got here and— Well, that's a story for another time. What you need to know is that things have taken a turn for the worse – as you said, Mina – because of the mine, and Mr Anhanga. He has subverted everything that made Grymm special.'

'Which was what exactly?' Mina sat back in the chair and crossed her arms. It was body language that said, *I don't trust you.*

Thespa looked like a woman who had decided that the truth was the best option. She took a deep, tired breath. 'Let's say you were a butcher and all you wanted was to be among the best butchers in the world. It's an innocent enough ambition. Then imagine that someone came along and just nudged you along a little. Sometimes it's a wife or a husband, a girlfriend or a boyfriend, a parent, or a close friend who provides the support to allow someone like that to follow their dreams. That's what Grymm does, but on a whole new, distorted level.'

'Like the baker!' cried Jacob. 'He wanted to put me in a pie, I'm sure he did.'

'You may pull a face, Mina, but it's quite possible. Mr Fleur has been promised much, I believe, and will do almost anything to get it.'

'By this Coathanger?'

'Yes. *Anhanga* appeals to the dark side of human nature, and somehow manages to steer these ordinary ambitions down a more shadowy path. Anhanga will whisper in our fledgling baker's ear that wanting to be *among* the best in the world is really just wanting to be second best. Why not' – and here her voice dropped a level, became quieter but more insistent, more persuasive – 'just be *the best*? Why not? Why not? Who would not want that? And, look! Here are the tools, here are the *books*, the old, banned books with their secret recipes. With these you can become *the best*.'

Jacob, who had been sitting there enthralled, his mouth open, swallowed hard. Mina too found herself under Thespa's storytelling spell.

'And the cost? Nothing! Well, nothing much. A favour here and there. But nothing that won't, in the long run, bring the person a little more glory, a little more profit. Just, say, fill an order for an unusual cut of meat.'

'The deer,' said Mina.

'The dog,' said Jacob.

Thespa curled a lip in disgust at Anhanga's tactics, held out her hand, palm up, and then slowly closed it. 'And before you know it, he *has* you.' The hand became a fist. 'And you are never the same again. I've tried to protect them all as best I can but . . . Anhanga's pull is getting stronger every day. I put more effort into Cleaver because . . . because . . . Well, let's just say I've got a soft spot for him.'

Mina remembered the man-mountain who had chased them up the street. *Soft* spot? For *that*?

'You really *are* a witch,' Jacob interrupted, excited by the prospect.

Thespa ignored him.

'I think you're lying.'

'Mina! I really, really don't have your little brother! I wish I did so I could give him back, but I don't.'

'Well, at least not telling us the whole truth. What do you know about this Anhanga? It's an odd name.'

'Isn't it just? It's also the name the Amazonian Indians give to the devil. Or *a* devil. A *baby-stealing* devil, actually.'

'You don't think . . . ?' Mina left the question unasked. It was too ridiculous for words. Or was it? Was it any stranger than anything else that had happened since they arrived in town?

'I think perhaps, yes,' said Thespa. 'I think Anhanga isn't human. Or at least not fully. I think he's a prankster who enjoys tormenting humans. He's like Loki, the Norse god of mischief. He is also said to fill people's minds with visions of the supernatural.'

At this, unnoticed by everyone else, Jacob looked down into his lap, startled by the reference to his experience at the funfair; To his . . . hallucination? Dream? Illusion? Delusion? There was something else there, he knew. Something sad. Something to do with the cool touch of the ring he had 'liberated' from the souvenir shop. Somehow Grymm had shown him what had happened to the carnival people, but there was something else, something underneath, something even worse beneath what he had already seen.

'It certainly fits in with what's happened to Cleaver and the rest,' explained Thespa.

'But why here?' asked Mina innocently. 'In the middle of nowhere? What does he want?'

'That, I haven't quite fathomed. Anhanga arrived a few years ago, when the work on the by-pass began. It was as if he got here just as we were "cut off" from the outside world. Nobody took any notice at first. And, of course, nobody much saw him unless they went up to the mine. And if they did *that*, they came back changed. *If they came back at all.* Take Margaret from the milk bar, for instance. She went missing in the first six months and hasn't been seen since. The city police came, but—'

'But we saw her!' shouted Jacob. 'Yesterday morning! She put maggots in my milkshake!'

'No, you saw her husband, Barton.'

'What?'

'That wasn't Margaret, that was Barton, her husband. He's gone a bit . . . funny . . . since Maggot disappeared. Guilt, I suppose. He wasn't much of a husband to her when she was here. They said he used to hurt her, that sort of stuff. Anyway, after she disappeared he gradually *became* her. He's convinced himself now that it's *him* that vanished.'

'Well, at least that explains the teeth and the wig.'

'And the leg.'

'The leg?'

'Maggot lost her leg in a motorbike accident in her teens. When Barton "became" her he *really* became her.'

'Oh my God! He cut off his own leg?'

'Of course not—' began Thespa.

'Flay did it,' offered Mina. It had come to her mind in a flash. She had no idea why but it just seemed to fit.

'Is she serious?' said Jacob.

'I'm afraid so.'

Mina paled and looked as if she were going to throw up.

'Anhanga has this . . . genius, I suppose you would call it for want of a better word, to make even the most bizarre request seem perfectly reasonable. He's very . . . *persuasive*.' Thespa slurped her coffee and shrugged. 'Grymm is an extraordinary place to live.'

'You're telling us.'

'You've felt it, haven't you, Jacob? Grymm has always had that something *extra*. The original inhabitants worshipped this place as part of their myths, the birth-place of the serpent god. It *is* a special place and it attracted the most unusual, special people; creative, interesting people who were pulled here by the legends, the land, the feeling that here was a place where great things could happen, away from the big cities and the great churning masses always wanting more, more, more.

'But somehow Anhanga has perverted that power. When Grymm looks past our masks – and we all have them, children, don't you worry about that – it used to see and accentuate the positive. When Anhanga looks past them, he sees the negative. He sees corruption, arrogance, conceit, ego. And he massages it and massages it and whispers in your ear until . . . until . . . anything can happen. Suddenly the most grotesque suggestions are feasible.'

'That's what happened to Fleur and Flay?'

'Yes. But so, so slowly that it was almost impossible to see it happening. The important thing is that Anhanga arrived and people began either changing or leaving or disappearing completely. Don't worry too much, though: I think Grymm *likes* you – both of you.'

'*Don't worry?* We're still missing Bryan, don't forget that. Has Anhanga got him? Is that it?'

'No. I don't think so. It's not his style. Too proactive. I've never heard of anyone being wiped out as if they didn't exist. That's unusual, even for here.'

'So what do we do?' Mina felt suddenly powerless and pathetic in the face of . . . *what*?

'Nothing for now. Go home. I'll see what I can find out and get in touch with you. Don't worry. We'll find him.'

'Nothing?' Mina was aghast. 'Nothing? That's all you can come up with?'

'I'm sorry, Mina – until I know more there's nothing *to* be done. Just be careful.'

Flay was gone when they emerged from Thespa's office. A few cars trundled slowly along the road, throwing up small red dust clouds. The drivers peered fearfully through dusty windows, looking out at the desiccated town like survivors of an atomic bomb who still can't quite get their heads around the devastation. The sky high above was still a deep royal blue, but the rippling heat haze, the dust and the sun–dried wood of the build-ings made it feel as if the town were enveloped in a red–brown bubble.

Mina squinted against the brightness and realized that what she was looking at could have been a sepia-tinged photograph of Grymm a hundred years ago. It looked like a Wild West town. She wiped sweat off her brow and puffed out her cheeks. She could feel her arms burning in the heat.

'And we thought we'd be bored here,' she breathed after a while.

'No such luck.' Jacob slung his bag across his back, making it rattle.

'What *have* you got in that thing?' asked Mina, for once with a little smile. 'And before you answer, I *saw* you take that stapler from Thespa's desk.'

'Stuff,' growled Jacob. 'Just stuff. OK?'

'Big baby. You'll get into trouble sooner or later, you little thief.'

Jacob just looked at her sullenly.

'Oh well, what do I care? Let's go home, eh? Maybe Bryan will have turned up and this will all have been a dream.'

It wasn't to be, though. Back home they found a dishevelled George sitting on the back porch drinking beer – one of many, judging by the empty cans around him – and muttering over dozens of rock samples and complicated reports and graphs. He was also in no mood to be disturbed.

'Go away. Busy,' he snapped. 'Unless you know what *this* is?'

The rock he held up meant nothing to them so they backed away slowly, as if retreating from a madman.

Mary wanted little to do with them either. Part of it was her annoyance at the morning's events, but she was also busy setting up her easel and a canvas, and cleaning brushes in the 'spare' bedroom. She was in no mood for Mina to point out that this invasion meant that she and Jacob had to keep sharing.

'Oh, do stop moaning, Mina. You'll live. You know, I brought all this stuff and forgot the paint. Maybe you can get some for me from the hardware store to-morrow? I can feel the muse coming on. I think this is going to be a great place to paint.' And she stood back to admire the placing of her equipment. 'Isn't the light wonderful? Now, I'm just going to have a little scribble with these pencils I found. You two can get your own dinner tonight, right?'

With George working and muttering out the back, Mina and Jacob were forced to defrost pizzas for dinner. *Again*. It was yet another reminder that their life in Grymm was going to be substantially different from anything that had gone before. Previously George and Mary were adamant that dinner was eaten at the table – no TV, no internet, no computer game was allowed to come between them and the evening meal that took place together as a family. It was sacrosanct, and sacrilege to think otherwise. But suddenly it had all been abandoned; their lives were being torn up and re-ordered – and not for the better.

Now, as they sat at the kitchen table morosely stuffing piping-hot pizza into their mouths, Mina wondered out loud where Bryan could have disappeared to.

'I was so sure it was Thespa but, I dunno, she seemed so . . . *adamant*.'

'What worries me,' said Jacob through a mouthful of pepperoni, 'is whether *we'll* be here tomorrow.'

8

It was a long night of interrupted sleep as both of them tossed and turned, expecting something and nothing, and waking now and then to make sure the other still existed – peering into the darkness to make sure that the shape opposite was a real person and not just a pile of pillows that treacherously resembled them. As dawn broke and the day's relentlessly bright light began to creep around the curtains, they emerged from their beds hot, tired and drenched in a sweat that wasn't caused only by the heat.

'I'm exhausted,' muttered Jacob into his pillow. 'That was a nightmare.'

'We're in *Grymm*,' snuffled Mina, feeling her spirits drop. 'Even when we *don't* have nightmares it's a nightmare.'

'Still no Bryan, then?' said Jacob after groggily lifting

his head up and listening to the house. 'It's too quiet for Bryan.'

'Who would have thought we'd ever find ourselves missing *him*?' Mina laughed at the absurdity of it. How could you hate something – *someone* – so much and yet . . .

'Do you think Thespa might have found him?'

'I don't think so. She seemed as shocked as us when we told her. Whatever happened, it's beyond her. She might still be able to help, though.'

'I hope so. It's all a bit scary. Especially when Mum and George are . . . I dunno, being all weird.'

'I think they're just doing what they would be doing if Bryan didn't exist,' said Mina, sitting up and shaking some shape back into her jet-black 'bedhead'. 'Dad's throwing himself into his work and your mum's getting back into her painting. It's probably a good thing.'

'For *them*.'

'Yes, for them. Makes you realize, doesn't it?'

'What?'

'What people give up. For us. For their children.'

'I s'pose.'

In the kitchen there was evidence that George had been and gone – the slaughtered remains of eggs, bacon and burned toast sat on the kitchen table next to a half-drunk cup of tea – but it was evidence of a lone breakfast. Of Mary there was no sign.

'Oh no!' shouted Jacob, his voice rising in a panicked crescendo. He looked around the kitchen, took a few halting paces here and there, not knowing what to do. Tears welled up in his eyes. 'She's *gone*! Mina, she's gone! Like Bryan! What are we going to do? Mina?'

Mina, who felt the panic rising in her chest like floodwater through a pipe, tried to keep calm. It wouldn't do for both of them to lose it – but what if it was just the three of them now? If Mary was gone, did that mean another of them would vanish tomorrow, and the day after, and . . . and what then? An empty house cracking up under the cruel heat of the desert? Is that what had happened to the previous inhabitants?

'Jacob? Mina?' The voice came from upstairs. 'Have you got a minute?'

'Mum?' Suddenly Jacob was a whirlwind, racing past Mina, throwing open the kitchen door and racing up the stairs two at a time. When Mina caught him he was standing in the doorway to the spare room, mouth agape.

Inside, Mary was standing to one side of her easel, grinning from ear to ear. Around her, on the floor, were various pots and jars filled with different-coloured liquids. Various paintbrushes stuck up from a few of them, or lolled precariously across the tops.

'So,' said Mary, 'what do you think? I've been up half the night.'

'It's . . . amazing,' stammered Jacob as he moved into the room and allowed Mina access. He was, she saw, gazing in astonishment at the picture that Mary had somehow painted without paint. It was a desert land-scape, she thought, but rendered entirely in browns and yellows and beiges. A few sketchy outlines here and there seemed to indicate that Mary had gained access to a pencil or charcoal, but the rest of it was made of . . . what?

'Coffee, tea and a few strands of saffron that I found in the cupboard,' she explained, as if reading Mina's mind. 'It's amazing what you can make do with when you have to. Basic rules, really: use what's at hand.'

'It's the desert,' whispered Jacob when his eyes had adjusted to the swirls and splashes. It was a striking representation of a desert clearing, even if it was made of last week's groceries, but there was something else. He felt as if he *knew* the place.

'Yes!' Mary clapped her hands in excitement. 'I just *had* to do it; it was like something was *forcing* me, forcing it out of me.'

'The rocks in the background . . .' said Mina. 'Are they – well, they look like something: a lizard, or a snake?'

'Do they?' Mary stared at her work for moment. 'I didn't really notice when I was working on it. It just came to me in a flash and I just *had* to paint it. Odd, really. I was awake most of the night but I don't feel in the least bit tired. Oh, I haven't been this excited since I don't know when. This is going to be a great place to work, I can feel it – there's just so much . . . energy here. I love Grymm.'

Love, however, wasn't the first thing on Jacob's mind. Anxiety? Something stronger? Fear perhaps. All he really knew was that there was something about his mother's painting, something familiar, as if he'd been there before. And it scared him.

'So, let's all go down and have breakfast! I take it we have to clear up George's mess? I thought so.' Mary smiled as she put an arm around their shoulders and led them to the door. 'And then you can go into town for me and pick up some paint from the hardware store; it's time to get serious.'

'I don't like it,' said Jacob as they approached the hardware store a couple of hours later. Thespa Grymm wasn't in her office so they hurried on past, keeping a wary eye on the butcher's and the baker's. 'It's – I don't know – I mean, a painting made of tea? Couldn't she wait?'

'And this from the boy who can't wait for the next *Batman* movie without getting his knickers in a twist?' said Mina, and ruffled Jacob's hair.

He, in turn, shoved her hand away and growled at her. 'Will you stop that? I'm not some pet monkey for you to pat. It really drives me . . .'

But Mina was on the move. Monkey? *Monkey!* She hurried up the street and then simply stood in the shadows opposite the hardware store. Bluehammer Hardware, Jacob noticed, also sold alcohol. Is that what she was interested in? There, in the window display, next to the saws, the hammers, the nails, the paints, the long-armed pink monkey and the lengths of wire, were cartons of beer and advertisements for whisky. Just another example of the people of Grymm trying *any-thing* to keep their heads above water.

Mina looked over at the gas station. Looked back again. Then she just lifted a hand and pointed across the street at the hardware store. *The monkey?* Jacob frowned. She was pointing at the monkey?

Mina continued to stare, and the monkey continued to stare stupidly back at her, its long arms and legs spread wide and suckered to the glass. The last time she'd seen it, it had been stuck to the inside of the 4WD that had stopped for gas.

'Mina?'

She stood her ground, though Jacob was certain he noticed her shoulders sag a little.

'Mina! Stop messing about. It's creepy enough here without you going all . . .'

She said something that he couldn't quite catch.

'What?' He came closer, still searching the street for signs of hostile life. 'What's wrong?'

'We've got a problem,' said Mina, still pointing at the monkey.

'Yes, it's very cute. You can buy it later. Come on.'

'Remember the jeep that was filling up when I found you at the baker's?'

'Sort of. So?'

'The monkey was in its window.'

Jacob's heart sank. What was she playing at? And then he realized: she was going to turn a simple job of buying paint into . . . what? He grabbed her arm and looked her straight in the eye.

'No! Let's just get the paint and go!'

She shrugged him off and started walking across to the store. 'I need to . . . I need to help . . . It's important . . . There's been too much selfishness in this town already. I can't just walk away.'

Jacob looked around wildly, suddenly seeing danger everywhere. All the cars had vanished and it was as quiet as the grave. Just as suddenly, Mina was across the street and almost at the shop door. There was no point in arguing with her, he knew that.

Inside, past the stiff-bristled brooms, mops and aluminium stepladders clustered around the door, were three long aisles packed with plugs, sponges, scrubbing brushes, curled lengths of wire, light bulbs, battery chargers, screwdrivers, and screws and nails of every width and length.

On a bright yellow chipboard wall just past the counter an exhibition of hammers, saws, mallets and wickedly sharp-looking chisels was lovingly arranged in order of size. And at the beginning of each aisle a bright plastic garbage bin was filled to overflowing with bargain basement items such as mosquito-repellent, lubricant and snakelike coils of hosepipe.

The third aisle, on the other hand, was nothing more than an enormous wall of beer. Carton after carton after carton of shrink-wrapped beer bottles stacked one on top of another until they almost reached the ceiling. And every one of them stamped WDM in bold red letters.

'At least Dad will like working there,' said Mina.

'That,' whispered Jacob in awe, 'is a *lot* of beer. Even George couldn't drink that much.'

'Very funny.'

'Look, just get the paint and let's get out of here.'

'OK, see if you can find anyone down those other aisles. I'm going to see if I can reach the monkey. I don't want the owner accusing me of stealing.'

'Sure.' Jacob, usually so sensitive about being ordered around but now just happy for Mina to have her own way with the stupid monkey, moved quietly across the front of the shop, glancing down each of the alleyways between the displays.

Meanwhile, Mina slipped behind the counter, reached into the front window and, with a series of soft plops as the suckers released their grip, pulled the stolen toy off the window.

'Anyone here?' she cried, cradling the monkey like a baby.

Jacob trotted back to the counter. They looked like salesperson and customer.

'Here, put that away quickly,' she said, handing the monkey over. Jacob snatched it with a glare and tried to stuff it into the maw of his bag. In his haste, however, he didn't open the bag wide enough and the monkey refused to disappear.

'Get. In. There. You. You. Monkey! Let's go, Mina. Mum will have to come back on her own.'

Mina seemed not to hear him. She was remembering the discussion with Thespa Grymm the previous day. It had left her head filled with a painful, jumbled whirl of bright colours, rampaging emotions and hellish images; she had felt like a car careening down a ravine, out of control. Now, suddenly, after a day's fermentation, it was like a missing cog had clicked back into place and the brakes were working again. She gazed lovingly at the big-eyed monkey as it seemed to fight back at the edge of Jacob's bag, and then at Jacob again. *Spot the difference* – she laughed to herself. Instead she smiled at him; it was a tired smile, resigned but also calm.

'Don't you think we should check out the back?'

'Yes. And no. It'll go all munted when we get back there – you know that, don't you? And this Bluehammer bloke will be as mad as a hatter.'

'Yeah, I know that. But what else can we do? We can't just leave him, whoever he is.'

Jacob knew what Mina meant: they couldn't just walk away and leave the jeep's owner to whatever fate Grymm had in store for him. Could they? How would they look themselves in the mirror if they walked away? He stood beside his stepsister and sighed loudly. He too remembered yesterday's discussions.

In that instant, one word sat in the silence between them, unspoken but as loud as a shout:

Timshel.

'I suppose you're right. But this time I'm going prepared.' And with that Jacob took off his bag, turned to the wall and pulled down the biggest hammer. 'And I'm out of there at the first hint of a cream bun.'

'Or a sausage,' laughed Mina as they moved off into the centre aisle, nails and nail guns on one side, beer on the other, flickering neon lights above them, armed with a steel hammer and a grinning pink monkey in a bag.

The avenue seemed to go on for ever, like some kind of optical illusion, or one of those dreams where the very thing you're trying to reach just keeps getting further away.

The far wall was made of the same kind of piss-yellow chipboard as they'd found at the front, but this one was festooned with small oil paintings and articles cut from the arts pages of every newspaper imaginable. The scarred workbench below it was covered with small sculptures in bronze, wood, paper, glass and ceramic. They were, in Mina's humble opinion, crap.

'Frustrated artist or what?' she murmured, just as a door cut in the chipboard to their left exploded outwards, slamming into the wall, and a tall, ginger-haired woman wearing an ankle-length skirt and an off-the-shoulder peasant-style blouse came bursting through with a shout. The skirt and blouse were decorated with intricate embroidery, covered in red-and-gold dragons breathing fire and attacking little villages of stick-like people. Her hair was pinned up behind her head with a silver, dragon-shaped clasp. The Dragon Lady of Grymm had appeared.

'Shoplifters!' she screamed. 'Help, police!'

Jacob, who was bending over the bench examining the artwork, jumped in surprise and accidentally pulled the head off a blown-glass clown.

'What are you two doing sneaking around my shop? Shoplifting, no doubt. Well, I've got you both on video so don't deny it. It's the slammer for you two reprobates, and then . . . then . . . the death penalty, I would imagine. Or life imprisonment at the very least, with perhaps a flogging thrown in. Twenty lashes for every dollar. I shall insist on that at the very least when the authorities get here, or my name's not Beersheba Bluehammer. And don't even think of trying to escape: there are laser beams at every entrance and exit. You would be cut down before you got two metres. Or the bloodhounds would hunt you down in some smelly drain somewhere during a thunderstorm. There's no escape, I can assure you of that . . . Why, the last felons to even *attempt* it . . .'

Mina and Jacob looked at each other and shrugged in confusion as this tirade – accompanied by a fluttering of hands in front of her face – went on and on and on.

Mina took the initiative. 'Ms Bluehammer?'

'. . . are still languishing in a dungeon somewhere trying to come to terms with the enormity of their crime — and all they stole was a tube of superglue and a six-inch nail . . .'

'*Ms Bluehammer!*'

'. . . see where *their* sticky, evil fingers got *them,* and believe you me, the same fate will befall anyone who steals—'

'*MS BLUEHAMMER! WE'RE NOT HERE TO STEAL THESE. WE WANT TO BUY THEM!*'

'Eh?'

'We want to buy them, not steal them. We're not thieves.' Mina had no idea where this idea came from — she had absolutely no intention of buying anything. It seemed to work, though, and the screaming banshee calmed down.

'Are you entirely sure, darling? You look a little shifty to me, and in my experience—'

'You scared us, that's all.' Mina was beginning to understand that the only way to get a word in edgeways with this woman was to just interrupt the babbling flow. She also remembered what Thespa Grymm had said about the people who were attracted to the town. This woman was obviously stark staring mad.

'Is *he* always this quiet?' The woman nodded at Jacob. 'I find quiet people quite unnerving. I can never tell what they're thinking. If I think something I say it. You always know where you stand . . .'

Jacob, in return, tried not to alert her to the fate of the decapitated knick-knack by looking at it. It was the world's ugliest, crassest clown, but you could never tell what anyone's reaction was going to be in Grymm. She was probably married to it or something.

'No, he's just a bit in awe of the . . . er . . . art.'

Impossibly, Jacob's eyes bugged out even further as Mina drew the madwoman's attention to the sculptures. He was sure the headless clown stood out like, well, a headless clown.

'Do you like them? Tell the truth now because—'

'Yes,' lied Mina. 'Are they yours?'

'Yes, but it's all my early work. I've gone on to bigger and better things now. In fact I was just working on something large out the back when—'

'Can we see it?'

'Well, I'm not so sure about that, you see, because it's not quite finished, and you might . . . But on the other hand . . .'

This time Mina decided not to interrupt while the woman argued with herself. Beersheba Bluehammer was tall and statuesque. Her pale freckled shoulders could have belonged to an Olympic swimmer. Or a bricklayer. Her feet – enormous big things poking out from her skirt – were bare apart from matching nail polish and several silver rings. These were echoed by the biggest hands they had ever seen on a woman. Big but also surprisingly delicate. The nails were painted red and the fingers were ringed with silver. Only her earrings, great hooped things that would have fitted around Jacob's neck, weren't silver. They shone like lopsided golden haloes in the shadowy depths of the shop.

Her head, though, was a different matter entirely. If ever a head was made to be working in a hardware store it was that one. The expression 'hatchet-faced' was long ago coined to describe someone with sharp features, but Bluehammer had a face that even *that* phrase didn't do justice to. Underneath a bright orange shock of frizzy hair that reminded Mina of the things her father used to scrub saucepans was a face that wasn't just *like* an axe, it *was* an axe. A freckled axe. You could have used it to chop wood.

And she had a nose that Jacob could imagine fixed to the prow of an ice-breaker as it ploughed through the frozen seas of the Antarctic. From the side it looked colossal, and yet from head-on its lack of flesh and anything resembling normal nostrils meant it almost disappeared from view. Both children found themselves wondering how she managed to draw in enough air through the tiny slits underneath that sharply angled shelf.

'. . . and yet I feel that if one doesn't try to expand the minds of young people, how will they ever be able to appreciate art? It's all very well saying, *I know what I like*, but what *does* one like if one doesn't understand . . .'

And then there were her cheekbones, great razor-sharp edges like the top cornerstones of a skyscraper over which her white, flaky flesh stretched almost to breaking point. And between *them*? Eyes like a hawk's, small, constantly flicking this way and that. Everything about her was reminiscent of the tools she sold in her shop: sharp-edged, hard, unyielding. It was as if someone had stretched human skin over a machine.

'. . . so I'd be honoured if you'd come and have a look at my little exhibition. One of these days I'm planning to move to a bigger location, somewhere I can really let my imagination run riot, do things on a scale as yet unimagined. Of course, it's a case of getting the raw materials, but *Mr Anhanga* up at the mine – he's *such* a sweetie, you know, and *very* much the collector – well, Mr Anhanga says if he's pleased with my latest piece I can put on a show in one of the bigger tunnels. Wouldn't *that* be something? Of course I—'

'Can we go out back now?' Mina eased past the wittering woman and stepped into her studio. 'I see what you mean about "bigger".'

The room was about the size of a basketball court

and filled with the paraphernalia of Bluehammer's art. Red paint had been splashed about the place in great crimson gobs while knee-high trestles nestled in corners with truncated lumps of wood held in the death grip of their vices. Saws, knives, chisels and choppers were strewn about the floor or left embedded in the nearest surface.

On the walls hung unframed canvasses that, as far as Jacob could make out, had been abandoned halfway through. Though he knew enough about art to realize that he could be wrong about that. On one wall was a representation of a window so perfect that he would have bet a week's pocket money it was real had it not depicted a countryside featuring a unicorn.

And among all this, great icebergs poking up above the disorder, were half a dozen or so exhibits covered in dustsheets. In the middle of it all stood one enormous fixture that almost reached the ceiling. If this *were* an iceberg it would have been the one that sank the *Titanic*.

'My babies . . .' breathed Bluehammer in their ears. 'Come see my babies.' She grabbed them by the arms and pulled them gently but insistently towards the first shapeless white bulk. 'I call this one "Cat's Cradle",' she crooned as she whipped the cover up and off with a flourish.

What she uncovered was a plinth, on which rested a

confusing concoction of coloured wire, pulleys, cogs, wheels and springs in the shape of a large cube that enclosed – and seemed to be attached to – a small ginger kitten. Mina gasped before she realized the animal wasn't real. Unlike Bluehammer's other attempts at sculpture, this one *was* a masterpiece. Every hair, every piece of fur seemed to quiver with life. It was only the softly sparkling but unblinking eyes that gave the game away.

'And it's interactive too,' boasted Bluehammer as she touched a red switch on the front of the piece. Suddenly, shockingly, the whole contraption flew apart, fracturing into half a dozen or so different sections that shot outwards from the main structure on ropes, large springs and pulleys. One moment it was a cube and the next it was a massive piece almost twice the size. Imagine watching a video of a clock being blown up and then freeze-framing the moment just after the explosion: it was just like that. And the pieces included the various limbs of the kitten figure, whose head, legs and body were now bouncing lazily on springs at different corners of the exhibit.

'Like it?' asked Bluehammer, flicking the switch again and smiling as the 'Cat's Cradle' clockworks began to whirr and clank and gradually bring the exploded kitten back together.

Mina found her voice with difficulty. 'It . . . it's . . . *amazing*.'

'*Bloody hell*,' murmured Jacob.

'It is something, isn't it, darlings? I'm very proud of it, although of course since I made it I've refined the technique. I think it illustrates the capricious nature of the universe and how—'

'Can we see some more?' Mina was anxious to keep exploring. She walked over to a larger white-covered object, this one just a little taller than Mina herself. 'What's this one?'

'Ah, now, that's one of my favourites.' Bluehammer looked disapprovingly back at Jacob, who was still watching the kitten put itself together. 'Do be careful with that, won't you, darling?'

'Yes, Ms Bluehammer.'

'Now, where was I? Oh yes, this next one was a great refinement of the "Cat's Cradle" technique. Help me pull this sheet off.'

Together they grabbed great handfuls of the heavy material and hauled it off to reveal a pretty tableau of a young girl about Mina's age standing underneath a dark, medieval castle-style gateway. She was made of china and she wore a weather-worn blue dress and a grubby white apron. Luxurious brown hair tumbled about her shoulders but her head was hanging down in such a manner that Mina knew immediately that she'd been, and perhaps still was, crying. Around her feet were half a dozen geese, frozen in time, looking every bit as life-like as the kitten.

'I call this one "Falada".' Bluehammer spoke with reverence, awe even, at the brilliance of her own creation.

And then Mina saw why the goose girl was crying. Nailed in the darkness underneath the gateway was the crudely decapitated head of a horse. Blood dripped from the ragged gash across its neck, down the wall onto the floor, where two of the geese waddled through it. But while she knew that the blood was fake, Mina wasn't too sure about the head. She began to circle the exhibit and, as she did so, a guttural voice issued, over and over, from the archway.

'Alas, young queen, how ill you fare!
If this your mother knew,
Her heart would break in two.'

At the other side of the sculpture, Mina's breath escaped her. Not in some great rush of air; it just disappeared and, for a while, she forgot to take in any more. For the horse's head and the geese had all been sliced in half down the middle. From this side she could see their brains and internal organs as if looking through glass.

'It's a technique called plastination. All the greats are using it these days.'

'What have you done?'

'Nothing much. It just arrests decay by sealing everything in a kind of plastic polymer. Fascinating, isn't it?'

'Are the horse and the geese . . .'

'Real? Oh yes, darling.'

'And "Falada" is . . .?'

'The horse. It's from a fairy tale that ends with the criminal being asked what should the punishment for such and such a crime be, not knowing that she's being asked to pronounce her own punishment. In fact that's the subject of another work-in-progress.'

'What is?' Mina wasn't the least bit interested but she wanted to keep Bluehammer's attention focused on her and not Jacob who, from what she could see, was attempting to cut the wires on 'Cat's Cradle'. Her stepbrother had hidden depths, it seemed.

'The punishment. You see, she decreed that the miscreant should be stripped naked, put in a barrel studded with pointed nails and harnessed to two white horses which would drag her around the streets until she was dead.'

'Charming.'

'Gruesome, isn't it? I thought I might—'

Her explanation was interrupted by a loud twanging as Jacob flicked the switch on 'Cat's Cradle' again and the whole thing blew up and flew into the four corners of the room with a sound like a grandfather clock falling over.

'Oops!' said Jacob with a sheepish look in their direction.

'You stupid boy!' roared Bluehammer as she flew back to see what damage he had wrought. In the confusion, Mina took the opportunity to slip away and start peeking under the rest of the dustsheets. They were not for the squeamish: Beersheba Bluehammer obviously liked using spare body parts in her work. They were animals, mostly, but also a few hands and arms that Mina couldn't be sure, in the semi-shadow, weren't real.

On the far side of the room the Dragon Lady and Jacob were scrabbling on the floor for the bits that had bounced away. Mina could hear Jacob trying his best to be as unhelpful as possible.

'Here's a piece – er, no, that's a lump of dried glue. At least, I hope it is.'

'Can't you just *stop* helping me?'

'But I feel bad. Hey, look, there's the kitten's bum!'

Finally Mina reached what she thought was the main exhibit. It stood three times as high as anything else, towering over her the way a cage towers over a trapped bird. She walked softly around the outside of the huge dome of a dustsheet, which was in fact several dustsheets sewn together, and wondered how to get it off.

Then she found a bell-pull; the sort of thing rich people used to have in their houses to summon the servants. She pulled it, and the coverings were released from the top like a trick in an expensive magic show.

Behold!

It *was* a huge birdcage! But one that bore – thanks to the huge cogs and cables and springs – more than a passing resemblance to 'Cat's Cradle'. Instead of a kitten it had a mannequin spread-eagled in its centre.

Mina goggled at this apparition for a second or two before its full, horrific purpose dawned on her and the monkey slipped from her hands. The dummy was dressed in cut-off blue jeans and a white T-shirt and was attached at the head, hands, arms, feet and knees to the machine. If this followed the same pattern as 'Cat's Cradle' . . . the result was too ghastly to contemplate.

'I see you've already made the acquaintance of my newest composition. Do you like it?' Bluehammer had come up behind her with Jacob and was now smiling over Mina's shoulder. 'Disarming, isn't it? I call it "Find the Lady". Have you gathered the principle yet? I see from your eyes that you have. It's too big to show you how it works in here, of course – it'd take the roof off – but once we've transported it to the mine for my exhibition . . . ah, then you'll see something . . . extra-ordinary. A one-off piece of performance art. I imagine if Mr Anhanga likes it – and he's a *great* patron of the arts, is Mr Anhanga – there'll be a few more shows . . . perhaps with the help of your good selves? Life, you see, is art; and art is life.'

'You're not going to put a real person in that thing, are you?' asked Mina.

'My dear girl! What do you think of me?' said Bluehammer in a voice that, to Mina, said one thing but somehow meant the exact opposite. 'Although it is an interesting idea, my dear, yes indeed. After all, death is very much a part of it, of life. Do you do much art yourself?'

'No, not really. But I know what I like,' said Mina, thinking, *And this isn't it.* 'Jacob's not bad at drawing, though. Eh, Jacob?'

But Jacob, who had been standing behind Bluehammer with a handful of parts from 'Cat's Cradle', wasn't listening. He had seen another of Bluehammer's pieces and slipped off to have a look at it. For standing in a far corner was a life-size replica of the clown that he had broken earlier, but made of bright blue plastic. It even had a long, thick, white wick poking out of its head.

'Cool,' he cooed. 'Hey, Mina, check it out. The face is really lifelike.' Then he did a double-take. 'Wow! *Really* lifelike.'

'*DON'T TOUCH THAT!*' screamed Bluehammer, almost flying across the room. '*DON'T TOUCH THAT WITH YOUR GRUBBY BOY FINGERS!*'

For the first time in their encounter Mina could finally empathize with Bluehammer: like most boys, Jacob was incapable of staying clean. He could scrub his face and hands to glowing pink perfection, but two seconds later he would have dirt under his fingernails and there would be a grubby mark on something he had touched.

Jacob jumped as if someone had stuck a needle into him, and pulled his hand away from the dazzlingly shiny surface before any damage could be done. Mina had never seen anyone so innocent look so guilty. She wondered if it was because he still had the little clown's head in his pocket.

'*AND DON'T STAND ON THE BASE, DON'T STAND ON THE BASE!*' Bluehammer roared while waving her hands around like demented butterflies. '*YOU'LL RUIN THE EFFECT! MY MY MY! HAVE YOU COME HERE TO DESTROY MY LIFE'S WORK, YOU MONSTROUS BOY?*'

When she had finished fluttering and fussing and

pulling Jacob away from her work, Mina could see why she was upset – the base of the 'statue' was a thick pool of the same blue plastic; or was it vinyl? Either way, it flowed down from the legs of the main statue into a make-believe puddle that doubled as the base holding it upright. The effect was of a large blue clown slowly melting into a puddle at what was left of his own feet. Unfortunately, the puddle now sported impressions of the underneath of Jacob's sneakers.

'Oops,' he muttered. 'Sorry about that. I thought it was, you know, like, hard plastic. How was I to know it was . . . er . . . what is it?'

'IT'S WAX, YOU STUPID BOY! WAX! DID THEY PUT YOU UP TO THIS? THE OTHERS? THAT . . . THAT FLAY? FLEUR? I COULD . . . I COULD . . . OHHHHH!'

Each word was spoken like the blow of an axe, her words echoing her face, which looked as hard as steel, eyes blazing, jaw clenched. Her breath came in short gasps through gritted teeth. So this, thought Mina, is what they mean by being speechless with rage. She and Jacob could only watch in silent and embarrassed horror as Bluehammer glared at the footprints, her hands opening and closing – first fists, then claws, fists then claws . . .

Gradually, though, the eruption subsided. Bluehammer

was still rigidly immobile but, like an athlete warming up for action, she slowly worked the kinks out of her neck and enormous shoulders with a series of bone-cracking stretches and exercises. As she did so, Mina examined the piece in more detail: Jacob was right – while the rest of the figure was a sketchy outline of a clown, the head was extraordinarily lifelike. So much so that she felt she recognized the face. And what a face! Behind the bulbous nose – blue instead of the traditional red – and underneath the big floppy hat, the features were a study in fear and agony. This was one clown who certainly never saw the funny side of things, that was for sure, thought Mina.

'It's creepy,' whispered Jacob in Mina's ear. 'It looks real but it's not, 'cos I touched it before she came over – it's hollow. The head, that is. A bit like yours. Ha-ha-ha . . .'

'*THAT'S IT!*' shouted Bluehammer, erupting again and stomping over to push them physically towards the door. '*OUT! OUT! OUT YOU GET! BOTH OF YOU!*'

'But Ms Bluehammer, we—'

'And *that*,' growled Bluehammer, snatching the pink monkey out of Mina's grasp, 'is mine!'

'Is it?' asked Mina as she allowed the woman to usher them to the door. 'I saw one just like it yesterday in the window of a four-wheel-drive that came into town. I thought it was theirs.'

'Well, you thought wrong, you *LITTLE THIEVES!* That was a present from Mr and Mrs Puzzlewick. And I saw no vehicle yesterday! *NONE!* Now, if you will, please leave my premises before I call the police *AND HAVE YOU LOCKED UP FOR TRESPASSING!'*

'But you invited us—'

'It's no good, Jacob, she won't listen,' interrupted Mina when they got to the door and were unceremoniously pushed through it into the main store.

'GO ON! GET OUT OF HERE! AND DON'T STEAL ANYTHING ON YOUR WAY OUT! I'LL BE WATCHING YOU! DON'T THINK I WON'T!'

Mina put her arm around Jacob in an unusual show of solidarity and began to tug him towards the exit at the far end. 'C'mon, Jacob, let's go. Thanks for showing us around, Ms Bluehammer. I'm sorry about the clown.'

'I SHOULD THINK SO TOO... and another thing...'

Beersheba Bluehammer's voice faded away as they got to the store entrance and back onto the main street.

'She's as mad as the rest,' muttered Jacob as the heat washed over them in shimmering waves you could almost see. At the far end of the street the figures of a few protesters from the mine milled around, their clothes faded by exposure, their shapes distorted by the heat haze. He squinted at them and then turned back to Mina. 'Still, at least she didn't try to eat us. That's a first. Pity we didn't find anything out, though. Or get Mum's paint!'

'Oh, but we did,' said Mina with a strange look in her eyes. Jacob couldn't make it out: was it fear or determination? Or a bit of both? 'You see, when I said I was sorry about the clown, I really meant it.'

'Eh?'

'The clown, Jacob. That lifelike face? I recognized it! It was the man who came into town in the jeep yesterday. I'm sure of it. Somehow Beersheba Bluehammer has used his face as the model for her statue.' Even with the hot anvil of the sun beating down on their shoulders they both shivered a little. Jacob's teeth gave an involuntary chatter.

'God,' he whispered. 'What did they do to him?'

9

'She did *what?*' asked Thespa Grymm when the children turned up at her door again and explained what they'd found at the hardware store. They followed her into the back office, where she told them to sit down. 'Are you sure?'

Mina sat upright in the armchair opposite Thespa and leaned forward. Even though the three of them were alone in the room, she whispered conspiratorially.

'It's odd, I know, but I remember everything so clearly because of the funny little man at the gas station. I thought there was something wrong with my eyes at first because he seemed all kind of fuzzy at the edges.'

'That'd be John Smith,' explained Thespa. 'He was boring enough *before* Anhanga got here but he's been fading out ever since. We call him Smudge.'

'That's it! That's it! He was just a sort of blur.'

'You should hear him *talk*.' Thespa yawned and rolled her eyes. The cigarette in her mouth had gone out and was stuck to her bottom lip. It jiggled up and down as she spoke. 'Go on – what happened next?'

'Well, nothing really. I was trying to find Jacob, who had wandered off *again*. The thing is, because this Smudge was so much of a, er, smudge, everything around him seemed super-real. Like, *really* focused. I'd recognize the driver of the jeep again anywhere.'

'Hmmmm.' Thespa shook her head. 'You know, I had higher hopes of Beersheba, but the changes have been taking place so, so slowly that it's almost impossible to see them happening. She was a great artist; eccentric, yes – but that's why people like her were attracted to Grymm in the first place. It fed their creative sides, their *egos*. It made them feel open and free and gave them the belief – no, not *gave* them – it *nurtured* their belief that they could accomplish anything. Now I'm starting to think I was wrong and the place is nothing but a big Venus fly trap.'

'So what do we do?' asked Mina, ignoring the look that Jacob gave her. *Do? . . . We?* said the look. *Do? We're going to 'do' more? Are you mad?*

'We can't just forget about him. Who knows what she's done to him?'

'Well, I think you'll find that whatever she's done to

him she doesn't have him now. You were given the guided tour, my dears. She wouldn't have done that with a captive in the place. No, no, no, I think he's been moved on.'

'Where to?' said Mina and Jacob simultaneously.

'Well, isn't it obvious?' Thespa squinted as she leaned back, struck a match and re-lit her cigarette, now hanging out of the side of her mouth. 'Think about it. Think about the wax, about the monkey. I would bet cash money he's at the Puzzlewicks' candle emporium – owned and operated by Frederick and Catherine Puzzlewick. I haven't seen them for quite some time. Whether that means they've come under Anhanga's influence or they've just been busy I don't know, so it would be best to be careful when we go up there.'

'Go up there?' Jacob's shock and horror at the day's events were beginning to wear off. 'Why would *we* go up there? What can *we* do?'

'Something. Anything. Can we leave him to his fate? Will you let Anhanga and the dark side of this town win? And, of course, look at me – I can't do it on my own.' She looked knowingly at Mina, guessing that the older of the two children would understand. She did.

'Timshel?' said Mina with a resigned shrug.

'Timshel,' agreed Thespa, and blew a cloud of blue-grey smoke in their direction.

Ten minutes later they were making their way along the street in the afternoon sun, hoping to rescue a man they had never met.

'This is a dream, right?' Jacob asked of no one and everyone. 'This can't be real. Any minute now I'll wake up and I'll have nodded off in the car, won't I? *Won't I?*'

'You wish,' said Mina. '*I* wish.'

'And my wish now, said Thespa with a lick of her lips, 'is for something to eat. Jacob? You look like you could do with something. Keep your strength up, eh? Ham sandwich? Mina?'

The sun was much lower in the sky when they finally left, and the shadows that accompanied them along the street were longer, thinner echoes of the three of them.

'It's getting colder,' whispered Jacob with a shiver. 'When did your dad say he was coming to pick us up?

'Five o'clock. With any luck we'll be able to get in, grab this man and get out of the factory without any fuss. Got anything in that little bag of yours that might help us right now?'

'A stapler?'

Mina barked out a laugh. 'You really are something, Jacob.'

'Thanks.'

They were silent as they passed the Most Magnificent

Pan-Demonium site, for it seemed to be emanating waves of fear and sadness and gloom and panic. It was as if whatever happened there had leached into the soil like an oil spill, contaminating it for ever.

'So what's the plan, Thespa?' asked Mina.

'Plan? I don't have one. I thought we'd just go in the front door and have a bit of a chat with Frederick and Catherine.'

'And say what? *Are you holding a captive in there?*'

'Something like that, yes.'

'When was the last time you saw these Puzzlewick people? As you said, they might have gone over to the dark side like Flay does from time to time.'

'Well . . .'

'You don't know, do you?'

'No, no, I don't. What am I – a fortune teller?'

'Well, that's just grea—'

'Mina?'

'Jacob?'

'I think she's right. Why don't we just go in the front door? It can't hurt. And maybe Thespa can help persuade the Puzzledicks—'

'*Wicks*, Jacob, Puzzle*wicks*.'

'Maybe she can persuade them to help us the way she can sometimes persuade Flay.'

'You know something, Jacob?'

'What?'

'You can be irritatingly right sometimes.'

'Thanks. I think.'

'But only sometimes. Don't get big-headed about it.'

The front of the Puzzlewick Candle Factory, apart from the huge and colourful sign, was painted a nondescript reddish-brown, as if to enable it to blend into the valley wall behind it. It looked as if someone had backed it into that spot as far as it would go and then driven off. The front door, a simple frosted-glass affair, was set off to the right-hand side, making the whole façade look a little askew. *That*, thought Jacob, *would be just about par for the course in Grymm.*

There was a little bell above the door that tinkled gaily when they entered. The showroom they found themselves in smelled of every perfume Mina had ever sniffed mixed with the essence of all the boiled sweets Jacob had ever eaten. The room had a sales counter running across the back, leaving just enough space for the three of them to spread out along it. Not that it was a small room, just that most of the available area was taken up by shelves laden with candles of all shapes and sizes and colours and smells: striped, spotted, psychedelic, you name it. Most of the samples on show, though, were novelty candles: wax fruit, birds, fish, dogs, cats, angels, cherubs and so on. Some of them were so realistic – the apples and bananas, for instance, even *smelled* like apples and bananas – that only the presence of the wick betrayed their true identity. There was even a huge log of wood and what looked like a leather-covered copy of the Bible. Mina was just wondering who would want a burning Bible when the door behind the counter opened and a tall thin man appeared. He stepped quickly across to the counter, laid two long, elegant hands on it and grinned at them.

'Thespa,' he simpered in a surprisingly high voice. 'Long time no see. What can we do for you on this fine, fine day?'

Thespa Grymm waited a second or two, peering at the man the way a scientist would peer at a particularly nasty microbe and taking the opportunity to shove yet another cigarette in her mouth. What she wasn't expecting – and it happened with an incredible speed – was for the man to reach over and rip it out again. *Whoosh*, *whip*, and the offending article was gone, down behind the counter. Thespa, for once, was speechless. Here was someone she couldn't bully or cajole or scare into doing her bidding. But there was something else; something that worried the children: there was fear. This wasn't the same man Thespa thought she knew. This was a version of a Puzzlewick that had been through the Anhanga mill and come out the other side as something far, far darker. Mina wondered what he had been promised: to become *the best* candle-maker in the world? Even though they had never met him before, Mina and Jacob knew that he had changed for the worse.

'Tsk, tsk, tsk,' said the man. 'You should know better, Thespa Grymm. Read the signs. *No smoking.* You know how dangerous that can be in a candle factory? One wrong spark, one little rise in temperature and *POOF!* Up it all goes.'

'Do that again, Catherine, and I will tear your arm off,' growled Thespa.

Catherine? Mina and Jacob looked at each other and then back at what was, evidently, *Catherine* Puzzlewick. Perhaps it was her clothes that had put them on so wrong a track: the black suit she wore hung on her like a deflated hot-air balloon. And the ṣame went for the white shirt and black bow-tie. She looked like an undertaker after a particularly drastic diet. Tall, with impossibly white skin – whiter even than Mina's – the woman also had white-blonde hair cut razor-short at the sides and gelled into long spikes on top. She wore bottle-bottomed glasses that made her dark eyes look even bigger, giving the impression of a huge but incredibly skinny snowy owl, and her face seemed devoid of any femininity. She was, thought Mina, sort of

233

. . . what *was* the word? Androg . . . androgist? Sexless. That was it. She could easily have been either a plain-looking woman or a good-looking, high-cheekboned man.

'My apologies, *dearest* Thespa, but rules are rules. Can't have you blowing us all to kingdom come, can we? And who are your little friends? You here to buy a candle? A souvenir of our fine community?'

Behind the glasses the distorted eyes goggled at them, moving quickly from one face to the next, as if in a race to memorize them all before she was tested on their individual characteristics.

'We're here for something else entirely,' said Thespa pointedly. 'And I think you know what it is.'

At that, the woman's eyebrows – also dyed white – drew together in a frown. Before she could reply, the door behind her opened and an exact replica of her walked in. Well, not *exact*, but near enough to make no difference. Frederick Puzzlewick was dressed the same as his wife; his hair was cut and dyed in exactly the same fashion. He too was as pale as bone and as thin as a stick insect. He had an Adam's apple, a *slightly* deeper voice and, when you got close enough, his features were coarser, but they were essentially the same. With their suits – once expensive but now shiny with wear – and their gelled hair, they looked like they had been made in the same mould. They also, Jacob noted to himself, both wore gold souvenir rings like the ones at Maurie's. They would have made a fine pair of candles for each end of a mantelpiece. Mina looked at Jacob as if to say, *I give up: nothing will surprise me now.*

'What's the problem, darling?' asked the newcomer. 'Oh, Thespa. What an honour. We don't see nearly enough of you in here. Candle for a special occasion, is it?'

'Thespa's angry because I took her cigarette away, dear.'

'Now, now, Thespa, you know that's—'

'Oh, do shut up, Fred. Where's the man from the jeep? I want him back.'

'Jeep? Man? We're afraid we don't know what you're talking about,' said Catherine.

Fred's busy eyes, enormous behind the thick glasses, smiled in agreement. 'But if it would make you feel better, why not come "backstage"?' he added with a smile. Even his teeth looked waxed. 'Take the grand tour? I'm sure these charming children would love to see how a candle factory works, wouldn't they?'

Mina and Jacob made it known that they would love – nay, adore – to go behind the scenes. It was, said Jacob before Mina could jab a warning elbow into his ribs, one of his life's ambitions; up there with bungee-jumping, abseiling, skydiving, white-water rafting, snow boarding and water skiing.

Catherine Puzzlewick loped over to the far end of the counter and lifted up a flap which allowed them to file in past her. At the head of the line her husband led them through the back door and into the factory.

Mina's first impression was of the noise – a constant roaring hum that was underpinned by the far-off rattle of metal against metal – and then of the smell, a disconcerting mixture of perfume, burning wax and engine oil. The front office was obviously sealed and soundproofed because conversation on the other side of the door was almost impossible.

'It must be the air con,' shouted Jacob in her ear. 'Remember what your dad said? About them having the mother of all air-conditioning systems? He was right.'

The source of the noise, though, wasn't immediately evident, for they had come to a stop in what seemed to be a shadowy stockroom lined with shelves. Through these they could see evidence of yet more shelving. Every wall was decorated with bright red danger signs warning them of the hazards of naked lights, of breathing in certain fumes, and advising what to do if they got acid on their skin.

'Acid?' shouted Mina to Frederick. At least, she thought it was Frederick.

'Stearic acid,' replied the neat figure next to her. 'It's a paraffin additive we use in candle-making to make the wax harder and also easier to get out of the moulds. It's not just a case of melting a few bits of tallow in a jar.'

'Tallow?'

'Animal fat. Candle-making started when people started dipping marsh straw in leftover kitchen fat. We've come a *long* way since then. Someone once said that candle-making today is a mixture of chemistry, art, imagination and . . . *magic*. I think that's probably true.'

As they passed between the floor-to-ceiling shelves, flickering fluorescent strips lighting their way, Mina noticed that they were stacked with case after case of different types of wax. Here and there a few cases had been ripped open and some of the twenty-kilo slabs of white wax taken out. Past the wax they came to a section devoted to great bulbous bottles of the oils used to give scented candles their smell. With the lights reflecting off the glass, it looked like some huge fairy-tale wall of glistening colours. They were called things like Cherry Blossom, Apple Surprise and Mango Daiquiri – all coloured accordingly. Despite the circumstances, Mina found herself pleasantly impressed – even if the mix of smells did leave her mouth, throat and skin feeling a little silky, as if she'd drunk gallons of the stuff rather than just passed through it. She turned to the Puzzlewick next to her again.

'No Eye of Newt or Tail of Rat?'

'No. We keep all that stuff upstairs, along with the dead animals,' laughed whoever it was. It was impossible to tell, in the half-dark, whether he, or she, or it, was joking.

At the end of the row they rounded the corner of the shelves, turned right, entered yet another aisle and found themselves walking back the way they'd come, albeit on the other side of the first row. It was like a dark but simple maze. This time the shelves were covered in padlocked wire-mesh doors and festooned with yet more warning signs. Behind these were industrial-sized cans of paraffin, large bottles of acid and something called polyethylene that, if the number of little symbols on the sides of the cans was any indication, would explode at the slightest touch.

'I can see why you're worried about the fire risk,' shouted Mina. She also quickly glanced round to make sure Thespa Grymm wasn't bloody-mindedly lighting up another cigarette.

'Yes. One spark and . . . *BOOM!* They'd find our corpses on the moon, most likely.'

'Cool!' bellowed Jacob. Mina could see that he was making a mental note of what was where; honestly, the kid was turning into some kind of manic urban guerrilla. For which she was eternally grateful – Grymm being what it was. She dreaded to think what he might be able to do with three hundred gallons of paraffin and a stapler.

At the end of the corridor of shelves they turned left and were confronted by a row of what looked like colour-coded plastic drinks bottles – red, yellow, ivory, purple, blue, green, orange and, oddly, coffee – filled with liquid dye. Opposite these was a wall of metal, glass and rubber moulds of all sizes and shapes: round, square, tall, short. Beyond these, a section devoted to cardboard boxes filled with wicks. These too came in all shapes and sizes.

'It's just round this last corner,' shouted the Puzzlewick in front of Mina. The noise of machinery had reached a crescendo now and was competing with the air-conditioning for supremacy. It was impossible to carry on even a shouted conversation. Not that Mina or Jacob needed to, their breaths taken away by the vast scene in front of them.

The space was entirely taken up with a huge silver-and-grey machine that chugged and rattled and rolled and clattered and clashed as it moved hundreds of wicks and moulds and mixtures around to meet each other at prearranged points. Whole rows of hanging white wicks were dipped into enormous vats of rust-proofed sheet metal filled with melted wax. In, out, move on. In, out, move on. Elsewhere, little gun-like jets squirted pre-set amounts of hot wax into moulds, which were then moved to one side to cool, obviously in preparation for another layer, another colour. The Puzzlewicks beamed at the sight of it.

'Like it?' asked Frederick.

'It's a bit noisy!' shouted Mina.

'Yes, indeed,' he agreed, and trotted off to one side to press a few red buttons on the wall. When he had finished, the clanking and the thundering ceased as the leviathan ground to a halt. 'How's that? Take advantage – can't leave it off for too long.'

'Much better,' said Mina gratefully, though she was still obliged to raise her voice because of the roar of the air conditioning. 'It's amazing. Do all candle factories have one of these?'

'Oh no, no, no.' Frederick was most adamant. 'No, this is all our own design. I don't think anywhere in the world has automated quite to this extent. We just need to fill up the reservoirs with fresh ingredients now and then, and Balthazar does the rest.'

'Balthazar?' said Thespa. 'I didn't know you'd named it, Fred.'

'It means "the lord of treasures", or something like

that. And it's certainly a licence to print money. Since we automated we've . . . well, we've doubled our capacity. For the miners, of course. Mr Anhanga's certainly got an eye for the . . . er . . . unusual, shall we say.'

'Is it happy like that?' asked Jacob. 'Turned off? Won't the wax burn or something?'

'Eventually, yes, but it's safe enough for now. It's all regulated by very expensive thermometers. As long as it stays below 190 degrees Celsius we're fine.'

'What happens then?'

'Well, that's the flash point of wax – the point at which it spontaneously combusts, bursts into flame. Now, what else can we show you? Well, nothing, to be honest. As you can see, we've nothing to hide.'

'What about up there?' snarled Thespa with a movement of her head towards the far right-hand reaches of the room. Mina and Jacob strained to see a staircase there – a metal staircase like a cage, with a padlocked door at the bottom of it. 'What's up *there*?'

'Nothing,' said the Puzzlewicks simultaneously.

'It's just a storeroom,' muttered Catherine. 'Have you got the key, Frederick?'

'Me? I thought you had it.'

'Didn't I give it to *you*?'

'No, I'm sure I—'

'Enough!' Thespa had reached the end of her tether. 'Give. Me. The. Key.'

Amazingly, the key was produced – seemingly out of thin air – and Thespa Grymm plodded over to undo the padlock that was keeping them from the upper reaches of the building. As she did so, one of the Puzzlewicks pressed the button to get Balthazar rolling again and indicated that they should follow Thespa. 'Honestly, there's nothing up there, but if you must . . .'

Initially, Thespa seemed disinclined to mount the stairs and just stood there at the bottom, her dark eyes wide open, peering up into the gloom ahead. Mina took hold of Jacob's hand in a gesture she hoped would be interpreted as the older sister being protective of her younger brother but was in reality just an opportunity to give his hand a warning squeeze. Jacob understood perfectly: she was telling him to be alert. This was all far too easy. But where Thespa went, they were going to follow. She was an adult, after all, so what could go wrong?

Hand in hand they entered what looked like a shadowy fire escape, a dark corridor of wire that led up to the next floor. Ahead of them they could see Thespa enter the square of light at the top of the stairs and disappear round a corner. The Puzzlewicks stayed at the bottom, all grins, encouragement and smirks. The weirdos couldn't keep those twisted smiles off their pasty faces. And in the shadows they looked like two disembodied heads floating in the dark.

It was enough to spook Jacob, who dashed up the rest of the stairs, pulling hard on Mina's hand, and didn't rest until he reached the light. Once there, though, they both wished they hadn't rushed. The area in front of them was the same size as the one below but looked bigger because it wasn't stuffed with shelving and machinery. The only thing of any size was a large covered truck parked off to the left-hand side. *On the first floor?* thought Jacob before noticing the large roller-door on the other side of the room. But even then – on the first floor? How did it get up there? The factory was backed up against the rock face – there was no room for a ramp or anything like that. This, though, wasn't the most significant thing about the first floor of the Puzzlewick factory; that honour was reserved for the hundreds, possibly thousands, of flickering black candles scattered about the place. It was odd, given the many danger warnings below them. They were placed on desks, in candleholders, in candelabras hanging by chains from the ceiling far above them, each with a small label attached. They stood on the sills of bricked-up windows and on the remains of each other, sitting on great pitch-black mounds of melted wax like trees on a hillside. They were long and short, fat and thin, round and square, and they gave off a foul-smelling odour.

'Yikes,' breathed Jacob.

'Oh. My. God,' agreed Mina as they strode over to examine the labels. Each one, they discovered, was covered in a hideously neat script that detailed the percentages of the candle's ingredients, the type of wick and the estimated burning time. And each was marked with a number.

'What are they trying to do?' asked Jacob.

'Something for Anhanga at the mine? Black candles? Black magic? Who knows.'

'Perhaps this will help,' said Thespa from across the room, where she had found a large old wooden filing cabinet filled with numbered cards. 'The Puzzlewicks are nothing if not efficient.'

The cards obviously corresponded to the candles still burning, and to many others before them. Whatever they were experimenting with, it had been going on for quite some time.

'What do those symbols mean?' asked Jacob, pointing to a series of neat little stick figures across the bottom of each card that were obviously meant to represent animals – horses, dogs, rabbits and so on.

'What was it Catherine said about tallow?' mused Mina. 'About how early candles were made from animal fat? They seem to be doing some experimenting . . .'

'Then what does this mean?' asked Jacob with a catch in his voice. He held out a card he had found further along the cabinet. On it was the little stick figure of a person. 'Does it mean what I think it means?'

Mina shuddered. Anhanga's pranks had taken an unexpected and unpleasant turn. Thespa avoided his eye and theatrically pulled out and lit a cigarette.

'That's a yes, then?'

They were still standing like this, gawping at the huge collection of cards, when Jacob saw something propped up in the furthest, most shadowy corner. Surely not . . .

The others followed his gaze, and then they all rushed over at once. There, in the corner, was what looked like another large blue statue. This time, though, it wasn't just a copy; this was the real thing.

The Puzzlewicks had turned the man into a human candle.

Mina imagined what he must have gone through, hands tied to his sides, dipped time and time again in hot wax, trying to keep it out of his eyes and nose and mouth.

It was monstrous.

More than evil.

Between them they hauled the rock-hard 'statue'

down and carried it, like a huge blue coffin, over to the candles, where there was more light. It seemed impossible that anyone could have survived, but Jacob refused to give up. He pulled the stapler out of his pocket and used the sharper edges to break the wax covering the face. As he did so, he knocked a table of black candles crashing to the ground.

'Careful there, Jacob, the last thing we need now is a fire.'

Jacob didn't care. He was looking down at the cold, waxy form of the man, his face exposed but the rest of him just a hard blue carapace. Somehow the weird wax had fused with his skin, or vice versa, making it hard to tell where he ended and the candle began.

'He's dead,' said Thespa. 'We're too late.'

'He can't be dead!' shouted Jacob. 'I saw his lips move.'

'He is,' confirmed Mina. 'You must have imagined it, Jacob. There's nothing we can do.'

'Exactly!' roared Jacob. 'Exactly! I *imagined* it and it happened! It's what happens in Grymm, isn't it? Imagine stuff? Except it never goes our way, does it? Still no Bryan, and now *this*!'

'Jacob . . .' Mina said, her voice soft. 'We can't save everyone.'

'Why not? *Why* can't we save everyone?' With that,

he ran off behind the truck and they heard a crescendo of banging as he took his frustration out on it.

Mina turned to Thespa, who was looking puzzled. 'Are you all right?' Perhaps the older woman had reached the end of her tether. She was no spring chicken, after all. 'Thespa?'

'It's all very strange, very strange indeed. This most definitely was not supposed to happen. Not at all. Listen, Mina, we need to get out of here. In this instance I think it *might* be best to get to a police station.'

'But I thought you said—'

'That poor man there is what is known as *evidence*. If the Puzzlewicks are arrested for murder, maybe we can get the inquiry widened, link it to what's happening at the mine. Don't you see? It's the first time Anhanga's left any physical evidence behind.'

'I see it all too well,' said Mina. 'And so should you.'

'What?'

'Don't you *see*? The Puzzlewicks *knew* we'd find him, alive or dead. We've been set up. What's the betting that the door downstairs is locked again – and have you noticed that the Puzzlewicks are nowhere to be seen?'

Thespa grimaced. 'Damn! Damn it!'

At the same time Jacob, driven by the need to do something – anything – rather than think about what he had seen, began searching in the gloom behind the truck and found that the roller-door was partially open at the bottom. Bending down, he looked under it to find a short concrete ramp that spanned the gap between the factory and the cliff face and then disappeared into a truck-sized tunnel leading upwards through the rock. Mina and Grymm were whispering to each other across the other side of the room, so he slipped quietly under the door and stood up in cool darkness on the other side. Water was trickling somewhere, and the smell of damp clung to his skin.

'Hello?' he said in a high, strangled voice that bounced against the rock walls of a tunnel that at first had seemed so big and now seemed much, much smaller. Ahead, though, he could make out a faint glow of daylight. Did the tunnel go right through the rock and out the other side? He made a decision and sprinted forward into the darkness.

The tunnel ended just a few minutes later, after a mildly strenuous uphill climb, and emerged on a small plateau from which the road descended into what was effectively a massive rock bowl surrounded by small cliffs. Spread out below was a jumble of pre-fabricated buildings thrown up around a giant hole in the rock face opposite, like the driveway and entrance to an enormous underground car park. It was also throat-searingly hot, and everything seemed to be covered in a watery brown gauze. Something had only recently come through. Another truck? Or something even bigger?

It was obviously a far-flung part of Anhanga's mine empire, thought Jacob. And then he heard something, a sound – something he recognized. And it was coming from the massive black maw below. He cocked his head to one side and listened. There it was again. A rustling. A whisper. *Yesss, bosssss.* Like a million spiders all scuttling together in the same direction. Where *had* he heard that before?

And then he saw the big, black, fat-bellied flies that had begun gathering on the rough boulders behind which he was sheltering. More and more of them were landing with horribly audible little thuds, like the first intermittent spatter of thick tropical raindrops. *Plop! Plop! Plop! Splat! Splat! Splat! Splat!* Suddenly the air was thick with them, whirring around Jacob's head and bouncing off his ears and forehead and cheeks, tiny furred ping-pong balls.

He waved his arms about and shook his head to dislodge them as they clustered around the edges of his eyes, nose and ears.

So many flies!

And then he remembered.

The funfair!

That was where he had heard the sound, and seen the flies. Soon there would be grey shadows. And . . . that thing.

Still waving his arms around at the flies, feeling their compact little bodies bounce like peanuts off his skin, he dashed back into the tunnel as if the hounds of hell were on his trail. And for all he knew, they were.

'*They're coming!*' he shouted – the first time he had dared open his mouth for a while – as he scrambled back under the roller-door. The flies seemed to disappear then, as if scared to enter the cavernous room. A few brave souls floated dreamily under the door but Jacob quickly dispatched them with some well-chosen whacks.

'Who's coming?' Mina seemed distracted.

'Them! From the mine! *Him!* Can't you hear it?'

'Hear what?'

'Listen!'

It was as faint as the pitter-patter of a mouse's feet across a stone floor at first, but soon they all heard it: the scurrying, the whispering. And they all recognized it too. It was the sound you heard as a child when, lying sleepless in bed at night, the night rustled around you; the noise you imagined cockroaches, spiders and earwigs made when they skittered across the floorboards under the bed and began to climb the legs.

Mina broke the spell first. She had no idea what Jacob was talking about but the look on his face was enough. Somehow he knew what was coming for them, and it wasn't good. She ran across to the top of the stairwell, shouting to Thespa to follow her. Jacob looked around the room for any other exit points. The lack of windows was an advantage now, but what about the big steel roller-door? He dashed over and stabbed at the red button on the wall marked OPEN/CLOSE.

Mina stood at the top of the stairs and peered down. 'There's no one there.' She grabbed Thespa's arm. 'Can you look around downstairs? See what the Puzzlewicks are up to?'

'Of course,' she replied, just as the roller-door behind them screeched into action. The noise was like fingernails down a blackboard and they both turned to see the great metal sections roll down to rest on the floor. 'What *is* he doing?'

'Don't know,' said Mina. 'Maybe he's just checking to see if we can get out that way . . . Go!' she told Thespa. 'And be careful.'

Thespa trod carefully down the stairs, inching her way into the unknown, while Mina ran over to where Jacob lay on the dusty, wax-splattered floor. She threw herself down next to him.

'Well?'

'Listen,' he hissed.

'What is it?' asked Mina.

'It's a tunnel. To the mine.'

'No – what's making that noise?'

'You really don't want to know.'

'You're right. I don't. Let's go.'

They got up and trotted back to the stairs to see how Thespa Grymm was getting on. There was no sign of her.

'Thespa?' shouted Mina. Her voice echoed in the stairwell. She tried again: 'Thespa!'

Silence.

Jacob sighed. Fine. It was up to *them* – him and Mina – now. 'She's gone. I'm going to have another look around up here.'

'Sure,' replied Mina absent-mindedly. Having spent days hating Thespa, she had now developed a soft spot for the woman. Anyone who refused to believe that Flay was all bad, or allow him to become so, at least had a good heart.

'Come on, Thespa! Come on!' She was about to give up when the old witch's thick black bulk came skidding into view as if the devil himself were on her tail.

'*GO!*' she screamed, nimbly taking the stairs two at a time despite her bulk. '*GO!*'

Mina started to run but then thought better of it.

Where would she run *to*? She turned back and crashed head-on into Thespa as she reached the top step. As they stared at each other in shock, the roller-door bent inwards with a crash and began to rattle. At the same time the truck roared into life, belching choking grey fumes into the warehouse.

Thespa Grymm turned to Mina. 'Look!' She pointed behind her, down the stairwell. Mina poked her head around the huge sweaty body to find Flay standing quite still and calm at the bottom of the stairs, looking up at them. Behind him, one to the left and one to the right, were the Puzzlewicks, grinning like bloodless lunatics. Unlike Flay they weren't armed, but their elegant hands were now curled into cruel-looking, oversized claws. One snickered. It was a spiteful sound that was immediately echoed by the other. Mina got the impression that they wanted to fly up the stairs and rip them to shreds.

It was not to be, though. Cleaver Flay was there, and Flay wanted them first. And he wanted Mina more than anyone; the *worm* who had caused such havoc in his shop. He was just a shadow framed in the light so she couldn't make out his eyes, but Mina would have bet the bank that they had changed colour again and were the deepest, darkest, liquid black. Black holes where the soul should be. He had a long pointed knife in one hand and a meat cleaver in the other. Both of them gleamed, as if smiling. Finally there was work to do. Despite the noise behind her Mina clearly heard his gritted whisper:

'Worm.'

'I couldn't stop him!' sobbed Thespa. 'Poor Cleaver.'

'Poor Cleaver? Poor *us* if he gets hold of us.'

'Who started the truck?'

'I'm hoping it's Jacob,' said Mina and, as if in response, Jacob's face appeared at the passenger window and he gave her a thumbs-up. With a glance down the stairs again – Flay was still slowly advancing and muttering – she pushed, pulled and cajoled Thespa over to the truck. Inside, Jacob was trying to work out how to put the vehicle into gear but was only succeeding in making awful crashing and threshing noises as the gears grated.

Mina shook Thespa's arm roughly. 'Can you drive?'

'Yes, yes, of course I can.'

'Let's go then!'

'Go? Where?'

Mina pointed at the roller-door, which was bending alarmingly. Clawed fingertips appeared underneath as it started to rise off the concrete flooring. 'First perhaps we should back it up against *that*.'

Thespa finally pulled herself together. They ran across the waxy floor, tugged open the truck's doors and piled in, pushing Jacob to one side. Thespa took a second to examine the controls.

'I thought you could drive!' yelled Mina, still trying to see if Flay had reached the top of the stairs. Jacob was squashed up against the passenger window with a huge smile on his face. He was at his best, thought Mina, when he was *doing* something.

'I *can* drive; I've just never driven something this big. Ah! That's it!'

With a sudden lurch the whole vehicle jumped forward and stalled. At the top of the stairs Flay appeared and glared at them. In his wake crept the Puzzlewicks, spreading out right and left as they entered the room.

'Maggots!' roared Flay.

Mina and Jacob slammed the locks down on the truck's doors. Thespa turned the key again but the engine just stuttered and coughed and spluttered. She stopped. 'Come on! Come on!'

Behind them a small, black, imp-like figure slithered under the door through the slimmest of cracks and stood up, raising its fists in triumph.

With another frantic turn of the key the engine roared into life and Thespa slammed the gears into reverse, gunning the accelerator at the same time. The truck shot backwards like a rocket, slammed into the roller-door and took the figure's head clean off. Before its decapitated body had hit the floor the whole thing vanished in a puff of smoke.

The pounding stopped. Mina, Jacob and Thespa whooped with delight and patted each other on the back – until, *BANG!* they looked up to find the bald, razor-clean head of Cleaver Flay staring at them through the window. He was hanging onto the wing mirror with one rubber-gloved hand and banging on the window with the other hand, now ungloved. The knife and the cleaver were tucked into his leather belt for the moment as he tried to force his way in. The knives would come into play, they knew, later.

His eyes were now mere slits behind which a dark liquid danced, and his full lips were drawn back in a snarl. And on one of his remaining fingers? A bright yellow ring.

The rattling, screeching and yattering behind them had also started up again; they could feel the blows now through the body of the truck. Something scuttled across the canvas behind them – a Puzzlewick, no doubt.

'*What now?*' screamed Thespa.

Mina and Jacob looked at each other and then at the far end of the warehouse, where the truck had been parked. Jacob shrugged. It was their only chance. What did they have to lose?

His sister turned to Thespa, who was staring in undisguised horror at Flay as he leaned backwards to take a swing at the side window with his enormous fist. It was no good trying to talk to her – and too late anyway – so Mina banged the gearstick into what she hoped was first gear and stamped her foot onto the accelerator, all the way to the floor.

The truck lurched forward but it was too late to stop Flay's fist hitting the window, which exploded into a thousand starry pieces. But the movement of the truck defeated him. He lost his footing and slipped downwards, his forearm hanging inside the cab for a few seconds before he disappeared behind them with a last shout of '*Woooormssssssss!*' and a thud as the truck picked up speed. The smell of burning rubber filled the cab and the huge vehicle thundered across the warehouse floor.

'What are you? My God!' shouted Thespa as she realized what the children were planning. All she had time to do was tense her arms on the steering wheel as, with a deafening crash, the truck struck the far wall and kept going. It plunged through the flimsy wood and plaster with the sound of a dozen car crashes at once, and then they were airborne, taking the *Puzzlewick's Candle Factory* sign with them as they went. All three of them screamed in unison and gripped the sides of the cab as the truck tipped forward and fell . . .

The impact when they hit the ground burst the two front tyres, shattered the windscreen and was enough to shake the fillings in their teeth. The truck bounced wildly a few times but stayed upright. It came to rest across the road that the children had driven in on. Steam spewed out of the engine. Glass fell. Then came silence.

'Awesome!' said Jacob eventually.

'Yeah, sure.' Mina sounded less than convinced. Mainly because she was picking bits glass out of her arms.

'Come on,' said Thespa. 'We're not safe yet.'

Mina and Jacob climbed out and raced round to help her; she was limping badly. Behind them the candle factory now sported a ragged hole in its top left-hand corner. Debris from the impact was spread across the road. Up in the hole itself they saw Cleaver Flay. He was battered and bruised but otherwise unhurt. Behind him they could make out darker shapes dancing around in anger at being deprived of their prey. The head of one Puzzlewick appeared, blinking and squinting in the sun before fading back into the shadows.

The three of them hobbled off at the double, and were racing back towards town as fast as their bruises would let them when the 'peace van' they had seen at the camp on their first morning came trundling along the road towards them. It slowed to a halt in a small cloud of red dust and the boy with the blue eyes peered out at them from the driver's seat. He seemed both amused and concerned. In the seat next to him was Eric Elland, buttoned up and with notebook in hand, as ever.

'Wow, what happened? Are you dudes OK?' said the boy, and leaped out to help them.

Mina blushed. The teenager – well, he could have been sixteen or twenty-six, if Mina was honest – was deeply tanned, with a lot of red dreadlocks, and eyes of the palest blue. A small gold ring pierced his right eyebrow and his tight white T-shirt bulged with muscles. Mina blushed again. He was gorgeous.

'Bit of a car accident,' said Thespa with a glare at the priest that persuaded him to put his pad down and help them. 'Nothing serious but we would appreciate a lift back into town. I know it's not far but . . .'

'Not a problem at all.' The boy smiled. 'Get in, get in.'

It wasn't a long trip but it was enough for Mina – normally tongue-tied in the presence of boys – to discover that the boy's name was Red and that he was eighteen and had been at the camp for a month, was a vegetarian and was being 'interviewed' by Elland for his so-called book.

'I think it's a great idea,' explained Red as he casually steered the beaten-up van back into town. 'Like, let the world know the truth.'

'The truth?' Jacob sat upright in the back.

'Yeah, man, about the mine. It's an environmental disaster, dude.'

Mina beamed at him. Jacob sighed in disappointment. Thespa tsk-tsked and returned to picking glass out of her arm. Elland sat in the back next to Jacob, making surreptitious notes.

In what seemed like seconds to Mina and hours to Jacob they arrived in Grymm proper. Mina shyly called goodbye to Red. And Elland, who waved happily from the back seat with his notebook in one hand and a pen in the other. With his big head, oversized smile and huge round glasses he looked like a great happy bug.

'Surely we're s-s-safe now?' said Jacob as they made their way along the boardwalk to the real-estate office.

'I think so, for the time being,' said Thespa. 'And look who's here! Perfect timing.'

The children glanced up to find Mina's father standing in the street next to their 4WD. He stared at the raggedy bunch approaching him: bruised, bloodied, dirty, their clothes torn, the children looked like they'd been through a war.

'What in God's name has been going on? What have you done to your head, Mina? Have you been fighting?'

Thespa quickly headed off any detailed explanations by telling him how she had crashed her car and flipped

260

over, becoming trapped, and how Mina and Jacob had helped to free her.

'Heroes, they are, Mr Lipton!' she declared. 'True heroes. I don't know what I'd have done without them.'

'Well, I'll be . . .' said George. 'Not bad for your first few days in town, eh? And you thought you'd be bored. Are you sure you're all right, Mina? That's a nasty graze on your head.'

'I'm fine, Dad, really. It's been all go, that's for sure.'

'Anything I can do to help, Ms Grymm?' Are *you* OK? What about your car?'

'Yes, yes, yes.' Thespa grinned. 'It's all under control. I'm fine. Just a little shaken, that's all. The car's a wreck but I'm OK. Thanks to these two. You just get these children home. They must be exhausted.'

George looked at the two of them with undisguised admiration. 'Well done, kids. I'm proud of you. You did good.'

'We certainly did,' said Jacob. 'But can we go home now?'

'Right, get your bikes and we'll be off.'

And they did just that, leaving Thespa Grymm, bruised, battered and limping, outside her office.

'*Will* you be all right?' whispered Mina before they got into the jeep. 'I mean, from, you know . . .'

'Ever heard the expression that an Englishman's

home is his castle? Well, this is *my* castle. They won't hurt me here. You go on home; you'll be safe there with your parents, I think. Safe enough. And thank you.'

'It was nothing,' boasted Jacob. 'Nothing at all.'

Thespa, though, had one more piece of advice for them before they left. She pointed at the pentacle around Mina's neck as they pulled away and mouthed the words 'Remember Bryan?'

Bryan! What were they going to do about Bryan?

Poo!

Which, when you thought about it, was the perfect word for Bryan.

10

In the time it took them to drive to the house, night fell with an almost audible thud. The last few hundred metres were a jet-black tunnel until they crested the final rise and the house came into view. With nothing but the night sky behind it, the lights shining from the windows looked like fireflies hovering in the chilly evening air.

'Home sweet home!' cried George. During the five-minute drive he had bombarded them with questions about their day and about Thespa's 'accident', questions that Mina and Jacob tried to answer as honestly as possible without actually being honest.

'Good day at work, Dad?' asked Mina, mostly to deflect any more questions but also because this was a different George to the grouchy one who had come home yesterday. It was the old George, to be sure, but somehow *more so*.

'Maaaarvellous!' he said, pulling up outside the front porch. 'Fantastic. Couldn't have been better. Not as exciting as your day, of course, but I think everything's going to be hunky-dory. Right, get your bikes off the rack and then come and help me with the stuff in the back.'

The 'stuff' turned out to be a few plastic bags of work files, some small boxes of mineral samples, and a large and heavy icebox that George insisted on carrying himself.

'You get the door, Mina. Key's in my top pocket. There! That's it. *Hey-ho, ho-hum, it's back from work we come!*'

'Are you sure you're all right?' asked Jacob as his stepfather wrestled the box out of the back of the jeep and supported it on his thighs.

'I will be when Mina gets that door open – this thing weighs a ton.'

'What's in it?'

'Ah-ha! Big secret! Show you later. Come on, Mina, I'm breaking my back here.'

The door swung open to reveal the hallway emblazoned with lights and smelling of lemon and beeswax. Mary, hair gathered in an untidy bun on top of her head, emerged from a side door wearing dungarees, bright pink rubber gloves and holding a filthy yellow duster.

'Hey! You'll never guess what the kids got up to today!' roared George as he burst through the door, slammed the icebox down on the floor and gave his wife a boisterous hug.

'Well, it certainly wasn't getting my paint,' groaned Mary over his shoulder as she raised a quizzical eyebrow. George was many things but he most certainly was not one given to over-enthusiastic displays of affection. Slow and steady, was George.

'No, no, no! No wonder they forgot the paint! No, they saved Thespa Grymm from her burning car! Real heroes, they are, according to Ms Grymm. You should see them! Have we got any ointment? They'll need plasters too.'

'What?' Mary threw the cloth down and took Mina's hand as she followed her father into the hallway. 'Oh my God! Your poor head! That looks painful! What happened? Jacob! Look at you!'

'It was just a car crash,' stammered Mina, both surprised and confused by her stepmother's concern. What had happened to the bitchy, frustrated artist? 'I bashed my head leaning in through the window, that's all.'

'That's all?' said Mary, examining the wound. 'It looks pretty nasty. We should get a doctor to look at it.'

'Out here?'

'Well, there must be a doctor at the mine, mustn't there?'

'*No!* No, really, Mary, I'm good,' insisted Mina. 'Really.'

'Yeah, it's no big deal, Mum,' added Jacob. 'We're fine. Really. Tired, that's all.' He was, at the same time, secretly pleased by the attention. A hero! Him! Even if it wasn't true.

'I should think so! Look at you both! You look like you've been in a war!'

'Hey! What about me?' demanded George. He pushed himself between them, grabbed Mary again and puckered up his impish face. 'Doesn't the man of the house get a kiss?'

'Get a room, *please.*' Mina grimaced.

'Good day on the job, dear?' asked Mary when George finally put her down.

'Fantastic! Maaaarvellous! Couldn't be better. Tell you all about it afterwards. Got to get this lot into the kitchen. Dinner's on me tonight.'

'I was going to do those pizzas that Ms Grymm left in the freezer for us,' said Mary. 'I got a bit sidetracked with my painting and tidying up the studio today. Haven't really thought about dinner.'

'Pizzas schmizzas – put them back. Throw 'em away. I've got something much better than that, don't you worry. Dinner in an hour or so, kids? Clean up that cut, Mina! Then you can tell us all about your adventures. You want to help me with this, Mary?'

'What's in it?'

'A surprise!'

'What sort of surprise?' asked Mina. 'We've had enough surprises for one day, Dad. Really we have. What's in the box?'

'Nothing for you to worry about, sweetness. You see to that head. There's some antiseptic cream in the bath-room cabinet, I think. Have a bath. Did you turn the boiler on today, dear? There you go! Have a *hot* bath. Relax. Pack up all your cares and woes.'

Jacob and Mina, however, were having none of it. Things had gone far too wrong already for them to walk away from the mysterious box without finding out what was in it. They followed their parents into the kitchen and watched them deposit it in front of the fridge. Mina realized that her heart was beating fast, too fast. Her voice was as hard as diamond. 'What's in the box, Dad?'

George flicked the clasps on the sides and snatched the lid away with a flourish to reveal an interior glisten-ing with ice-cubes and thick red cuts of meat.

'*Voilà!*' he said like a magician who had just pulled a crocodile from a wallet. 'What about that lot then? Got it from a guy at the mine. Cheap as chips. He was almost giving it away. Luckily nobody here's a vegetarian, eh?'

'What,' asked Jacob, 'is it?'

'What do you mean *what is it*? It's meat. All sorts of stuff. Beef, chicken, lamb – that looks a little bit like liver . . . er . . . brains? Might give those a miss, eh, kids? And I think there's a kidney or two in there at the bottom. Are you two all right? You've gone very pale.'

Mina and Jacob exchanged sickly glances and began to edge towards the door. 'We're good, we're good,' said Mina weakly. 'We'll just go get cleaned up.'

'Be careful of the water, you two,' warned Mary. 'The plumbing's a bit ancient and the taps tend to explode a bit at first. You don't want to get scalded. Are you *sure* you're OK? Mina?'

'It's just been a long day,' said Jacob as they climbed the stairs. 'By the way, Mum – sorry about the other day. You know? The baby thing? It was stupid.'

'Yeah, sorry about that,' echoed Mina. 'And about the paint . . . It just slipped our minds.'

Mary frowned good-naturedly at them, then at George, who was loading meat into the freezer and whistling. 'Apologies? Hugs from George? What's going on?'

'Nothing,' said the children.

'Hmmm, a likely story. I'll give you a shout when dinner's ready, OK? And don't worry about the paint –

I gave Ms Bluehammer a call to ask about art classes and she brought some up this afternoon. I knew you'd forget. She's quite nice, isn't she?'

The children stared at her in undisguised surprise: *Bluehammer? Quite nice?*

'Anyway, we'll talk about it over dinner. You heroes get yourself cleaned up.'

Upstairs, Mina and Jacob headed for the bedroom. It was tidier than before and a chest of drawers had been moved in, but Jacob's bed was still in the same place. He threw himself down on it and stared at Mina with eyes as big as saucers.

'What are we going to do now? I'm starving but . . . I can't eat any of that stuff downstairs. It could be anything.'

'Or any*one*,' whispered Mina as she kicked off her trainers and sat on the edge of the bed massaging her feet. 'It makes me feel sick just thinking about it. Dad thinks he's got a bargain, though. He'll bug out if we don't eat it.'

'And he's in such a good mood too.'

'A bit *too* good. It's like he's taken a happy pill.'

'Yeah. No job's *that* good. Is it?'

'No.'

There was a moment's silence before Jacob continued in a small, hesitant voice: 'Mina, all that really *did* happen today, didn't it? I didn't dream it, did I? Did *we*?'

'I hurt too much for it to be a dream. Look at your T-shirt! Look at those bruises on your arm.'

'So, what now?'

'First, a bath. After that . . . dinner, I suppose. There'll be vegetables and stuff, won't there? We'll have to . . . I dunno . . . just not eat the meat. Oh, look, I don't know. I'm starving and I can't think straight when I'm starving.'

'No, I mean, what do we do now? About Grymm and . . . and Bryan . . . and Bluehammer and Anhanga?'

'To be honest, I don't know and I don't care. Not right now. I ache all over and I'm hot and sweaty and my hand hurts. I *need* that bath.' Mina looked at Jacob and smiled. 'And so do you. You smell worse than Bryan. And before you ask, no, I don't know what to do about him, either.'

When they went back downstairs an hour later – washed, wearing fresh clothes, their wounds cleaned – the first thing they noticed was the mouthwatering aroma of roasting meat. It drifted up the stairs as if it had been waiting for them; warm, enticing, comforting, seductive.

'Ohhhhhhhh,' groaned Jacob. 'That smells . . .'

'Disgusting. It's disgusting. Right? Jacob? Don't fall

for it. Don't forget what happened at Fleur's.'

'But what if it's just, you know, just lamb or something?'

Mina stopped at the foot of the stairs and grabbed him by the shoulders. 'It's *not*. It's from the mine. It's trying to . . . to . . . trick you.'

'Trick me? It's just a lump of meat.'

'Well, yes, but what *type* of meat? People have been disappearing in Grymm, Jacob. Where do they go? What if it's one of them? What if it's frozen Doberman leg?'

'Do you think it could be?'

'Could be what?' asked George, who had just at that moment come out of the kitchen in a blare of fluorescent light, heat and the sound of meat sizzling.

'Nothing, Dad. What's for dinner then?'

'Roast pork!' He closed his eyes and breathed in deeply. 'Smell that! Roast pork with lovely crackling. Should be ready in about half an hour. How's that? Come on into the sitting room. I'm just telling Mum about my new boss.'

'Mr Anhanga?' said Mina, as if her father had said a dirty word. 'You *met* him?'

'Of course! I'm going to be working very closely with him. How did you know his name?'

'Heard it a lot in town today,' explained Jacob as they edged into the sitting room. 'Hi, Mum.'

'Come sit down, you two.' Mary smiled and patted the threadbare sofa beside her. Now that the rooms had been cleared of the debris of moving, the true nature of the house they had moved into became apparent. It was gorgeous, an architectural gem with every possible detail in perfect condition, from the leaded casement windows to the art nouveau-style wrought iron of the gas fire in the chimney grate, to the matching wooden mantelpiece and the brass fingerplates and doorknobs.

So perfect was it that, for the first time, Jacob and Mina noticed how faded *their* furniture was. The sofa, the coffee table, the armchairs – everything seemed bleached in comparison to the room itself, which looked brand new even though it must have been built at least a hundred years ago. Even the carpet and the wallpaper were bright and cheery, if a little floral and old-fashioned.

The only thing missing, thought Mina, was a coffin in the corner, so much did it resemble a funeral parlour in an old movie. Perhaps if they opened up the double doors at the back of the room, the ones that led through to the formal dining area, they'd find one there. Yeah, and knowing their luck Cleaver Flay would leap out of it.

'So, tell me all about your heroics today,' Mary was saying. 'I'm told *Ms* Grymm was raving about you.

That's a bit of a change from before. I'm glad you're on better terms with her now. I thought she seemed nice enough.'

'She's all right, but we'd rather hear about Dad's new boss,' said Mina as she folded herself into the nearest armchair and slipped her hands inside her black sweat-shirt.

'Yeah, the accident was nothing, Mum, really,' said Jacob as he cuddled up to Mary. 'Thespa crashed her car, the door got jammed and we helped open it. That was it, really.'

She ruffled his hair with one hand and leaned forward to pick up her wine glass with the other. She took a sip and seemed to relax. 'Just like that? Is this like you getting home from school and just saying "good" when I ask you how the day went? "Good". Fair enough, young man. So, George, how did your day go? And don't say "good".'

'Oh, pretty good,' sniggered George as he lay length-wise on the other sofa and balanced a half-empty glass of beer on his ample stomach. 'Yeah, pretty good.'

'George!'

'Sorry, sorry, sorry. Well, it was . . . interesting. Yesterday was all a bit confusing, to be honest, but today I spent the morning just sorting out my office, reading reports, meeting people – you know, just getting the feel of the place. I thought it was going to be pretty boring stuff but it's fascinating, *intriguing*. They're looking for deposits that, well, seem . . . Oh, it's all too technical to go into now. But it was when I met Mr Anhanga that things got a little odd.'

'Odd?'

'Well, normally the mine manager's office is some- where near the entrance to the mine. Stands to reason, right? But Anhanga's is hundreds of metres *underground*.'

'That seems to be taking your job a little too seriously,' offered Mary with a laugh. 'Don't you start digging an office in the garden, will you, dear?'

'Not like this one, I won't. It's reached by an elevator and there's no other way in or out. It must have been more or less dug by hand. There's no way you could get any heavy machinery or trucks down there. Seemed like a waste of time and effort. I've never seen anything quite like it, to be honest.'

George sat up, as if his story were too big to be told lying down. 'It's this large cavern, painted red – well, sort of burgundy . . . and . . . it's odd, really.'

'What?' blurted Mina and Jacob in unison.

'Well, he's got all this magic stuff down there.'

Mina glanced surreptitiously at her stepbrother. 'Magic? Black magic? Stuff like that?'

George threw his head back and guffawed. 'Black

magic? Mina! Where *do* you get your ideas from? No, you know, *magic* magic. Rabbits out of top hats, saw the lady in half, card tricks. He's got quite a collection. All sorts of odd-looking cabinets and props. Says some of them used to belong to Houdini himself. He's very good too.'

'Houdini?'

'No, Anhanga. He's always fiddling with something: packs of cards, coins, playing tricks. It's more than a hobby, that's for sure . . . and . . .'

'And?' prompted Mina.

'And I quite liked him, to tell the truth. Seems to know his onions. We talked about the mine, about how he heard about my work, and how he thinks I'm – get this – *one of the best geologists working in my field* . . . which is why he offered me the job. How's *that* then?'

'Oh, George!' chuckled Mary. 'No wonder you were in such a good mood when you got home. That's marvellous news!' She raised her glass in a toast. 'Cheers!'

'Cheers!' George smiled, and finished off his beer. 'Aaaaah! Smashing.'

Jacob and Mina joined the chorus of approval but inside they both felt increasingly nauseous. This was *exactly* what Thespa Grymm had described as Anhanga's modus operandi: the flattery, the stroking of the ego.

Soon it would be promises, a little favour here, a corner cut there. The phrase 'one of the best geologists' stuck in Mina's mind. Pretty soon Anhanga would be whispering in her father's ear that he could be *the best* in the world if only . . . if only . . .

'So what's he like, Dad?'

'Who?'

'Mr Anhanga.'

'Didn't I say?'

'No, not really.'

'Well, he's a bit intense at times, but then again—'

The sentence was cut short by the jangling of the old brass bell behind the front door. George jumped to his feet. 'No need to explain now. You can see for yourself.'

'See for myself?' Mina felt Jacob scoot over to stand behind her as she stiffened.

'Yes. That'll be him now.'

'Who?'

'Mr Anhanga. I invited him over to dinner.'

The figure that confronted them as they sidled into the hallway behind their parents was a bit of a let-down. When George opened the door, their visitor was motioning to the driver of the long black limousine that had dropped him off, and all they could make out was the back of a tattered black overcoat.

What they saw beyond this disappointingly sober shape, on the other hand, was shocking to the core: as the electric window of the car slid smoothly up they saw the bottomless dark eyes and shining bald head of Cleaver Flay. Jacob, hanging onto the back of Mina's sweatshirt, was trembling. 'I thought Thespa said we were safe here.'

'We are, we are,' hissed Mina with more confidence than she really felt. Why was she angry with *Jacob*? Get a grip.

'Mr Anhanga,' said George, stepping forward with hand outstretched. 'Thanks for coming.'

'Much thanks for inviting me,' said Anhanga in a dark and accented voice that sounded to Mina and Jacob like the carapaces of thousands of insects scrabbling over each other. 'Very decent of you, Mr Lipton.'

'George, please. This is my wife, Mary, and behind her are Wilhelmina – Mina – and Jacob.'

Anhanga, when he stepped into the hall and they could get a good look at him, was still a let-down. Of medium height – certainly no taller than George – he looked like . . . like nothing at all. Under the bedraggled topcoat he wore a black three-quarter-length frock coat, and under that a waistcoat and shirt of the same colour. His black hair was cut razor-short, like a helmet, on his small round head. Try as they might, neither Mina nor Jacob could find anything to pin their preconceived ideas on to. He was evil personified, wasn't he? He was corrupting Grymm, turning the locals into bizarre interpretations of their deepest, darkest desires. And here he was, in their house, shaking hands with Mary and smiling charmingly. There were no fangs, no talons, no claws, no horns; there was just an ordinary man dressed like a magician who'd hit hard times. And that *face*. A round face with high cheekbones and not an ounce of fat on it. It was a face so commonplace, so mediocre, that you'd see it a dozen times every day. He could have been anyone – the man in the souvenir shop, in the newsagent's, the butcher, the baker, the— That was *it*! Anhanga's face seemed to be an ever-shifting combination of his victims. He didn't just seduce and corrupt them, he *sucked* part of them into himself.

And as he turned from their parents to look at them directly for the first time, they saw faint, fleeting images of Flay, Fleur, Bluehammer and many, many more. They looked like people trapped under the ice of a frozen lake. All the good in them was there, drowning in the murky waters at the core of Anhanga's soul.

And Anhanga saw that they saw.

'And you musts be Jacob and Mina,' he whispered. 'I hears you was quite the heroes today.'

Once again, his voice brought to mind dank

underground nests teeming with hard-backed insects. He pronounced every word with care, not at ease with the language. And in doing so he gave life to each one, hatching them from some pulsating egg sac in his mind and sending them out to skitter, featherlike, up the children's spines and into their brains.

They found themselves involuntarily touching their ears, expecting to find some many-legged insect trying to wriggle its way in.

'My! Good news travels fast here,' laughed Mary with a proud glance at the 'heroes'.

'Yesses, I hears they were . . .'

The children froze. Would he tell their parents about the factory? They had, after all, destroyed a whole wall and written off a large truck. George might even lose his job.

'. . . very braves.'

'Yes, we heard that too. We're very proud of them. Can I take your coat, Mr Anhanga?' said Mary.

'I'd rather keep it on if you don'ts mind, Mary. I feels the cold.'

'Not a problem, Mr Anhanga. Come into the lounge and have a drink. I can always turn the heat up.'

'No, please, I'm fine,' said Anhanga. 'But a drink would be belcome. After *you*.'

Jacob and Mina staggered aside as he scuttled past

them, led by Mary and followed by George, who frowned at them as if to say, *Buck up, you two, let's not have a repeat of your little performance with Ms Grymm.*

In the lounge, George and Mary set about making Anhanga welcome with drinks and a selection of peanuts, dips and olives. He, in turn, perched on the edge of an armchair, the layers of his clothing gathered around him like folded wings.

But while Mary and George fussed around him, chatting inanely about the mine, the future, the move from the city, all Mina and Jacob could do was sit tensely together on the sofa opposite him as if in a double-sized electric chair. They were mesmerized by his every move, by how his cheap, stained clothes seemed to shine in the dim light, how the layers appeared to part and shiver and fold over each other with the noise of eggshells rubbing against eggshells.

And all the time he chatted to their parents, smiling at their jokes, complimenting them on the nibbles, on the roasting smell emanating from the kitchen, he stared at Mina and Jacob with fascination. No, not so much stared as *examined* them, for his eyes never stopped moving, taking in every twitch and movement, every detail of their postures, clothes, hair . . . *pores* even. It was the look of a predator stalking its prey.

And then he picked up an olive . . . in both hands

. . . and began to take tiny, tiny bites out of it. With this simple act, everything came together in their imaginations: the layers of black, shiny clothing, the threads hanging off here and there, the noise, the odd, skittering walk. Anhanga was like an insect, a giant, flying, vampiric cockroach-thing.

He smiled again then, the same non-smile as before, and they suspected he had *let* them see his true form. Not only that, but when George and Mary both had their backs turned for a moment, he suddenly shimmered, rose up a little and shook himself so that his wings shuddered, opened and closed.

In that instant they saw that the frock coat and the waistcoat were merely part of the monster's multi-sectioned abdomen, and there, *there*, in the shadows of the overcoat, were several folded insect-like legs that clawed against each other in protest at being contained in such a manner. Or did they? Was it just Grymm again, playing tricks on them? Or were they doing it themselves?

'So, children, how do you likes Grymm so far?' he asked them in his strangely garbled voice, as if his vocal cords were caught mid-transformation.

Mina could take no more. With a strangled cry she leaped up and dashed from the room. Jacob sat there for a moment longer, transfixed by the puzzled stares of George and Mary, before he ran after her.

'Delayed shock, I think, Mum,' he shouted over his shoulder. 'From the accident. I'll see if she's OK.'

Upstairs, he followed the retching sounds to the locked bathroom door. He knocked delicately. 'Mina? It's Jacob. Let me in. Let me in. I've got an idea.'

The door was unlocked, wrenched open savagely, and a dishevelled Mina appeared just long enough to grab Jacob by the shirt-front and pull him inside.

'What?' she barked. 'What? I don't know whether I can keep this up, Jacob. He . . . he's . . . *ugh*!'

'Yeah, and so was Thespa when we first met her, and we imagined she was a witch.'

'You mean . . . ?'

'I reckon we're letting our imaginations run away with us. Again. Everything we've heard today convinced us old Coathanger was a monster and so when he turns up here . . .'

'*We* turn him into one? Oh, Jacob, you're a genius!'

'Yeah, all right, all right, just don't start again with the hugging and the kissing and stuff.'

'Sure. So what now?'

Jacob raised a curious eyebrow. Wasn't it obvious? 'Well, we go back down there. We just have to convince ourselves that he's just a man. Probably not a very nice one, but a man, not some sort of insect person.'

'Ugh! When all those legs started moving——'

'Mina! There were *no legs, no wings, no insect bits.* OK?'

'You're right, you're right. I'm letting myself get carried away. Oh, Jakie, when will this all stop? I'm so *tired.*'

'Me too. Let's just get through dinner in one piece. Then we can sleep. C'mon, let's make sure your dad's not getting sucked in by Anhanga any more than he already is. You with me?'

'Yeah. Do I look all right?'

'Apart from that bit of carrot on the side of your face, you look fine.'

'What? Where? Oh, you horrible beast!'

'Serves you right for the *Jakie.*'

'Did I say Jakie? Did I? It's a term of endearment, honest. Jacob? Jacob! Wait up!'

By the time they got back downstairs Mary and George had thrown open the big double doors leading to the dining room. They'd pulled out all the stops for this dinner with George's boss: dining table, place mats, embroidered napkins, the best silver, the best china. The main lights had been turned out, leaving the room lit by candles in large, multi-armed candlesticks.

With the large lump of crisp-looking pork as the centrepiece to the table, surrounded by silver serving platters heaped high with steaming, glistening vegetables, the effect was of decadent opulence. Jacob was reminded of Dickensian Christmas scenes, of tables piled high with goodies while, outside, beggars starved in the street. Of course, Dickens never mentioned the occasional fat and seemingly well-fed fly that had to be shooed away from the table.

George, who was just cutting into the meat, gave a cheery hello as they returned and sat down. They could see their dark, distorted reflections in the windows that ordinarily looked out over the parched back yard.

'Are you all right, sweetness?'

'Yeah, just a bit of delayed shock, that's all, Dad. An early night'll fix it, I reckon.'

Mina turned to Anhanga, who was sitting at the head of the table to their right. He looked, once again, like a magician whose act wasn't playing too well. Any trace of giant cockroach was gone. *Jacob was right.* 'Sorry about that, Mr Anhanga. Too much excitement in one day.'

'Not to worries, my child. I trust you is feeling better?'

'Much.'

'Good, because your parents, they have prepared a' – and here he waved a hand at the spread before them – 'a *feast*.'

'Oh good,' muttered Jacob.

'A bit of everything, Mr Anhanga?' asked George.

'Just a very few vegetables, George, but do not hold backs on the meat. I *love* something recently deceased on my tongue.'

'Well, I don't know if this was *that* recent but the guy at the mine insisted it was the best.'

'Trust me, George,' said Anhanga with a quiet laugh, 'if it came from the mine it most certainly was only killed recently.'

'Really?' said George. As he carved and placed piles of the pale white meat onto everyone's plate, Mary added vegetables, waved away a couple of persistent flies, and served the finished dishes, Anhanga first. 'So someone round here keeps pigs? It seems an odd place for a piggery.'

'That is one of the joys of Grymm,' said Anhanga with relish. '*Nothing is quite what it seems*. We might be a long ways from anywheres but nobody can holds a candle to our Mr Flay. He has skills beyond compare.'

Mina and Jacob, up to now contemplating the plates piled high with food before them, looked up sharply.

'Well, he's done a good job here,' mumbled George through a mouthful of food. 'Thish ish delishous.'

'George!' hissed Mary.

'Do nots worry, Mary. Is good to see a man enjoys his food. Not so, children?'

285

'It smells great,' said Jacob. 'That crackling looks brilliant.'

It obviously wasn't what their 'guest' was expecting. Out of the corner of his eye Jacob could see Anhanga scowling. What was it he'd told Mina? *We just have to convince ourselves that he's just a man.* And if it worked for the man . . . then this was just an ordinary roast dinner. And the more he told himself that, the more appetizing it looked. From her little smile, he knew that Mina was thinking the same. Anhanga wasn't going to spoil this for them. They just had to concentrate. Anhanga, he saw, was finding it hard to contain his anger.

Bite me! Suck that!

'This is great.'

'Mmmmm,' agreed Mina, stopping only to wipe some gravy off her chin. 'Trrific. Oops.'

You'll see, you'll see! Fee fi fo fum, I smell the blood . . .

'You're a mucky pup,' scolded her father good-naturedly. He was, Mina realized, more contented than he'd been in a long time. Certainly since her mother had died. And why wouldn't he be? He had his new family around him, a good, well-paid job and a boss who seemingly thought he was the bee's knees. Mina found herself both happy for him and at the same time immensely sad that it was all a lie. And that somehow she and Jacob had to try to take it all away from him.

The dinner was a great success, with even Anhanga seeming to relax and enjoy himself. He was now a far cry from the sticky, rustling cockroach *thing* that had so sickened her earlier – thanks, Mina was sure, to Jacob's level-headedness. And if they could do *that*, then maybe, together, they could do anything if they put their minds to it.

Mary poured herself some more wine, picked a waterlogged fly out of her glass, and suggested in a tone that wasn't a suggestion at all that Jacob and Mina clear the dishes away and wash up 'while the adults talked'. Mina bristled but Jacob took the lead and quietly began doing as he was told. This was no time, he told Mina in the kitchen, to lose focus.

Afterwards, when they were sitting around the dining table drinking coffee and hot chocolate, Anhanga wondered if it would be 'appropriate' to perform a few party tricks. 'I always carries my cards with me,' he explained, reaching into an inner fold of his jacket and pulling out a sealed packet. 'Closes to my chest. Ha–ha! Is a joke, yes? Closes to my chest?'

George and Mary laughed quietly, lulled by the dim lighting and the relaxing flicker of the candle flames, and settled down under the spell of Anhanga's deep, droning voice and flickering fingers. The children weren't so easily persuaded. Anhanga seemed, to Mina at least, to have aged. Here was a being, she thought, who has been talking, persuading, wheedling, playing tricks, parlour or otherwise, since time began. But somehow, it didn't matter. All that mattered was the tale, not the teller.

'Magicians . . . *tricksters*,' whispered Anhanga as he tore open the pack and began shuffling the cards, 'has always been among us. Often they was also storytellers, telling tales and using sleight of hand to confuse and amaze their audiences in return for, perhaps, a meal or a beds for the night. They aroused wonder, and *dread*, in their primitive audiences as they sat around their firesides at nights . . .'

He fanned the cards out with smooth, practised dexterity, showing them that it was an ordinary deck. Both sides. Hearts. Diamonds. Spades. Clubs. It was a gesture that said, *Trust me, I'm not here to trick you.*

'That wonder and dread has today been vanished from our lives and homes by the inventing of electrickery; why be afraid of the night when we can banishes it with the flick of a switch? Why gape at a card trick when you can shines a bright lights on it and expose it for what you always knew it was: a trick of the light, a twist of the wrist? Which is why we sit here among the tallow and wick of days gone by, to allow the night in, just a little. To give the darkness the idea that here, perhaps, is somewhere it can gain a foothold. And to fool ourselves that this might just matter, that magic might actually still be out there, begging to be let in.'

Gradually they drifted deeper and deeper until the room became insignificant, as if seen through the wrong end of a telescope. All that mattered was the cards as they twisted and slid around and against each other. Flick, flick, *flick*. There they all were, sitting around a candle-lit table, listening, listening and watching.

'Pick a card,' whispered the magician with a knowing smile. 'Pick a card, George . . . any card.'

As George contemplated the proffered pack, Anhanga turned to face the children. 'The secret is to makes your . . . *victim* believe that he, or she, is making a choice on their own. They're not. They never are, or the trick wouldn't work.'

As he talked, Mina gradually got the feeling that he was talking just to her and Jacob.

'Today, George,' said Anhanga, looking not at him but at the children, 'today would be good.'

George finally plucked a card from the pack, looked at it and, in time-honoured fashion, put it back.

Anhanga looked angrily at him. 'Who told you to do that? Who tells you to put it back? How ams I supposed to find one card amongs that lot? Jesus, George!'

And with that he threw the cards down, face up,

scattering them across the table. 'What was it? What card did you pick?'

'The f-f-five of clubs,' stammered George, not sure if this fit of pique was part of the act or not. Mina and Jacob froze, too scared to move. There was an increase in the buzzing from the flies that seemed to follow Anhanga around. Would he show his true colours? Was this *it*? Would they all disappear now like the fairground people? Would Thespa find the house empty tomorrow, the front door flapping in the hot desert wind?

'Find it!' hissed Anhanga. 'Find the five of clubs and we'll start again. *Noch einmal. Une autre fois.* OK?'

George quickly shuffled through the pack as Mary and the children watched in fascinated, horrified silence. Anhanga too watched, like a vulture perched patiently on a mountain top as its next meal slowly expired in the valley below.

'It's not there,' said George finally. 'It's gone.'

'Well, thanks you, George.' Anhanga grinned. 'What good is a fifty-one-card pack? It's justs as well that I brungs a spare. Now what did I do with it?'

Then, suddenly, his right hand whipped out like a striking snake and brushed past Jacob's left ear. Jacob grunted, jumped backwards and raised his hands in defence until he realized that Anhanga was now holding a five of clubs.

'There it is! No thanks to you, George. Luckily Yacob here had that particular *carte* in his ear. Thank you. Thank you.'

'That was amazing, Mr Anhanga,' said Mary with an excited clap of her hands. 'We're so close but I just didn't see anything. Really quite wonderful. Tell us how you did it.'

'Ah,' said Anhanga with a bobbling shake of his head, 'if I did that then the magicians' guild would track me down and . . . kill me.'

'Ha-ha-ha! They take these things seriously, don't they?'

'And then they would kill you . . . and then they would kill your whole family.'

Silence again, then. A hot, humid, sweaty desert silence. A fly passing slowly in front of Anhanga's face. Just for a heartbeat or two before he gave a laugh – a sound that was high-pitched and somehow not funny at all. 'Yes, Mrs Lipton, they take it very seriously. Now, children, has anyone got a coin?'

And so they played on into the evening as the candles flickered and Anhanga made coins appear and disappear, changed cards from hearts to diamonds and back again. And all the time he wove word spells about magicians past and present, about the joys of misdirection and the beauty of well-executed sleight of hand.

Finally Mary yawned and eased herself upright. 'Would you like another cup of coffee, Mr Anhanga?' she asked.

'That would be lovelys.' He grinned, plucking another coin out of thin air. 'Blacks with no sugars, if you pleases.'

Then, when Mary and George had disappeared into the kitchen, he turned to the children, leaned towards them conspiratorially, and grinned even wider, showing a set of eerily white, almost pointed, teeth. His eyes sparkled with mischief and . . . *joy*? Yes, thought Mina with a shock, *joy* – he's *loving* this. It's all just a game, another trick, to him.

'Have a goodly times today, did we?' he hissed. 'Don't worries – I suspects there's much more where that came from. I is going to rings the changes in grey old Grymm. Oh, you have *no idea*! But you will, you will.'

'What do you mean?' croaked Mina, her voice sounding too high and too young in her own ears.

'Mean? Oh, before you two beautifuls arrived it was all too easys. These . . . these . . . mugs here are too simples, yes? You know? Whereas you twosome – there's something differents about you twos. Grymm *likes* you. The town, that is. And that changes everybing.' He paused again, looking deep into their faces, assessing, wondering, plotting. And then he seemed to come to a conclusion. 'You know, I think our little worldy here is going to be much more *funs* with yous in it. *Much* more funs. Yessiree Jimbo.'

'Who are you?' asked Mina with a sneer.

'Mina, Mina, my little wormy Wilhelmina – I'm the Anhanga. That is all. I'm on the lookyout for some funs and games here in funny old grim old Grymms. And I think you two munchkins will provide it. Has you not guessed yet? Has you not read your fairy tales? Oh, the young peoples, the young peoples with their modern world. No history, no histories. Has you not seen that you has all passed through the lookings glass, beyond the rainbows? Does you not remember the Brothers Grimm? Jacob and Wilhelm? And their nasties stories? Has you not thought about it? Oh yesss. So, shall we let the games begins? Ho-ho-ho! There'll be laughter and tears before the fat lady sings! Which reminded me: how *is* Thespa?'

'She's fine, no thanks to you.'

'Good. Was she any helps in finding Bryan? Ooh, I can sees from your faces that she wasn't. All talks, that woman. All talks. What would you thinks if I told you I have him, all tied ups in a nice neats little bundle?'

The children stared at him in astonishment until Jacob found his tongue.

'Where?'

'Well, that would be tellings, wouldn't it? No, no, no, you don't gets Bryan back — and he's safe and sound, to answer your next questions. I think we'll just sit tighted and sees what else Grymm is going to serves up.'

'You talk as if the town's alive,' said Mina.

'Oh, but it is, little Wormina, it is. After a fashions. Dead and alive, I like to calls it. Dead and alive. A warning, though: have your funs, enjoys our little towny, but don't interferes with *my* business. Not all fairy tales are for children, you sees. And—'

Before he could go on, the kitchen door opened and Mary returned to the room. His voice changed again. 'You see, children, the trick is to be one steps ahead, to know what your enemy — sorry, audience — is eshpecting, to make them looks over *here* when they should be looksing over . . . *there*. Learn how to do that and . . . and . . . well, the world is yours . . . Ah, coffees! Thanks you, Mary. You is most kindliness. And I hears on the gropevine that you is an accomplished artist! Would it be impertinent to ask to sees your works?'

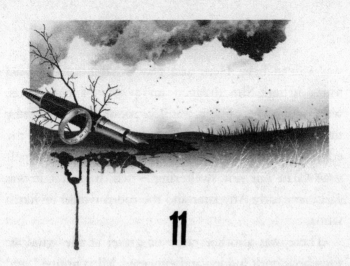

11

Mina was dreaming of an insect-faced magician in black top hat and tails throwing daggers at his beautiful assistant through a pane of glass, when she realized that it had, as dreams do, drifted almost imperceptibly into reality. Not all of it, of course – just the faint tinkling noise as the daggers seemingly passed through the glass *without breaking it*.

One moment it belonged to another time and another place, surreal and vaguely impossible, and then it also began to sound very much like small stones rattling against a window. Without it, she suspected later, she would have slept for ever. Or at least until some gorgeous prince had fought his way across the burning desert to kiss her pale, death-damp lips.

Instead she bolted out of bed. She remembered: this was *GRYMM*. Nothing was as it seemed. Yesterday it was a dead baby, Fleur and Flay; what horrors would today bring? She dragged on a pair of old shorts, wondering what time it was. The room was dimly lit by the chinks of faded pink light that crept around the edges of the thick curtains Jacob's mother had put up. It was warm but not sweltering – which meant it was early, *very* early. Any later and the room would be like a sauna.

There was another rattle of gravel at the window, somehow both sudden and expected. Mina jumped, and frowned. Should she look? *What* was out there? With another start she wondered if perhaps she was *still* dreaming; hadn't the episode with Bryan seemed real enough?

One thing was for sure: dream or not, she wasn't facing this thing alone. She tiptoed across to the slight figure half tangled in its light bedsheet and placed a gentle hand on its slim, tanned shoulder. Jacob was frowning in his sleep. Or rather, the half of him she could see was frowning – his features were squashed against the pillow as if he had been dropped from a great height and landed on his face.

'Jacob! Jacob? Wake up! Jacob.'

'Go away,' was the response, achieved without moving a muscle, without opening his eyes.

Mina shook him again. 'Jacob!' she hissed. 'There's

somebody – some*thing* – outside. Please! Wake up! Remember where we *are!*'

Like a dissected frog touched by electrodes, Jacob leaped up and out of bed. He was wearing only striped boxers and was a little unsteady on his feet, and still half asleep, but ready for action. Sort of: he was still clutching his green bag.

'Wha? Wha?'

Mina couldn't help but smile at this skinny apparition – hair askew and eyes wobbling wildly in their sockets. She grabbed him gently by the shoulders and tried to bring him back down to earth. 'Jacob, it's me, Mina. Wake up. I need you to wake up, OK?'

Gradually his eyes began to focus on her face. He looked, she thought, like a drowning man surfacing. But not in a panicked way – more as if he had finally accepted his fate and was puzzled that living was an option.

'I was dreaming,' he mumbled. 'Dreaming about . . . What's that noise?'

'That,' explained Mina as she released him and tossed him his jeans and T-shirt, 'is why I woke you up. I think someone's trying to attract our attention, and I'm not checking this out on my own.'

Wide awake now, Jacob got dressed and joined Mina at the window. In unspoken agreement they each grabbed one side of the curtains and – one, two, *three* – yanked them apart. Quickly they pressed their faces against the glass – there was no way they could sleep with the windows open no matter how hot it was – and peered down.

They were expecting . . . anything. Fleur with a suspicious meat pie, maybe; Cleaver Flay waving a severed head, even. What they got was Jacob's mother, standing at her easel in the bright early morning light and throwing what looked like handfuls of dark dirt – at least they hoped it was dirt – at a shock of a painting that looked like the end of the world seen through the eyes of a madman. Bits of the sodden earth clung to parts of the canvas while the rest dribbled down like snot on a toddler's top lip. In the middle of it all, pulled together with bits of wood and wire, was what looked like the smashed remains of Grymm itself.

When Mary, in a paint-spattered shirt and jeans, turned to look at them, they noticed that she was wearing a gold WDM ring and her teeth were filed to vicious points—

Then there came another rattle of gravel on glass, and Mina sat bolt upright in bed.

A dream! It was *all* a dream. A dream within a dream! Except the rattling at the window was still going on.

With a weird feeling of déjà vu, she tiptoed across

to Jacob. Sure enough, he was frowning in his sleep. 'Jacob! Jacob? Wake up! Jacob.'

'Go away.'

'Jacob! There's somebody — some*thing* — outside. Please! Wake up! Remember where we *are*!'

'Wha? Wha?'

'Wake up. I need you to wake up, OK?'

'I was dreaming . . . What's that noise?'

'I think someone's trying to attract our attention, and I'm not checking this out on my own.'

As in Mina's dream, Jacob got dressed and joined her at the window. Would her dream come true? Would Jacob see his mother painting the end of the world? She grabbed one side of the curtains and yanked them apart to reveal . . . Thespa Grymm, throwing handfuls of dirt up at them. When she saw them she waved and mimed for them to come outside.

'It's only Thespa.' There was something akin to relief in Mina's voice.

'It's weird,' said Jacob as they watched the chunky black figure mouth words and wave her arms around. She seemed desperate to talk to them. 'I'm actually glad to see her.'

'Maybe she's found Bryan.'

A heavy silence descended at the mention of their missing brother and they quickly busied themselves getting ready to face whatever Grymm – the town and its namesake – was going to throw at them. Mina, in particular, was impressed with Jacob's reaction – he was displaying a maturity she hadn't seen before. Maybe she was going to have to raise her own game; get past the pettiness and jealousy.

They crept through the still sleeping house, down the stairs, into the hallway, through the laundry and out the side door. The sun was just poking its head over the horizon, bathing the desert, Grymm and them in a soothing pink glow. It looked peaceful, warm and, yes, almost beautiful.

Thespa was waiting for them at the corner of the building, where she enthusiastically embraced them both in turn. Jacob wrinkled his nose in disgust over her shoulder, but despite the alarming lack of deodorant he was pleased that she was there – she was warm and cuddly and safe, and proof that not every adult in Grymm was *completely* mad and bad. When everything was said and done at least they still had Thespa – odd as she was – and their parents. It wasn't *all* bad. Was it?

'After yesterday's antics I thought I'd see how you are. So, how are you?' she asked, sticking a cigarette in her mouth and flicking open her lighter. She sucked deeply of the smoke and exhaled it through her nose. Jacob thought it was one of the most revolting things he had ever seen. It was like watching a gargoyle's head just before it spontaneously combusted.

'Well, we had an unexpected visitor last night.'

Thespa looked shocked. 'You did? I really didn't think he would send anyone, not after—'

'He didn't send anyone. He came himself. For dinner. Dad invited him.'

'My, my, my! And?'

'And nothing. He came, had dinner, did a few card tricks and went home. We went to bed before he left but we heard him talking to Mum and Dad for a while, and then he was gone. He was—'

'Weird,' interrupted Jacob. 'He talked foreign, like, and he said he was looking forward to us being here. Said Grymm would be more fun with us in it. *And* he said *he's* got Bryan.'

'He was *laughing* at us,' snarled Mina. 'He thinks we're *funny*. He thinks it's all a big game, said it was a fairy tale.'

'To a certain extent he's right, of course. Not about being funny, Mina, so calm down!' Thespa took a huge suck on her cigarette that made the end glow like lava. 'No, you stirred things up somehow. Things *are* different now. I'm not sure about Bryan, though; it's not Anhanga's style. Not so far anyway.'

'Well, I don't care,' said Jacob emphatically. 'I've had

enough of it. This isn't our fight.' He held his hands out in exasperation and as he did so, something in his bag – as usual slung over his shoulder – rattled, metal on metal, and once again Mina wondered what else he had collected.

'So we just give in? Forget everything that happened yesterday?' said Mina.

'Yes! No! Oh, I don't know!' Jacob glared at Thespa, who was watching their exchange with a fascinated frown, and jabbed an angry finger in her direction. 'It's *her* fight. This is all about *him* and *her*. How did we get mixed up in it?'

'Jacob,' said Mina tenderly. 'What about Bryan? *He's* our fight, isn't he?'

Jacob stopped in full flight, his words dying in his throat as he realized that he *had* forgotten all about Bryan. And yet last night he'd gone to bed praying for the return of the poo machine. They were only talking about him moments earlier! Was this another of Grymm's insidious effects? Out of sight, out of mind? Was he too starting to forget his half-brother? He suddenly felt ashamed, and guilty.

Mina, for once, didn't follow up on her advantage, and instead felt like giving her stepbrother a hug. She wanted to let him know that she understood. She was also finding it harder to remember what Bryan looked like. And Jacob, well, he looked so young, and so alone. She took a step forward, putting a hand out to touch his arm, unsure whether it was the right thing to do but needing to do something.

'It'll be all right, Jacob – we've got each other.'

He turned away from the physical contact but at least managed a croaked, 'You're right, you're right.'

'So what now?' Mina asked Thespa Grymm.

'I'm not sure,' whispered Thespa, polluting the crystal-bright morning air with another mouthful of cigarette smoke. 'I think Anhanga had a busy night last night . . . You know the mining protesters?'

The children nodded, and Mina thought involuntarily about Eric Elland.

'They're gone.'

'Gone?'

'Yes. The tents and stuff are still there but the camp's abandoned. It looks like they left, or were made to leave, in a hurry.'

'Like the funfair people?' asked Jacob, recalling his 'vision' of their fate.

'Just like that, yes.'

'They're gone.' There was a note of dread in Jacob's voice that made Mina's flesh crawl. 'Gone', she thought, could easily have been replaced by 'dead'. '*He's* taken them into the mine.'

'And?' asked Mina with a sinking feeling in her stomach.

'I'm not sure but it's nothing good,' said Jacob.

'No, it's not.' Thespa grimaced. 'But look, it doesn't matter. What matters is finding— What's that noise?'

On the one hand, the noise that reached them faintly from the front of the house made a change from Bryan's nerve-shredding screeches, but on the other, it was something the children had never, *never*, heard: their parents arguing.

Mina ran across to the back door and wrenched it open just in time to catch the shrill noise of her stepmother screaming, 'And don't come back! I hate you!'

There was a moment's silence – before the kitchen door was flung open and slammed with enough force to make the whole house shake. Outside, the 4WD coughed into life and roared off with a tyre-burning shriek.

What on earth was going on?

'It's Mary and Dad,' muttered Mina to Jacob, who just looked back at her uncomprehendingly. 'That was them shouting at each other. It sounded serious. *Really* serious. Oh, Jacob, you don't think they're going to split up, do you?'

Yet another of their deepest wishes seemed on the verge of coming true. Mina and her dad would be together again, two against the world. Jacob wouldn't have to put up with Wilhelmina the witch any more, or with George's awful jokes. And yet the thought of the other not being around was suddenly too awful to contemplate.

'Is it Grymm, do you think?' asked Jacob.

The kitchen was a mess. Neither of them had seen anything quite like it. A box of cornflakes had been up-ended across the table and there were scrambled eggs on the floor. Two wet tea bags sat on the kitchen counter in the middle of spreading brown pools. Several slices of blackened bread smouldered in the toaster.

And in the middle of all this sat Jacob's mother. She was nursing a cup of tea and looked up at them in surprise, as if coming back from a long way off. 'Ah! Kids! Ms Grymm! Help yourselves to breakfast. I'm on strike until your father apologizes.'

'For what?' asked Mina.

'Oh, just something small that got out of control, that's all. It's fine, it's fine. It'll be fine. Hey, Jacob, what about a nice cup of tea for your mum? This one's luke-warm. Ms Grymm? Can I get the kids to make you a nice tea? Coffee?'

'Er . . .' For once Thespa Grymm seemed at a loss for words.

'Are you all right?' interrupted Jacob, alarmed.

'Nothing that a fresh cup of tea won't solve,' said Mary. 'And, Mina, how about some toast? With strawberry jam, please. Don't you think it's amazing, Ms Grymm, how spoiled children are these days? Never lift a finger to help, expect everything to be done for them. It's our own fault, of course, because we indulge them too much. So, what's it to be, children?'

They just gaped at her.

'Nothing? Right. Fair enough. I'll be upstairs painting if you need me. I think I should concentrate on my painting again rather than running around cleaning up after everyone, don't you? Beersheba thinks I should.'

'Beersheba?' blurted Mina.

'Yes, seems she runs art classes at the back of her store. She's very accomplished. I might just take her up on her offer. She was very complimentary about *my* work, that's for sure.'

'But—'

'But, but, but . . . Now off you go. My apologies, Ms Grymm, but I'm at the end of my tether. Yes, off you go, kiddiwinks! Off you go. Leave Mary to slave at home. I'll cook and clean and dust and rub the brass till it shines. George can bury his head in his geology books or rock samples, trying to impress his new boss, and everything will be spick and span when you get back. Or maybe it won't.'

And with that she walked out of the room and stomped upstairs, a door slam the final punctuation.

'What,' said Mina, mostly to herself, 'was that all about?'

'Your mum will be fine, I know she will,' said Thespa. She didn't sound convinced. 'It's just an argument. Don't worry. All parents have them.'

'Ours don't,' corrected Jacob. 'Never. They never argue.'

'Perhaps they were due one, then?'

'She said she hated him.' Jacob was now close to tears. 'I don't get it. She talks about my dad all the time but she never says anything about *hating* him. George is going to leave us like my dad, so why—?'

'I think, Jacob,' whispered Thespa, 'that you are too young to understand.' She put a pudgy arm around his shoulders and looked into his face. A stale miasma of cigarette smoke and underarm sweat enveloped him. 'You have to realize that love and hate are not two sides of the same coin.'

'What?'

'Hate is not the opposite of love, my dear boy. The opposite of love is indifference. The opposite of hate is indifference. I think that's why your mother feels at ease talking about your real father – she just doesn't *care* any more. Do you see? She's angry with George because she loves him so much. Only someone you love could drive you so completely mad.'

'Shows what you know,' sulked Jacob, his arms folded across his chest.

'Oh, believe me, I know about this stuff. I wasn't always such a . . . witch, you know. There was a time when— A tale for another time, perhaps.'

'It's this town, isn't it?' said Mina. 'Or the visit from Anhanga last night. Or both. They'll be as mad as you lot before long. No offence.'

'None taken. And you may be right. Or it may just be a silly domestic argument – probably not the first but certainly the first they've had in front of you two – and it will all blow over by dinner. Either way, I think it's time I went back to my office to see if I can think of a way to get your Bryan returned to you. What are your plans today?'

'N-nothing much,' stammered Mina. 'I think maybe we should stay here. See what's happening with Mary. Clean up the mess in the kitchen.'

'Good idea. I'm off then.'

As she made to leave, though, Jacob had one more question. 'Thespa – how did you get up here? It's too far to walk.'

'On my broomstick, of course. I parked it out the back.'

Jacob goggled at her: so she *was* a witch after all. They stepped out into the warm bath of the day and watched as Thespa Grymm waddled round the far corner of the house and came back with . . . a small red 125cc motorbike.

Mina smiled. 'You are such an idiot.'

Thespa, on the other hand, just winked at him knowingly as she threw a ham hock of a leg over the slim motorbike and settled her gargantuan bottom on the little seat. The bike groaned under the weight and sent out a series of clicks and twangs that Jacob suspected were Morse code for 'H–E–L–P–M–E'.

'It turns into a broomstick just round the corner, Jacob,' she laughed around the inevitable cigarette before turning the key and bringing the machine to life with a throaty roar. With a not-so-dainty thrust of her foot, she clanked it into first gear and, holding grimly onto the handlebars as if the bike were a horse that wanted to buck and throw her off, she gently hit the gas, put–putting away with a gentle fart, hardly even disturbing the gravelly sand.

They watched with amusement as the tiny bike bounced slowly along the rutted road with the large black-clad figure of Thespa Grymm in her open-faced black helmet balanced precariously on top of it like a sack of coal on a pogo stick.

'She looks like a cartoon character,' said Jacob. 'Do you think it does turn into a broomstick round the corner?'

'I doubt it.' Mina shrugged. 'That's bike's suffering enough – I can't imagine a broomstick that could carry her, can you?'

'So what now?' asked Jacob. He knew the answer but wanted his fears confirmed.

'Now we clean up the kitchen and make your mother tea and toast.'

Later, as they cycled into town, Grymm served up yet another surprise. The anti-mining protesters' campsite was a disaster zone. The tents had been pulled to the ground and slashed to pieces, the oil drums pulled over, the fires kicked around until the embers had set fire to anything flammable. A few placards remained but the rest had been trampled or burned. Jacob stopped and let his bike fall to the ground. He felt sick and scared and angry all at once. Of the protesters themselves there was no sign.

'Oh. My. God,' gasped Mina. She got off *her* bike and laid it carefully down. The first thought in her mind was of the yummy Red. He was *gone*. Gone. She felt her heart sink. And she didn't even *know* him.

'They've all *gone*,' echoed Jacob. 'Really gone. Vanished.'

He was right, but words didn't do justice to the feeling of desolation that hung over the area. In the background the wire fence around the mine seemed to hum mournfully as a heavy warm breeze blew through, taking smoke from the few small fires that still smouldered and dispersing it. An armed sentry stood in the shadow of the gate office and watched them without interest. The world went on but this little piece of it felt . . . tainted. Something had sucked the life out of the place and replaced it with an emptiness, a moral vacuum, that smelled of vindictiveness and death. Here, thought Jacob, *timshel* meant 'thou *must* do evil'.

'Like the people at the funfair, do you think?' asked Mina. *Where was Red?*

They didn't know what hit them, Jacob just knew it. There would have been no warning – or at least none that they would have recognized. A few extra fat and self-satisfied flies here and there, an irritation around the communal cooking pot? Whatever those things were, they had swept out of the mine like a jet-black tsunami of hate, ripping and chittering and . . . *eating*.

'Just like that, yes. I think so. I think Anhanga lets them' – he wanted to say *devour* but he knew that Mina was soft on the Red boy and changed his mind – 'have their fill every now and then.'

'Them?'

311

'Those things we dreamed about.' Jacob's voice cracked with emotion. 'You know, the ones who . . . you know, with Bryan.' He knelt down then and reached for a handful of red earth. He couldn't tell if it was naturally red or stained with blood.

'We're going to find him, OK?' said Mina, thinking also of Red. 'We will. I know we will. And we'll stop Anhanga while we're at it. I promise.'

'How? We're not even sure what he's doing, or why,' argued Jacob. He squinted up at her, grimacing against the sun. Mina was just a dark shadow against the bright blue sky.

'Well, we know he runs a sad and cheap jewellery business from a failing mine and has managed to corrupt almost everyone in—'

'Jewellery!' shouted Jacob, slinging his green bag off his shoulders. As he dug around inside it, he went on, 'It's the jewellery! The rings! Every time I touch one it feels odd. I *see* things! Look!'

From the depths of the bag he pulled out the ring he had stolen from the souvenir shop. It glinted gold in the sun as he slipped it onto his finger.

'You stole one, didn't you?' exclaimed Mina. 'From Maurie's Mementoes. You crafty little thief! I knew you were up to something. Jacob, that's . . .'

Jacob stood there, staring vacantly into space.

'Jacob?'

For a moment he was completely motionless, his breath coming in short gasps and the blood draining from his face. Eventually, pale as death, he grabbed Mina's hand and held it tightly. 'Oh, Mina. *I see it.* See *them.* All of them. It's not just Grymm. Not any more. It's not just happening here. He's sending them . . . *it* . . . all over . . . It's *out.*'

'Out? Out where? What happened?'

'That's the thing. It's the ring – I see them all. *Everyone* who wears one of the rings. And they're not all here in Grymm.'

'Where are they then?' asked Mina.

'Out there,' said Jacob with a wave of his hand. 'With everyone who's ever passed through Grymm and bought one of those crappy rings.'

'But why?'

'Think about it. Anhanga . . . Loki – who cares what he's called – I think he just wants the world to be as nasty as possible. And he's found a way to do it. I *see* them, Mina,' wept Jacob, now too upset to try to stem his tears. 'Don't ask me how, but I see them.'

'Who?'

'Well . . .' He closed his eyes, concentrated. 'There's a woman in Washington who thinks her husband is having an affair because he works late a lot. It *used* to be an idle thought but now she's obsessed with the idea. She *thinks* she knows who the other woman is . . . and she's bought a gun.'

'You can't possibly—'

'Or there's the man in London who stays at home and looks after the children while his wife works. It's getting too much for him, driving him crazy. They never stop crying and moaning and want-want-wanting, the little b—'

'Jacob—'

'Or perhaps the guy in New Delhi whose wife's snoring has kept him awake for years. A pillow over the face would do it. That's all. And then he could get a good night's sleep.'

'Jacob, stop, you're—'

'And if she turns that friggin' map round one more time I'm gonna get the tyre-iron out and—'

'Stop it! You're scaring me!'

'A little rat poison in the bitch's sugar should do it; it's about time I won something for best cheesecake . . . And who's to know . . . I could be the best if only he were to fall under a bus . . . It's a long way down . . . No, no, don't cry again, not while I've got the knife—'

'Jacob!' Mina finally slapped Jacob hard across the face. With her other hand she grabbed his finger, ripped the ring off and threw it far away across the deserted camp.

'Wow!' said Jacob.

'Sorry, but you got a bit scary there – are you OK?' Mina was staring at Jacob like she didn't know him.

'I don't know. I kind of got into their heads and couldn't get out. It's horrible! He's using whatever it is that makes Grymm weird and incorporating it in the rings! Or maybe it's already *in* the metal, I don't know.'

'And all *that* really is happening?'

'Sort of. I don't think there are many of them out there yet. But they *will* be. And soon. Think about it – the world going mad bit by bit. Anhanga would love it.'

'And Dad's at the mine now, wearing one of those rings, and Mary's still at home doing God knows what. We have to go. We have to go now.'

'Well, yes, I suppose . . .' mumbled Jacob.

'But not to Thespa.' Mina was suddenly sure that Thespa Grymm wasn't the person to talk to. 'Don't you get the feeling she's holding something back? That there's something she's not telling us?'

'I thought that right from the start. She knows more than she's letting on.'

'OK, well, there's one man in town who might know.'

'As long as it's not Cleaver Flay,' said Jacob, who had

no intention of going near the butcher ever again.

'No, no, not Cleaver – the priest guy? Elland? If anybody knows what Thespa's hiding it will be him.'

'He's certainly the most normal person we've met here. Can we trust him?'

'I dunno, but what choice do we have? He's a priest! And we need help.'

'OK. Where did he say he was working?'

'In the church, going through the parish records.'

'That's where we'll go, then.'

'It's a plan. And, er, sorry about the slap.'

Jacob smiled and touched his face where it still stung. 'Just don't do it again or I'll have to cut your head off and suck your eyes out of their sockets.'

'Don't joke like that, Jacob,' said Mina, picking up her bike. 'Not here, not now.'

'Who's joking?'

St Stephen's church *was* easy to find. A tall red-brick building, it stood alone on the very southern edge of town, surrounded by vacant lots. It was as if the rest of Grymm had shied away from it, turning its back on a leprous intruder. As they approached, Jacob thought it looked like one of those old pictures of the London Blitz, where whole streets were bombed flat except for one solitary building that had somehow escaped.

316

On the way they had ridden along the length of the main street, subconsciously giving a wide berth to Flay's, Fleur's and Bluehammer's shops, and turned into a side street that headed due south. It was here that Mina stopped for a moment, making Jacob screech to halt behind her.

'Whoa! What did you do that for? I nearly ran into you.'

'Sorry. Just a bit hot, that's all. I need a drink. You should have some too. Keep hydrated.'

'Thanks, Mum,' grumbled Jacob, but still stretched down to grab his water bottle.

From their vantage point they could see, off to the right, the ramshackle backs of the main street shops. Past them, the forbidding wall of Cleaver Flay's abattoir loomed outwards; a dead-end in more ways than one.

The other side of the street was lined with old one- and two-storey houses built from whatever flotsam and jetsam their occupants could find, and then abandoned. Cardboard, the tops of old tables, rusty corrugated iron, slabs of breeze block; it was a lesson in makeshift architecture. Wire fences sagged out front, no longer able to protect the houses they had once surrounded. In one garden a washing line was punctuated with coloured pegs bleached by the sun. Here and there among the detritus a few hardy cactuses survived –

though they seemed to be frozen in time, caught in the act of breathing in, a final sucking up of the last few molecules of moisture from the dust and then . . . nothing.

'Can it get much hotter?' Mina murmured to herself. She tipped a little water into her hand and patted it around her neck. Her white T-shirt was plastered to her back with sweat, and there were dark, wet patches under her arms. If Jimmy Flynn could see her now. Or Red.

'You ready?' She glanced at Jacob, who had squirted the dregs of his water over his face and was wiping it backwards through his black hair. With his prominent widow's peak he looked, she thought, like a Chinese Dracula.

'What?' he said. 'What's so funny?'

'Nothing. You OK to go? It looks like a bit of a ride.'

'Yeah, let's go. Let's get this over with. Do you think he can help us?'

'Who knows? It can't hurt, though, can it?' said Mina with more confidence than she felt. 'We'll do this, and before you know it we'll have Bryan screaming in our ears again.'

'Who'd have thought it?' Jacob was as surprised as anyone at how much he wanted the hated Bryan back again. He stood up on the pedals and pushed away from Mina. 'Let's go. Last one there's a girl.'

As they rode onwards, the houses on either side began to peter out – not so much that they weren't there but more because they had been cannibalized by unknown hands or had simply collapsed under the weight of a sun more punishing than any bulldozer. With the road not too far ahead of them undulating in a heat haze, and the wood of the buildings on either side faded to an almost uniform snow-white bone colour and texture, Jacob and Mina felt like they were cycling through the scorching Martian equivalent of an elephants' graveyard.

Gradually the houses dwindled, each more dilapidated than the last, each more covered with dust and sand, until they disappeared entirely. To Jacob they looked like the skeleton of some huge and ancient beast that had charged through the desert but had somehow been swallowed up by the earth itself, floundering around as if in quicksand and gradually, inexorably, disappearing.

'And I thought town was the middle of nowhere,' said Jacob as they cut across an empty corner towards the church.

They propped their bikes against the wall and went in. It was cooler inside, but not much – the large stained-glass windows on either side saw to that as they focused the sun's rays like magnifying glasses. But despite the long oblongs of brightly coloured light that fell across one side of the interior, it still took a moment or two for the children's eyes to get used to the general gloom.

'It's not much to look at, is it?' Jacob pointed out needlessly.

'It's a church, dumbass. What were you expecting? Choirs of angels? God?'

'Well, given that it's in Grymm . . .'

'Hmm, I see your point. Hello? Anybody there?'

Mina's shout echoed around the church, off the walls, around the pews, against the altar and the large statue of an agonized Christ on the cross at the far end. It bounced high up into the timber rafters that supported the pitched roof and fell, dead and ignored, at their feet.

'Mr Elland?'

Again, nothing but a dead echo.

'I hope we haven't come out here for nothing,' grumbled Jacob.

As they spoke, though, a bright light cut through the gloom to the right of the altar as a door they hadn't noticed before swung open. Light from the stained-glass windows twinkled off two huge, glittering eyes as the shadow of a head poked through the gap.

'Can I help you?'

'Mr Elland?' asked Mina, stepping forward, followed by Jacob.

'Yes,' said the voice. 'Can I help you?'

'I bloody hope so,' whispered Jacob to Mina as they walked over to him.

'Ah! Jacob! Mina! To what do I, er, owe this, um, honour?'

'We just wanted to talk to you about something,' explained Mina as they arrived at the door. She heard the rustling echo of her own voice fade away above her, like the final, panicked spasms of a pigeon caught in the rafters.

'Well, come, come in then,' he said, and promptly disappeared behind the door. From inside whatever room it was they heard chairs being dragged about. 'Come in. Come in, come in out of the heat. It's the only room with, air, er, air-conditioning so it's wonderfully cool.'

They entered hesitantly, fearful that Grymm would live up to its reputation and greet them with something grotesque or out of kilter. Instead they found a room stacked – occasionally in neat piles but mostly tumbling haphazardly across the floor – with pieces of yellowing paper and dusty editions of what looked like old newspapers. There was the smell of long settled dust and musty sweat. It was, at least, cooler than outside.

'Welcome to my humble abode,' said their host,

sitting behind his stacked desk. He was holding an old-fashioned fountain pen in one hand and smiled a disarmingly genuine smile.

Jacob and Mina, standing side by side, grasped each other's hands and said nothing. The man nodded. It was as if he understood and accepted their reticence.

'Sit! Sit down, sit down. Make yourselves at, um, home, please.' He gave them a lopsided smile that was both amused and sad, as if he knew exactly what they were going through.

Mina sat down opposite him but Jacob moved off and began poking around the piles of papers that had slithered off their stacks like landslides. He had the air of someone who had one ear and one eye on the lookout.

'So what can I do for you?' asked Elland.

'Well, we've got some questions. About the town. We thought you might be able to help.'

'Oh yes, yes, indeed, please do, fire away!'

Jacob and Mina glanced at each other: had they finally found an adult in Grymm who wasn't insane? An adult who might even believe their stories? Might even help them? Mina, though, still wasn't ready to trust him.

'Can I ask you, Mr Elland, why you're writing a book about Grymm?' she asked.

'Isn't it obvious?' As he rubbed his hands together with delight at the idea, the children both noticed that the fingers on one hand were stained red. They also noticed with relief that he *wasn't* wearing a fool's-gold ring. 'Grymm, where *nothing's quite what it seems*? Heard that? Right? From Thespa? Right? Am I right? Certainly not, er, from Cleaver – he's a man of few words, right? Lets his "work" speak for him, hmm? If this isn't a, um, a story worth telling, then what is? The godless town that went mad and died of selfishness . . . eh? Eh? What a story!'

Jacob held up a copy of an old newspaper and blew off a layer of dirt. 'And all this stuff?'

Elland bounded over enthusiastically, reminding the children of an over-excited Labrador. He thumped a hand down hard on one of the piles, sending a cloud of dust into the air. 'Research. Research. Research for the who, the what, the where, the why and the when of it. It's all here, you see, the whole of it. Grymm. All the little, er, secrets, the little vices, all the . . . well, *everything.*'

'But why hide out here?' Mina was finding the man's enthusiasm disconcerting. 'Why not just take all this back to the city? Write it there? In comfort.'

'What? And let *everyone else* know about this place? And anyway, I'm the parish priest. Free accommodation and, given the, er, size of my congregation – *zero* – not much work to do. And this is *mine*. This is my passport to, you know, um, fame and fortune. There'll be prizes, of course, when this comes out. No point being second past the whatsit – the, er, post, eh? Eh? Second best is the same as last, right? Good enough isn't good enough, eh? Am I right? Of course I am. Ask Anhanga. *He* knows. Clever man. Knows a good story when he sees one.'

Jacob sighed; so Anhanga had got to him too. 'How long have you been here?' he asked.

'Long? How long?' Elland pondered the question for a moment and then dismissed it with a wave of a hand and a shake of his head that almost dislodged his spectacles. 'Long as a piece of string. It will take, ah, as long as it, ah, takes – a book is only as good as its research. There's history here, you see – long before your time, or my time. *History*' – he said the word as if it had ten times as many letters in it – 'is here and now, and also then and there. It's the key; the key to it all.'

'Yeah. I see what you mean,' said Mina, not seeing at all. Jacob, meanwhile, was rummaging through a pile of papers that threatened to tumble off an old, wheeled office chair. He stopped when he noticed a faded, sepia-toned photograph taped to the wall nearby.

'Mina!'

'What?'

'Look at this!'

'Ah-ha!' Elland grinned as he followed Mina over. 'The protagonists! Well, some of them, anyway.'

The photograph – cracked and torn and mended and creased and re-mended with now-desiccated tape – showed a group of men and a few women standing around what the children took to be the entrance to an old mine. They were all dressed in the old-fashioned clothes of a century or more ago – too hot and far too heavy for either the terrain or the climate. Some struck haughty attitudes; others hefted shovels or pickaxes. One figure, a man obviously more important than the rest, stood a little further in the foreground. He wore a black suit, black hat and sported suitably dignified mutton-chop whiskers like overgrown grey hedges that needed shearing.

'The founding fathers of Grymm,' Elland chortled.

Mina leaned in and squinted at the caption under the photograph. '*In the foreground . . .*' she read out loud. '*Oh!* It says that's Mr Henry Grymm.'

'Yeah,' agreed Jacob, 'he looks just like Thespa, with a beard.'

'There is a bit of a likeness, isn't there?' agreed Elland. 'Got that photograph from Mr Anhanga.'

'You've met him?' asked Mina as they peered at the hirsute ancestor of Thespa Grymm.

'It's him I have to, er, thank for being where I am,' he babbled. 'I was just going to write something short for the parish newsletter when I found out about the, um, massacre of the native tribes for the land; pretty cold, *that* was. After that it was Mr Anhanga who, you see, uh, put me on to all the rest of it – the "accidental" deaths of the Chinese miners who struck gold . . . the deaths, the disappearances and . . . of course, somewhere along the way I lost my, you know . . . God.'

He paused and squinted at them, eyes blinking and brow furrowed, as if weighing up how much he could tell them, trust them. Then, like the blind rattling down behind Cleaver Flay's front window, he obviously decided that he couldn't. 'Well, as you can see, it's a *big* story. Won't go into details just yet, eh? Right? Sure you understand. Top secret and all that, eh? I can trust you two to keep it under your hats, right? Right?'

'Sure, sure,' agreed Jacob quickly. He was certain that Mina felt the same – that it was probably best just to agree with Eric Elland for the time being.

'One thing, though . . .' added Mina. 'What's the story with the rings? I see you're not wearing one.'

'The rings? The rings! Yes, yes, stay away from the rings. They make you *do* things. *Let* you do things. It's all the, er, badness, you see, the *rage* that seeped out of the burial grounds where the original settlers disposed of the bodies.'

'Bodies?' said Mina and Jacob in unison.

'Oh, yes, didn't you know?' Elland shuffled through

the papers on his desk and came up with a sheaf of handwritten pages. 'Didn't Thespa *tell* you, the naughty old witch? Here, here, here . . . let me read you some of my, er, pages. The manuscript, you see. First draft, of course, so, well, you know. Ahem! And I quote: *While gold ushered the township into existence, the land . . . the land, with all its secrets, has always been here, and was known by many other names before the white man arrived and "claimed" ownership. What the indigenous people called it has been lost in time. A word, a name, an explanation, that existed for 40,000 years died one vast, dry, white-hot day when white men herded hundreds of indigenous men, women and children into a natural stone amphitheatre and shot, clubbed or knifed them all to oblivion. The sun wasn't the only merciless thing that day.*

'*Perhaps that name was the final word on the lips of the last man to die, staring at the cloudless sky as his blood was sucked thirstily into the ground beneath him. Perhaps it was a curse. Perhaps it was simply the saddest dying words in the world: "I wish . . ."*

'*There were certainly curses on the lips of the Chinese miners who discovered a massive seam of gold in Grymm fifty years later. As the charges the white men had laid behind them brought the walls of their tunnel down around their ears, they called on ancestors halfway around the world. Their screams embedded themselves into the very earth itself as those unlucky*

enough to survive the initial blast lay trapped deep under-
ground, their flesh shredded, their bones smashed.

'*And, high above them in the earth, did the shallow-buried,*
bleached bones of four hundred natives stir in response? In
anger? In revenge? And sitting above it all, the town of
Grymm rode into the world on a golden wave of prosperity.'

He stopped there, dipped his fountain pen into the
inkpot on the desk and added a squiggle before looking
up again. 'Hmmm, not bad, if I, er, say so myself. And
a Grymm has had a hand in it *all*, you see. Thespa's
Grymm's ancestors are *why* the town's so . . . er . . . So
you see, you see? It's *in* the gold, all that rage and, um,
hatred. Thespa's people came here and, well, you see, just
decided that they wanted these lands and began, um,
cold-bloodedly massacring the native tribes. Most were
just, er, buried where they fell. And then, decades afterwards, came the deaths of the hundred or more Chinese
miners who struck gold in the 1880s and were
"accidentally" buried in a mine explosion . . .' Elland
paused and buried his head in his hands. When he lifted
it again, he looked fifty years older and there were tears
in his eyes. His stuttering manner of speech had also disappeared. 'My God, children, can you imagine it? So
much *death*. So much *rage*. So many voices crying out. Is
it any wonder Grymm is stricken the way it is? I've
prayed for their release but I don't think God is

listening. Not to us, anyway. Not out here. Grymm was built on – quite literally built *on* – death and greed and hatred and destruction. And I believe that . . . *badness*, that *rage*, has seeped out of those burial grounds. I think it has seeped out from those bodies, from those angry souls, and I think it has infected whatever they're digging out of the ground at the mine. I think it seeped into the gold somehow.

'Have you noticed how so many people in town are wearing those awful rings? Or some other piece of tacky jewellery? I see that you have. Well, that's the other thing – I think the rings accelerate whatever has been happening in Grymm. Think about it – all that hatred, all that fear, all that thirst for revenge . . . all *that* concentrated in a ring or a bracelet or an earring. Have you not noticed it, Jacob? You of all people?'

Jacob just stared blankly at the man. What *was* he going on about? 'Eh?'

'The miners, Jacob, the miners were all Asian men. Hundreds were killed or trapped deep underground when those charges went off. Can't you feel them? Feel their anger?'

And then Jacob got it: even here it never ended. 'What? Because I'm half Chinese? Because my dad—' Rage forced him to choke off the words. He sat down on a chair and seethed quietly at the man.

'I'm sorry, Jacob, but blood is, er, thicker than water, as the cliché goes. I thought you might have had some, um, *affinity* with the fate of these men. I see I was wrong. My apologies. But mark my words; you too, Mina. Stay away from the, ah, rings. They make you . . . *do* things. *Let* you do things you wouldn't normally do. I'm convinced of it. It's all here, in the church records. Oh, they left acres of parish records, those long-ago monsters in the shape of Christian men. Acres of, you see, um, *tales* about their deeds, their pride in the town they created. It makes me sick to think about it.'

'Our parents . . .' whispered Mina. 'They got some of that jewellery on the first night we got here. It was a present from Mr Anhanga at the mine. It might explain why they were arguing this morning.'

'Just be careful. From what I've seen it doesn't happen overnight. You might find it really was just a petty spat and nothing to do with the rings at all,' said Elland soothingly. 'I don't want to, um, scare you unduly.'

'Nothing could scare us unduly after three days here,' snapped Mina. 'One last question, though – what's with the fountain pen?'

'The electricity supply isn't too good out here. Lost a couple of early drafts like that.' Elland grimaced at the thought of his lost words and wandered over to his desk.

He sat down, one hand absent-mindedly patting the top of a pile of paper that the children assumed was his work-in-progress. It was covered in scribbles. Mina decided that Eric Elland could do with a few hand-writing lessons – it looked like a spider had scuttled through a bottle of spilled red ink. 'Typewriter ribbons have all, er, gone. Used them up early on.'

'So what do—? Ouch!' Mina jumped as Jacob trod on her foot.

'Sorry, Mina,' said Jacob with a surreptitious glare and an almost imperceptible nod of the head that said *Shut up and let's go*. She frowned in return and began looking around for whatever it was that had spooked him.

'Thanks for helping us, Mr Elland,' Jacob was saying as, again, he edged towards the door, 'but we really need to get going. Mina?'

Mina saw it then. Or rather *them*. Dozens of tiny puncture marks on the inside of both Elland's arms. She looked at Jacob, as if to confirm what they meant. He nodded and then looked meaningfully at the desk again. *The pen*, he mouthed. *The pen*. And there it was, sitting there on the table, a shiny golden nib spattered with Elland's blood. He might not have been *wearing* a ring but Anhanga had made sure he'd gone one better – he was dipping the infected gold directly into his veins.

'Let's *go*,' said Jacob.

'Thanks, Mr Elland,' Mina said, trying not to look at his arms or the manuscript or the pen.

'Good luck,' replied Elland. He hadn't moved from his desk – his obsessive determination to get back to his book now almost palpable. 'Let me, er, know how you get on! You might get a whole, um, er, chapter to yourselves!'

'Yeah,' whispered Jacob to himself as he and Mina left. 'A whole chapter to ourselves *if* he doesn't run out of blood first.'

12

Back on the main street, they were surprised to find the place, for once, alive and full of people. Burly miners in sweatshirts that lived up to their name were ferrying covered trays from the bakery to a large truck that idled at the kerb, belching grey smoke. The same was happening at Flay's shop, with Flay himself coordinating efforts so that nothing would get dirty. He was dressed, as usual, in his striped apron, boater and faintly ridiculous yellow rubber gloves. As they cycled by – giving him a *very* wide berth – he glared at them and growled under his breath.

Further up the street Beersheba Bluehammer supervised the loading and strapping of her large 'Cat's Cradle' exhibit onto a flatbed truck, helped by Inky Bugleslab and Smudge from the gas station.

The sun wasn't yet at its height but the slight shimmer of heat along the street gave the scene a surreal, other-worldly look — as if someone had waved a magic wand, awoken all the courtiers in Sleeping Beauty's palace and they had staggered out into the real world through centuries of dust and cobwebs.

'What's happening?' asked Jacob of nobody in particular.

'No idea,' said Mina. 'Perhaps Thespa will know.'

Inside the office, before Thespa could greet them or even wrestle her bulk up from behind the desk, Mina went on the attack. 'You lied to us!'

'Quite possibly.' Thespa scowled through the habitual pall of smoke. She settled back and eyed them up and down. 'I lie about a lot of things. I could say I quite like your pendant, for example, but I wouldn't mean it. What did I lie about that's got you so hot under the collar? Are you all right, Jacob? You look a little warm. Want a cold Coke?'

'About the town. About your part in it.'

'Who's been . . . ? Ah, that. Yes, well . . . Look, please sit down. You're making the place look untidy. Pretty please?'

Mina and Jacob did as they were asked, a little taken aback by the change in tone. Thespa looked embarrassed more than anything else. And as they sat, she stood up and lit a cigarette, even though she'd just put a lit one in her ashtray. She winced as smoke drifted into one eye.

She looked, thought Jacob, like a huge one-eyed fish, goggling at them from the depths.

'You've been talking to Eric, I take it? Yes. Yes, I can see you have.'

'Yeah.'

'I am starting to dislike that man, I really am. Would feeding him to Cleaver be out of the question?'

'Mr Elland told us all about you killing those people,' spat Jacob. Even to himself he sounded like a child singing 'Na-na-nana-na!' What an idiot.

'Me? I most certainly did *not* kill anyone. Now, my ancestors . . . well, they were a different kettle of fish completely.'

'Why didn't you tell us?' asked Mina.

Thespa snarled at them, grey teeth gritted in a grimace full of hatred and contempt. A fleck of errant tobacco stuck to one front tooth so fascinated Jacob that he had trouble *not* looking at it. Thespa slowly pointed at them each in turn, flicking her cigarette around with practised ease and holding it like chalk towards a blackboard.

'Look at you, and you: *Oh, Thespa Grymm's a witch; oh, Thespa Grymm's stolen our baby; oh, Thespa Grymm's from a long line of mass murderers.* You are *children* – you would *not* have understood, and anyway, I do *not* have to explain myself to *you*.'

'You feel guilty, don't you?' said Mina in surprise. It had come to her in a flash: Thespa Grymm had stayed there in the desert, watching her friends and neighbours become monsters, because of her guilt at what had been done in her name so many, many years ago. 'You *can't* leave. Your conscience won't let you but you don't know what to do to stop it.'

'Yes, well, thank you for your profound insight, Mina,' said Thespa, turning away. Was she crying? 'But it's all too late. Have you seen what's happening out there? Something *big* is going on, and my invitation seems to have been lost in the post. I think before the day is out, we will find out what Anhanga's doing and—'

'But I *know*,' interrupted Jacob. 'I *know* what he's doing.'

'You do? How?'

Jacob's explanation was drowned out by the roar of a large truck bearing the initials WDM as it thundered past the door.

'What?'

'It's just that, well, it's the rings, you see. They *tell* me stuff. They've been telling me stuff since I got here but I didn't realize until today. Not really. The thing is, I now realize it's not just Grymm that'll be affected. He's going to send them out, hundreds and thousands of them, all over the world. The madness . . . Oh, I can't remember – it was so clear when I was wearing the ring.'

'You put one *on*?' gasped Thespa. 'Jacob, that's so, so dangerous. You never know what—'

'Luckily I took it off him and threw it away,' said Mina.

'Yes, but you didn't' – Jacob smiled as he dug into his green canvas bag and pulled out a shining gold ring – 'get this one.'

Mina grinned at him. 'You little thief, you took *two*?'

While Mina was marvelling at her stepbrother's audacity, Thespa was lunging towards Jacob. '*No!*' she yelled.

But Jacob was too fast for her: he tipped his chair backwards and fell to the floor, just out of reach of her grasping hands. As he did so, he slipped the ring onto his finger . . .

This time, though, he didn't see the demon-thing, didn't see the madness that Anhanga was intent on unleashing upon the world, didn't see the rocks crushing the life out of the miners or the blood-covered Grymm family bludgeoning natives to death . . . This time was all the more shocking for the peacefulness of the scene before him. Expecting hell on earth, he instead saw a quiet desert clearing, enclosed by a ring of rocks that looked vaguely like a sleeping dragon, and dotted with a few dry, utterly defeated trees whose branches creaked uneasily in a skittish breeze as warm as the air from a hair-dryer.

But he didn't just *see* it; it was much more than a vision – it was as if he was actually there. He felt the wind ruffle his hair, felt the burning heat of the sun on his forehead and cheeks. A bead of sweat ran down the middle of his back. He knew there were patches of sweat under his arms. And there was the *smell*; he knew that smell. It was the smell of meat that you take out of the fridge only to find that it's way past its sell-by date, sort of gamey and sickly sweet. But the source wasn't just a dodgy steak, and that knowledge started a nameless fear nibbling away at his innards. Despite the heat, he shivered as a cold wave of revulsion, and the urge to puke, rolled over him.

The soil in the clearing, he noticed, was red and rich and undisturbed; there were no animal prints – no lizard had ever skittered, tail swishing, across *this* stretch of ground. Indeed, nothing living, Jacob realized, ever ventured here. For this was where *it* happened. Where *they* happened. This was where God or whatever had given the inhabitants of Grymm the choice – *timshel* – and where they had failed so miserably. And despite the years in between, despite the earth and rocks and dust and sand that had been piled on top of bodies long turned to dust and bone, the stench of putrefaction still rose up out of the depths and clung to the surface.

It was like a thin coating of rancid oil covering everything. Jacob held his hand out in front of him and seemed to feel an oily resistance as it moved through the air. No wonder nothing moved here. He brought his hand back and examined it. It felt dirty, as if something inhuman had seeped into his skin through the pores. *So this is what evil feels like*, he thought. *Or hate? Or fear? Or vengeance?*

And then he realized something else – it was the clearing in his mother's painting!

And then it was gone.

'Jacob! Jacob!'

He opened his eyes to find Mina and Thespa crouching above him. Thespa had something akin to understanding in her eyes. Mina shook him roughly and then clasped him to her. She had ripped the ring off his finger, he knew, and tossed it into a corner. It was OK, though. He knew he wouldn't need it again. 'Jacob? Are you all right?' she cried.

'I . . . I think,' he stammered, 'I think I have a plan. But we're going to need Mr Elland. We'll have to go to the mine and we'll need a diversion . . .'

'Elland?' Mina was aghast. 'But he's been' – she struggled for the right word – '*contaminated* by Anhanga.'

'Exactly,' said Jacob.

★ ★ ★

Later that afternoon, as the day's shadows grew longer, three shapes disengaged themselves from the darkness around the remains of the truck that still sat like a squashed bug by the side of the road into town. The ragged hole in the wall of the Puzzlewicks' candle factory had been patched up badly and hurriedly.

'If I'm right,' said Thespa as they approached the building, 'they'll be up at the mine with the others, doing whatever it is they're doing today.'

'What if it's locked?' Jacob was keen to break into his bag of mischief and wreak a little havoc.

'Out here?' Thespa laughed. 'Not a chance. Who's going to steal anything? And what? A candle?'

As before, the bell behind the door tinkled merrily when they entered and they were hit by the sweet smell of wax and perfume and acid. The machine that the Puzzlewicks called Balthazar was ratcheting and banging on, noisy as ever, as they threaded their way through the factory and up the stairs to where they had fought their battle with Flay and the Puzzlewicks. It all, thought Mina, seemed so long ago. The blue wax 'body' was gone but the candles were still flickering.

They each grabbed a candle and moved off into the tunnel beyond the roller-door. Suddenly all three candles guttered in an unexpected breeze.

'If these go out I'm going to scream,' warned Mina in a high, strangled voice that bounced against the rock walls enclosing them. The tunnel, once so big and so cool, now seemed much, much smaller and much, much hotter.

'Me too,' said Thespa.

'Me three,' said Jacob. 'But it's not far now.'

Thespa was panting heavily when they emerged onto the plateau overlooking the mine buildings.

'*We're in,*' whispered Mina as they hunkered down behind a tumble of boulders.

But where previously the great rock bowl below had been empty, now it was a carefully controlled ballet of monster trucks, rigs, eighteen-wheelers, lorries, vans and forklift trucks, all weaving in and out and past each other without incident. And in between, a host of men in dusty jeans, work boots and sweaty shirts walking, talking into radios and passing on orders with shouts and well-rehearsed signals. There were also massive vehicles with giant wheels which dwarfed the men in hard hats. They could feel the rumble of these leviathans even up where they were hiding.

'Just watching them,' puffed Thespa, wiping the sweat off her brow with a stained handkerchief, 'is making me tired. My, it's hot up here.'

'Where is everyone?' asked Jacob.

'There are about fifty people down there. Isn't that enough for you?' Mina waved a large fly away from her face.

'No, I mean Cleaver, Fleur and the rest. Weren't they coming up here?'

'Whatever's happening is probably happening underground,' suggested Thespa. She waved a hand in front of her face to scare off a couple of flies. 'And have you noticed something else?'

'What?'

'The flies?'

'The flies,' said Jacob. 'Of course. Too many of them. On the backs of the men who came to town. Every time Anhanga's involved. In my vision of the fairground people . . . and when I was up here last.'

'Flies, yes, and where there are flies there's . . . decay. There's evil here for sure, children,' whispered Thespa. 'We must be extra careful.'

'Look!' Jacob was suddenly alert, the word whispered but also urgent and clipped. They followed the line of his outstretched finger and saw what had grabbed his attention: three figures leaving one of the flimsy buildings. It was Cleaver Flay and, loping along in front like some evil upright cockroach, the black-coated figure of Anhanga. They were heading across the open ground to a pair of wooden doors set in the mouth of a smaller cave entrance much like the one in which Mina, Jacob and Thespa now hid. It was a door none of them had noticed.

'Oh, Flay . . .' murmured Thespa.

Anhanga held up a hand and stopped so suddenly that Flay almost collided with him.

'Shit!' whispered Jacob, ducking. 'How could he hear that?'

Thespa glared at him to be quiet. Below them, Anhanga did the same thing to *his* companions and paused, head cocked to one side, as if unsure of what he had heard, if anything. His gaze swept across the cliffs surrounding them, across the scurrying men and the vehicles, across the entrance to the candle factory tunnel. Several of the men faltered in their work as they felt his stare pass over them.

Jacob, Mina and Thespa froze, unable even to wave away the flies that now settled on them, for fear of Anhanga seeing or hearing them. They each closed their eyes and gritted their teeth as the insects scurried back and forth over their skin, flying up and plopping down again, investigating tightly pursed lips, ears and the corners of eyes. Mina felt the bile rise in her throat.

She was just about to give in to the impulse to wave them away when a series of guttural clicks echoed around them. *Chit-chit-chit-chit-chit*, they went, on and on, surrounding them, washing over them. And they knew that it was Anhanga, searching them out with some kind of bizarre echo location. One move and he would know they were there.

CHIT . . . CHIT . . . CHIT-CLICK-CLICK-CLICK-CLIKCLIKCLIKCLIKCLIKCLIKCLIK-CLIKCLIK . . .

Even the flies stopped moving.

CHIT-CLICK-CLICK-CLICK-CLIKCLIKCLIK-CLIKCLIKCLIKCLIKCLIKCLIK . . .

Jacob, Mina and Thespa held their breaths.

CHIT-CLICK-CLICK-CLICK-CLIKCLIKCLIK-CLIKCLIK . . . CLIK, CLIK, CLIK . . . CLIK.

And then it stopped. The flies resumed their investigations, and the three intruders breathed a sigh of relief. When they dared to look out from their hiding place, Anhanga had resumed his ungainly walk across the clearing. Even from where they crouched, it seemed as they could hear the scurrying of insects as his clothes swished back and forth. Finally he reached the sun-bleached wooden doors at the base of the cliff, where Cleaver Flay, his bullet-like bald head shining in the sun, undid the padlock and moved aside to allow him to enter. He, in turn, surveyed the area with his blank, black eyes before stepping backwards and gradually, eerily, bit by bit, fading into the darkness behind him.

'That was close.' Jacob collapsed into the dirt and gulped down the air he'd been afraid to breathe in case Anhanga heard it. But that was impossible, wasn't it?

'Too close,' said Mina, waving her hands angrily about her head to get rid of the flies. She was oddly pleased to feel the light *pock* against her palms as she connected with them. 'Are you all right, Thespa?'

'I'm rather disappointed.' Thespa smiled grimly. 'I expected him to have grown horns at the very least.'

'Be careful what you wish for . . .'

'You're right, we mustn't allow ourselves to get carried away. Much of the power of any bully comes from *our* fear. Isn't that right, Jacob? Jacob?'

But Jacob was gone, crawling crab-like down the incline, skittering from one bit of cover to another. A rock here, a discarded piece of machinery there. He didn't even look back.

'What is the matter with him?' growled Mina. 'He'll get us all killed.'

'I think,' mused Thespa, 'that's what he's worried about. Come!'

Jacob reached the doors without being seen, and slipped inside what turned out to be a small dark cave with two passageways leading off from the rear. In the cool stillness he crouched behind a packing case and waited just in case Flay came back. He waited in tense silence until a hand clamped onto his shoulder and he jumped backwards in fright.

'Are you all right?' asked Mina.

Thespa kneeled behind her, agony etched on her face. 'My knees can't take much more of this,' she complained as her joints made a noise like two dry old bones being rubbed together. 'Ooooh.'

'And my heart can't take much more of *that*!' hissed Jacob. 'You scared the life out of me!'

'Well, you shouldn't have run off like that,' said Mina, slapping him on the shoulder. 'From here on we stick together, OK? No running off. Right? *Right?*'

'Yes, Mum.'

'Good. Now which way did they go?'

The two paths confronting them were dimly lit by a series of weak light bulbs strung along the ceiling. One led to the left, one to the right.

'I don't know; they were gone by the time I got here. Eeny-meeny-miny-moe?'

'I think not,' said Thespa. 'Listen.'

At first there was nothing, but gradually they began to make out the faintest of sounds coming from the left-hand tunnel — impossible to identify what, but it was their only clue. Thespa raised her eyebrows questioningly. 'Shall we go?'

Before venturing down the tunnel Jacob quietly

closed the gates to the outside and armed himself with a shovel he found leaning against the wall. He hefted it in his hand and smiled. Mina raised her eyes to the heavens and gave Thespa a theatrical shrug. 'Rambo rides again. Got anything else back there?'

'There's a sort of small sledgehammery thing, but it's quite heavy.'

'I'll take it,' said Mina. 'It might come in handy if we have to deal with Flay again. Sorry, Thespa, but he's over on the dark side, you know he is.'

'Yes, dear, but a *hammer*?' She watched Mina struggle to get the rock-breaker above shoulder height. 'And it's so heavy. Look at you – you're more likely to do *yourself* an injury than Flay.'

'He's got feet, hasn't he?'

'Yes, well, as long as you don't drop it on *mine*.'

The tunnel twisted and turned and, at times, dropped away so steeply that they were forced to edge forward on their backsides. The lights grew dimmer too, and fizzed here and there as water seeped in from above.

'I'm *cold*,' said Mina, shivering.

'Me too,' said Jacob, who was holding the shovel out in front of him like a lance. He glanced back at Thespa, for once envying her the layers of clothes she wore, and in doing so accidentally ran the metal spade straight into the wall.

CRRAAAANNNNNG!

The sounds ahead of them, which, little by little, had been growing louder, ceased, and in the silence they heard the patter of tiny feet.

'Rats?' whispered Mina.

'No,' said Jacob. He had a good idea what was coming. 'Get back.'

They scurried back until they reached a slight turn in the tunnel where a light bulb had burned out. Jacob forced them along a little further and then hunkered down in the darkness with the shovel held behind him like a baseball player waiting for a pitch.

The sound of feet was joined by the prattle of some gibberish tongue. Jacob had heard something like this before, at the fairground, and at the candle factory. And then, as if on cue, something came trotting round the corner – a single dark-grey imp with eyes like a cat and little, perfectly formed hands and feet that ended in razor-sharp talons.

A small gasped '*Oh!*' escaped. It wasn't much of a noise but it was enough. The imp noticed her and Thespa, and broke into an impossibly wide smile that revealed double sets of teeth like a shark. A pitiless snickering came from its throat and it began to advance on them. It didn't see Jacob or spot the shovel as it came slicing through the air until it was too late.

Whoosh! Thunk!

The snickering ended in an abrupt cough of air from its little lungs; air that escaped from the hole where its head used to be. Then it – and its head – disappeared in a putrid puff of smoke.

But no sooner had the smoke and the smell wafted away than another imp rounded the corner and saw them. This one wasn't quite so stupid. It ducked under the swinging arc of Jacob's weapon and leaped onto his right leg, hanging on like some sort of emaciated and evil koala. Jacob stumbled backwards and tried to shake it off while at the same time stopping it from biting his leg off by thrusting the shovel blade between them.

'Mina!' he hissed. 'Help!'

But Mina, who could hardly lift the heavy hammer, was unable to get a clean shot at the snarling, drooling little monster for fear of hitting Jacob. If she swung and missed she knew she could easily break his leg. A few tentative and half-hearted jabs did nothing at all – the imp didn't even notice her.

Then, to make matters worse, a third imp appeared, only this time somehow clinging to the roof like a large four-legged spider – with a wicked-looking curved knife clenched between its silvery teeth. It snickered wildly, seeing Jacob defenceless and vulnerable, and advanced on him from above. As Mina looked on helplessly, it grabbed the knife with one hand and readied itself to leap. Mina gasped, and the breath left her as she realized she was too far away to do anything about it. Suddenly it looked like she would lose the stepbrother she had so despised – and she felt part of herself drain away at the thought of it.

'Jacob!' she cried, and was about to go on when the breath – what was left of it – was knocked out of her body and the words snatched from her throat. She was bowled over backwards towards the tunnel wall and the hammer ripped from her grasp. She had time to wonder whether another imp had found its way round behind them when she slammed into the wall and her head exploded with stars.

The next few seconds were a blur, but she regained enough sense to realize that it was Thespa Grymm who, moving faster than you would ever have thought possible, had crashed into her and was now pulling the hammer back behind her head. In a blur – and a waft of sweaty armpits – Thespa launched the hammer down the tunnel like a javelin. It turned over and over in the air, just missed Jacob, and smashed into the face of the knife-wielding imp with a sound like the top of a soft-boiled egg being cracked open.

Caught in mid-leap as it sought to plunge the knife into Jacob, its little legs still continued working while the top of its bald, round head shattered, spraying a green, jelly-like substance against the wall and onto the floor and roof as it cartwheeled through the air. With a soft squidge – and a clatter as the knife dropped from its senseless fingers – it splattered, pulverized, onto the stone floor. And then it was gone, leaving behind only the smell of something long dead.

Mina could only gape at Thespa, who shrugged.

'School shot-put champion,' she explained.

Jacob, meanwhile, was still trying to lever the second attacker off his leg, unaware of the danger he had been in. 'A little help here, please?' he grunted.

But as Thespa and Mina advanced, the imp, seeing it had lost the element of surprise and that its companions had perished, loosened its grip a little and was tossed to the floor. Jacob shifted his grip on the shovel handle and used it like a baseball bat to thump the creature in the chest with the flat side. With a screech it tumbled backwards, head over heels, and slammed into the wall, stunned.

In an instant Jacob was upon it, the edge of the blade pressed deep into its neck, keeping it pinned against the rock wall. When it regained its senses it began to twist and turn and hiss and spit, grabbing the edges of the weapon holding it down and trying to wriggle away. It was as if it didn't know what a dire predicament it was in, or simply didn't care if it died.

'Kill it,' hissed Mina as she went to pick up the hammer. But Jacob hesitated. Now that the cut and thrust of the fight was over he was in two minds about killing the thing in cold blood, no matter how unnatural or evil it was. Could he do it?

One thing was for sure, the thing understood English. At Mina's instruction, it redoubled its efforts to get free. Not to escape, they were sure of that; it just redirected its hatred towards Mina, spitting and snarling, gnashing its rows of sharp teeth and hurling guttural phrases at her which didn't need any translation.

'She's right, Jacob,' whispered Thespa; she was pressed up against the rock face, wheezing as quietly as she could. 'There could be more. And we certainly can't let it go.'

'But—' began Jacob, only to fall head first as Mina, intent on doing her bit, brought the hammer down on the thing's head with a wet splat and it vanished in the usual puff of putrid smoke.

'You might have warned me,' he hissed.

'Shhhhhh,' said Mina, and motioned them both to drop back into the shadows. 'Thespa's right – there might be more of them.'

They waited a minute. Two. Three. Then Jacob slowly put down his weapon and exhaled, long and slow. There had been only three of them. They were safe. For now.

'Yurgh' – Mina grimaced – 'those things smell worse than Bryan *ever* did.'

'I think it at least proves that Anhanga's been dabbling in a lot more than mining,' said Thespa. 'We must be more careful. There are probably thousands of these things.'

A little further on, a little deeper, a little colder, they came to the end of the tunnel and were confronted by the source of the noises that had led them to this under-world: a massive subterranean chamber full of stalagmites and stalactites. In the feeble glow from light bulbs high above them, Thespa, Mina and Jacob emerged onto a natural balcony high above the cavern.

At the opposite end of the chamber, on a slight rise, twenty or more large trucks sat in front of a roller-door similar to the one at the candle factory.

'The rings,' muttered Jacob, 'ready to go out.'

In the space between, some sort of party was in full swing. There were a few of the remaining inhabitants of Grymm here and there, tottering unsteadily between ice-laden barrels stuffed with canned beer, and a dozen or more burly miners in black scattered among them like blowflies stuck in a vanilla pudding. Mina could see

Maurice Au down there, Margaret from the milk bar, Inky Bugleslab too.

'Look,' said Mina, and pointed across to the right-hand side of the cavern.

It was Cleaver Flay, enormous and spotless in his whites, straw hat and striped apron. His leather belt of knives was tied around his bulky waist and he used them with skilful precision as he sliced bite-sized pieces of meat off a pig carcass that turned slowly on a spit. With deft movements he flicked the chunks across onto a folding table, where Maggot was sweatily folding the meat into buns and handing them out to the guests. As if on cue, the smell of roasting meat wafted up to them. Jacob could feel his mouth watering. Thespa licked her lips and sighed.

'Elland should be in position by now,' whispered Mina. 'Do you think he's OK?'

There was no time for a reply.

'Ah-ha!' shouted a voice the children recognized. It was Anhanga. He was in the middle of the crowd, a black-suited cockroach scuttling from guest to guest. He turned to look up at them. 'Jacobs! Meeeena! What a lubbly surprise. And you've brought a friend. Thespa? I thought as muches. Charmed, I am sures. Do come down and join us – this is an importance day. Come, come, come down. Join us.'

A dark presence behind them was revealed as a Neanderthal-looking miner who had loomed up silently out of the darkness. There was no escape. He escorted them down a flight of stairs and along to the edge of the party before quietly withdrawing. Anhanga came over to greet them. Again, Jacob and Mina couldn't get the image of a giant insect out of their minds. He leered at them and seemed to shiver with pleasure. And again they heard that low chittering, as if a whole nest of cockroaches had just woken up and begun to skitter about. Thespa, on the other hand, seemed immune to him and just sneered and snapped out another cigarette.

'I wouldn't if I was you,' said Anhanga. It wasn't a request.

'Oh?'

'Too many explosivenesses aroundabouts. One bit of ashes and . . . *booooom*.'

Thespa nodded and put the cigarette back in its box. She seemed uncharacteristically quiet. Jacob suddenly realized she wasn't really taking much interest in their meeting with Anhanga. Instead she was standing a little on tiptoe, scanning the crowd. What *was* she looking for?

Anhanga, though, was still talking. 'Well, what a pleasure to sees you both again. And so soonish.'

He moved away with small, dancing steps, further

355

into the crowd, encouraging them to follow him. He gestured to something way off to the left and began walking in that direction. The crowds disintegrated as he tottered towards them, a parting of the waves – but only, thought Mina, because the waves were afraid of what direct contact with this monster might mean.

'Jacob,' said Anhanga, 'would you like something to eat? You look famished. Look, Mr Fleur has brought some of his wonderful pastries with him. I'm sure a boy likes yourself could eat himself to death.'

And there, before them in all his pasty white glory, was the towering and rotund figure of Malahide Fleur, standing beside a table groaning with pastries. Bigger in all respects than even Cleaver Flay, he seemed to take up so much space that the cavern, for a second, didn't feel big enough for them all.

'Boy!' he intoned in a deep baritone that stretched the word out for several seconds. He peered down at Jacob and Mina with eyes so deep set in the fat of his face that they looked like raisins pushed into an uncooked loaf. 'Good to see you both again. Sticky bun?'

The pudgy hand that held out a finger bun oozing with strawberry jam and cream was attached to an arm that was as much fat as Cleaver Flay's was muscle. He jiggled the offering in front of Jacob's eyes and the ripples ran backwards up his arm and disappeared under his shirtsleeve. As if in answer, the jowls under his chin wobbled too.

Jacob was torn. He was hungry, and the bun did look appetizing, and one little bite wouldn't hurt, would it? He reached out.

'Jacob! I think we need to talk to Mr Anhanga in private, don't you?' said Thespa, and gently took his hand. Mina, already starting to think a *mille-feuilles* mightn't be a bad idea, snapped out of the spell too.

'Oh, you is a spoilsporty,' tutted Anhanga. He didn't seem annoyed at all, Mina realized. He just wanted to see what mischief he could wreak. He couldn't help himself.

'So what's the occasion?' she asked, to change the subject.

Anhanga whirled round and pointed to each of the trucks at the far end. 'Our trucks start to leaves today . . . all loaded with trinkets for the peoples of the Earth. Out into the greats wide vorld. Taking our hopes and fears and . . . dreams . . . with it. Hee-hee-hee. And so, we cereblate!'

Thespa, who was still holding Jacob's hand, felt a tremor run through him.

He had been right – *it* was about to escape. They had to stop it.

'Of courses, this is just the beginnings, stage ones of

the great plan,' purred Anhanga. 'We have been vorking hard hard hard towards this day. And vere is plenty mores where this is comings from once eeny meeny Mina's daddy helps us find the deep stuff, the new streamings deep down under us. But you haven't comes here for this.'

He whirled round with a flourish and headed off towards an elevator door set into the cavern wall nearby. Over his shoulder he snapped, 'Flay! Fleur!'

As Mina, Jacob and Thespa fell into step behind Anhanga, the two man-mountains, in turn, took up positions behind them like some sort of praetorian guard.

The elevator that led down to Anhanga's underground office was nothing more than a wire cage suspended over a deep vertical tunnel not much bigger than the cage itself. As they each got in, it creaked alarmingly and trembled and swayed from side to side, scraping the rock of the shaft and sending out screeches like nails down a blackboard.

Jacob couldn't help but look upwards, trying to make out the size and condition of the cables holding it in place above the abyss.

'Don't worries, Yakob,' sniggered Anhanga from where he nestled in the corner, almost hidden by the bulk of Flay and Fleur. 'It's perfectly safes. I think.'

Jacob, in turn hidden behind Mina and Thespa, clutched his green canvas bag closer to his chest. He looked a little sick in the eerie, bloody pink wash sent out by the elevator's red light bulb.

'You know, you should get rids of that thing, little boy,' sneered Anhanga. 'You is like a little babies, sucking on your comforts blanket. Ha!'

Before Jacob could answer, Flay hit the DOWN button and the cage's concertina doors closed with a crash. Mina reached out and grabbed her stepbrother's arm as, with a sudden and stomach-churning downward jerk, the elevator began its journey into darkness – a tiny red light moving through layer after layer of history.

'I don't like this at all,' she said. 'Stop fidgeting, Jacob!'

'It's not me! It's the elevator!'

'Will you two be quiet!' hissed Thespa, who was gripping the sides of the cage as if her life depended on it. 'You're behaving like children.'

Mina scowled. 'Very funny.'

Jacob just closed his eyes, shifting his bag nervously from hand to hand, and rode the rest of the way down in silence. The closer they got to the source of the badness in Grymm, the more his head hurt. It was as if the rings he'd tried on had left bits of themselves on his skin – only a molecule perhaps, but the murdered voices from the past were inside his skull, trying to get out. There was death just ahead, they said. But whose?

To keep this new anxiety at bay he concentrated instead on the small sounds: the creaking, the scraping of the cage on the tunnel walls, Mina's breathing, Thespa's lungs wheezing, the rustle of her many layers of clothing, the increasing cold after the browbeating heat on the surface, the slight thud as they reached the bottom, the rattle as the doors slid apart.

He opened his eyes to . . . Anhanga's office.

And it was more or less as George had described it – a large cavern carved out of the rock and painted red – but he really hadn't done it justice. The room was magnificent; magnificent and yet grotesque at the same time. The walls were covered in bookshelves, paintings and framed antique maps. To their right, a series of glass-topped exhibition cases like the ones you find in museums held other artefacts documenting Anhanga's obsession with magic. A large executive desk stood in the middle, surrounded by boxes and glass-fronted cabinets which held top hats and stuffed rabbits and Tarot sets and oversized playing cards. A saw-the-lady-in-half box was positioned off to the left-hand corner, the saw still embedded halfway through it.

And hanging from invisible wires that must have been attached to the shadowy cavern roof were dozens and dozens of posters, new and old, for magic shows: from Harry Kellar, Burling Hull, Chung Ling Soo and Harry Houdini all the way up to Copperfield, David Blaine and Criss Angel.

As they marvelled at this impressive display, Anhanga slipped away to stand behind his desk, his black clothes gathered around him like a cocoon. He really did look like an insect with a human head, thought Jacob. This close to the source of the town's power it was hard not to let every stray thought, every infinitesimal image, take on a life of its own.

He sat there and just scrutinized them, with a look on his face that was close to disappointment. It was all just too *easy*, his expression said. And as their thoughts began to run riot, so Anhanga started to change. Gradually he seemed to come apart, as if every bit of him were a different insect, all moving in different directions. He was a man, a *thing*, made up of every kind of revolting, dark creepy-crawly you can imagine – and a few more besides from places deep under the earth where no human had ever been. And they – beetles, cockroaches, earwigs, centipedes, spiders, worms – all slithered and scuttled and oozed and slimed, their hard carapaces and thick wings keeping up a constant chitter-chatter as they bumped into each other and clung together with a combination of thousands of clutching, clicking legs, webs and drooping strands of sticky, regurgitated mucus.

Just watching this made all three of his prisoners itch. Mina scratched at a non-existent earwig that was trying to burrow its way into her brain; Jacob was convinced the sweat rolling down his back was a cockroach; and Thespa began to feel as if tiny burrowing worms were writhing just under the surface of her skin.

And all this kept together by the sheer willpower of the entity that was Anhanga. And all that fuelled by hatred and vengeance and the deadly secrets of a town called Grymm.

And then, to their surprise, from the darker depths of the cavern behind him, two pale grinning faces emerged. It was the Puzzlewicks, stepping slowly and carefully, like oversized stick insects, into the glow of the table lamp on Anhanga's desk.

'Thespa, my dear,' said one of them, pointing a deathly white and bony hand in her direction. 'We haven't seen you since . . .'

'. . . you drove a truck through our factory,' finished the other.

'Nice to see you, Frederick, Catherine,' said Thespa dully. 'Up to no good again?'

'Just helping the Anhanga, that's all,' whispered one in a voice that dripped a mixture of love and disgust. Mina noticed that rivulets of melted black wax had solidified on the Puzzlewicks' hands. At least, she thought it was wax. Who knew what they were doing back there in the shadows? In the dim light it could have been wax, ink, or blood. Further back, in the direction they had come from, Jacob, Mina and Thespa heard a faint rustle of movement. Anhanga noticed their interest and smiled.

'Would you like to sees the rest of my little worlds?' he asked after he had, quite literally, pulled himself back together. 'I sees you would. Come. Come.'

He stood up and disappeared – almost floated, it seemed – into the darkness from whence the Puzzlewicks had come, expecting them to follow. Which they did, propelled none too gently by Flay and Fleur. For a moment they were blind, staggering into a darkness so profound as to be almost palpable. All three held their hands out in front of them, expecting at any moment to walk headlong into a rock face. Instead, a faint greyness appeared ahead and gradually grew into a half-moon shape through which they passed into a cavern as large as the one where the loaded trucks were parked above them.

Flickering fluorescent lights around the walls just above head height threw a sickly glow over everything, somehow both revealing *and* hiding the astonishing scenes before them.

Off to their left, a small army of black-eyed imps, mere shadows in the shadows really, swarmed over the fallen rock face with alarming dexterity. There were thousands of them, of all shapes and sizes, some like large deformed cats, others like stunted hairless black rats. They clambered over rubble, rock and each other, disappearing into crevices and holes, collecting little handfuls of glittering ore which they then deposited into the steaming maw of a machine that extended up, up, up into the shadows above them. They were like a colony of ants, intent on one thing and one thing only: serving the king of the 'hive' – Anhanga.

'Do you likes them?' he chuckled, throwing an arm around each of the Puzzlewicks. In return they rubbed themselves against him and purred like kittens. 'I've got Frederick and Catherine to thank for zem, really. Of course, I supplies the recipe but my friendlies here did all the cookings, as it were!'

Mina gazed upwards to where the vast, brass-coloured machine, a seemingly cobbled-together concoction of awkwardly welded metal panels and tubes and hissing pipes, vanished into the darkness above. 'And that?' she asked.

'Oh, that goes ups and ups and ups and . . . well, you gets the idea. And you've seen some of it before, of courses, in the candles factory.'

'It's Balthazar?' squeaked Jacob.

'Yes — impressiveness, isn't it? It takes the ore — such a lovely mix of iron pyrites and all those years of hates and despairing — and converts it into the lubbly jewelleries that's going to go out into the world and spread the Gospel of Grymm. I loves it! Thespa? Impressiveness? After alls, your family started this.'

'This isn't a game. People are going to get hurt.'

'Yes,' said Anhanga sadly, hanging his head as if in shame. 'Yes, yes, they are.' He then waited a beat and carried on, 'It's just so . . . *deliciousness!*'

Games, thought Jacob. *It's all just games. Until someone loses an eye. Or a leg.*

'So' — Anhanga smiled — 'to what do I owe the pleasures of your company?'

'We want Bryan back,' said Mina.

Anhanga chuckled, and was echoed sycophantically by the Puzzlewicks. The imps also joined in, snickering from the shadows but not ceasing in their work. 'Bryan? Oh, *him*. No ideas. I didn't takes him.'

Jacob and Mina stared at each other in dismay. All this, and Anhanga never knew? He had to be lying — didn't he?

'Don't play games with us. He's gone, disappeared as if he never existed — and you did it!' shouted Mina.

'Me?' Anhanga's confusion seemed genuine. 'I don't

have the little thing. Certainly nothings to do viz *me*. And anyway, you *hates* Bryan. You both does. More than you hate each other.'

'Yes, but that's no reason to . . .' stammered Mina. 'I mean, Bryan can't help it, can he? He's just a baby.'

'Indeed he is. Or *was*.'

Both children leaned forward at this change in tense: he'd killed him after all! Bryan was dead!

'No, no, no – *I* don't have Bryan; *you* does.'

'*We* do?' they said in unison.

'Well, *I* certainly don't knows where he is.'

'You don't?'

'*We do? You don't?* Comes, comes, you can does better than that.'

'I don't think *we* have to do better than that,' said Mina tersely. Jacob was glad she'd spoken up because he was beginning to think Anhanga had a point. 'I think it's up to *you*' – and here she pointed an accusing finger at the man – 'to explain what's happening here. We arrived here not a week ago with a mother, a father and a baby brother. Now the brother's gone, we've spent days running away from mad people, our parents are in danger of going the same way as the rest of you lunatics, and *you* seem to know exactly what's going on. I think you *do* know where Bryan is.'

Mina was surprised at her own audacity; if her father

ever caught her talking like this there'd be hell to pay. But then, as far as she was concerned, she'd already been *through* hell, paid, and come out the other side.

'Wrong on all counts, my feisty Wormina. I am *nots* behind what you so charmingly calls *all this*. Well, yes, I am. Ha-ha! Most of it, in facts. *BUT*, I most debinitely do *not* know what *you* have done with Bryan.'

'There you go again: *we've* done nothing with Bryan. We woke up one morning and he'd been wiped off the face of the earth. How could we have done that? And don't call me Wilhelmina.'

'Yeah,' said Jacob, who thought he should at least bring something to the conversation. 'Suck on that!'

'Charmed, I'm sures,' sneered Anhanga before turning his attention back to Mina. 'Listen. You've no doubted realized by now that Grymm isn't a normal, eberyday sort of town, right?'

'With knobs on.'

'Thanks you once again, Jacob. Your contribution is proobing to be priceless.'

'Why don't you leave him alone and get on with it?'

'Such guardianship, Mina! This time last weeks you wouldn't have given Jacob the times of day. The only person you despived more than *Jacob* was . . . was *Bryan*, wasn't it? And why did you dislikes that charming libble bundle? For coming along and spoiling your littles

367

family unit? For being the son of the woman who takes your daddy away from you? Be honest.'

Mina gritted her teeth and tried not to pout, blush or cry. She failed on all three counts. 'Things change,' she said, sniffing back tears. 'I've changed . . . It's been a long week.'

'Thinks back. Who would have gained most from ze disappearbance of Bryan? Me? I didn't even *knows* Bryan. Never met the little . . . and don't wants to. Babies? *Urgh*. Between two slices of bread, perhapsly, but . . . anyway, the two people in the worlb who most desired to see the backs of baby Bryan were . . .'

'Me and Jacob . . .' Mina felt something warm and wet start gurgling in her lower intestines. It was the sick, bubbling feeling you get when you begin to understand something that you'd rather not. Or when you've got diarrhoea.

'Indeeds. And knowing Grymm the ways you do, at least *now* . . . don't you thinks it's pobbissle that the town has the powers to granted your most cherished wishes?'

'So what you're saying,' said Mina, 'is that, deep down, we wanted Bryan to disappear so much that Grymm granted our wish. *We* did it.'

'I'm afraided so. Ironics, isn't it?' Anhanga chuckled. 'With your imaginations, by dear Wormina, and Jacob's connection – as itty-bitty small as it may be – with the

Chinese mining men, you quite literally *changed reality*. Poof! Magics! Abracadabra! And shitty poo-bum Bryan is . . . gone.'

It was the last thing the children had expected to hear, but suddenly it all made an awful, bizarre sense. At least as much sense as anything in Grymm. Silence descended on them and their jaws dropped in shock. They had wished with all their hearts that Bryan would disappear . . . and he had. They quite literally wished him out of existence. What was it Thespa had said? Mina wondered. That Grymm can sometimes grant your deepest desires? It was a sobering thought. They'd been hunting *themselves* all along.

'Mina?' said Jacob guiltily, his voice quavering. She said nothing because she had nothing to say and didn't trust herself not to break down. And this was most certainly *not* the time to lose control. Instead she just reached out, took his hand and gave it a squeeze that spoke volumes. It said, *We'll get him back, I know we will. We wished him* out *of existence – somehow we'll wish him* back.

Anhanga, who had been studying their reaction intensely, giggled and waved a hand to encompass everything around them. 'As for all the rests, yes, that's all my doings – in so far as I has took advantages of what was already here. Oh, children, when I gets here and

369

finds out what they lovely townspeople of Grymm had done all those years ago – twice, for cryings out loud – it was a dreams come true, if you'll pardon the pun.'

'What do the rings do?' asked Jacob. He was still holding his sister's hand but his voice was steady and strong.

Mina wriggled her hand so that their fingers were interlocked. *Together*, the action promised, *we're stronger than him. If we can wish a baby out of existence, what can't we do?* She also knew that Jacob was back on track and that they needed to buy some time.

'Ah, you more than mosts should knows that, my boy. All those deads miners crying out to their homeland, begging to lives, begging to dies, all unheard, all so angry, so disappointedment, so desperate for revenges, yadda yadda yadda . . . and above *them* the bones of the natives people. Insults piled's upon injuries, quite literalement. Hee-hee-hee. How could it *not* affects their surroundings?'

'The gold?'

'Yes, Jacob. You sees it, don't you? Sometimes? Right now too, I expects. This closes to the source, as twere. Bloods really are thicker than waters. You can thank your father for that if you ever sees him again. Oh my, this is wonderfuls.'

'But what does it do? I sort of get it but it's hard to

sort it out in my mind. It's like trying to get your head around infinity.'

'Try. Please do try. Your mother's turnings into a painting madwoman; imagines what a contest we can stirs about between her and Beersheba? Sharpened brushes at twenty paces, I should thinks! Hee-hee! And who *knows* what forms it will takes wiv your father. You see, the rings lets the wearer's worst thoughts come to the surfaces. All the stuffs that you normally keep hiddenly is allowed out.'

'Like wishing Bryan would disappear.'

'Yes. In a ways. But with adults it's difference.'

'Different?'

'I see where he's going with this,' interrupted Thespa. She addressed the children directly. 'You were both pretty open about not liking Bryan, weren't you? Because you could be. Because you are children and most of what you say doesn't matter.'

'Speak for yourself, Einstein.'

'Think about it, Mina! When you scream at your father and say *I hate you* and run off slamming doors, do you think he believes you?'

'Well . . . no.'

'But if *he* said it to *you*? That would be different, wouldn't it. Wouldn't it?'

'Well . . . yes.'

'You see, adults keep a lot more stuff inside. *A lot more*. And a lot deeper. What if your mother was even the tiniest bit irritated about staying at home and tidying and washing and cooking and never having time for her painting – the one thing that made her *her* and not some motherly drudge? What if she held even the smallest grudge that George sat down, ate his breakfast and went to work without ever clearing up?'

'Hang on, that's my mum you're talking about. I'm sure—'

'Jacob! Think about it. *What if . . . what if* your mother thought that – only occasionally maybe, and in some dark, secret place? She'd never say it out loud because it wouldn't be worth it. She *knows* your dad works really hard. She *knows* he goes to bed late after a hard day's work and gets up early. She *knows* all that, and yet, deep down, what if a small piece of her resented it? And what if something got past those defences and that little thought, that little shard of nastiness, of truth, eventually works its way to the surface like a glass splinter? And then the fun begins.'

'And that's where the jewellery comes in?' asked Mina.

'Yes!' barked Anhanga. 'And suddenly alls that buried emotions is released. Can't you hears it? Can't you hears them, Jacob? It's the final mad laughly of the people

Grymm killed all those yearses ago . . . They might still be buried but they're digging up one large – how does you say? – *shitstorm* instead.'

'Well, *you* are,' argued Mina. '*They're* not doing anything. You are. Without you most of this wouldn't be happening.'

'Oh, Mina, Mina, Mina . . . I'm just a catalystic. Without me it would still happens – just a lot slowerly. In fact, you could says I was helping to righted an ancient wrongs.'

'You don't care about right or wrong,' Mina spat back. 'You just want to create havoc. That's why you're sending truckloads of the jewellery out into the world. You want to spread misery as far as you can.'

'Oh, all right,' simpered Anhanga quietly. 'You gots me. I confesses! It's truly. I'm a real natsy man.' He looked at them all with utmost contempt and crinkled his lips into a hateful sneer. 'So *sue me*.'

The words were obviously a code because, as he said them, Cleaver Flay slipped like a giant wraith between Mina, Jacob and Thespa and the exit to the next room and the elevator, cutting off any chance of escape. His mutilated hands rested lightly on the brown leather belt that held his prized collection of knives. His huge face broke across the middle in a pitiless smile. 'Wormsssss,' he growled.

'So what now?' asked Thespa. She drew out a cigarette and placed it in her mouth without lighting it.

Anhanga smiled sadly and gestured for the Puzzlewicks to advance left and right. Behind them the blackness suddenly lit up with what looked like dozens of bright yellow cats' eyes. Only much, much larger. And the imps' snickering stopped.

'Well, as much as it pains me, I don't thinks I can let you go backs to the surface. Not now. Not now you knows so much about my plans. So I think we comes to the parting of the vays. Oh, and I think you knows by nows that your diversion thingy didn't work.'

'It didn't?' said Mina and Jacob.

'No, no, no, no. We caughts you, didn't we? Poor Eric was no helps at all.'

'What have you done with him?' snapped Mina.

'With him? Nothings. We just ignoreds him. He "got away" with a mechanical diggers and was last seen heading into the deserts with its. He'll be back, poor mans. It's bery, bery hots out there, you knows. Hee-hee. Now shall we all adjourns to my officeness? It's so much more comfortably.'

And with a nod of his head he set the Puzzlewicks, Flay and Fleur into motion, closing in on his three captives and hustling them back into his Houdini room. Once there, he sat down on a chair that was more throne than anything else, and smiled at them. But then his smile faltered. There was something wrong. He felt it. Mina; Jacob; Thespa – they were too calm by far. He tensed up as the creatures that gave him coherence faltered.

'What?'

'Can you feel it?' Jacob was the first to speak. 'Can you?'

The Puzzlewicks stood stock still. Fleur and Flay came to a halt, puzzled at the turn of events. A flare of fear crossed Anhanga's face. It was fear of an unknown.

'Flay,' was all he said.

Jacob jolted, expecting Cleaver Flay's sharpest blade to come whizzing through the air.

But . . . nothing.

He turned to find Thespa stepping forward to confront Flay, who thrust a gleaming, razor-sharp knife towards her but didn't make contact. She laid her hands on his enormous, mutilated fist. 'Husband,' she crooned. 'Don't do this. You're better than this.'

Husband? Mina and Jacob looked at each other in astonishment. Again. Now that *was* a surprise.

Cleaver Flay's almond-shaped eyes locked onto Thespa and he cocked his head in puzzlement. He looked like a drowning man staring up at them from the bottom of a deep but crystal-clear lake. His expression

375

said *How did I get here?* and all the tension drained away from his rubbery features as he smiled at Thespa.

'Thespa?' he said.

'Do I have to do everythings myselves, Flay, you *moron*?' screamed Anhanga. 'Remembers what I promised you!'

Then it was Mina's turn to talk. 'We know all about you, Mr Coathanger.'

'*Know?*' screamed Anhanga, his cockroach identity starting to reassert itself. 'You know nothings!'

'We know something you don't, that's for sure. We know that Elland wasn't the diversion. How's that for starters?'

'You . . . what?'

'Elland isn't the diversion, you little bug – we are the diversion,' said Mina calmly. 'Even as we speak, Mr Elland is using that digger to begin the recovery of the bodies.'

'*Bodies?*' Anhanga seemed to have lost the power of speech. The word came out as a strangled cough.

'The natives – the ones murdered by Thespa's ancestors. We – well, Elland at the moment – but *we* are digging them up . . .'

'And the Chinese miners, don't forget them . . .' said Thespa.

'And we're going to give them a proper burial,'

finished Jacob. 'It's only a start because it could take days or weeks to find all of them, but as you know, here in Grymm, it's the thought that counts.'

'It's all they ever wanted,' added Mina, quietly praying that they were right. 'They want recognition of what was done to them. Some sort of justice. And, unlike Thespa and everyone else, Jacob could *see* where they're buried; they've been telling him – the miners, anyway – ever since we arrived. I think you'll find that your jewellery, when Mr Elland's finished digging, will be worthless.'

'But Eric's *mine*!' roared Anhanga. 'I owns him! He wouldn't—'

'Oh, he would,' explained Thespa, 'when it was explained to him what a smashing final chapter it would make for his book: the discovery and recovery of the unquiet dead. You worked on him a bit *too* well: he knows everything about the town and he would do *anything* for an exclusive story, wouldn't he? We just used your own tactics against you. And he's sooo pathetically *desperate* to please you.'

'*NOOOOOO!*' Anhanga began bristling under his long frock coat. A few millipedes and worms fell to the floor and began wriggling away. Was the monster about to reveal himself completely? He seemed to brace himself against his 'throne', preparing for an attack.

'And as for you,' added Mina in a voice that sounded calmer than she felt, 'we're just not interested any more. You're nothing.'

'Whats . . . ?' The monster hesitated.

'Yes, we're over it. All of us.'

'But you can't—'

'It was something that Thespa said this morning about love and hate. I realized that you feed on them both, don't you? People either adore you – like Mr Elland and Ms Bluehammer – or hate you, like us. It nourishes you either way.'

Thespa, now holding hands with a docile and somewhat stunned Cleaver Flay, took up the attack as Jacob and Mina backed away towards the elevator.

'*Indifference*, Anhanga. They learned what I knew all along but didn't realize was important: that indifference is the opposite of hate. And indifference is where this all started; the indifference of us – the townspeople past and present – to the fate of the natives and to the miners. In that case indifference bred hatred from the dead, and they learned how to take a modicum of revenge on the town that killed them.'

'You can't . . . you can't . . .' Anhanga seemed to shrink before their eyes as more and more insects fell away from him, as if the mind keeping him – them – together was finally weakening. His face, which until now had seemed the most human part of him, began to waver and droop. A long pulsating white worm slithered between his lips and dropped onto the desk, where it writhed and looped crazily around on itself.

Jacob swallowed, trying to keep what felt like a thick ball of vomit down. He felt any calm he had gained start to drop away. This wasn't the plan. They were supposed to remain relaxed and, well, indifferent. They knew now what Anhanga fed on but . . . but when your enemy has just coughed up a worm – especially given Jacob's own experience with maggots – it's hard to stay cool.

Mina too was wavering. A few of the worms and pupae that had fallen off Anhanga were slithering towards them and she had to tiptoe this way and that to avoid them. They were like nothing she had ever seen before and left disgusting pools of pink slime, like snot tinged with blood, behind them as they inched towards her and, occasionally, lifted up their eyeless snouts to sniff the air. Something rotten throbbed inside them – she could see through their transparent, sausage-like skin. *Fee fi fo fum, I smell the blood . . .*

It was all Anhanga needed, that few seconds of fear. It seemed to energize him. He pulled himself upright, picked the long worm off the desk in front of him and introduced it back into his body through an earhole.

There was a small sucking sound and the worm was gone.

Behind him the darkness came alive too. The entrance to the cavern behind was invisible but it didn't take a genius to know that the imps were swarming out. They finally emerged like a jet-black tsunami, along the floor, across the walls and ceiling. In amongst them the Puzzlewicks and Fleur were pale ghosts.

'Come, my sweets, come,' crooned Anhanga.

Suddenly a single imp launched itself from its perch on the ceiling. It flew through the air like a bat, arms spread wide, talons at the ready, mouth as wide as a shark's, with about the same number of teeth. It was aiming at Jacob and Mina.

Anhanga let out a snickering sigh, a breath of triumph. It was the beginning of the end.

But before the imp could reach them a whooshing sound filled the air.

It was the sound of Cleaver Flay's huge arm swishing down from behind them.

Silver sparkled even in that dim light.

And the imp fell at their feet, sliced in half by Flay's sharpest, deadliest knife.

With a soft *whump* it disappeared.

Anhanga looked at the spot it had occupied with a puzzled frown. With a flick of his wrist he sent several more imps swooping towards them. And, *slash*, *slash*, *slash*, Cleaver Flay's knives – one in each huge mutilated hand – made short work of them.

Mina and Jacob began to find their confidence again. And Jacob was convinced that the work Eric Elland was doing in the desert was helping to negate the evil influence of the rings.

'So, you see,' said Thespa, appearing from behind Flay's huge bulk and ushering the children towards the elevator, 'our indifference to you and your plans will, we hope, appease the dead. From now on you're just a man with twenty trucks full of cheap jewellery in your pocket and no tricks left up your sleeve. I mean, look at yourself.'

And it was true.

As the seconds ticked by and the uneasy truce continued, Anhanga's hold on the situation – and his shape – loosened. He looked like an onion being peeled apart, layer by layer, insect by insect, worm by worm, until he was no longer manifesting any of his insect persona. A few glimpses could be seen as his anger increased, but overall he grew smaller and smaller. Finally he stood before them as a man – an evil man whose looks at that moment could kill, but a man only. Behind him the Puzzlewicks hesitated. Malahide Fleur suddenly looked around as if surprised to find himself in an underground 'dungeon' rather than his beloved kitchen.

It had worked! Mina and Jacob exchanged surprised looks and then bolted for the elevator. Behind them they heard Anhanga screech in frustration. The doors slid open almost immediately and they tumbled in – Mina holding the door open, Jacob by her side, and Thespa Grymm holding the mutilated hands of her husband. When they were all safely in, Mina stabbed at the UP button. The doors seemed to take an age to close, and they could only watch as Cleaver Flay turned round, slipped nimbly between the closing doors and stepped protectively between them and Anhanga – who leaped towards them screaming, 'This isn't over yets! This isn't over yets! I'll kill you all, I'll—'

He was stopped mid-sentence just as the doors closed.

'That should take care of that ba—' Mina hesitated as she noticed Thespa crying. Flay! 'Oh, I'm so sorry, Thespa. We didn't know.'

Jacob too suddenly realized what they had done. They might have got rid of the Anhanga-monster but they had probably killed Flay at the same time.

'He saved us,' said Thespa, smiling grimly. 'That's what matters. In the very end, he saved us. And I love him for that.'

At the top they sprinted out and ran for their lives through the astonished party-goers, who seemed confused and dazed, and back up through the tunnels until they burst into the blinding white-hot heat. Anhanga had set off the emergency sirens, and men were running back and forth, trucks and cars skidding in the gravel as they tried to find out what was wrong. Far off, on the other side of the mine, they saw George emerge from an office with a crowd of other men and jump into a truck. They also saw a small group of dreadlocked figures scuttling out of a doorway on the far side of the compound. One of them had bright red hair.

'Dad!' shouted Mina. 'Red!'

'They can't hear you,' said Thespa, pulling her towards the path. 'At least they're safe. Come on – let's go this way. It's quicker.'

With a quick glance at the confusion around them, Mina nodded and followed Jacob up the path towards the candle factory. They ran without looking back, but both of them knew enough about Grymm to realize that nothing was quite what it seemed. Anhanga might only be a man now, but he was a man with murder in mind and an army of supernatural imps. He would most certainly come after them. And who knew how long his transformation back to mere human might last now that they weren't there? No, sir, they certainly weren't safe. Not yet.

They tumbled down the stairs inside the factory three at a time, stumbling and cracking their arms and legs against the metal but not noticing the pain. And there, at the bottom of the stairs, Jacob stopped in his tracks. 'I've got an idea. Get Thespa out and take cover,' he told Mina.

'What are you going to do? We need to get out of here . . .'

Jacob grinned widely at her and pulled his bag off his back. 'I need to leave a bit of a crumb trail for Anhanga, get him to follow us in here. I'll give him a fairy tale he'll never forget.'

Mina hesitated and then saw what he was looking at. 'Got it,' she said with a grim smile. 'I know what to do. You just be quick, yeah?'

'I promise,' he said, and gave her a quick peck on the cheek. 'And if you ever tell anyone I did that, I'll kill you myself.'

'Keep going, Thespa,' shouted Mina, 'and I'll catch you up.'

A few minutes later the two of them were crouching behind the wreck of the truck outside the factory, but there was still no sign of Jacob. Mina was starting to panic. Should she go back? What if Anhanga had got him?

'Where is he?' whispered Thespa. 'What's he doing?'

Then the front door burst open and Jacob came flying out as if the devil himself were on his tail. For once he wasn't carrying his canvas bag. 'Get down! Get down!' he shouted, his face a mixture of mischievous delight and complete and utter terror. He skidded to a halt next to them.

'Are you all right?' asked Mina. 'You scared the life out of us.'

'I'm fine, I'm fine. I scattered all my stuff along the trail and then left the bag with a hole in it. They're coming.'

'You did what?' snarled Thespa. 'You led them right to us?'

'Sort of,' said Jacob. 'Sssshh.'

Then, as if on cue, the front door crashed open again, and there stood Anhanga, his face contorted with rage. His eyes were red holes that burned with malice and rage and evil. The space behind him in the doorway was packed with his cat-eyed imps.

'Oh crap,' said Mina. 'It didn't work.'

'We,' said Jacob, 'are *munted*.'

But as he said this, a small *whump* reached them from the factory. Then another. Anhanga looked behind him and then back at the children. His snarl of animal rage and surprise was lost in the massive fireball that blew the roof clean off the factory, and exploded and

385

roiled, red, yellow and black, into the clear cobalt sky.

The fireball engulfed Anhanga and his demon army and ripped them into millions of fiery pieces. The shock wave of the explosion blew Thespa, Mina and Jacob off their feet, and a massive red and yellow cloud mushroomed into the air. For a moment they just lay on their backs and stared at the sky; then burning debris began raining down.

Mina was first to her feet, pulling frantically at Jacob and Thespa. 'Come on, come on!' Her voice seemed to be coming back to her through cotton wool.

Jacob, his head ringing, couldn't hear her at all. He watched, dazed, as she stood above him and shouted soundlessly.

'Get up! Let's go. It might explode again.'

Then, like air rushing in to fill a vacuum, everything came back at once. The heat, the wind, the flaming rubble around them, Mina shouting, Thespa stumbling sideways and falling over, blazing meteorites thudding into the dust and, oddly, the splash and splatter of hot melted wax as it started to rain down around them. As they watched, the remains of the candle factory slowly toppled into a crater-sized hole that they knew led straight down to Anhanga's lair.

Thespa laughed. 'Balthazar! You two blew it up!'

13

By the time they had got themselves together and limped back to town, everybody was out in the street watching the dark mushroom cloud as it spread into the cloudless sky like ink in water. What few inhabitants Grymm had left stood around in the searingly hot sun – ants mesmerized by something beyond their comprehension.

Beersheba Bluehammer, Inky Bugleslab, Maggot and a straggle of mineworkers came rushing headlong into town in a battered truck as if the devil were on their tails. As they slowed down, Bluehammer leaped out, gave a long, keening cry and ran off along the street towards the candle factory. Maurice Au was standing outside his souvenir shop in a daze. All the shine had left him, and he seemed to sense that his shop had just suffered a catastrophic failure in the supply line.

Mina, Jacob and Thespa just stood in the middle of the street, smiling. The sun was low and the shadows long. It was still warm but the sweltering heat had passed.

'Is it over?' asked Mina sadly.

'I hope so,' muttered Jacob. 'I'm shattered.'

'Me too,' said Thespa. 'Come on. Let's get out of the sun. Such as it is.'

Two minutes later she was throwing herself down on the sofa in her office. 'I need a drink,' she said.

Mina dropped into an armchair and winced as she picked a few blobs of cold candle wax off her arm. Jacob just stood in the middle of the room. He seemed, thought Mina, lost without his bag – that bloody bag!

'I'm sorry,' he said to Thespa. 'Sorry about . . . your husband.'

'Oh, Jacob, you have no reason to be sorry. Cleaver was— Oh my God!'

They turned at once to find the massive bulk of Cleaver Flay standing in the doorway. He was covered in soot and wax and dirt and other stuff that none of them wanted to think about. There was a large gash on his bald head and cuts up and down his forearms. Mina jumped up, grabbed Jacob and pushed him towards the back of the office. If Flay had turned again, they were in big trouble. 'We need to get out of here!' she shouted.

'Wait!' It was Thespa. 'Look!' She was pointing at Flay's huge hand – where yet another finger was missing: the finger on which they'd last seen a shining gold ring was now just a bloodied stump.

'Thespa?' said Flay. He sounded tired, empty, beaten. He took a clumsy step forward and held out his other hand, palm up. In it was the missing finger, still sporting the ring. 'I think . . .'

He got no further, just toppled slowly forward like an ancient redwood tree being felled, and hit the floor with an agonizing crunch. As Thespa rushed towards him the ring bounced and bounced and bounced and came to rest between Jacob's feet.

'Don't!' screamed Mina.

'What?' Her stepbrother grinned as he kicked the ring across the room. 'How stupid do you think I am?'

Even Thespa, who was kneeling next to the unconscious bulk of Cleaver Flay, laughed.

'So what now?' asked Jacob. 'What now?'

'Nothing. Nothing at all,' said Thespa. She moved Flay's head so that he wasn't leaning on his own squished nose and lit a cigarette. A great grey cloud of smoke issued from her lips and drifted up towards the ceiling. 'We do nothing at all. Well, I see to what's left of Cleaver and then we go and make sure your parents are OK.'

'But all that . . . evil . . . all that *hate* that's already made it out into the world . . . ?' whispered Mina.

Jacob nodded in agreement. 'What do we do about *that*?'

'As I said: nothing. Welcome to the real world, children. It's already out there – you can't put that particular genie back in that particular bottle. As The Beatles said, *Let It Be*.'

'Who?'

'Jacob, Jacob, Jacob – what *do* they teach the young these days?'

They pushed and pulled and dragged the unconscious figure of Flay onto the sofa, patched up his hand, and then, in a car borrowed from Inky Bugleslab, Thespa Grymm drove them back to the house. Grymm, though, hadn't finished with them yet. As they clambered, exhausted, out of the car, an ear-shrivelling, blood-curdling scream echoed from inside the house and shot out across the desert.

Thespa looked at them in shock. 'What, in God's name, was that?'

Jacob and Mina looked at each other in sheer delight, excited grins spreading across their faces. '*BRYAN!*' they shouted in unison, and dashed into the house, up the stairs two at a time, towards the source of the nail-shredding caterwauling.

With Thespa huffing and puffing behind them, they burst into the bedroom in a windmill of arms and legs. It had been transformed again. There were clothes and boxes everywhere, the tangle and detritus of a family that have just moved into a new house and haven't yet had time to unpack properly. Bryan's favourite clown mobile was hanging off the handle of a drawer and there, in the midst of it all, was Bryan's cot.

And standing in front of that was Jacob's mother. She looked exhausted, dark circles under her eyes, but at least she was smiling. To begin with anyway – it faded immediately.

'My God,' she said, staring at the two bedraggled figures in front of her. 'What happened to you?'

There was no time for explanations, though: the children ran across and peered in, hesitantly at first, given Grymm's propensity for surprises – but there he was, moon-faced and scowling and flushed pink from all the screaming. He looked at them, smiled and farted.

It was their Bryan all right.

Mina picked him up, tears in her eyes. They touched his fat cheeks, held his chubby fingers. In return, for once, he smiled at them and gurgled.

In the meantime Thespa Grymm had silently entered the room and made another discovery. She had found a large two-seater pram that the children had overlooked.

She grabbed the handle and pushed it gently towards them.

'Now, now, now,' she said as they billed and cooed over their not so long-lost half-brother. 'Don't play favourites.'

Favourites?

Thespa wheeled the pram round, and Jacob and Mina came face to face with . . . two more Bryans, identical to the one Jacob now held in his arms. One of them let out a fart that sounded like it had lumps in it. Wet lumps. The other lifted his pudgy arm and slapped the first one in the face. Then they both began to cry.

They looked from baby to baby, and then at Thespa, who grinned.

'What? Never seen identical triplets before?' she asked above the cacophony.

Mina gaped. Jacob mouthed words but nothing came out.

Thespa laughed loudly. 'You know' – and here she winced at the noise issuing from the Bryan triplets – 'you two are going to have to be *much more careful* what you wish for.'

THE END